THE LYME
BROOK MIST

THE LYME
BROOK MIST

ANTON CORVUS

Matador
9 Priory Business Park,
Wistow Road, Kibworth Beauchamp,
Leicestershire. LE8 0RX
Tel: 0116 279 2299
Email: books@troubador.co.uk
Web: www.troubador.co.uk/matador
Twitter: @matadorbooks

ISBN 978 1838595 265

British Library Cataloguing in Publication Data.
A catalogue record for this book is available from the British Library.

Printed and bound in the UK by TJ International, Padstow, Cornwall
Typeset in 11pt Adobe Garamond Pro by Troubador Publishing Ltd, Leicester, UK

Matador is an imprint of Troubador Publishing Ltd

For Leo – an adventure…
…I hope you like it!

CONTENTS

CHAPTER ONE

THAT BROUGHT
THE FOG AND MIST

I T WAS A DAMP and chilly winter morning – the 15th of December 2018, the penultimate Saturday before Christmas. A thick blanket of fog had descended over the Westlands, the area just to the west of the market town of Newcastle-under-Lyme where Leo Marcus lived. Leo's father was at the desk in his office, reading one of the obscure books which so fascinated him, all the while checking the things which the book said on the internet; he was something of a sceptic, Leo's father, and hardly, if ever, trusted any single source of information.

"Dad, can I go meet my mate, Sam, in town?" asked Leo, walking into his father's office. His father looked out of the window.

"Hmm … it's extremely foggy today," he replied.

"It'll be alright in town," insisted Leo.

"Which route will you be taking?" asked his father.

"I'm going to meet him in Lyme Valley, between the bridge and Homebase," answered Leo.

"Right," said his father, "very good. Be careful, though… in this fog." He turned to his windowsill and took the small brass pot in which he kept some loose change. "I imagine you'll be in need of some funds… you'll be going for lunch in Subway I suppose?" Leo's father knew well enough that Leo liked to go to Subway whenever he went to Newcastle.

"Oh, yes, please," replied Leo cheerfully. His father delved into the brass pot, removed three two-pound coins and held his hand out towards Leo.

"Will that be sufficient?" he asked.

"Yes, that's fine, thanks," replied Leo happily. His father stood up and peered out of the window again. His office window faced into the back garden of their home; it was impossible even to see the back gate leading to the garage.

"This fog really is terrible," mumbled Leo's father.

They both walked out into the hall and towards the coat hooks near the front door.

"You'd better put your parka on, Leo," said his father, opening the front door to gauge the temperature. Leo pulled his parka off the peg, put it on and zipped it up halfway. "You have your phone?" he continued rhetorically. "It's fully charged, I hope?"

"Yes, Dad," replied Leo, moving it from his trouser pocket to his coat pocket. "I just unplugged it, so the battery's full."

"Very good. Be careful, then," said his father.

"Is that Leo going out?" shouted his mother from upstairs.

"Yes, I'm going meet Sam in Castle," Leo shouted back.

"You're going *to* meet Sam…" admonished his father, who often corrected him for the omission of prepositions "…and the town is called *Newcastle* not *Castle*," he added. Leo had a propensity for abbreviation which his father liked to correct.

"Well, it's dangerous going out in fog like this!" warned his mother, appearing at the top of the stairs holding some laundry.

"It'll be fine, mum," replied Leo. "I'll be extra careful. I only have to cross one road; I'm going through Lyme Valley."

"We've already had this conversation, dear," said Leo's father, dismissively.

"Well, be very careful, then!" conceded his mother with a still anxious expression.

"I will!" Leo smiled and walked out through the door towards the front garden gate. "Be extra careful on the pelican crossing!" his father called after him. "The visibility is very bad today – it's the worst fog I've seen in a long time!"

"I will, Dad, see you later!" replied Leo as he disappeared through the gate and into the fog. His father shut the door and returned to his office and his obscure book.

Leo was 12 years old, almost 13 in fact, and quite an informed and knowledgeable boy. He naturally liked to play computer games, as do most boys and girls of his age, but he also enjoyed reading, which he did very frequently – albeit not frequently enough for his father's satisfaction, but one might suppose that to be not an uncommon observation of parents towards their children. He liked to read about science and history mainly but loved funny and trivial books too. He also liked to watch videos on YouTube about all manner of different subjects.

As he walked along towards the pelican crossing on Clayton Road, the fog became even denser, and as he reached the crossing, he even briefly entertained the possibility that his parents' warnings about the fog being dangerous might be justified. He pushed the button and waited for the green man to appear, which it soon did. Notwithstanding that under normal conditions that would have been sufficient for him to proceed, he listened very carefully for the sound of any oncoming traffic over the beeping of the crossing and only stepped out onto the road once he was satisfied that it was safe to do so.

Once safely across the busy main road, he felt considerably more at ease and started to ponder about what he and Sam might get up to once they reached the town centre. Other than going to Subway or McDonald's – he hadn't yet decided for definite between the two in his own mind, and being a considerate sort of young fellow, he would anyway need to take his friend's preference into account – what else could they do?

The amusement arcade just outside the Vue Cinema was always on his itinerary for a trip to town, but he didn't have enough money for more than about fifteen minutes in there. "The cinema itself?" he wondered. He hadn't bothered to look what was on, so that was a decision only to be taken once in town, and with only six pounds in funds, it was not a strong contender. As he proceeded along Buckmaster Avenue and reached the top entrance to the Lyme Valley Parkway, he considered the mundanity of living in Newcastle-under-Lyme. "Never much to do in Castle," he mused, failing to observe his father's admonition on abbreviating place names, "same old, same old … nothing eventful or extraordinary ever happens here – always just the same old Castle!"

Leo's view wasn't entirely fair in actuality because Newcastle-under-Lyme did usually host an annual travelling fairground over the Easter weekend in Goose Street, and another one around mid-October in Lyme Valley, at the same time as the annual fireworks display. There was also the annual switching on of the Christmas lights, although Leo never considered that event to be too much of an excitement.

As he continued along the path which runs down into Lyme Valley proper, the fog got thicker and thicker, and by the time he reached the bend in the path at the end of the treeline, he could barely see a few yards in front. In fact, and notwithstanding that he had followed the same route hundreds of times in his short life, and thus knew his way around Lyme Valley like the back of his hand, if it were not for the path being tarmacked he would undoubtedly have lost his way.

So he continued on, looking down at the path now rather than forwards, as that was the only way to gauge that he was still going in the right direction. When he reached the bottom of the path, where the circle with the benches is, he very nearly walked into the Lyme Valley Parkway metallic sign that rises from the centre of the circular area. "Great," he muttered in a sarcastic tone; "I can't see a damn thing now!"

By now he could see that the fog was being created from a mist that was actually rising from the surface of the Lyme Brook itself which runs the whole length of Lyme Valley thereby giving it, and the town of Newcastle-under-Lyme, its name. The mist was rising in swirls or vortices and moving outwards from the brook – which he knew was there but couldn't actually see.

Leo stopped walking and paused for a moment in a spot just past the metallic sign. He could not see the bridge over the brook although he knew for certain it was there and not more than three or four yards in front of him. He continued on slowly and cautiously but had to bend forwards at this point just to keep sight of his own feet. In addition to the eerie swirls of mist coming from the brook, there was an uncanny silence which was absolute, creating an atmosphere of sinister creepiness which sent a tingle down his spine.

Also, no dogs were barking – a most unusual circumstance for a Saturday morning in Lyme Valley – and he could not hear any traffic noise even though London Road, the main A34 dual carriageway, was only thirty to forty yards in front of him on the other side of the bridge.

As he reached the edge of the bridge, he moved a little to his left so that he could take hold of the steel railings to guide his steps. He kept going but very slowly, just one measured step at a time. He looked down, but he could not see past his knees, then to his left, but he could only barely see his fingers clasping the railing. As he reached what he supposed was the halfway point across the bridge, the railing abruptly ended, and he felt polished stone through the tips of fingers. He drew still closer to the left so that his thigh brushed against what was no longer a railing, but in fact, a wall of good quality cemented brick topped with stone. As he continued on, the surface of the bridge felt different too. He stooped down to investigate: cobblestones.

"Mum will be pleased," he thought; Leo's mother often complained about the council's persistent neglect of the parkway. "They've finally decided to make some improvements to the Valley," he mumbled to himself, although he considered it somewhat odd that the tarmac path had been replaced by cobblestones.

He carried on across and finally reached the other side, indicated to him by the termination of the edging wall which he had been using to guide himself. Bending down once more, just to make sure he was still on the path, he turned to his left to head along the line of the brook and towards Brook Lane.

As he continued on, swirls of mist continued to ascend from the brook, which was now to his left, and yet the viscosity of the fog overall seemed to dissipate with each step he took. Before too long he could see his feet clearly enough again and the grey close-cut cobbles beneath them. He glanced at his watch to check the time, as he told his friend that he would meet him along the path which he was now on at 10:30. His watch showed 10:34. Following a habit almost certainly learned from his father, he pulled out his mobile phone to check the time on that also – also 10:34: so he was late.

"Can't be helped in fog like this," he thought. "Sam's probably late too." He carried on but was able to pick up his pace slightly as the fog continued to lift. He started to muse to himself as he walked that the mist was itself at least something unusual. He couldn't see more than three or four yards to either side or get much of a sense as to how far along the path he'd gone, but two things did strike him as rather odd: the first being that the path was far more winding than it had been when it was tarmacked, and secondly it was still uncommonly quiet – in fact it was silent. After a few more minutes, the fog had cleared sufficiently for him to be able to see not only the brook but also the far bank. He looked anxiously to his right hoping to see the playground where the zip wire is, but he couldn't see it at all – just grass; then, at first very faintly, and as he continued to walk along, more clearly, he thought that he could make out the outline of a canal barge. As he followed the path as it turned towards the right, the view became clearer and clearer: it was, in fact, a canal barge. Leo stopped dead: there was no canal running through Lyme Valley!

"What's going on here?" he asked himself, still standing motionless. He edged forward a few steps towards the barge. As he did so, he could see a row of stone and brick edging and beyond that a canal – quite a wide canal in fact. He shook his head, disbelievingly. He took another a few steps forward, and then a few more. All manner of confusing thoughts ran through his head. Because it was winter and the last few weekends had been very wet, he hadn't been through Lyme Valley for several weeks, so of course, some public works could have been carried out since he was last here, and yet, he could scarcely believe that the council would decide to run a canal through Lyme Valley. He took out his mobile and called Sam's number – nothing. He looked at his screen – no signal AND still showing 10:34! "Oh great," he scoffed under his breath, "now my phone's broken or the whole network's down… maybe the fog's affected the reception?"

He went into his phone settings, scrolled down to "System" and then tapped it and went into "Date & Time". Sure enough, it was set to "Automatic". Although he'd rarely had occasion to unset that setting, he thought maybe the fog was so interfering with the reception that he'd better switch off *Automatic* and then see what networks were available; he did so. Then he glanced at his watch again – also 10:34 … but his watch was analogue! "What?" he muttered.

Just then he heard footsteps and the sound of faint whistling coming from the direction in front of him: someone was approaching from the direction of Brook Lane. The footsteps were weirdly loud – although quite far away – and like the sound of horse's hooves actually rather than regular footsteps. Sometimes people did ride horses through Lyme Valley, but it was unusual, and it hardly seemed like the weather for someone to be going horse riding. He looked at his watch again more closely: the second hand was frozen at fifteen seconds past. He shook his wrist and tapped the glass but nothing – still stopped dead. He checked his mobile screen again: still 10:34, no network signal, no 4G.

The footsteps and whistling got closer. Leo recognised the tune but couldn't name it: it was a classical or operatic tune – he recognised it from his father's playlist. "Weird..." he thought "... and what's happened to Sam? I hope he hasn't fallen into this new canal!" The fog continued to clear. The rolling mist that had been rising from the brook had stopped completely, and the surface of the brook had become almost clearly visible, although fog still hung above it and overhead. The footsteps and whistling got louder still, and the outline of a figure started to appear, albeit indistinctly, about thirty yards along the path in front.

Leo squinted as he tried to make it out. He – and Leo assumed it was a *he* as the figure was over seven feet tall – walked quite unhurriedly along and continued to whistle as he approached. As he got closer, Leo started to make out horns protruding from the sides of the top of his head as if he were wearing some type of Viking style helmet. It was difficult to see, but as he came closer still, Leo realised it was not a Viking helmet at all, but what he perceived to be a full face mask of a bull, topped with a flat cap.

Had it been Halloween, Leo might not have thought so much of it; but it was an odd costume for the Christmas season. The man was otherwise dressed very well, although quite quaintly to Leo's estimation. As he drew nearer still, Leo noticed that he had hooves instead of feet and hands; and they really appeared to be hooves, and made the sound of hooves as he walked. "Some kind of animal stilts?" Leo asked himself. "And hoof-like gloves?"

As the figure reached a distance of about seven to eight yards, Leo's curiosity turned into terror and thoughts of Theseus and the minotaur ran through his mind. It became almost certain that what Leo had at first thought was a full face mask was in fact not a mask at all – if it was a mask, then it was of the quality of a blockbuster movie, it was no mere plastic or rubber theatrical piece – but the most compelling giveaways were undoubtedly the sound of the figure's breath, which was a bellowing, and the sight of its voluminous exhalations condensing in the cold, damp air.

"A man couldn't breathe like that…" thought Leo "…not even if he really tried to."

Leo glanced down at the figure's hooves again – they were real hooves all right, as were the ones protruding from the sleeves of his tweed jacket – actual, real bull's hooves with a central split. Leo's mind just blanked.

Automatically, and without any intentional thought, he turned in panic, as if to run in the opposite direction, but he immediately ran into another figure which had approached unheard behind him. He looked up and gasped in horror. A six-foot tall, sandy-brown coloured bear, standing perfectly upright – just upon its back legs, looked down at him through a set of gold-rimmed spectacles.

CHAPTER TWO

ADVERSITY MAKES STRANGE BEDFELLOWS

"GOOD MORNING," SAID THE bear. "You seem to be in quite a rush, young sir!"

"Please don't kill me!" gasped Leo, stepping back and holding the palms of his hands out in front of himself.

"Kill you?" repeated the bear quizzically. "Why would I want to kill you?"

"You might want to eat me…" suggested Leo meekly – it was the first thing that came to mind.

"Why would I want to eat a boy?" asked the bear incredulously. "I'm a vegetarian: I eat berries and roots," he added in a tone of voice which indicated he was somewhat mystified as to why Leo would immediately jump to an expectation of being eaten.

"But are you actually a bear or is that just a really, really good costume?" asked Leo, recovering his composure slightly.

"Of course I'm a bear," said the bear. "Do I not look like a bear?" he asked.

Leo looked at the bear again more closely. He was easily six-feet tall, maybe a little taller, although not quite as tall as the bull, who was now standing directly behind Leo, although Leo hadn't noticed.

Starting at the top, the bear wore: a black bowler hat; gold-rimmed half-moon spectacles; a white, and very crisply starched, winged-collar dress shirt with a maroon tie, having diagonal thin, grey stripes; a black waistcoat adorned with a golden chain, which was obviously attached to a pocket watch – but Leo couldn't see that; a black woollen frock coat, such as a groom might wear at a wedding; greyish pinstriped trousers; and, rather curiously, a pair of bright red woollen socks but no shoes.

"Hmm... yes, actually... you do look exactly like a bear..." said Leo hesitantly "...except you're wearing clothes and speaking."

"Why wouldn't I be wearing clothes and speaking?" asked the bear suspiciously.

"Anyway..." mumbled Leo "...I'd better be going, I'm late." His panic level had certainly reduced as the bear seemed quite cordial and not at all threatening, but the intrinsic strangeness of the situation nevertheless seemed to suggest an exit would be appropriate.

Leo smiled politely, then made a one-hundred and eighty-degree turn and ran directly into the bull who had been standing behind him. He again gasped and took a step back. The bull was bent forward slightly, and like the bear, was standing just upon its back legs. It examined him with some curiosity. The bull was a little taller than the bear and of a reddish-brown colour.

Like the bear, he was well dressed. He had a flat cap in tweed, a white, winged-collar shirt very similar to the bear's but with a cravat style tie rather a normal tie, which had a pattern of red and green paisley print. Over his shirt, he wore a yellow waistcoat, chequered with green and red stripes, and crossed with a silver watch chain, and over that, a tweed sportsman's jacket. A very baggy pair of brown corduroy trousers adorned his legs. Unlike the bear, he had nothing on his feet, or more correctly – his hooves. Leo looked over his shoulder at the bear and then at the bull again; if he were the type of boy to faint, he would most certainly have fainted at that moment.

"Good morning," said the bull.

"I really need to be going," stuttered Leo.

"Where will you be going to?" asked the bear.

"To meet my friend, Sam," said Leo.

"Where do you intend to meet him?" asked the bull.

"At the side of Homebase," said Leo.

"Homebase?" repeated the bull questioningly. "Where or what is Homebase?"

"It's the DIY store," said Leo, pointing to where he thought Homebase should be. The fog had cleared very substantially in the last few minutes thanks to quite a brisk west wind. Leo looked over to where he thought Homebase should be, but there was no Homebase, just some Victorian-looking industrial buildings and a large grey gas tower looming up in the background behind them.

"And where is this so-called DIY store supposed to be?" asked the bear.

"It's supposed to be there," said Leo, as he continued pointing to where it very clearly wasn't.

"What is a DIY store?" asked the bull.

"It's a shop where you can buy DIY stuff," said Leo.

"And what is DIY stuff?" asked the bear.

"You know…" started Leo "…DIY stuff."

"Actually, young sir, we don't know…" started the bull.

"That's why we're asking," interrupted the bear.

"Well," said Leo, "I'm surprised you don't know, but DIY stands for *Do It Yourself*, and Homebase sells tools and supplies for decorating and renovating and plumbing and light-fittings and that kind of thing."

"So it's like a builders' merchants?" asked the bear.

"Hmm… yes," said Leo, "I guess you could say that."

"And this shop is supposed to be just over there, where the canal ends, and the goods yard is?" asked the bear.

"Exactly," confirmed Leo.

"But it's not there," said the bull.

"No, it doesn't seem to be," said Leo.

"But you seemed initially to be quite convinced that it should be there?" retorted the bull.

"It was there before," insisted Leo.

"I see," said the bear with a quizzical expression.

"So, how can you account for its absence now?" asked the bull.

"Well…" began Leo "…I'm not sure really."

"So where are you going to meet your friend?" asked the bear.

"You can't meet someone by the side of something that isn't there," added the bull.

"Well said, Bull," added the bear, looking at his friend. "That's logical."

"Anyway, I really need to find my friend, so I'll have to be going," said Leo, trying to excuse himself.

"We could come with you," said the bear.

"Precisely," added the bull, "we may be of some help to you."

"Especially since you don't appear to know where anything is," added the bear.

"That won't be necessary," said Leo. "I can manage on my own well enough, thank you anyway."

"No doubt of it, young sir," said the bear, "but nevertheless, you don't quite seem to fit in here. It might make more sense for the two of us to accompany you…"

"Just for a while," interrupted the bull, "until you find your way around, you know?"

"It really won't be necessary," said Leo politely but firmly.

"May we take it that you are in some manner dissatisfied with our company?" asked the bull sulkily.

"Hmm ... no," replied Leo, not wishing to be offensive. "It's just that my mother always says that I shouldn't talk to strangers."

"Why does she say such a thing?" asked the bull.

"Because strangers could be kidnappers or murderers," said Leo matter-of-factly.

"But surely a stranger could just as well be helpful?" proposed the bull.

"That is more probable," added the bear; "modern criminology reveals that the overwhelming majority of people in a society are not criminals but rather law-abiding citizens who mean no one any harm."

"Besides," added the bull, "if you never talk to strangers, then you will never make any new friends. You see, besides your immediate family, you must necessarily meet everyone whom you will come to know for a first time, and at that time, such persons are by definition strangers."

"Precisely," confirmed the bear, waving his left paw through the air and then stroking his chin.

"In any case," said the bull, "do please allow us to formally introduce ourselves ... now that we've had such a lengthy chat as strangers." They both smiled.

"I'm Mr Bear," said the bear, offering his paw which Leo shook, "but please do call me Bear."

"And I'm Mr Bull," said the bull, similarly offering his right hoof – which Leo also shook, "but my friends just call me Bull."

"And you are, young sir?" queried Bear.

"I'm Leo," said Leo.

"Ah, a Leo," said Bear enthusiastically. "Which means *lion* in Latin, I believe."

"That's right," confirmed Leo.

"So, a lion, a bull and a bear – we shall make a great company," said Bull with a profound and contented grin.

Oddly, curiously – and certainly inexplicably – in that one moment, Leo felt entirely at ease with his two new acquaintances.

It made no sense that Lyme Valley had changed beyond all recognition; it made no sense that he was standing next to a canal that didn't exist; it most certainly made no sense that he was speaking comprehensibly to a bull and a bear dressed in the clothing of Victorian gentlemen, and yet, despite his initial trepidations, once they had stated their names and he his, he felt unaccountably at ease in their company. It was as if, at the risk of his venturing into some manner of fatalism, he had been intended to meet them, and they him. It was as if their meeting had been ordained in advance and meant to be.

CHAPTER THREE

THE LION, THE BULL AND THE BEAR

"SO, MASTER LEO," SAID Bull, "now that we're no longer strangers, please allow us to assist you in finding your friend."

"Indeed," added Bear. "We know the area very well."

"So," continued Bull, "what we know so far is that you had arranged to meet your friend at the side of this so-called Homebase DIY store which we now all agree is not where you supposed it to be."

"I don't know why it isn't there," said Leo perplexedly and looking again towards Brook Lane.

"Maybe we should take a closer look," suggested Bear, "although I'm quite certain there is no such place."

"Let's walk along in that direction," said Bull, leading the way. The distance to Brook Lane was very short. As they walked along by the side of the brook, the canal continued to their right, and there were several other barges moored at the side. The canal widened towards its terminus in the goods yard, no doubt so that barges could be turned around once loaded. A railway line also started towards the end of the canal which ran off to the north-west, crossing Brook Lane by means of a level crossing. As they reached Brook Lane, it was clear that the buildings they had seen belonged to the goods yard and that Homebase was in fact nowhere to be seen.

"This makes no sense," said Leo, "everything is different to how it should be! And there's no sign of Sam anywhere!"

"How old is your friend ... Sam, is it?" asked Bull.

"Yes, Sam," confirmed Leo, "he's twelve, the same as me."

"Perhaps he's still in school," suggested Bear, "taking out his gold pocket watch and checking the time – it's only around eleven, too early for lunch break."

"But it's Saturday," said Leo, "and we don't go to school on Saturday."

"No, it's Friday still," said Bull. "It won't be Saturday until tomorrow, and that's not for definite." Leo looked rather confused.

"But it's definitely Saturday," said Leo, "because if it were Friday then I'd be in school myself, and I'm not, so it must Saturday."

"That's an entirely illogical proof of it being Saturday," retorted Bull.

"Quite so," agreed Bear. "If the only evidence you can muster that it's Saturday is the fact that you're not at school, then it could equally well be Sunday."

"Or worse..." added Bull "...you could be a truant!"

"In either case, your absence from school does not prove what day of the week it is," concluded Bear.

"But I can prove it's Saturday," announced Leo confidently.

"And how can you do that?" asked Bull inquisitively. Leo reached into his coat pocket and pulled out his mobile phone. He pressed the side button and the time, day and date immediately displayed on the screen.

"There you are," he said, holding the phone towards the two of them, "Saturday 15th December."

"What is that?" asked Bear with an astonished expression.

"It's my mobile phone," replied Leo rhetorically.

"My goodness," said Bear, "I've never seen such a thing."

"Me neither," said Bull. They looked at each other and then at the phone again.

"What does it do?" asked Bear.

"Are you kidding?" asked Leo.

"Not at all," said Bear defensively. "We've never seen such a thing before. No one else has one of those. Where did you obtain such an item?"

"My dad bought it from Amazon," said Leo, still rather puzzled by their ignorance.

"Your dad?" asked Bear. Leo Nodded.

"Is your father an adventurer, then?" asked Bull.

"A what?" replied Leo.

"An adventurer?" repeated Bull. "Does he travel the seven seas in search of items like that?"

"Hmm… no," said Leo. "Why would he do that?"

"You said that it came from the Amazon," retorted Bear; "and the Amazon is far away across the ocean and in the southern hemisphere, I believe."

"No, no… not THE Amazon, just Amazon," clarified Leo. "You know, the online store?" They looked at each other and shook their heads confusedly.

"What is an online store?" asked Bear.

"Is it a shop that hangs from a line?" queried Bull with a squint.

"But, my dear fellow," said Bear, directing his comment to Bull, "how would a customer get to the shop if the shop were hanging from a line? It would require all the customers to be tight-rope walkers or acrobats of some nature, and imagine the required tensile strength of the line itself, in order to support a shop in mid-air…"

Leo looked on confounded as they continued to speculate between themselves how an online shop might operate.

"No, no, no," he said finally. "You're misunderstanding the meaning of online – it's nothing do with a clothesline, fishing line, steel line or any other kind of line. It just means the internet, that's all!"

"Internet," muttered Bull incredulously. Bear shook his head.

"You know? The internet... www dot, the World Wide Web?" said Leo.

"A worldwide web, you say?" challenged Bull. They both appeared to be very shocked.

"It must be something to do with the Spider Company," suggested Bear.

"But if this web you speak of really is worldwide, then why isn't it here and visible in Altcastle?" asked Bull.

"Visible where?" demanded Leo.

"Here, in Altcastle," repeated Bear.

"What is Altcastle?" asked Leo bewilderedly.

"It's here. Our town. Our borough. Where we live. Where we're all standing now," replied Bear rhetorically.

"But this is Newcastle," said Leo shaking his head. "Newcastle-under-Lyme."

"No," said Bull, "this is Altcastle-under-Lyme NOT Newcastle-under-Lyme."

"Wait a minute," said Leo, "I know where I live and where I woke up this morning. I've lived in this town my whole life; I was born in this town. This is Newcastle-under-Lyme, in the county of Staffordshire, England."

"I'm afraid not, dear fellow," said Bull "this is most certainly Altcastle-under-Lyme, in the county of Altfordshire, Altland."

"That's crazy," insisted Leo, "I know where I am!"

"It would seem not," said Bear, pulling a rolled newspaper from his frock coat hip pocket. He unrolled the newspaper and showed the front page to Leo.

"You see," he said, pointing to the newspaper's header, "it clearly says, and I quote *The Local Daily Newspaper of Altcastle-under-Lyme Town & Borough.*"

"And furthermore," added Bull, "you can clearly see that the date is *Friday 14th December.*"

"And this is today's copy," added Bear.

"It's completely mad," said Leo, "and furthermore, what kind of newspaper is called *The Daily Tale*? It's like some kind of joke!"

"We can assure you, Master Leo, it's no joke," said Bull: "The Daily Tale is the well-established newspaper of the whole borough."

"Incredible!" protested Leo. "I've never heard of anything so mad in my entire life." The two of them chuckled cheerfully.

"Then we're all in good company," laughed Bull; "you with your gadget that shows the wrong day of the week and your fantastical notion of an immense spider's web spanning the whole world, and us with our newspaper – the name of which seems so entertaining to you!"

"My mobile does not show the wrong day of the week," Leo protested again. "Today is definitely Saturday! That newspaper must be yesterday's."

"No, I have yesterday's here in my pocket," said Bull, removing a folded paper from the pocket of his jacket. "I kept it for the chocolate biscuit coupons."

"And what is the date on that?" asked Leo. Bull unfolded it and showed it Leo.

"Why, Friday the 14th of December of course," he said, "the same as today!" Leo stood up straight, took a deep breath and then exhaled sharply.

"So that must be the same paper then, you have a copy each," exclaimed Leo.

"No," said Bear, "you can clearly see that they're from different days because the headlines are different." Leo looked at both front pages and notwithstanding that the date on both was Friday

14th of December, all the rest of the two front pages were in fact completely different, from the news items to the adverts.

"But don't you both see that it's completely insane! How can today's newspaper and yesterday's newspaper have the same date?" he demanded.

"Because it was the 14th of December yesterday and it's also the 14th of December today," said Bull in a tone of voice which indicated his incredulity at Leo's lack of comprehension.

"I think it's been the 14th of December for at least three days now," mused Bear.

"It could even be four days," added Bull pensively, "one loses count, you know." Bear's eyes turned upwards as he stroked his chin in a deeply thoughtful pose.

"Yes, yes… could be, old boy," he mumbled. Leo shook his head, disbelievingly.

"But how can it possibly be the same day for four days in a row?" demanded Leo. "It's impossible!" he added indignantly.

"There you go again," said Bear, "with your illogical protestations. Who says it can't be the same day for several days? Her Worshipfulness – the Right Honourable Lady Debra Sipby, Countess of Altcastle – decides what day it will be the next day each evening once she has received the shopping reports from the town's retailers."

"Exactly," confirmed Bull.

"But how does that work?" asked Leo.

"She's very commercially minded, you know, the Countess. When she gets the reports from the shops, if they haven't taken enough money that day – based on the expected takings for the time of year, you understand – then it just stays the same day, over and over again until enough money has been taken," explained Bull, "and when enough money has been taken then it can be the next day."

"Exactly," said Bear. "Simple!"

"Of course, if the townspeople don't behave and buy enough goods, it could be the same day for ages, and then Mipas would never come because it would always be the 21st of December, for example, and never get to the 25th," continued Bull.

"Well, no one would want that," added Bear, "as everyone loves Mipas, especially children, so people need to buy enough from the shops so that the day can move on and Mipas can arrive."

"What's Mipas? "asked Leo.

"Why it's the 25th of December of course; when children get presents and humans eat poor old turkeys," said Bear.

"But the 25th December is Christmas!" said Leo.

"No, it's definitely Mipas," said Bear.

"It's mad," said Leo, "I've never heard anything like it! So first of all, this countess just makes it the same day over and over again for as long as she likes basically, and then even worse, Christmas is called Mipas which doesn't mean anything and sounds a mad, made-up word!"

"Exactly so regarding the dates," said Bear, "but I really don't quite understand what you have against Mipas! Everyone loves Mipas and people are happy!"

"I remember one year when Mipas didn't arrive until the late spring," said Bull, "but that was a long time ago. People are much wiser these days and get out shopping and doing their bit for the Altcastle economy, but from what we hear from our friends in the retail business, it may even be Friday for several more days yet."

"Indeed," confirmed Bear, "sales have been slow again this year as most people already have everything they need, you see."

"And because everything made in Altcastle is of such a high quality and standard of workmanship, it's very unusual for anything to wear out or break," added Bull.

"Yes, that's right, Master Leo, it can be quite a problem," said Bear. "In fact, Bull, do you remember that year when we had the kettle thefts?" Bull pondered a moment.

"Ah, yes," he said. "I remember that!"

"What happened?" asked Leo.

"Well," explained Bull, "kettles are made at the Altutton Iron Works, but the owner complained to her Worshipfulness one year that nobody wanted to buy any more kettles because everyone already had three – some people even had four, I believe – and then there was a mysterious spate of burglaries all through the borough over a period of about two weeks…"

"It was reported in The Daily Tale," interrupted Bear excitedly.

"…many people speculated that the Countess had had something to do with it in order to improve kettle sales, as the only items stolen by the burglars were kettles…"

"Bit of coincidence, eh?" said Bull with a wink.

"…so we suspect, as do others, that the Countess had organised the burglaries herself…"

"It was also particularly unusual as there is generally no crime in Altcastle," interjected Bull.

"…and furthermore," continued Bear, "almost exactly the same thing had happened a few years before during the Great Button Thefts when the haberdashery shop wasn't doing very well, and dozens of people reported that the buttons had been stolen from their shirts while hanging out on the washing line."

"I see," said Leo. "But how does she get away with it. It seems very obvious what went on, even to me and I'm only twelve. Why didn't the police look into it?"

"The Constable works for the Countess, of course," laughed Bear, "and he was conveniently on his annual holiday on both occasions – staying in the countryside we believe – some even said it was probably the Constable who had carried out the burglaries…"

"But not publicly, obviously," interjected Bull.

"It seems very corrupt," mused Leo.

"Well, that's how Altcastle runs, you know," said Bear. Leo pulled out his phone again and re-checked his watch: both still read 10:34 and his mobile still showed no signal and no 4G.

"Problem?" asked Bull, looking at Leo's expression.

"My mobile and watch both say 10:34 still," he replied. "They've been showing 10:34 for ages now. They've both just stopped at that time for some reason. What time is it?" Bull pulled out his silver pocket watch.

"Eleven-twenty," he said; "and still no sign of your friend!"

"But my friend was going to meet me in Newcastle, and this is now Altcastle, so I guess that means he's waiting for me somewhere else ... I don't get what's happened, but something really weird has happened for sure," mused Leo. "I mean there's a canal here that shouldn't be here, Homebase has literally disappeared, and I'm talking to you two – which is also highly unusual, to say the least." Leo pondered a moment, and then an expression of terror flashed across his face. "Wait a minute!" he exclaimed. "If I really am in Altcastle, does that mean that my house isn't there anymore? Has my house disappeared just like Homebase? What about my mum and dad?" He looked suddenly panic-stricken again at the thought of it.

"Where do you live?" asked Bear.

"Just at the edge of the Westlands," said Leo.

"Westlands?" retorted Bull confusedly. He looked at Bear blankly.

"Perhaps he means the Altestlands?" suggested Bear.

"Ah, so you live at the farm?" asked Bull.

"No," said Leo, "there are no farms in the Westlands."

"Hmm…" mused Bear, "…we'll come with you to investigate … I'm afraid there is nothing but farmland in the Altestlands…"

"Oh no," said Leo.

"If, of course, the Altestlands is the same place as your Westlands, which it may not be," added Bear, seeing Leo's concern.

"Anyway," said Bull, "let's not get too despondent – let's all go and see."

"Yes, OK," agreed Leo.

The three of them proceeded back along the path by which Leo had arrived at the spot where he had met them. They walked at a very brisk pace, and Leo had to almost jog to keep up with them his legs were quite a bit shorter than theirs. The fog had mostly lifted by this time and visibility had greatly improved. The canal was now plain to see as was the brook, which looked both much higher and much cleaner than Leo remembered it. As they carried on along, Leo could clearly see that that the playground was not there at all and there were only fields full of sheep where the Lyme Valley Parkway had been.

"Has there ever been anything here?" asked Leo.

"No," said Bear, "not as long as we've been here – just fields with the canal running through."

"How long have you lived in Altcastle?" asked Leo.

"Oh," said Bull, "I think we've been here for a few decades, but it's difficult to keep track of time in Altcastle as it's a bit variable…"

"The Countess, you know," interjected Bear knowingly.

"Yes, I understand," said Leo.

They soon reached the bridge over the Lyme Brook, which was now clearly visible and constructed of very high-quality stone and brick: it looked nothing at all like the bridge that Leo knew. As they crossed the bridge, the cobblestone path veered round to their left; there was no path towards the west going up the hill, just a field full of sheep.

"This way," said Leo, leading them across the field; Bull and Bear followed compliantly. As they ascended the hill, which should have led up on to Buckmaster Avenue, Leo could quite clearly see as they climbed that none of the houses was there. They soon reached the summit, and Leo gasped as he surveyed nothing but fields.

"Well?" asked Bear.

"Looks like nothing I know is here," said Leo despondently. He continued westward, and they all soon reached Clayton Road which was there and exactly where it was supposed to be, albeit surfaced in cobblestone rather than tarmac.

"My house is over there," said Leo pointing to the south-west.

"I doubt it," mused Bull, half under his breath. Leo proceeded on, to where the shops are – or perhaps more accurately, were. He looked out towards the west: nothing but fields, trees, cattle and sheep.

"My house is gone!" he said. "All the houses are gone … and the roads … everything!"

"Maybe, they're not gone," said Bear reassuringly.

"What do you mean?" asked Leo; he was despondent.

"Well, I've been thinking, Master Leo," replied Bear, "there are strange circumstances afoot here. Although we've only just met you, you are clearly not a silly boy…"

"Not at all," interjected Bull, shaking his head.

"…you know that you live in Newcastle, not in Altcastle. You know where your DIY store should have been. You think that it's Saturday because I believe that where you came from it is in fact Saturday. Your clothing is not in any way similar to any clothing we have ever seen before. You have a gadget which appears to be self-illuminating, although such a thing is not possible. Your watch has stopped dead at a certain time, your gadget too, and finally, the house you live in is not here, nor is there any trace that it ever was – in other words, it is not gone but was in fact never here."

"Yes, yes," mused Bull.

"What are you saying?" asked Leo.

"It is my now firm belief," attested Bear, "that by some unknown means, you have crossed into an alternate reality!"

"So Master Leo's house is, in fact, still where it was?" asked Bull.

"Precisely," said Bear, "but it exists in another version of reality … just not in this one."

"I've seen movies about this type of thing," said Leo.

"Movies?" asked Bull.

"It's a long story," said Leo, realising immediately that neither of them would know what a movie was.

"Quite," said Bear understandingly, "we can save that for later."

"So," said Leo, "you really think that everything is OK in my reality?"

"Yes," said Bear, "I really do."

"But some things are the same," protested Leo, "the Lyme Brook is still where it should be, the basic geography is as it was…"

"Maybe the timelines have diverged in some way at some point in the past so that both our Altcastle and your Newcastle share a common history," suggested Bear, interrupting him.

"Maybe," muttered Leo, "but how has this happened? And if it's true, how can I get home?"

"Those are good questions, Master Leo," admitted Bear.

"And what about my parents?" asked Leo.

"I am sure they are fine, back in your own reality," said Bear.

"But they'll be worried! They'll think I've been abducted!" said Leo anxiously.

"Perhaps not," said Bear thoughtfully. "Your gadget still shows 10:34, does it not?" Leo checked his mobile again.

"Yes, 10:34," he confirmed.

"So, maybe it's still 10:34 in your reality, and nobody has missed you?"

"Could be," mused Leo.

"Maybe when you get back, it will be the same time as it was when you left," suggested Bull.

"But how can I know?" asked Leo.

"Let me think," said Bear. "Does your watch still say 10:34?" Leo checked his wrist.

"Yes," he confirmed.

"And is your watch a mechanical device like ours?" asked Bear.

"I think so," said Leo.

"How is it powered?" asked Bear.

"I have to wind it up every day," said Leo.

"So it is entirely mechanical … and have you wound it today?"

"Yes… I mean… I think so," confirmed Leo.

"Can you check?" Leo tried to rotate the winding cog between his forefinger and thumb, but it hardly moved at all, indicating that it was fully wound.

"So, it is fully wound but the second hand is still stopped," mused Bear.

"What does it mean, old boy?" asked Bull.

"I'm not sure, but it surely indicates something about time standing still," said Bear. "There is no plausible scientific reason why a mechanical device that is fully wound should suddenly stop functioning at a specific moment in time, and it is all the more unusual as the gadget stopped at exactly the same moment – it must indicate something about time being frozen in the reality that the watch and gadget came from!"

"Remarkable deduction, Bear," said Bull.

"But how can we be sure about any of this?" asked Leo. "It's just a theory!"

"We must confirm our suspicions with an expert," declared Bear.

"And do you know an expert on the subject of travelling between alternate realities?" asked Leo.

"Well," said Bear very definitely, "we do know a very clever fellow who knows pretty much everything that can be known!" Bull and Bear looked at each other and then said in unison:

"The indomitable Doctor Toad!"

"Who is the indomitable Doctor Toad?" asked Leo.

"He is the wisest fellow in the whole borough. The wisest fellow anyone has ever heard of, in fact…"

"Or even imagined," added Bull, cutting his friend off in mid-sentence.

"And where does he live?" asked Leo. "Can we go to his house?"

"Therein lies a small problem," said Bear. "He lives in an invisible airship, and therefore one must make an appointment to meet him at a pre-agreed time and location.

"We have only met him very occasionally," added Bull, "over the years we have been here in Altcastle."

"Indeed," said Bear, "he is a very private sort of fellow."

"So how can we contact him to arrange a meeting?" asked Leo.

"He is contacted by the use of smoke signals," said Bull. "It is a thing well known amongst the more enlightened residents of our borough."

"Exactly," said Bear, "we must make a fire on high ground and then employ traditional techniques to send a message to him specifying when and where we wish to meet him. Once he sees the smoke signals from the gondola of his airship, he will know where and when we wish to meet him."

"But how will we know if he has even seen the smoke signals?" asked Leo.

"Unfortunately," said Bear, "we cannot know that for sure until we go to the rendezvous point and he either turns up or doesn't – I'm afraid there's no other way."

"It's not a very efficient method of communication," observed Leo.

"Possibly not," agreed Bear, "but it's all we have for communicating with the skyborne."

"So how shall we proceed?" asked Leo keenly. "I would really like to know that my parents are not worried about me and then once I know that, I can concentrate on finding a way back!"

"Then, we shall proceed immediately," avowed Bear.

"Indeed: immediately!" agreed Bull.

"Yes, but how?" repeated Leo. Bear swept his right paw through the air with a flourish and then lifted one of his claws to the sky.

"A singularly good question!" he said.

"Indeed," said Bull, undertaking a similar gesticulation.

"Do either of you have any idea how to make smoke signals?" asked Leo suspiciously.

"Hmm…" mumbled Bear, stroking his chin, "…actually not. You, Bull?"

"I, of course, know how to make a campfire; but as to then using smoke to make signals which contain an actual message, I believe I might struggle somewhat," said Bull.

"Somewhat?" challenged Leo.

"Well, you know…" he said, shaking his head "… actually I haven't the foggiest idea."

"No pun intended," chuckled Bear, looking up at the sky. Actually, while they'd been talking the fog had disappeared entirely, and the sky was now a deep blue with some patches of white cumulus clouds scattered around.

"So what can be done?" asked Leo.

"Back to town!" shouted Bear in a loud voice. "We must go to the public library and find a book about smoke signals." Bull pulled out his pocket watch and flipped open the cover.

"Hmm… it's already 12:10pm, and the library closes for lunch between 12:30pm and 1:30pm."

"Yes," agreed Bear, "we shall never make it to the library from here in twenty minutes."

"Right after lunch, then?" suggested Bull.

"Indeed, after lunch, it is," agreed Bear.

"And what shall we do about lunch?" asked Bull. "Are you hungry, Master Leo?" Leo hadn't really noticed being hungry as he'd clearly had other more pressing matters on his mind. Finding oneself unexpectedly in an alternate reality rather takes one's mind off other more mundane issues – like having lunch – but now that Bull had mentioned it, he did notice that his stomach was rumbling a bit.

"I wouldn't mind a small snack," said Leo.

"Shall we have a picnic?" suggested Bear. "I really like picnics. In fact, I know a great song about bears and picnics!"

"Please don't start singing it again!" said Bull forcefully. "And in any case, as I pointed out the last dozen times that you insisted upon singing it – it's about Teddy Bears not Syrian Brown Bears like you!"

"It's still about bears," insisted Bear. "There's no song about bulls having a picnic, not even Teddy Bulls."

"I don't think there's even any such thing as a Teddy Bull," interjected Leo.

"Oh yes, there is," said Bull, "my friend's young daughter had one – don't you remember Bear?"

"Hmm… yes, vaguely, but I thought it was a cow rather than a bull," mused Bear, trying to recall the item.

"Anyway," said Bull, "it's hardly the weather or time of year for a picnic, is it? And secondly, a picnic involves having sandwiches, cakes, biscuits and a flask of tea, and we don't have any of those things!"

"Finally, you've made a valid point, Bull," said Bear.

Just then they heard the sounds of a handbell ringing and of horse's hooves galloping on cobblestone. The sounds seemed to come from the direction of the town. They all turned towards the north to face the brow of the hill and sure enough within a few seconds, first the hat, then the face, then the body and finally the horse beneath the rider, appeared at the brow of Clayton Bank.

"It's the Town Crier!" exclaimed Bear. The fellow was dressed in an old-fashioned red topcoat, with a cape lined at the edges with golden lace embellishment. He had a white, ruffle collar, a red waistcoat, black breaches, white stockings and buckle shoes. On his head he wore a black tricorn hat, also edged in gold lace, and a large feather fluttered from one side. His horse was well-groomed and was pure white. The Town Crier continued galloping from the brow of the hill at some speed, all the while ringing the bell vigorously and repeatedly shouting: "Oyez! Oyez! Oyez! Beakery abroad! There's beakery abroad!"

Within seconds he arrived at the spot where the three of them were standing and stopped dead. He peered down directly at Leo and shouted again: "Beakery abroad! Everyone to the Guildhall immediately!" Leo looked up at him with a rather shocked expression. "Well?" he demanded. "What's you waiting for?"

Leo looked at Bull and Bear who were just standing there smiling, as though amused by the scene.

"What shall we do?" asked Leo of Bear.

"We?" demanded the Town Crier. "Who's WE? Is you blinking royalty, young fellow?"

"Hmm… no, but…" started Leo in reply.

"But nothing!" shouted the Town Crier. He seemed to be very irate. "You's already late, you is! The meeting was called over half an hour ago, it was!"

"But how can I be late for a meeting which I didn't even know I had to go to?" protested Leo.

"Didn't know?" yelled the Town Crier. "That's no excuse, is it! Making up excuses is beakery, so it is! Pure beakery! I'll be reporting you to the relevant authorities, I will!"

"Better head off to the town," said Bull. "Or you'll be in trouble."

"What about you two?" asked Leo.

"What two?" demanded the Town Crier. "There's only one of me!"

"I wasn't talking to you," said Leo.

"Was you talking to me horse, then?" asked the Town Crier.

"I was talking to these two," said Leo, pointing to Bull and Bear.

"These two whats?" laughed the Town Crier. "You's as mad as hamsters isn't you! Here? Has you escaped from the Loons Demented? I saw them coming in on the Keele road this morning, ready for the Mipas Fair."

"We should point out, Master Leo, that the Town Crier cannot see us at all," said Bear.

"We're completely invisible and inaudible to him," added Bull.

"Why is that?" asked Leo, to Bull and Bear, not taking on board the full implications of what they'd just told him and not realising the question "Why's that?" would appear to the Town Crier to be directed at him.

"Why is that?" screamed the Town Crier. "Because it's the bleeding fairground opening soon, that's why! Now stop your cheek, and be off down to the Guildhall or I'll be fetching the Constable to deal with you, so I will!"

"OK," said Leo, "don't panic. I'm going!" Leo set off up the hill along Clayton Road. Bull and Bear went with him, unseen by the Town Crier.

"That's more like it," shouted the Town Crier, "and be quick about it… late you is!"

"OK," shouted Leo over his shoulder, "I'm hurrying!" The Town Crier grunted then set off southwards again at a brisk canter, once again ringing the bell and shouting "Oyez! Oyez! Oyez! Beakery aboard! Beakery abroad!" As they reached the brow of Clayton Bank, they looked back to see him already well off in the distance.

CHAPTER FOUR

A CURIOUS CASE
OF BEAKERY

L EO, BULL AND BEAR continued on down Clayton Road
towards the town. The area just below the brow of the hill
and to the east was far more heavily wooded than it was in
Leo's reality and he could hardly see the town centre, only glimpsing
the towers of St Giles' and St George's occasionally between the
tree trunks. There were also a few tall, industrial chimney stacks in
the distance that were not there in his Newcastle.

"So how come that guy couldn't see you two?" Leo asked them.

"He's too stupid," said Bull.

"Only wise people can see us or hear us," said Bear. "I was
quite surprised actually when you bumped into me," he added. "I
never expected it; that's why I didn't go around you or move out of
the way – I anticipated you would just walk straight through me
as most other humans do."

"That's what normally happens, you see," said Bull.

"You mean like a ghost?" asked Leo.

"Exactly," said Bear.

"So you do have ghosts then, in your Newcastle?" asked Bull.

"Well… we don't exactly have them," explained Leo. "I mean, they're not like everywhere. I've only ever seen one myself, but we know about ghosts. There are lots of shows on TV and Netflix about ghosts which I think are quite interesting,"

"What are TV and Netflix?" asked Bull.

"Really?" asked Leo rhetorically. "Netflix – I get that you don't have because you don't have the internet, but you must have TV. Televisions have been around since just after the war so you must have televisions."

"No, we've never heard of such things," said Bull.

"What war?" asked Bear, interrupting the TV discussion.

"Well, the Second World War of course," said Leo emphatically.

"Why is it called a *World War*," asked Bear.

"Because the whole world was involved," said Leo, "well almost the whole world – some countries weren't involved, but most were."

"Why was it called the *Second* World War?" asked Bull, placing emphasis on the word *Second*.

"Because it was the second time the whole world was at war at the same time," explained Leo.

"I've never heard of any World War," said Bear, "not even a first one, let alone a second one!"

"And are there more world wars after this second one?" asked Bull.

"Not yet," said Leo, "but my dad says there might be one someday if crazy politicians keep acting the way they do."

"How's that?" asked Bull.

"Well," said Leo, "my dad thinks countries should mind their own business a lot more than they do and stop bombing other countries and trying to overthrow their governments."

"What's bombing?" asked Bull.

"Seriously?" retorted Leo. "How different things are here! Bombing is when aeroplanes drop bombs."

"What are aeroplanes?" asked Bear.

"Hmm… how shall I explain, that?" muttered Leo. "They are machines with wings that fly through the sky."

"Like airships or air balloons ?" asked Bull.

"Yes, a bit like that, but much faster and with wings for lift instead of gas," answered Leo.

"But how can they stay in the air?" asked Bear. Leo was a keen reader of science books and had read one about aerodynamics, although he felt somewhat underqualified to fully explain the principles of aerodynamic lift and drag.

"It's difficult to explain," he said, having decided that was the best answer. "But maybe if we sit down with some paper, I could have a go."

"Maybe, later then," said Bull, "as it sounds a fascinating matter."

"Indeed," agreed Bear, "but let's get back to this Second World War business. Who was this war between?" he asked.

"Well basically it was Germany and Japan versus everybody else," said Leo. He liked history and was quite knowledgeable on the subject.

"Germany and Japan?" queried Bull.

"I think he means Altmany and Altpan," suggested Bear.

"Oh, I see," said Bull, "and you say it was just them versus everybody else?"

"Yes… mostly just those two… there were some other countries also on the same side, like Italy, Hungary, Bulgaria, Romania… and Finland, sort of…"

"That will be Altaly, Altungary… hmm… Altugaria… let me see… Altomania and hmm… yes, Altinland," interjected Bear for the benefit of Bull's comprehension – as he wasn't as quick as Bear at translating normal place names to Altland place names.

"That doesn't seem very fair at all," opined Bull. "It seems the sides were less than equal. Who set the rules for that?"

"Sounds like a hamstery type of business to me," interjected Bear.

"Well… hmm… no one actually set any rules: wars don't have rules," said Leo, shaking his head in consternation at their ignorance.

"It is a strange reality that you're from, Master Leo, when things that should have rules don't have any," said Bull.

"Indeed," agreed Bear enthusiastically, "everything should have rules; that's only fair!"

By this time they had reached the bottom of Clayton Bank, where it meets Brook Lane, close to the point at the north end of Lyme Valley where they had first met. The Lyme Brook, canal, railway lines and goods yard could be seen now very clearly on their right.

They continued across the Brook Lane bridge, which went over the brook, and walked over the railway tracks in the road which formed a level crossing in this reality. As they continued walking towards the town centre, Leo noticed some additional railway sidings and some workshop type buildings on their left, and beyond that was a gas works with two large grey towers – no such things existed in Leo's Newcastle.

On their right, where Lyme Valley Road and Hatrell Street were in Leo's reality, was a large, open field and a huge number of half-assembled stalls, tents and other items that one might expect to see at a fairground, although no-one was about at all and it looked as though the whole site had literally been abandoned in mid-assembly.

"What's going on there?" asked Leo.

"That's the site for the Mipas fairground," said Bull, "it's due to open soon, I'm not exactly sure when. Do you remember Bear?"

"I think it's supposed to be Saturday, but now that it's been Friday for so long it might be earlier," said Bear. Leo shook his head again – he had still not gotten his head around how it could be the same day for several days.

"But where are all the people – the whole site appears as if it's been abandoned in a hurry?" he asked, returning his attention to the site of the supposed fairground.

"They were probably summoned to the town centre like you were, and just had to down tools and rush off," speculated Bear.

"I should think that's it, Bear," agreed Bull.

As they continued on along Brook Lane past the gas works, which also looked abandoned with not a soul in sight, they approached a crossroads with a road marked *Goose Street* going off to their left in a north-westerly direction and another marked *Stubbs Gate* to their right going off towards the south-east. On the corner of Stubbs Gate and Brook Lane stood the Boat & Horses Pub: it was the same building, and it stood in exactly the same spot as in Leo's Newcastle-under-Lyme of 2018. Leo stopped dead and looked at it.

"What is it?" asked Bear.

"It's exactly the same!" declared Leo happily.

"It's an old public house," said Bull.

"Yes, it's an interesting matter," said Bear, "we must remember to tell the indomitable Doctor Toad about everything that is the same in both versions of reality – that will no doubt aid him in determining what has gone on."

They soon came to the crossroads, and Leo only then noticed the large and rather grandiose four-storey building on the opposite corner of Stubbs Gate to the Boat & Horses Pub. The building had very tall wooden double doors which were impressively finished and studded with brass. Above the doors ran a sign: *Registered Office of The Daily Tale Newspaper Limited.*

Just outside the main doors, in Stubbs Gate, was a small newspaper stand, still containing some newspapers with a small stool stood next to it, which was vacant – most probably because its occupant had also been summoned away by the Town Crier. Leo went over to the newspaper stand and examined the front page of the newspaper on top of the pile. The front page was identical to the one which Bear had shown him earlier with the date reading "Friday 14th December".

"Is this building there in your reality?" asked Bull.

"No, this would be the entrance to the carpark of the apartments," said Leo.

"What is a carpark?" asked Bear.

"It's where you park your car," said Leo rhetorically. "But I guess you won't know what a car is," he added after thinking about it. The two of them looked at each other and shrugged.

"We know the word, car," said Bull, "it means a vehicle with wheels, but no-one really uses the word very much, most people would use the word carriage as in railway carriage rather than railway car."

"Hmm…" mused Leo, "I think that may also be something for later then."

"Of course, old boy," agreed Bear. "Let's add that one to the list for a later discussion."

"Quite so," agreed Bull, looking at the time on his pocket watch again. "We had better be getting along, or we'll miss the excitement!"

The three of them continued up the hill towards the town centre. In Leo's Newcastle, the incline they were walking up would have still been Brook Lane, but he noticed a sign on the side of a building which read *Penkhull Street* so he concluded that in Altcastle, Brook Lane must have finished at the crossroads. Penkhull Street was also much narrower than the top of the Brook Lane which he knew and had a mixture of both shops and private houses on either side. The shops were of a curious nature to Leo's mind and seemed like buildings from the set of a Sherlock Holmes or other Victorian drama.

As they continued on towards the levelling of the hill, he saw how different the road layout was, and yet some of the buildings at the top did seem familiar to him. As they rounded the bend of Penkhull Street, he saw the Guildhall with its imposing clock tower in front of them.

"That's identical," he exclaimed, pointing to it.

"You mean the Guildhall?" queried Bear.

"Yes…" said Leo "…the two pillars in stone, the clock tower and even the clock face with its Roman numerals… all exactly the same!"

"Well, that's splendid," said Bull, "but are you sure that it's *exactly* the same?"

"Yes," said Leo, "really *exactly*… identical in every way!"

"Then Altcastle and Newcastle were at some point in the past actually the same place, for certain!" concluded Bear. "This will be essential information for the indomitable Doctor Toad, and could be key to explaining what has occurred…"

"And getting me back home!" said Leo.

"Indeed," confirmed Bear.

They continued to walk along what was in Altcastle called Penkhull Street, towards the Guildhall where a large crowd of several hundred people was gathered in front of it and spread out on either side. Due to his height, it was difficult for Leo to see what lay beyond the crowd, but clearly, the crowd were faced towards the Guildhall, and a brass band was playing. He recognised the tune but couldn't quite place it. As they got closer still, Bear noticed a discarded wooden crate and pointed it out to Leo, who collected it to stand on top of. Having obtained some viewing height, he could see that a stage had been erected in front of the Guildhall's great twin Doric pillars.

The stage was just under the same breadth as the building itself and was covered by a white and black chequered awning supported at its four corners by large iron poles and two additional poles in front of the pillars to prevent it from sagging over such a length. The stage was about three yards deep and had a dark-wooden lectern at its centre facing the crowd. There were two rows of small potted conifers either side of the lectern and a row of wooden chairs at the rear, the central one of which was throne-like and had a crest on its upper back panel.

There was additionally a bunting of orange and black triangular cloth flags hanging all-round the awning. The whole setup looked positively Halloweenish and seemed quite inappropriate for Christmas – or even *Mipas*, as they say in Altcastle.

The three of them were at the back of the crowd, but a few more stragglers continued to join the assembly with each passing second – similarly late to have heard about the requirement to attend, Leo assumed. Several men in blue and white striped aprons and straw hats moved throughout the crowd selling pies and other pastries. There was a definite party atmosphere and a raucous noise of chatter and laughter as they all waited for whatever was about to happen.

As people were continuing to turn up, Leo surmised that the show was not about to start yet – whatever the show was going to be. Immediately in front of Leo, two old ladies were chatting away merrily. He couldn't exactly hear what they were saying over the din of the crowd but could just about make out the words "beakery" and "abroad".

"What is this *beakery abroad* business anyway?" he whispered to Bear, who thanks to the crate was now about the same height as him and standing just to his right.

"Well, Master Leo," said Bear, "as stated: someone has perpetrated a beakery."

"But what is *beakery*?" asked Leo.

"What?" scoffed Bull, who was standing to Leo's left. "You don't know what beakery is?"

"As far as I am aware," replied Leo, "there is no such word in the English language as beakery!"

"What language?" retorted Bull.

"English!" repeated Leo.

"But who speaks this English?" asked Bull. Bear remained silent and looked extremely thoughtful, stroking his chin again.

"I do… you do… we do… we have all been speaking English since we met!" said Leo.

"Not at all," said Bull, "we've all been speaking Altlish, everyone in Altland speaks Altlish."

"Curious," said Bear, coming back into the conversation, "very, very curious…"

"What is?" demanded Bull.

"I was going to remark earlier – then it slipped my mind as so many astonishing things have been said by our new friend – but what I had thought was: how remarkable it is that Leo speaks almost perfect Altlish even though he has come from a different reality."

"Then this means that Altlish and English are almost identical languages," said Leo.

"Precisely," said Bull, "and whatever the differences are now, those differences have only developed since the two timelines of our respective realities have diverged – which we now know from the Boat & Horses Public House and the Guildhall cannot be more than two centuries ago at the absolute most. In fact, the divergence probably occurred much less than two centuries ago, but we will have to work it out in more detail when we meet Doctor Toad."

"Yes," agreed Leo, "that sounds right as other than *beakery* and *Mipas*, most words are the same and have exactly the same meaning. Of course, some words like *abroad* are a bit weird as no one would say that something was *abroad* in my reality – it's like a very old fashioned way of saying *about* or *going around*, but I get what it means."

"Fascinating," said Bull, "but what is the word for *beakery* in English then?"

"I don't know," replied Leo, "because you still haven't told me what beakery is yet."

"Well," started Bull, "it's simple, very simple… it's hmm… it's… how would you say it is, Bear?"

"It's just beakery!" said Bear. "Everyone knows what beakery is, even babies and dogs…"

"Cats, too, most probably," added Bull, "and birds… especially clever ones like parrots and ravens."

"Quite so," agreed Bear.

"So what is it then?" asked Leo.

"It's when a person does something bad… like dropping their food on the floor…"

"Or spilling their tea on the tablecloth," interrupted Bull.

"That's right… or spoiling something," Bear continued, "or making a mess, or forgetting someone's birthday…"

"Or forgetting to water the plants, or not buying something on the shopping list… or not keeping a room tidy," added Bull.

"Exactly," confirmed Bear, "they're good examples – in fact, any type of hamstery business is beakery!"

"Hamstery what?" scoffed Leo.

"Hamstery business?" repeated Bear hesitantly, half realising that Leo had no idea what he was talking about.

"So hamstery business is the same as beakery?" asked Leo.

"Pretty much," said Bull.

"I would definitely say so," said Bear. "If someone has perpetrated beakery, one could equally well say that such a person had engaged him or herself in a hamstery business, eh Bull?"

"Quite so, Bear," confirmed Bull.

"It's all madness," said Leo. "I've never heard of anything like it and furthermore…" Leo was cut off in midsentence as the brass band abruptly stopped playing and an incredibly loud fanfare of trumpets sounded, bringing the entire crowd to a state of immediate silence.

A smartly dressed man with a very tall, black top hat stepped up onto the stage. He was quite short, had a lot of stubble and appeared to be in his late thirties. He was wearing a black frock coat, a greyish waistcoat over a white winged-collar shirt with an orange silk tie, and grey pinstripe trousers. On his feet, he wore shiny black shoes with white buttoned spats, and about his neck hung an ornate and bulky, golden chain of office.

"That's the Lord Mayor…" said Bull "… Mr Woodhay."

"He works for the Countess," added Bear. Leo nodded.

The trumpets sounded again. The brass band had departed from the scene, and Leo could see two trumpeters standing either side of the stage dressed in dark-orange, gold-braided livery and wearing what appeared to be riding helmets. The helmets were black. The trumpeters had white gloves on their hands and wore white trousers with black knee-length boots. Their trumpets were unusually long, and a half-orange half-black flag – divided diagonally – hung from each of them with what looked like a coat of arms in the middle. Leo couldn't see the coat of arms very clearly from where he was standing towards the back of the crowd, but it looked very much like an orange and black shield placed over a white or light-grey background with a golden castle and a spider's web on it.

"We shall wait a few moments for confirmation from Mr Summoner that all those duly bidden are in attendance… as far as possible," said the Mayor.

"Who's Mr Summoner?" asked Leo in a whisper.

"That Town Crier fellow, we met earlier," said Bull. Leo nodded. Just then the sound of the Town Crier's bell could be heard again behind them and also the sound of his horse's hooves as it trotted over the cobbles.

"Oyez! Oyez! Oyez! Beakery abroad!" he shouted as he rode around the crowd to the front of the stage, still ringing his handbell enthusiastically. Once in front of the lectern, he dismounted and handed the reins of his horse to a smartly dressed boy of about Leo's age who gave it an apple and led it away. The Town Crier removed his hat and bowed to the Mayor.

"You may inform her Worshipfulness, the Right Honourable Countess, that I have summoned all them not essentially employed, in all close districts to attend, your Worship," said the Town Crier in a loud, formal and clear voice.

"Very well, Mr Summoner, you may be dismissed," said the Mayor.

"Very kind, your Worship," replied the Town Crier, bowing again and replacing his hat on his head; he headed off, around the side of the Guildhall.

"Hear Ye! Hear Ye!" shouted the Mayor in a voice so loud it seemed far more than necessary at the same as banging a gavel on the lectern several times. A hushed silence moved through the crowd. "There's beakery abroad in Altcastle!" he shouted. "A beakery has been reported!" A sonorous gasp grew up from the crowd, accompanied by a wave of chatter.

"Ooh... a beakery, Vera!" said one of the old ladies directly in front of Leo.

"Ooh... I wonder what is today, Gladys?" replied the other.

As other members of the crowd were similarly oohing and aahing, the Mayor banged his gavel again three times. Bull and Bear looked at each other and giggled.

"Order! Order!" shouted the Mayor, banging his gavel again each time he did so. "A beakery has been perpetrated of the most unspeakable hamsteriness!"

The crowd once again broke into a subdued chatter.

"Order! Order!" shouted the Mayor again, yet again banging his gavel. He seemed to enjoy banging his gavel and allowed no opportunity to do so to elude him.

As he continued banging away merrily, some other people climbed the steps of the stage and took seats, although no one sat in the central throne-like chair which remained vacant. Two other people, dressed very similarly to the trumpeters, walked up to the sides of the stage on wooden stilts – giving them a height of above ten feet at least. They stopped at the sides of the trumpeters. Each was carrying a large folio of approximately one yard in width and a foot in height, and embossed on the cover with what appeared to be the same coat of arms as was on the trumpeters' flags. The folios were held with their spines at the bottom.

"Who are they?" whispered Leo to Bull.

"They're the prompters," said Bull. "You'll see what they do very soon!"

"Order! Order!" shouted the Mayor again. The crowd once again fell silent. "I will now hand over to the town's magistrate, Mr Justice Bender," announced the Mayor.

One of the prompters let the cover of his folio drop open to reveal a white page with the word "CLAP" in large black letters. Everyone immediately started to clap and continued doing so as the Mayor took a seat, and another man stood up.

He was unmistakably the town's magistrate as he was wearing a long black judge's gown and a white judge's wig. He was quite old, at least sixty, and wore the same type of gold-rimmed half-moon spectacles as Bear. He seemed to linger for quite a few seconds after standing up and appeared to sway from side to side. He then removed a silver hip flask from inside his gown and took a generous swig of whatever it contained. Replacing his hip flask, he stumbled towards the lectern, still swaying from side to side, and almost tripping up over his own feet as he did so. Bull and Bear laughed quite loudly, Leo less so. The rest of the crowd continued clapping as though nothing in the least bit unusual was going on.

"Is he drunk?" whispered Leo.

"I expect so," said Bear; "he usually is."

"Drunk as a skunk on the bottom bunk," added Bull, laughing.

The Magistrate eventually made it to the lectern and held on to it with both hands to steady himself. Once he had recovered his balance, he again reached inside his gown and took out some papers which he just about managed to place down on the lectern in front of him. He looked down and started to squint at the papers. The prompter with the "CLAP" sign closed his folio and the other prompter simultaneously let his open to reveal a page with the word "SILENCE" – also in bold black lettering. The crowd fell silent. Just then two additional prompters appeared, dressed the same as the other two and also on stilts, and took up positions next to their colleagues either side of the stage.

"Now then," started the Magistrate, still squinting at the papers in front of him, and without looking up. "Hmm… hmm… hmm… who am I?" he asked, turning round to look at the Mayor.

"The Magistrate of Altcastle, my Lord," answered the Mayor as quietly as he could.

"What's that?" said the Magistrate. "Do speak up, please!"

"The Magistrate of Altcastle, my Lord," answered the Mayor again but this time more loudly.

"Who is?" asked the Magistrate in a confused tone. Many people in the crowd started to giggle at this point.

"You are, my Lord," said the Mayor.

"Ah, yes, that's right… so I am… well spotted," mumbled the Magistrate. He turned back to the crowd and banged the gavel three times while shouting "Order, order, silence in court!" He possibly hadn't noticed that no one was in a court. Everyone fell silent as the Magistrate squinted at the papers before him again.

"Order! Order!" he shouted, banging the gavel again; even though in Leo's estimation, there was no disorder that needed to be ordered as everyone was already silent and just waiting for him to say something.

"It is my painful duty…" said the Magistrate in a loud and very serious tone of voice. "It is my painful duty… my painful duty…" He stopped and turned around to the Mayor again. "What is my painful duty?" he asked.

"The beakery, my Lord… it's about the beakery," said the Mayor.

"There's been a beakery, you say?" asked the Magistrate in a surprised and startled tone.

"Yes, it's all on that paper in front of you," said the Mayor. The Magistrate turned around again and inspected the paper for the umpteenth time.

"It's gibberish!" he exclaimed. "It makes no sense at all! It's not even written in Altlish!" The Mayor jumped up and went over to the lectern. After looking at the paper himself, he discreetly turned it the other way up – the Magistrate had been trying to read it upside down.

"Start here," said the Mayor, quietly pointing to the paper.

"Order, order, silence in court!" shouted the Magistrate. "It is my painful duty to report the perpetration of a singularly foul and unsociable beakery…" the prompter on the extreme left let go of his folio cover to reveal a page with the word "GASP" on it – the crowd all took a sharp intake of breath which was extremely coordinated and made quite a loud noise, creating an atmosphere of real suspense. "Yes, shocking it is!" added the Magistrate in answer the crowd's gasp. The prompter closed his folio.

"It's a shocking beakery, Gladys," said Vera.

"Ooh, it must be, Vera," said Gladys, "if his Lordship says so."

"Order, order!" shouted the Magistrate. The crowd fell silent once more. "This is a most serious matter!" exclaimed the Magistrate. "No stone will be left unturned… and that's the case as it stands!" He nodded to himself in a self-congratulatory manner.

"But what's the beakery?" shouted a woman in the front row.

"The beakery?" asked the Magistrate, squinting at the paper again. The Mayor, who had remained standing behind the Magistrate, took a pencil from his pocket and pointed to the paper again.

"Ah, yes…" resumed the Magistrate "… the beakery was perpetrated at approximately eleven o'clock this morning in the lavatory of Mother Hubbard's tea rooms. The perpetrator had the audacity to leave the toilet seat in an upright position…" starting from the left, each prompter let go his folio cover in timed two-second intervals revealing the words "Ooh", "GASP", "SHOCK" and "HORROR". The crowd reacted accordingly in what could only be described as a frenzy of astonishment and indignation.

Bull, Bear and Leo all laughed out loud and uncontrollably, although upon realising that he was the only one who could actually hear Bull and Bear, Leo decided to tone down his laughing a little in case someone heard him.

"Ooh, Gladys, you can't believe your ears," said Vera.

"Ooh, you can't, Vera," said Gladys. "Whatever next, I wonder? I've never heard anything like it, I haven't. It needs stamping out right away!"

"Ooh, it does Gladys," agreed Vera.

Although both Leo and his father were frequently admonished by his mother for the same indiscretion, he could hardly believe such an offence warranted summoning several hundred people and bringing the entire town to a standstill, not to mention actually dispensing a rider with a handbell to summon people from the roads leading to the outlying villages. Perhaps the most astounding thing of all though, was not that those in power in Altcastle thought that the beakery merited such a treatment, but that those whom they had called to assemble seemed to be in such complete agreement with them – a fact which was amply demonstrated by the people's reaction to the announcement and the continuing chatter.

"Order, order, silence in court!" shouted the Magistrate, banging his gavel so vigorously that it bounced out of his hand and had to be caught by the Mayor. The prompters closed their folios, and then the one on the left opened his again on "SILENCE". The crowd fell silent. He closed his folio.

"There will be a most thorough investigation conducted by the Constable," continued the Magistrate, "but, as that may take some time to complete, I have no alternative but to find everyone guilty!" The prompter on the right displayed "CLAP", which most people did, although not very enthusiastically.

"Wait a minute!" shouted a well-dressed girl a little older than Leo. Everyone stopped clapping.

"Yes?" asked the Magistrate peering at her over his spectacles.

"Well, your Lordship, a girl or a woman wouldn't have left the lavatory seat up: only a boy or a man would have done that," she said. "So, that means that all girls and women are innocent!" The Magistrate reached inside his gown again, removed his hip flask, and took another large swig. As he did so, the Mayor whispered something into his ear. The Magistrate's eyes opened wide, and he pouted his lips and nodded.

"That young lady is Polly Sipby," said Bull.

"She's the niece of the Countess, so Justice Bender will no doubt take some note of her comment," added Bear. Leo nodded.

"Order, order!" he shouted, banging the gavel, which the Mayor had returned to him. "After careful consideration and long deliberation with the jury…" there was, of course, no jury at all "…I have decided that the young lady is quite correct in her analysis of the beakery, and I hereby declare that all girls and women are now NOT GUILTY!" A loud and spontaneous round of applause arose from all the females in the crowd: the prompters just stood there and looked at each other blankly.

"Wait a minute, wait a minute!" shouted a very smartly dressed man at the front. He was wearing a long, black caped-cloak and a black top hat. His left hand was covered by a folded newspaper, and in his right hand, he carried a black walking cane with an ornate silver cobra's head on the handle. The clapping stopped.

"Yes, Mr Cromwell?" asked the Magistrate.

"You've already given the verdict, my Lord," said the man. "You can't change the verdict – not once you've given it, it's not lawful!"

"Oh," said the Magistrate, putting his hand to his chin and slightly covering his mouth.

"That's Ebenezer Cromwell," said Bull.

"He's a damned hamster if ever there was one," added Bear. "The fellow can't be trusted at all."

Sighing could be heard coming from many of the females whilst the males all seemed very supportive of this latest gambit and started talking amongst themselves. The Mayor once again whispered something into the Magistrate's ear, and he again looked both elated and enlightened.

"Order, order, silence in court!" he shouted, still not seeming to notice they were not in court. The crowd fell silent almost before the prompter on the right had time to display his "SILENCE" page, which he quickly closed again. "You've made a very compelling point," said the Magistrate, pointing to Mr Cromwell. "Therefore, all girls and women are guilty again!" He banged his gavel down hard. Gasps, sighs and mutterings could be heard rising unprompted from the females. "But…" he continued – to a newfound silence "…notwithstanding their obvious guilt, they are all hereby granted a full and unconditional pardon. So rules this court!"

He banged the gavel down hard again, and a wave of euphoria spread amongst the females, once more accompanied by an equal amount of gasps, moaning and "it's not fair" mutterings from the assembled males. The prompter on the left opened his folio at "CLAP" and all the girls and women readily obliged, most males much less so. The Magistrate took his seat again and yet again had recourse to his hip flask, this time waving to all the ladies as he did so. Ebenezer Cromwell looked most displeased.

Leo was utterly astonished by the proceedings and found the whole system of justice – if it could even be so described – entirely bizarre. It actually seemed as though the whole thing had actually been designed as some kind of crazy Christmas pantomime in which the audience all participated gladly as extras – as part of the fun of the show.

Mayor Woodhay once more took to the lectern.

"I will now call upon the Honourable Chairlady of ACES, Mrs Sarah Pod, for a few brief words relating to this shocking beakery." All prompters displayed "CLAP" as Mrs Sarah Pod came to the lectern and the Mayor returned to his seat.

"What are ACES?" asked Leo.

"Altcastle Close Eye Society," said Bear.

"Always keeping a *close eye* out for any beakery," added Bull mockingly.

After a decent time, the prompters displayed "SILENCE", and Mrs Pod readied herself to speak.

"My dear, fellow citizens," she started, "as you all know, the Altcastle Close Eye Society, or ACES, as we are better known, has a long and proud history of keeping a close eye on all matters relating to good and citizenly conduct and remaining ever vigilant and watchful for the pernicious tentacles of hamsters and any beakeries they may see fit to perpetrate…"

"Hamsters don't have tentacles," whispered Leo. Bull and Bear just smiled.

"…in our ancient and loyal borough so happily governed by our dear Countess and Lord Mayor." The prompters displayed "CLAP", "VERY", "LOUDLY and "LOUDER". Everyone obliged. "SILENCE" was again displayed once the Mayor was satisfied.

"In order to defeat the forces of hamsterism, so cruelly thrust upon us all again this very morning, ACES is pleased to announce that we will be once again offering generous numbers of chocolate biscuit coupons to any and all citizens of Altcastle who offer information leading to the arrest of the perpetrator of this latest beakery. All coupons will be distributed by the good Constable himself…"

"Or not," muttered Bear.

"That's why he's so fat," chuckled Bull.

"…so, as we, at ACES, always say:

A snitch a day keeps the hamsters at bay,
So don't let beakery have its way,
Go snitch now, and don't delay!
(No Evidence Required)

Thank you all and a Merry Mipas!"

The prompters again displayed "CLAP", "VERY", "LOUDLY and "LOUDER". Everyone again obliged but even more enthusiastically this time.

"Must be the promise of chocolate biscuits," commented Bear.

"Quite so," agreed Bull.

Mrs Sarah Pod returned to her seat, and the Mayor once again took to the lectern. As he stood up, it started to sleet lightly, and the prompts changed to "SILENCE". The Mayor looked up to the sky, and a few umbrellas went up in the crowd.

"Order, order!" he called out, banging the gavel. "Given the change in weather, I shall be brief … just a few announcements, and we'll be done. So, firstly, I'm pleased to announce that Punch & Judy will be playing from today right up until Mipas, right here in front of the Guildhall…" there was unprompted and spontaneous applause at this "… and tomorrow morning, please do join the *Protest Against Savers* starting here in front of the Guildhall at nine o'clock sharp! Free hot cocoa will be served to all!"

"What about chocolate biscuits, your Worship?" shouted one boy.

"Yes, I'll see what I can do," said the Mayor raising his forefinger and smiling. "Thanks for asking! Well, I think that will be all for now. Thank you, everybody, good day!" And with that, he and all the other dignitaries scurried away in the direction of the Ironmarket as did the prompters and trumpeters.

"Ooh… what a pity, Gladys, I was really enjoying that meeting," said Vera.

"Ooh, yes, so was I, Vera," agreed Gladys. "Why don't we go to Mother Hubbard's Tea Rooms and have a nice cup of tea and some Altstanton Cake?"

"Ooh, yes, let's," said Vera, "then we can have a natter about who we can snitch on this week. I've already got a few ideas."

"Ooh, yes, that'll be lovely, it will." And they too departed the scene.

"Well, Master Leo, what did you think of that?" asked Bear.

"Amazing!" said Leo. "But not in a good way! I've never witnessed such total nonsense in my entire life. I think the whole town, and everyone in it, is completely mad!"

"Present company excepted, eh?" asked Bull opening his left eye wide.

"Of course," agreed Leo.

"But isn't your Newcastle like this?" asked Bear.

"Not even slightly," said Leo.

"What a pity," lamented Bull. "It must be very boring."

"I suppose if you like this kind of thing, it would be," agreed Leo.

"Well," said Bear, "looking up at the Guildhall clock, it's half past one already, and the library will be open again by now. Shall we go and search for a book about smoke signals?"

"Oh, yes," said Leo, "I'm still worried about my parents. If time hasn't stopped and it's also 1:30pm in my reality, my parents will be going mad by now because I haven't called to say I'm OK."

"Do your watch and gadget still say the same time?" asked Bull. Leo checked them both and nodded.

"Yes, exactly as they were," he said.

"Very good," said Bear, "then I am sure it is still 10:34 in Newcastle, but let's make haste and contact Doctor Toad in any case."

CHAPTER FIVE

THE LIBRARY OF
INOFFENSIVE BOOKS

BEAR LED THE WAY. They walked north-west along the High Street towards the Ironmarket, the street that runs perpendicular to the High Street in both Altcastle and Newcastle. As they did so, Leo noticed that the Police Station was situated on the south-eastern corner of what was in his Newcastle the Lancaster Building, but the narrow passageway connecting High Street and Ironmarket was in just the same location. As they rounded the corner and headed right, Leo immediately saw a grand and imposing clock tower towards the left. By now the sleet had turned to snow, and quite a gusty wind had blown up.

"What's that building?" he asked, pointing.

"That's the Municipal Hall," said Bear.

"That's where we are going," said Bull. "The library is in there."

"Is the Hall not there in your Newcastle?" asked Bear.

"No," said Leo, "the building that is there in my reality was the library, but that is closed down and empty now, but it wasn't a beautiful building like that one anyway."

"What a pity that the Municipal Hall isn't there anymore in your reality. I think even above the Guildhall, it's the finest Building in Altcastle," mused Bear.

"Yes, it looks it," agreed Leo.

"But why has Newcastle's library closed down?" asked Bull.

"The library has been moved inside the new civic building now as not as much space is needed for books as it used to be. I guess because most people don't read as many books anymore as they used to," said Leo, "and when they do, they read them on their phone or on a tablet."

"They read books on a tablet!" exclaimed Bear.

"They must be incredibly short books," declared Bull. "Either that or the writing must be minuscule."

"Indeed," agreed Bear, "one couldn't possibly fit very many words on a tablet."

"And what if the reader fell ill," added Bull, "and needed to take the tablet for medicinal purposes?"

"What a bizarre practice," mused Bear, "one could lose one's book merely by developing a headache!"

"Indeed," added Bull, "the whole notion is ridiculous."

Leo shook his head despairingly and sighed. As they had by this time walked the length of Ironmarket and reached the Public Library, he felt it might be better to explain the concept of tablets later.

"Ah, here we are," said Bear. They turned left under the arch of the Municipal Hall and entered the library.

It was, in Leo's opinion, how a library should look. He stopped for a moment in the foyer and marvelled at how delightfully antique it all was with its dark wood panelling and shelving, and its gas-lit chandeliers. Near to the front desk, on the wall, was a large official-looking sign in a gilded frame which read:

Any and All Beakeries Observed in this Library
are to be Reported Immediately to the Relevant
Authorities Without Undue Delay.

~ By Order of ~

The Worshipful Countess of Altcastle-under-Lyme

The Right Honourable Lady Debra Sipby

Next to the sign was a notice board promoting various bodies and groups. The ACES had a notice encouraging snitching and signed by Mrs Sarah Pod. Underneath that was a notice of a meeting to be held in the Guildhall on Sunday 16th December by TAGS, which apparently stood for "The Altcastle Goodbers Society" and just to the left of that was another notice designed around what looked like the picture of a whippet with antlers advertising the giving out of cocoa and chocolate biscuits to anyone who turned up for the meeting – that was issued by MOAB, which had "Mooses Of Altcastle Borough" written in small print underneath and that one was signed by one Mr Arthur Pod Esquire – the husband of Sarah Pod maybe? Curiously the main thrust of the notice seemed to be the encouragement of moose-like behaviour which Leo considered somewhat strange, to say the least.

On the extreme right of the notice board the largest notice, actually more like a poster, was advertising something called the "Mayor's Mipas Magpie March" and had a large sketch of the High Street with the Guildhall in the background and a line of hundreds of people walking in a conga-like line, bent forward with their hands behind their backs. The Mayor himself was leading this madness in his best top hat. Unsurprisingly by this stage in Leo's adventure, the official patroness of the said Mayor's Mipas Magpie March was given as The Right Honourable Lady Debra Sipby.

"They're all deranged here," muttered Leo under his breath.

Once Leo had finished inspecting the notice board, they walked on past the front desk and into the main library which had a multitude of signage to indicate all manner of subject matter, although the majority of the signage indicated science subjects like botany and ornithology, hobbies like floristry and painting, cooking, poetry and fiction. There seemed very little in the way of either history or geography, both, or either, of which were the headings under which Leo might have expected to find a book about smoke signals. They walked around for a few minutes looking at the various categories.

"Why are there so few books about history?" asked Leo.

"Too violent, I expect," suggested Bear.

"The Countess doesn't approve of people reading about wars and that type of thing," added Bull, "better to read about beekeeping and how to make honey, or how to arrange flowers nicely."

"Precisely," agreed Bear, "or about cross-stitching or how to make sushi. All those tales of the past can elicit unpleasant thoughts you know, and make people feel sad when they should be feeling happy."

"But that will result in widespread ignorance," protested Leo, "I've read dozens of books about history and wars."

"Well, you won't find many here..."

"Or even any," interjected Bull. "In fact, it will be a lot quicker if you ask the librarian, Mr Zenodotus. I think he's Altreek, but he's lived in Altcastle for a long time, so his Altlish is very good. He can't see us exactly, but we always get a distinct feeling that he half senses us, so he must be quite wise. We'll stay back here so as not to raise any suspicions against you."

"Right," said Leo. "I'll go and ask him."

"Don't forget to be polite," said Bull.

"What do you mean?" asked Leo indignantly. "I'm always polite!"

"Of course, of course," spluttered Bull apologetically. "I just meant that in Altcastle, children always address older gentlemen as *Sir*, so don't forget or he'll think it odd."

"Especially in view of your clothing," added Bear.

"My clothing?" queried Leo.

"Haven't you noticed that you are dressed somewhat oddly by Altcastle standards?" asked Bear. Leo looked down at his tracksuit bottoms and trainers. "The parka coat is passable as explorers wear them, but the material and stitching are most unusual and in any case why would anyone of your age be wearing one in a town?"

"And as for the shoes and trousers, no one here will have ever seen such things. It's only because of the bad weather and all the excitement of the beakery that no one has noticed thus far. So just don't speak strangely, that's what we're saying," added Bear.

"Right," said Leo, "got it."

Leo walked over towards Mr Zenodotus. He was quite an old looking chap, well over sixty, with a bald head and very short, white bristly hair on the sides and back. He was quite portly, and the faded leather-covered buttons of his herringbone waistcoat appeared as if about to pop, as did his watch chain. He wore a shortish jacket in charcoal grey cotton and a white shirt with a black necktie. He had one pair of full circle gold wire spectacles on his face, and another pair hung around his neck on a chain.

"Excuse me, Sir," said Leo as politely as he could. Mr Zenodotus put down the books he was working with and turned around.

"Yes, young fellow, how can I help you?" he asked.

"I am looking for a book on the subject of smoke signals, Sir. Would your library happen to have such a book?" asked Leo, feigning as well as he could the way in which Bull and Bear spoke.

"Hmm…" mused Mr Zenodotus, scratching his chin "… smoke signals, eh? A most curious choice of subject, if I may say so." Leo just smiled. Mr Zenodotus looked around the hall of the main library as if in search of some inspiration. "Ah," he said finally, lifting his forefinger in the air, "I think we might just have…" He wandered off towards the end of a long bookcase against one of the walls, appearing to mutter to himself as went. Leo followed him and noticed that it said "Other Countries" on the signage above the shelf. Mr Zenodotus started to run his finger along the edge of the shelf.

"If we have anything it will most certainly be in this section, although I must say that in more than thirty years of working here, I have never come across any book specifically on the subject of smoke signals," commented Mr Zenodotus as he continued looking. "Hmm…" he muttered once again, before pulling out a largish volume entitled "Encyclopaedia of North Altmerican Cultures". It seemed to have many hundreds of pages.

"It is, I fancy, a most singular subject which you have chosen, young fellow," said Mr Zenodotus, as he opened the book and turned to the index at the back. He languidly went through the index pages until he came to "S". "Ah," he said finally, "here we are! Pages 189 to 201." He turned to page 189 and then handed the book to Leo, who took it from him gently. "Will that do?" he asked. Leo skipped through the pages, which seemed to contain what he was looking for – there were instructions on how to burn wet and dry straw, how to use a wet blanket, appropriate siting, wind speed and direction; in fact, everything Leo might have expected. There were even a good number of pencil sketches showing the techniques.

"This will do very well, Sir," said Leo finally. "May I borrow it?"

"Of course, young fellow," said Mr Zenodotus, "that is the whole purpose of a library! You do have your library membership card on you?" Leo's heart sank: of course, he had no library card! He thought for a moment.

"I'm afraid I left it in my other coat – I just put this one on because of the weather," he said – it was the best he could come up with. Mr Zenodotus eyed Leo up and down and took particular note of his coat.

"Hmm…" he said, "well it is a singularly fine coat. Why in fact, you look like a polar explorer," he added with a chuckle. Leo just smiled again and nodded. Bull and Bear were watching from a distance as best they could and trying to monitor what was going on. Leo looked over at them and grimaced.

"Well," said Mr Zenodotus, "you seem like a goodber, so I suppose it will do no harm if you take it away today and get your card stamped tomorrow … but do not forget, as it is technically against the rules, you know."

"I will not forget, Sir, I assure you," Leo replied.

"Very good, then, I hope you find what you are looking for and enjoy learning about it," said Mr Zenodotus with a broad and friendly smile.

"Thank you very much, Sir," said Leo. "You have been most helpful."

Mr Zenodotus nodded, "Good day, young fellow."

"Good day, Sir," said Leo. He turned around quickly and returned to Bull and Bear. Before any of them spoke, they exited the library and the Municipal Hall, and returned to the Ironmarket where it was still snowing but only very slightly.

"So, old boy?" asked Bull.

"All good," replied Leo. "It seems this book will do. It has good instructions on making the fire and all that. Looks like we'll need a thick blanket. I think for more detail; we'll need to go somewhere to read it."

"Does it explain how to make words and numbers using the smoke?" asked Bear.

"I didn't see that," said Leo, "but I've only skimmed through it yet. It does show how to use a blanket to make different signals, though."

"As you say, we need somewhere quiet to read it," agreed Bear, looking up at the clock of the Municipal Hall which read ten minutes to two.

"Maybe we could get a small snack somewhere?" asked Leo. "I'm quite hungry now."

"Of course, dear fellow," said Bear, "I fancy we'd quite forgotten about lunch."

"It was all the excitement of the beakery," said Bull, "a case like that was enough to distract even the finest mind. What would you prefer for lunch, Master Leo?"

"I noticed there are quite a few pie shops and that type of thing; of course my usual eateries aren't here."

"What are your usual eateries?" asked Bear.

"Mainly I go to McDonald's or Subway," said Leo.

"What curious trading names exist in your reality," mused Bull.

"You do have some money, though?" asked Bear rhetorically, while fumbling around in his frock coat and waistcoat pockets. "I'm afraid I spent my last ha'penny on this morning's Daily Tale … do you have any, old boy?" he asked, referring to Bull.

"I'm afraid not," he replied after checking his pockets. "All my money is in the tin at home, I never imagined we'd need any money today."

"Nor I," concurred Bear.

"It's fine," said Leo, pulling out his three two-pound coins: "I have six pounds."

"Six pounds!" exclaimed Bull. "My goodness, you're a wealthy fellow!"

Leo appeared to be somewhat shocked: he didn't consider six pounds to constitute much wealth.

"Just a moment," said Bear regarding the three coins in Leo's palm, "what are they supposed to be?"

"They're two-pound coins," retorted Leo.

"Two-pounds coins, you say?" scoffed Bear.

"But pounds only come in notes!" said Bull incredulously.

"And even then, they don't come in a denomination of two!" added Bear.

"Well, they're fine in Newcastle," said Leo.

"I'm afraid they'll be of no use in Altcastle," lamented Bear.

"Then what can we do?" asked Leo.

"We could go back home and fetch some," said Bull, "but it's a long walk."

"Wait a minute, old boy," said Bear to Bull in a delight of realisation, "didn't we leave some money with Emma Jency several months ago, just in case we were embarrassed one day."

"Indeed we did, old fellow," confirmed Bull, jovially slapping Bear on the back. "All's well then: we can just go now to Emma's shop."

"Who is Emma Jency?" asked Leo.

"Emma is a most remarkable custodian of all manner of things," said Bull. "One simply makes an assessment of any item or items which one might run out of, or otherwise be in need of in an unexpected emergency, and then one simply deposits a small supply of such items at Emma's shop to be collected at some future point when the need arises. In the meantime, Emma will take good care of the items in her custody."

"Why does she offer such a service?" asked Leo. "I've never heard of such a thing."

"She does it because she's Emma Jency," said Bear, "and that's what Emma Jency does!"

"How much did we leave, Bear? Do you remember?" asked Bull.

"No... actually I don't. Not exactly, anyway... but it was about ten shillings I reckon," replied Bear thoughtfully.

"Shillings!" exclaimed Leo. "Are you really still using shillings here?"

"Why would we not be using shillings?" asked Bear indignantly. "Don't you have shillings?"

"No," said Leo, "just pounds and pence."

"What? And no shillings?" spluttered Bear.

"No, they went out with decimalisation," said Leo.

"Decimalisation?" retorted Bull. "What is that?"

"That's when pounds, shillings and pence were replaced with just pounds and pence," said Leo.

"Why would anyone do such a heinous thing?" asked Bear. "What happened to all the shillings?"

"I don't really know," said Leo. "It happened a long time before I was born, but my dad told me all about it and how his favourite chocolate bar immediately went up in price in the new money."

"I thought as much as soon as you mentioned it," said Bull. "It sounded from the start as if some kind of terrible scam."

"I don't think it was actually a scam," said Leo, "it was just progress."

"Progress? It's an odd name to give to a scam," said Bear: "when the price of a fellow's chocolate bar suddenly goes up, then that sounds like a scam to me!"

"You might be right," said Leo, "as I said: I don't know a huge amount about it."

"Well," said Bull, "at least if a pound is still two-hundred and forty pence, I suppose it may not be too bad, but it still sounds incredibly inconvenient having no shillings." Leo thought for a moment.

"Actually," he said, "a pound is only one-hundred pence, not two-hundred and forty."

"There we are then!" stated Bear triumphantly and raising a claw of his right paw in the air: "a scam of historic proportions, just like I told you! A full one-hundred and forty pence lost per pound: outrageous!" Leo nodded in agreement although the maths had quite lost him.

"Good, good," said Bull, "now that we've resolved that small matter of financial beakery, let's be off; then we can get Master Leo a pie or sandwich to eat. Emma's shop isn't far; it's in Red Lion Square. Do you know it?"

"Yes," said Leo, "it's at the end of the High Street."

"That's it," said Bull slapping him on the back, and the three of them set off down the Ironmarket at a brisk pace.

CHAPTER SIX

A PLACE FOR
EVERYTHING

THEY SOON REACHED THE end of the Ironmarket, turned to their right into the High Street and were soon in Red Lion Square. The tower and roof of St. Giles loomed large over the rooftops to their left.

"The church looks exactly the same," said Leo, "as do the buildings at the end."

"Old buildings again," mused Bear, "it's significant for sure that all the really old buildings are the same in both Altcastle and Newcastle. Once we've obtained some money for food, we'll get on to signalling the Indomitable Doctor Toad, and I'm certain he will be able to make a valid conclusion based upon our observations of what is different and what is not." Leo nodded stoically.

"I hope so," he said.

"Here we are," said Bull: "Emma's shop."

Leo looked up at the signage above the shop, which read: *Miss Emma Jency's Box & Tin Emporium*. The shopfront looked tidy and neat. There was a retractable awning over the main window and the door – which was on the extreme left of the building. Next-door, to the shop's left and adjoined, stood the "Globe Commercial Hotel" – a Georgian-looking building. Both the hotel and Emma's shop were of three storeys.

"Shall we go in?" suggested Bear. Leo nodded, and Bull opened the door allowing first Bear and then Leo to enter. As the door had opened a small bell had been rung, and just as Bull closed the door behind himself, a woman of about twenty-five appeared from a small door marked *PRIVATE* and entered into the shop space behind a wooden counter with a glass top. She had flaxen hair which was plaited and tied-up into a bun, dark brown eyes and a pale milky complexion. She was dressed in a cotton ankle-length floral print green dress, with a white lace collar and buttoned bodice. The skirt of the dress was circular but not overly so, and the garment was obviously designed for work rather than ostentation. She wore lace-up black leather ankle boots with a small heel on her feet.

"Ah, Mr Bull and Mr Bear," she exclaimed in a salutatory tone, "how very nice to see you both!"

"Good afternoon, Miss Jency," they both replied in unison, tipping their respective hats.

"She can actually see you?" asked Leo quietly.

"Of course," said Bear, "we told you that wise people can see us, and Miss Emma Jency is certainly one of the wisest people in Altcastle."

"Allow us to introduce our new friend, Master Leo," said Bull holding his hoof out towards Leo.

"How do you do?" said Emma, coming out from behind her counter and offering her hand.

"Very well, thank you, Miss Jency," replied Leo, very politely, while shaking her hand. She smiled and bowed her head very slightly.

"I feel sure that there will be no need for such formality," she said, "you may call me Emma. May I call you Leo?"

"Sure," said Leo.

"So, gentlemen," said Emma, turning her attention to Bull and Bear, "what brings you to my shop today?"

"Our young friend is in need of some sustenance, and unfortunately we find ourselves with insufficient funds to finance its provision," said Bear.

"I see," replied Emma. "So you have come to collect some *Emma's Money*?" she added, returning to the rear of her counter.

"Indeed," replied Bear.

Leo scanned his eyes around the shop. It was certainly not misnamed as a *box and tin emporium* for it contained shelf upon shelf of tins and boxes of all shapes and sizes. In the window, there was a display of over fifty items at least, and on the floor, there were several very large boxes and some trunks, some of which looked like ones that might contain pirate treasure. The tins and boxes on the shelves comprised a very eclectic collection with some painted, some plain, some varnished, some unvarnished – in all, just about every type of box or tin that anyone could possibly desire. The shop also had a fireplace with an ornate surround and mantelpiece. There was a bucket of coal on one side and a box of chopped logs on the other. The remnants of a fire smouldered in the iron grate.

Emma opened a small drawer in the bureau behind her counter and pulled out a silver tin with a "V" etched neatly onto its lid. She opened the tin and looked inside.

"You have ten shillings and sixpence," she said cheerfully.

"That's sixpence more than we thought we had!" said Bull with a wide smile.

"Always better to have more than less!" replied Emma.

"Indeed," agreed Bear.

"How much do you need?" asked Emma.

"Let me see," said Bear, "we'll need a few pence for lunch… maybe some more for supper if we're still out…"

"We need to buy a blanket too," added Bull.

"Yes, I'd forgotten about that," agreed Bear. "So, I think five shillings will be more than enough."

"Of course we'll be back tomorrow to replace what we're taking today," said Bull.

"Naturally," said Emma.

"You see, Master Leo," said Bear, "wise creatures always remember that whenever they have need to call upon Emma, they should always replace whatever they have taken as soon as possible afterwards so that they always have an emergency supply that never runs dry."

"Yes, it seems a good system," agreed Leo while looking at the small tin with its hinged lid. "But may I ask, Emma, how do you remember whose tin is whose?"

"Well," said Emma gently, "if you have been here in Altcastle for any length of time, or even more than a few hours, in fact, you will have no doubt noticed that very few people are at all wise. Accordingly, with so few clients for my service, it is not considerably difficult for me to recall whose tin is whose: I currently have only seven depositors in fact."

"I see," said Leo smiling again. He had immediately liked Emma, and it seemed to him that she was in fact, quite wise herself.

"How do you know he's not from Altcastle, he could be from one of the outlying villages?" asked Bear with a suspicious squint.

"Well, it is rather obvious from your attire, Leo," she replied addressing him rather than Bear, as it might well be considered somewhat rude in polite company to speak about someone in the third person when they are present, and Emma Jency did most certainly appear to be quiet proper in her manners. Leo smiled and looked at his trainers again.

"The coat is just plausible, though highly unusual," she said, holding her hand out and tipping it about its axis, "but the trousers and footwear are clearly not from Altcastle; and since it is most unlikely that you have been given either an import license to obtain goods from elsewhere, or a pass to leave the Borough and go shopping elsewhere, I deduce that you are not from the Altcastle Borough."

"Hmm… we've always said that Emma Jency's a wise one, eh Bull?" said Bear.

"Indeed we have, Bear… indeed we have," chuckled Bull.

"So, where do you think I'm from, Emma?" asked Leo, fascinated by the interaction and enjoying the fun of it.

"Well that, I fancy, cannot be deduced without more information, but I would certainly venture that you are not only an alien to Altcastle but also to Altland. Where are you from, may I ask?"

"I am from Newcastle-under-Lyme, which the three of us have now worked out is actually in an alternate reality to Altcastle-under-Lyme, but at some point in the past was the same place," stated Leo matter-of-factly.

"The two towns probably exist in the same space at least, but not it seems at the same time; as time appears stalled in Newcastle-under-Lyme but continuing here… it's most perplexing," explained Bear.

"How incredibly fantastical," exclaimed Emma. "So how did you get here?"

"That small matter, we have not been able to work out yet," said Bull, "so we intend to consult the Indomitable Doctor Toad to see if he can throw any light on it."

"And I suspect," said Emma, "that it is for such express purpose that you wish to purchase the blanket which you referred to earlier?"

"Indeed," spluttered Bear, "what powers of deduction you have!"

"A Sherlock Holmes type, eh, Leo?" commented Bull.

"Indeed," said Leo with a nod. He was becoming quite used to the way in which Bull, Bear, and now Emma, all spoke and rather enjoyed copying it when the opportunity arose. "Indeed" was not a word he had previously used very often.

"I am surprised, though, to hear you mention Sherlock Holmes. So you do know who Sherlock Holmes is?" asked Leo to Bull.

"Of course," said Bull, "everyone has heard of Sherlock Holmes."

"Curious," said Leo.

"What do you find curious?" asked Emma.

"That not only are some buildings the same, and the older ones at that, but also Sherlock Holmes is known in both realities – also an old series of stories, although not that old. It would be interesting to know when Sherlock Holmes was first published," mused Leo. "Because if Newcastle's and Altcastle's timelines have diverged from a common history, then it must have been both after the buildings were built and after Sherlock Holmes was first published."

"Fascinating," said Bear; "truly fascinating! You are using the publication date of a story about a detective who uses deductive logic to logically deduce when the timelines diverged!"

"Sherlock Holmes would be proud!" said Bull.

"Indeed," said Bear, Leo and Emma all together in unpremeditated spontaneity. Everyone laughed.

"Returning to the topic of Doctor Toad," said Bear, "do you know of him, Emma?"

"Indeed, I do," said Emma, "I have had occasion to consult the good Doctor myself on several occasions."

"I see," said Bull, "then you know about the smoke signals?"

"Of course," confirmed Emma, "one must send the smoke signals from the top of Bunny Hill just to the north of Rowley Wood."

"I know Bunny Hill," said Leo, "I play with my friends there."

"Is it the same Bunny Hill?" asked Bear.

"It lies just to the south of Altbridge," said Emma.

"So… Altbridge here would be… hmm… Seabridge, I guess. So, yes," said Leo, "that's right then – same place! It's funny all the place names here start with '*Alt*', but the endings are the same as in my reality… except the Guildhall is still called the Guildhall and not the Althall or something like that, and now Bunny Hill is still called Bunny Hill and not Altunny Hill or similar. I wonder why it's like that?"

"Maybe Doctor Toad will be able to answer that," said Emma.

"Yes, hopefully," said Bear. "And so, Emma, it seems with this new Bunny Hill information, you know more than we do about Doctor Toad."

"Not an unusual circumstance, old boy," said Bull, chuckling.

"Quite so," confirmed Bear. "So, we now know that the preferred high ground from which to send the smoke signals is Bunny Hill. Leo has obtained a book from Mr Zenodotus..." Leo held up the book to show Emma "...so, we are going to consult that to find out exactly how to make the necessary smoke signals."

"May I see?" asked Emma. Leo placed the book down onto Emma's counter and opened it at page 189. Emma started to look through it.

"The main problem I suspect," said Bear, "will be to make an intelligible message."

"Quite so," agreed Bull, "I have no clue how to do that; hopefully, the book will tell us... unless you already know, Emma?"

"One must use Morse code," said Emma, "but I am not entirely sure of the exact mechanism for creating the short and long bursts of smoke, although I fancy some form of a chimney would be easier to use than a blanket."

"How did you contact Doctor Toad?" asked Bear.

"I employed the services of one Captain Bellamy, a dear old friend of the family," said Emma.

"Hmm... yes, I've heard of the fellow," said Bull, "although I don't think we've met him... or have we met him, Bear?"

"No... I don't believe so, old boy," said Bear.

"Where does he live?" asked Bull.

"In a cottage just to the south of Altridge," said Emma, "but that is about three miles from here and..." she looked at the carriage clock on her mantelpiece "…it is already half-past two."

"And the smoke signals will not be visible after the sun has set of course," mused Bull.

"Precisely," said Bear, "so we have very little time to get a message to Captain Bellamy to ask him to signal Doctor Toad."

"It is far too late in the day for any of us to make it to Altridge on foot and for the Captain to then go to Bunny Hill, light a fire and then send a signal," said Bull.

"There are more efficient methods of sending a message over such a distance," said Emma. "Come into my parlour, and we can write out the message that we would like the Captain to signal. My friend Nevermore will then take it to his cottage."

"Odd name … I don't think we've met your friend," said Bull, "he's a quick-footed fellow, then I take it?"

"Not exactly *quick-footed*," said Emma, "but quick, certainly." Emma smiled and went through the small doorway into her parlour; the three of them followed after her.

Her parlour was quite large – not as big an area as her shop floor but spacious, nonetheless. There was a fireplace with a Minton tile surround and ebonised mantelpiece above – somewhat deeper than the one in the shop and easily deep enough to have space for two oil lamps, a large wooden cased carriage clock, some framed photographs and some books. The walls were papered in a green print of swirling vines and leaves, and a green and red patterned rug adorned the boarded wooden floor. There were two armchairs either side of the fireplace, a large sideboard and several occasional tables, two large bookcases, a large circular dining table with a paisley print tablecloth and four dining chairs, a writing desk with its own chair and lastly but by no means least, a large wooden frame on which perched a jet black raven who looked at the three of them closely as they entered.

"Good afternoon… good afternoon," said the raven once they had all filed in.

"Good afternoon," said Leo, Bull and Bear.

"Please take seats as convenient," said Emma, collecting a fountain pen, a pot of ink and some paper from her writing desk. All four them took chairs at the dining table.

"So this is my dear old friend and companion, Nevermore," said Emma, looking at the raven.

"Why is he called Nevermore?" asked Bull, developing his earlier comment of it being an odd name.

"I think I know," said Leo.

"Do you indeed?" said Bear. "Then please enlighten the two of us."

"Is he named after the raven in Edgar Allan Poe's poem?" Leo asked Emma.

"He is, indeed," said Emma with a smile.

"Hmm… eh, Bear?" said Bull. "It's no wonder the fellow can see us."

"Quite so, quite so, Bull," agreed Bear.

"Do you know the poem?" asked Emma.

"Yes," said Leo, "my dad used to read it to me when I was young – it's one of his favourites. Do you happen to have a bust of Pallas around somewhere?" asked Leo with a smile.

"I am afraid that I do not," said Emma, "although I would certainly like to acquire one if the opportunity should arise."

"Bust of who?" spluttered Bull.

"Pallas, my dear fellow," said Bear.

"Never heard of him," scoffed Bull.

"Her," said Leo.

"Really?" muttered Bull, with a squint.

"Shall we compose the message?" asked Emma, glancing at the clock on her mantelpiece.

"Indeed," agreed Bear. Bull continued to eye Leo shiftily as if to marvel at his knowledge of Edgar Allan Poe and Ravens.

"So, shall we suggest a meeting place and time?" asked Emma.

"That would seem best," said Bear. "Somewhere we won't be seen, but then again somewhere that's also close enough for us to be able to get to easily."

"What about the cemetery?" suggested Bull. "If we make the meeting after dark, it will be deserted as there is no lighting."

"That seems to be a good idea, Mr Bull," said Emma.

"There you see, Bear: Emma says I've had a good idea," said Bull smugly.

"It was bound to happen one day," said Bear. Leo giggled.

"So I will write: Dear Doctor Toad, please can you meet us in the Municipal Cemetery, At five o'clock this evening regarding a most curious matter, Yours sincerely, Mr Bear & Mr Bull?"

"That sounds perfect," confirmed Bear.

Emma wrote out the message on a long, thin strip of paper, then rolled it up and placed it into a small tin cylinder no more than an inch high. She then attached the cylinder to Nevermore's leg.

"Please take this, my friend, to Captain Bellamy and ask him if he might be so kind as to signal Doctor Toad before the sun sets," she told Nevermore.

"Very well, Emma," said Nevermore, hopping off his perch onto the back of her hand. Emma proceeded into her kitchen and opened her back door.

"Please also convey my kindest regards to him," she said.

"I will," said Nevermore, and he stretched out his wings and flew up into the sky. Emma returned to the parlour and retook her seat.

"He's an incredibly useful fellow," said Bull.

"Indeed he is," agreed Emma.

"How do you know Captain Bellamy, if I may ask?" queried Bear.

"He was a friend of my mother," said Emma.

"Is he a military captain?" asked Leo.

"No, he was a seafarer," said Emma. "Of the private sector, I believe."

"I seem to recall some rumour that he was linked to piracy," said Bear.

"I fancy we shall say no more about that," admonished Emma somewhat indignantly.

"Quite so," said Bull looking at his friend huffily and then holding his hoof to his mouth to clear his throat. Bear sat back with a chastised expression.

"He is an extremely agreeable gentleman," said Emma, "and a longstanding client. His absentmindedness makes him a frequent visitor to my shop almost every other time he comes to town."

Just then, the sound of the Town Crier's handbell could be heard in the street outside and within seconds his gruff voice also.

"Oyez! Oyez! Oyez! Punch and Judy at three o'clock!" he shouted.

"O jolly good," said Bear. "I've been so looking forward to the commencement of the Mipas Punch and Judy season!"

"He does so love Punch and Judy, Emma," said Bull. "I shall be compelled to watch the whole season no doubt, even though it's the same thing over and over again – nothing ever new, nothing varied, nothing which it is not sufficient to have seen once!"

"Oh please, dear fellow, don't be such an awful bore," said Bear.

"And do you like Punch and Judy, Leo?" asked Emma.

"Well," started Leo hesitantly – not wishing to offend his friend, Bear, "I can certainly watch it, although…"

"There you are Bear," said Bull, interrupting him, "even Leo doesn't care for Punch and Judy!"

"He never actually said as much," complained Bear.

"It's incredibly boring," said Bull. "Nothing but slapping and walloping and messing about with sausages!"

"It's beakery, Sir; pure beakery to say such terrible things – an outrage against decency in fact!" protested Bear.

"Oh, dear, Mr Bull, I think you may have upset your friend," said Emma.

"No doubt he'll get over my comments a good deal quicker than I'll get over watching the nonsense for an hour a day between now and Mipas," said Bull. Leo and Emma laughed to see their sparring. "I agree with Bull," she mouthed to Leo silently.

"Let's be off then," said Bear, standing up, "it's almost three o'clock now!"

"Very well," agreed Bull.

"I do so admire the part with the sausages and the crocodile, you know," said Bear.

"We know… we know," mumbled Bull. "We shall return afterwards of course," he added. "I expect your feathered friend will have returned by then."

"I expect so," said Emma looking over at the clock, "whilst your gone, I will cut some sandwiches for you, Leo. Would that be fine?"

"Oh yes, thanks," said Leo, "I'm quite hungry now!" Emma, Bear and Bull all stood up, and Emma went off into the kitchen.

"So," said Bear, "we'll be back in about half an hour. It's a pity that you'll miss the show, but I suppose you'll have a chance to see it later."

"Oh, he will for sure," said Bull, "and I think the sandwiches will do him better."

"See you later," said Leo; Bull and Bear departed for the Punch and Judy show.

CHAPTER SEVEN

AN ALTERNATE
TEA-PARTY

—————————

"DO TAKE OFF YOUR coat, Leo, and make yourself at home. Put some more coal onto the fire, if you are feeling cold," Emma called from the kitchen.

"OK," he said, getting up and placing his coat on the coat stand next to the door by which he'd entered the parlour. He then proceeded to the fireplace and started to examine the coal bucket, fireguard and grate. He had never before had even the slightest interaction with an open fire – his own home had no fireplace of any description, having only a combi boiler powered central heating system operated from a wi-fi based control panel. He very cautiously removed the fireguard then took the coal tongs and lumped on five pieces of coal one by one. Feeling reasonably satisfied that five were enough, he hung the tongs back up and replaced the fireguard.

"Will you have tea?" called Emma.

"Oh, yes please," he called back.

Leo sat back down at the table and started to survey the pictures and photographs hanging on the wall of Emma's parlour. It was a wide-ranging collection in terms of both style and content, with post-impressionist and pre-Raphaelite pieces and a very large reproduction in oil of Botticelli's *The Birth of Venus* directly over the fireplace, which Leo considered somewhat risqué given Emma's apparent Victorian propriety.

"Here we are," said Emma, coming back into the parlour with a tray holding a charming china teapot with matching cups and saucers, tea plates, milk jug and sugar bowl. The spoons appeared to be of sterling silver as did the tea strainer and sugar tongs. She laid the tray down on the table.

"Very nice," said Leo; he was more accustomed to a mug.

Now that Leo had removed his coat to reveal a brownish polyester polo shirt, he looked even more out of place in his current surroundings.

"I fancy we shall have to find you some alternative clothing for the remainder of your stay in Altcastle," mused Emma looking at him, "those clothes are a certain giveaway that you do not belong here."

"Yes," he replied, ponderously looking down at his attire.

Emma reverted to the kitchen and soon returned with a three-tier cake stand, also of china, but of a slightly different pattern to the tea set. It had crustless sandwiches on the bottom tier, a variety of butterfly cakes on the second and a selection of petits fours on the top tier.

"Please do help yourself, Leo," said Emma. Leo's hungry eyes lit up. He took two sandwiches and put them onto his tea plate although the first one didn't stay long on the plate and was very quickly devoured. Emma sat down, set out the cups and saucers, and placed the tea strainer over Leo's cup.

"More tea?" she asked him very earnestly, but with a wry smile.

"I haven't…" he started to say, but then he smiled too, realising that she was playing a little game with him. "Yes, please," he answered instead.

"It's Darjeeling," she said, "my favourite… I do hope you like it."

"Yes, I like Darjeeling," said Leo, "we have it at home."

"Oh good," she said. She finished pouring Leo's tea and moved on to attend to her own cup. Leo added some milk to his tea and also a lump of sugar. He generally never took sugar, but he was so fascinated with the fact that the sugar was in cubes and could be served with such wonderfully quaint silver sugar tongs, that he decided he would have some on this occasion. "So, you are very familiar with *Alice's Adventures in Wonderland*, then?" asked Emma.

"I am, indeed," he answered, again emulating her manner of speaking. "It was the first whole book that I ever read. My dad is a big fan of Lewis Carroll."

"How delightful," she said. "I am also very fond of Carroll. I have all of his works."

"My dad does too. He often says that it's such a pity there are only two books in the Alice series and that one day when he has time, he might write a book himself along similar lines."

"Really? And about a girl called Alice, who enters into a strange and fantastical world?" asked Emma.

"Perhaps not about an Alice, or even a girl, but certainly about a child who finds him or herself in a strange and fantastical world, and then meets with all manner of unusual characters and bizarre situations," answered Leo. "He'd probably put a slightly different spin on it to Alice, but it would be along similar lines, I think… he once said that he might even make me the main character and include allusions to other books and authors I like, in addition to Alice and Lewis Carroll."

"Well, that does sound intriguing; I would certainly be interested in reading that," said Emma. Leo quickly ate his second sandwich, which was of thinly sliced cucumber; the first one had been of cheddar cheese. He was not overly fond of cucumber sandwiches, but he was very hungry and in any case did not wish to appear rude. He again eyed the cake stand voraciously as he swallowed his last mouthful. "Take some more," said Emma, "I will only be taking the two that I have, as I had lunch at one."

"Thanks," said Leo, taking a further three, but trying as best he could to select the ones with the cheese. "Shall we save some for Bull and Bear?" he asked.

"No need," said Emma, "they hardly ever eat sandwiches. They mostly eat some type of vegetable and berry soup, which Bull makes for them. Mr Bull is uncommonly fond of soup, I believe. He described it to me once; it sounds utterly revolting, I must say… but please do not mention that I said as much."

"I won't," agreed Leo.

"Are the sandwiches all right?" asked Emma.

"Oh, yes," he said, "I actually prefer sandwiches with the crusts cut off, but we never have them at home as it's too much trouble."

"I see," said Emma, "I always give the crusts to Nevermore. He likes them."

"Yes," said Leo, "if I leave my crusts, I always put them out for the birds." He continued munching away on his sandwiches and had soon finished them, turning his attention immediately to one of the chocolate butterfly cakes which seemed to be beckoning to him.

"Do take a cake, Leo. There is no need to be shy," said Emma, noticing his interest. He did as directed. Just as he was eating his cake, and Emma was pouring them both some more tea, they again heard the Town Crier's handbell ringing outside.

"Oyez! Oyez! Oyez!" he called. "Beakery abroad! There's beakery abroad! All to the Guildhall at half-past four!" The bell continued ringing, and he continued shouting out his message. "Beakery abroad! All to the Guildhall at half-past four!" they heard again as he continued down the street.

"My goodness," said Emma, "whatever is happening in Altcastle? There has not been a beakery for over three weeks, and now there have been two in just one day!" Just as she had finished speaking, they heard the sound of the bell tinkling as the shop door opened. Before Emma had even had a chance to stand up, Bull and Bear stormed into the parlour in an agitated fluster.

"You won't believe your ears!" cried Bear.

"Another beakery!" added Bull.

"Yes, we have just heard the Town Crier," said Emma. "What is it this time?"

"Mr Punch has gone missing!" said Bear excitedly.

"Oh, dear!" exclaimed Emma. "What a tragedy!"

"Yes," lamented Bear; "he gave an inspiring performance in scene one, but after being smashed by Judy with a wooden bat and some sausages, he never re-appeared for scene two…"

"And no one knows where he is or what has happened to him!" interjected Bull.

"A rumour soon circulated through the crowd that he's been kidnapped!" added Bear.

"No! Really?" said Emma. "Kidnapped? In Altcastle? It cannot be so!"

"I think it's something to do with GOTCHA and Ebenezer Cromwell and his boys!" suggested Bear keenly.

"You always think GOTCHA is behind everything!" scoffed Bull.

"What is GOTCHA?" asked Leo.

"It stands for Guild of The Covered Hand Associates," said Emma. "They are a scurrilous secret society run by the noted scoundrel Ebenezer Cromwell."

"You remember, he was complaining about the Magistrate's verdict earlier," said Bear.

"Oh yes, I remember," said Leo.

"Anyway," said Bull, "there's no evidence that either GOTCHA or Ebenezer Cromwell are behind the disappearance… or even that Mr Punch has been kidnapped. He may just have been taken ill or something else quite innocent."

"I doubt that very much," said Bear shaking his head solemnly. "It's most unusual in the middle of a show... very disturbing indeed, I have to say!"

"No doubt more information on the incident will be revealed at half-past four," said Emma.

"No doubt," agreed Bear.

"Perhaps, you will have some tea, to calm your nerves?" suggested Emma.

"I will," said Bear. "Oh, I will, yes. It's all been most unsettling...many of the smaller children are crying their poor eyes out, sneeped they are, beyond measure." Emma went to the kitchen to fetch two extra cups and saucers.

"There were sneepsters all abroad," agreed Bull.

"What are sneepsters?" asked Leo.

"People who are sneeped, of course," responded Bull.

"Anyone who has been, and persists in a state of being sneeped is referred to as a sneepster," explained Bear.

"And *sneeped* means upset," added Emma.

"Yes, I know the word *sneeped*; we have that in my Newcastle, but not *sneepster*," said Leo.

"How fascinating," mused Bear, "what a terrible paucity of language you have in your reality: no *beakery*... no *sneepsters*... why, it's difficult to imagine how any of you manage to communicate at all!"

Leo smiled at Emma, who was pouring Bear his cup of tea.

"Well, we just about manage," he said.

"Here is your tea, Bear," said Emma handing it to him.

"Thank you so much, dear lady," he said earnestly.

"Would you care for a cup of tea, Mr Bull?" asked Emma.

"Why not," he replied, sitting himself down at the table, "we shall have to wait until at least twenty-five past four now to walk up to Penkhull Street and hear what has become of poor old Mr Punch."

"Indeed," agreed Bear, also taking a seat at the table and eyeing the butterfly cakes with a good deal more than mere curiosity.

"Do both help yourselves to anything you fancy," said Emma.

"Most kind... most kind," muttered Bull. He took two cakes and several petits fours. Bear shook his head disapprovingly, but no more than five seconds later took one cake and two petits fours himself. Emma smiled to herself.

"I will leave the pot here," she said, putting it down, "then you may all help yourselves."

"So," said Bear, with his mouth still half-filled with cake, "what did you find to talk about while we were away?"

"We spoke mainly about Alice," said Emma.

"Alice who?" asked Bull.

"Alice, as in *Alice's Adventures in Wonderland*," replied Emma.

"And what did you say of it?" asked Bear.

"Oh, how much we both admire the book and the work of Carroll in general," she said.

"Ah, quite so," said Bull; "it's the finest of literature."

"It is indeed," agreed Bear, "but please don't get carried along too far, old boy, and start singing... or even worse – composing lines for the poetry competition."

"Are you thinking to enter this year, Mr Bull?" asked Emma.

"I am, in fact... although Bear is actively trying to discourage it... as usual," lamented Bull.

"Oh, Mr Bear," said Emma, "surely you could indulge your friend a little at Mipas."

"Well," said Bear, "I just can't take his singing of *Beautiful Soup* at all hours, and as to his composing, the metre never seems quite right to me, you know."

"My metre is as good as anyone else's," complained Bull, "and furthermore, my rendering of *Beautiful Soup* has been widely praised by those whom I think it acceptable for me to refer to as cognoscenti of Carrollian matters."

"Really?" questioned Emma.

"Indeed," attested Bull, putting a hoof to his mouth and clearing his throat most expressively.

"I would really like to hear you sing *Beautiful Soup*," said Leo.

"As would I," said Emma. Bull pulled in his chest with pride and looked at his friend, Bear, sneeringly. Bear shook his head mournfully.

"Shall I proceed immediately?" he asked, with a broad smile.

"Please do," said Emma. Bear hung his head in despair, and Leo laughed. Bull stood up and was about to start when there came a tapping on the window. They all looked round; it was the beak of Nevermore against the glass. Emma went immediately to the back door and opened it, upon which Nevermore hopped from the windowsill onto her hand.

"All well, my friend?" asked Emma.

"All well," confirmed Nevermore. "Captain Bellamy sends his compliments. He went directly to Bunny Hill as soon as he had read the message and sent up the smoke signals. I saw them in the sky behind me as I glanced back while flying home."

"Very good," she said, "you have done well." She returned to the parlour and Nevermore flew from her hand onto the table.

"A little cake will be most welcome," he said, looking at Leo.

"Which one would you like?" asked Leo. Nevermore tilted his head to one side and looked at the selection on offer.

"Vanilla if you please," he said. Leo took one of the vanilla butterfly cakes and put it onto the tea plate which he had been using himself, then pushed it over the table to where Nevermore was now standing.

"Most kind," he said, tilting his head to the other side before starting to peck at his cake. He ate the cream first.

"We were just about to hear Mr Bull sing *Beautiful Soup* from *Alice's Adventures in Wonderland*," said Emma, "I feel sure that you will appreciate that too, Nevermore?"

"Indeed I will, Emma," agreed Nevermore. Bull's face lit up as he inhaled deeply and then began his performance:

"Beautiful Soup, so rich and green,
Waiting in a hot tureen!
Who for such dainties would not stoop?
Soup of the evening, beautiful Soup!
Soup of the evening, beautiful Soup!
Beau--ootiful Soo--oop!
Beau--ootiful Soo--oop!
Soo--oop of the e--e--evening,
Beautiful, beautiful Soup!

Beautiful Soup! Who cares for fish,
Game, or any other dish?
Who would not give all else for two
Pennyworth only of beautiful Soup?
Pennyworth only of beautiful Soup?
Beau--ootiful Soo--oop!
Beau--ootiful Soo--oop!
Soo--oop of the e--e--evening,
Beautiful, beauti--FUL SOUP!"

As he finished and made a small bow in favour of his audience, everyone applauded loudly, even Bear. Nevermore flapped his wings together in front of himself so vigorously and for so long that Leo wondered how it was even anatomically possible for a raven to do that.

"Excellent!" said Emma. "You do have a most attractive voice, Mr Bull." Bear sneered sulkily and helped himself to another of the petits fours.

"I think there's no subject more worthy of singing about than soup," said Bull.

"Do you sing. Bear?" asked Leo.

"Certainly not," he spluttered, almost choking on his chocolate at the very thought of it.

"What about you, Leo?" asked Emma.

"Not at all," he said, shaking his head. "Do you?"

"I fear that I have quite a terrible singing voice," said Emma.

"Quite right… quite right…" muttered Nevermore. "Mostly on washing day," he added.

"Oh, really," rebuked Emma, "we have guests!" Nevermore just shrugged and carried on pecking at his cake. Emma looked over at the clock on the mantelpiece.

"I had better arrange for the alternative clothing for you, Leo," said Emma, "as we shall need to leave before too long to find out what has happened to Mr Punch."

"Do you have any boys' clothing?" asked Bear.

"I do not," replied Emma, standing up and collecting her coat from the coat stand by the door, "but I fancy that if I go over to George the Tailor, I should be able to borrow something which we can use for a few days." She put on her coat and buttoned it up, then took a small black bonnet from her sideboard and a pair of silk gloves. "I shall not be too long, Leo: George's shop is just along the High Street."

"Shall I wait here?" he asked.

"I think that will be best," replied Emma, "as he will find your clothing odd if you come with me. I will simply say that my nephew from Altgerheads is staying with me – that is a sufficiently faraway place I think, for us to say that you are from." Leo tried to work out what *Altgerheads* corresponded to back in his own world, and it took him several seconds before he came up with the answer: Loggerheads.

"Yes, it must be about ten miles away," he said.

"I think so," agreed Bear. "It's a long journey even by horse or carriage."

"And I don't think many would walk it," said Bull; "it's not a place anyone from town would often visit if at all, so no one would know who is from there or not."

"That is settled then," said Emma, "you are now Leo from Altgerheads!"

"OK," said Leo with a smile. "That sounds fine!"

"And you'll soon look like a farmer!" chuckled Bear.

"What is your shoe size, Leo?" asked Emma.

"Six," said Leo.

"Very good," she said with a smile. "As for the clothing, I fancy I shall be able to trust my eye." Emma left the parlour and exited into the street via her shop.

"While we wait for Emma," said Bull, taking a small notebook and pencil from the inside pocket of his jacket, "why don't we write out the points that we need to raise with Doctor Toad. I was thinking to do it, earlier."

"Good idea, old boy," agreed Bear, "we certainly don't want to forget any vital piece of important information."

"OK, great," said Leo, "what shall we start with?"

"Let's start with buildings that exist in both realities," suggested Bear.

"OK, so…" started Leo, thinking back from the beginning of his adventure and their first meeting, "I think the first building that is the same is the Boat & Horses Pub…"

"Yes, yes, that sounds right," said Bear. Bull made a note.

"The big office of the newspaper was completely different, as was the street that leads up into town and the gas works – all of that was different. Some of the buildings on either side of the High Street, or Penkhull Street as it is here, they seem the same, but the business names and outside appearance are so different I can't be sure. Then onto the Guildhall: that's exactly the same."

"Saint Giles' church and also the building at the end of Red Lion Square," added Bear. Bull continued to note it all down.

"Let's also note down that we all know of Sherlock Holmes and Alice," said Leo.

"Yes, that's an important point," said Bear. "It may be a useful exercise to try to find other authors and books that exist in both realities."

"We have all heard of E. A. Poe," interjected Nevermore.

"Well remembered," said Bull, noting it down also.

"Can you think of any other famous books you have read, Leo?" asked Bear. "I think we seem to be looking at the period around the end of the nineteenth century."

"Is it 2018 here?" asked Leo. The matter of what year it was had not previously come up.

"I believe it is," said Bear ponderously.

"But you're not sure what year it is?" asked Leo somewhat astounded.

"Well, dear fellow, you must understand," said Bull, "such things are of little importance in Altcastle. Additionally, it's no easy matter to keep track of time when the Countess makes it the same day for days on end just as she pleases and then also does the exact opposite when that suits her."

"So, sometimes days go missing as well?" queried Leo.

"Indeed," said Bear, "why, January is a typical example. As most people don't like January because the nights are dark and Mipas is all over, the Countess might skip as many as ten days of the month to make it February sooner."

"That's right," confirmed Bull, "I think even this year the 6th of January – that's the end of the Mipas season, you might know – was followed by the 7th as one would expect and then the next day was the 13th…"

"Or maybe even the 14th," interjected Bear.

"And also, let's not forget, that sometimes it's a different day in the afternoon than it was in the morning," said Bear.

"Yes, that's where the phrase *Friday all day* or *Tuesday all day* comes from, you know. For example, one might ask someone what day it is, and they might say it's *Wednesday all day today*."

"Precisely," agreed Bear, "because it can happen that it's not *Wednesday all day* at all, and around two o'clock in the afternoon, it just changes to *Thursday!*"

"That's completely mad," said Leo. "I don't understand how this Countess can get away with such things."

"Well, she's the Countess, you know," said Bull.

"But the most confusing thing of all is when time goes backwards," said Bear.

"Oh, yes," nodded Bull, "that can trip up quite a few people. Do you remember when Mr Punch complained during the summer season that he'd had to do extra performances for the same wages?"

"I do in fact," said Bear; "I felt quite sorry for the fellow actually."

"What happened?" asked Leo.

"Well," said Bull, "as I recall, it was a particularly lovely day in July, and a lot of people were in town strolling around, going for a drink, buying ice creams et cetera, so the Countess decided to cash in by adjusting the time. Mr Punch performed his show at six o'clock and then again at seven o'clock as usual, but just as he had finished his last show at around seven-thirty, the Town Crier appeared and declared that it was going to be six o'clock again..."

"The Guildhall clock, Municipal Hall clock and all other clocks in the town were also set back to just before six o'clock as well – don't forget that bit," interjected Bear.

"That's right," agreed Bull, "so what happened was: it became six o'clock again, and all the clocks started striking six, so Mr Punch had to do the six o'clock, and seven o'clock shows all over again for a second time. Now obviously because it was getting darker, the Countess couldn't repeat the process again and was forced by the angle of the sun to allow time to continue as normal after this revision, but nevertheless, Mr Punch did four shows that evening instead of the usual two."

"And when he went for his wages," continued Bull, "after the booth had been all shut up for the night at eight o'clock, he asked for extra ha'pennies, but the owner of the Punch and Judy Company, a deeply unpleasant man called Pierre La Falot, refused to pay him any extra because it had only ever been eight o'clock once and he said that Mr Punch is only paid at eight o'clock."

"I see," said Leo, "it's not easy to follow, but I think I get it. What happened next?"

"Mr Punch argued that if he'd already been paid at eight o'clock and the time had been set back to seven o'clock, for example, he wouldn't have expected to be paid again at the second eight o'clock because he wouldn't have done an extra day's work," said Bear. "So, if the time revision worked in his favour, he would be fair about it, so to speak."

"But as the time revision ordered by the Countess had worked against Mr Punch," continued Bear, "then the owner should be fair about it and pay him some extra ha'pennies for doing more shows. You see, Leo?"

"I do see," said Leo, "although it's quite confusing – I mean the idea of first eight *o'clocks* and second eight *o'clocks*; but, I think I agree with Mr Punch in this situation, and he should have received some more money."

"I feel the same," said Bear, "but he didn't get any extra."

"In fact, I think he got beat with a stick for the asking!" added Bull.

"Yes," said Bear mournfully, "I believe he did."

"That's really awful," said Leo.

"And now he's been kidnapped," added Bear, "poor old fellow!"

"We still don't know that for sure," said Bull.

"What other time anomalies does the Countess create?" asked Leo.

"Oh, all sorts," said Bear.

"Too many to think of really," added Bull. "Time is very messy here."

"One of the most outrageous examples," mused Bear, "was when she decided to make it the previous Tuesday on one Thursday afternoon. As you can no doubt imagine, that caused great confusion as not only the day but also the date changed that time."

"Yes, even the normally equanimous Mr Zenodotus complained on that occasion, because people were returning books to the library before they had borrowed them!" chuckled Bull.

"And Mr Justice Bender had to let someone off for a beakery perpetrated on a Wednesday because his lawyer argued that he couldn't have done a beakery on Wednesday 15th because it was still Tuesday 14th and his client couldn't have committed a crime in the future," laughed Bear.

"I think that was the circumstance which most dissuaded the Countess from doing it again," said Bull, "because she missed out on collecting the fine for the beakery!"

Just then the shop doorbell tinkled.

"I am back," called Emma. She soon came into the parlour carrying a large bundle wrapped in brown paper and tied with string.

"I think you will find everything you will need to look like a proper Altcastler in here," she said, handing the parcel to Leo.

"Thanks," he said, taking it from her.

"You may use my spare bedroom to change," she said, pointing to a small door in the corner of her parlour, to the right of the fireplace, "it is the first room on the left at the top of the stairs."

"OK," said Leo getting up. "Be back in a few minutes." He headed off to change.

"All well?" asked Bear.

"Yes, no questions asked by George," she replied, "the story was well received."

They continued to chat amongst themselves for a few minutes until Leo returned looking distinctly different. He had a white, winged-collar shirt with a blue cravat tie. Over that he wore a smart three-piece suit in grey herringbone with black ankle boots, and he carried a charcoal grey overcoat, striped woollen scarf and a tweed, flat cap with him.

"My goodness," said Bear, "you look quite the young gentleman, so you do!"

"Doesn't look like an Altgerheads farm boy at all," mused Bull.

"Does it all fit well enough, Leo?" asked Emma.

"Perfectly, thank you," he said.

"Good; then we had better be off," said Emma. "Keep an eye on the shop, Nevermore, though I expect everyone will be at the meeting."

"Very well," said Nevermore.

Leo put on his overcoat, flat cap and scarf, and they all walked from the parlour into the shop.

CHAPTER EIGHT

KIDNAPPED

THE FOUR OF THEM stepped out into the street, which was now showing a light dusting of snow, and made their way along the High Street, heading towards the Guildhall. The sun had already set behind the rooftops of the High Street's western shops, and the town's lamplighters were busy at work. An atmosphere of excitement and trepidation permeated the cold winter air as hundreds of people made their way to find out what had happened to Mr Punch. As they reached the stage in front of the Guildhall, they could see that the dignitaries were already in place, sat on the row of chairs at the back as they had been earlier; and as before, two trumpeters and two prompters stood either side of the stage ready for action once the crowd had fully assembled.

"It seems like quite a gathering," said Leo.

"Most of the townsfolk hold these events in higher esteem than the theatre, Leo," said Emma.

"There's that hamster, Cromwell," said Bear, pointing to him. He was walking along the opposite side of the High Street and was accompanied by five or six other men, all tall and burly. He was still carrying a folded newspaper over his left hand with just the tips of his gloves poking out.

Bull, Bear, Leo and Emma had soon joined the back of the crowd and Leo once again made use of the same crate that he had stood upon earlier so that he could see what was going on.

"Let's just move a little to the left," he said to the others, noticing that Gladys and Vera were there. "I don't want to miss the running commentary from those two!"

Emma smiled, and they all moved up. Everything on the stage was just as it had been earlier except that a white and red striped Punch and Judy booth had since been erected in front of it, about five feet to the left of the central lectern. In front of the booth, there were four rows of chairs and those who had turned up earliest now occupied them. There was a clamour rising from the crowd as they waited and yet again an almost party-like atmosphere. The crowd was at least twice the size of the one earlier, and as the four of them waited, more and more people continued to turn up. Finally, the Guildhall clock chimed four-thirty, and upon the last chime, the four trumpeters sounded a fanfare and two prompters, one from either side, displayed "SILENCE".

The Mayor stepped up to the lectern and once again attacked it with his gavel in a frenzy of delight while shouting his usual refrain of "Order! Order!"

The crowd fell silent, and one could have heard a pin drop.

"A most foul and dreadful beakery has been perpetrated!" he said in a loud and solemn voice.

"Ooh, Gladys! It's foul and dreadful this time," said Vera.

"Ooh, it is, Vera. What a business it must be!" agreed Gladys.

"I will now call upon Constable Cuffem to relate the particulars of the matter!" The Mayor resumed his seat, and the Constable stood up and proceeded to the lectern.

"Evening, all," he thundered.

"Evening, Constable," most people chanted back in a school assembly type manner.

"As his Worship, the Mayor, has just explained, a beakery of the most serious gravity has been perpetrated," said the Constable in a slow, plodding monotone voice with great emphasis placed on at least the first, and often the second, syllable of each word.

"Ooh, *serious gravity* it is, Gladys," said Vera.

"Ooh, heaven help us, Vera, whatever next I wonder?" said Gladys.

"It is my sad duty to report," continued the Constable, "that Mr Punch has upon this very afternoon been kidnapped by a person or persons unknown!" The prompters let go of their folio covers to reveal the word "GASP", but before anyone in the crowd had a chance to oblige, an incredibly squeaky female voice chirped up very loudly,

"Oh no, he hasn't!"

The crowd now gasped of their own accord.

"Who said that?" demanded the Constable.

"It's beakery!" shouted the Magistrate, jumping up from his seat and spilling some of the brown liquid from his hip flask. He sat straight down again.

"Looks like he's on the scotch tonight," said Bull. Bear nodded.

"As I was saying," continued the Constable, "Mr Punch has been kidnapped..."

"Oh no, he hasn't!" repeated the same squeaky female voice. The crowd broke into an uproar and started looking around for the culprit.

"Silence! Order!" shouted the Constable and then he took out and blew his whistle three times – probably preferring that to the gavel from force of habit. The crowd fell silent again. The Constable coughed to clear his throat and then resumed,

"As I was saying... Mr Punch has been kidnapped..."

"Oh no, he hasn't!" repeated the voice.

"It's beakery!" shouted the Constable. "I won't have it, I won't!" he continued in an even stronger and more determined voice:

"MR PUNCH HAS BEEN KIDNAPPED THIS AFT…"

"OH NO HE HASN'T!" screamed the squeaky voice. At this, the Magistrate again jumped to his feet and this time went straight to the lectern, took up the gavel and started banging away for all his worth.

"BEAKERY! BEAKERY!" he shouted at the top of his voice while banging the gavel like a man possessed. "It's eakery, freakery, squeakery, beakery, I say!! Stop interrupting the Constable! I won't have it, I won't! It's against the law!" he bellowed while jumping about with such gusto that his hip flask jumped out of his pocket and his wig fell off. The crowd just looked on in silent amazement.

"I think he's a tad upset," said Bear.

"Hmm… it would seem so," agreed Bull. The Mayor got to his feet, collected up the Magistrate's things and helped him back to his seat. He replaced his wig and had a liberal swig from his flask.

"Now then, now then," continued the Constable, "we'll be having no more beakery…

"Oh yes, we will!" called out the squeaky voice.

"What's that? What's that?" shouted the Constable in an agitated manner. The crowd remained silent. "As, I was saying," he continued, "Mr Punch has been kid…"

"Oh no, he hasn't!" yelled the voice again. The crowd gasped, and the Magistrate again got to his feet and went to the lectern, pushing the Constable to one side.

"I'll deal with this myself!" he screamed. "I've never witnessed such infamy! Never in all my born days!" He paused while his eyes eagerly scanned the whole crowd over the top of his glasses as if he expected by such means to identify the source of the voice. He picked up the gavel and banged it twice.

"Now then, the facts of this case are very clear…"

"Oh no, they're not!" shouted the voice. The Magistrate's face turned redder than a ripe tomato, and he banged the gavel in a fit.

"MR PUNCH HAS BEEN KIDNAP…"

"OH NO HE HASN'T" shouted the voice.

"Constable!" shouted the Magistrate. "Arrest that voice immediately!"

"Yes, m'Lord," replied the Constable, before blowing his whistle three times and running around the stage aimlessly – as he had absolutely no idea where the voice was coming from.

"Voice!" he shouted. "You are under arrest!"

"Oh no, I'm not!" shouted back the voice. The crowd again gasped and then erupted into chatter.

"Ooh, I've never seen the like, Vera," said Gladys.

"Ooh, heaven preserve us," said Vera, "I'll need the doctor if it carries on!"

"This is a much better show than the earlier one," said Leo.

"Ooh, it is!" said Bull laughing in mockery of both the proceedings and the old ladies.

The Magistrate banged his gavel, the Constable blew his whistle, the Mayor shouted "Order! Order!", but order there was not.

"I shall report this to the relevant authorities!" shouted the Magistrate at the top of his voice.

"You are the relevant authorities!" shouted back the Mayor.

"Ah, yes… so I am… that's a good point… what shall I do then?" he asked forlornly as the crowd continued to chatter away and no one took any notice of the prompters' folios which read "SILENCE".

"We'd better be off to meet Doctor Toad," said Bear to Leo, looking up at the Guildhall clock. "We need to be at the cemetery by five." Leo nodded and discreetly stepped down from his crate.

"Will you come, Emma?" asked Bull.

"I had better stay here," said Emma, "someone will likely notice if we both leave. Watch out for the Town Crier as you go, Leo, or he will send you right back."

"OK, see you later," said Leo, and he, Bull and Bear slipped away into Friars' Street which in the Altcastle reality was little more than a dark alley.

"In one respect it's a good thing they haven't bothered to light the lamps down here," said Bull.

"But in another…" said Leo, "I can hardly see my feet let alone where I'm going."

"Hold my paw," said Bear. "We bears can see in the dark." Leo took hold of Bear's left paw, and Bear guided his steps until they got to the crossroads formed by Goose Street, Lower Street and Blackfriars' Road. There was a little more light once they passed the crossroads as the moon had risen and was at its first quarter, though the continuing presence of cloud didn't help the situation. They proceeded quickly along Blackfriars' Road, crossed the bridge over the Lyme Brook and then turned left into Friarswood Road.

Unlike in Leo's Newcastle, there were no houses along Friarswood Road, just allotment gardens and on the right, there was a large industrial building with a sign outside which read "Friarswood Silk Mill". The Silk Mill was all in darkness, and its gates were closed, no doubt because everyone employed there had gone to the meeting in town. They continued quickly on, keeping a lookout for the Town Crier, and had soon enough turned into Cemetery Road and reached the tall iron gates of the cemetery itself. Unfortunately, the gates were locked.

"Oh no," said Leo, "what shall we do now?"

Bull looked around for a few seconds, paying particular attention to the lodge which sits just a few yards to the right of the cemetery gates.

"I don't think there's anyone in the lodge," said Bear, "there's no light from any of the windows." Bull nodded in agreement but continued to look around.

"So, you will have to climb over," Bear said to Leo. "Be careful of the spikes on top."

"What about you two?" asked Leo, but even as he was still speaking, they both walked through the gates as though the gates were not there, or as if the two of them were ghosts.

"Neat," he muttered. "How do you do that?"

"Actually," said Bull, "we don't know – we just know from experience what we can walk through and what we can't."

Leo quickly climbed over the gates, letting himself down judiciously the other side. The cemetery's main avenue was heavily treelined in Altcastle just as it is Leo's Newcastle, which obscured the now cloud-masked moon. The presence of only very faint moonlight made it difficult to see anything; there were no gas lamps in the cemetery nor any other light source.

"Now, the question is," mused Bull, "where will Doctor Toad meet us?"

Leo peered up the incline into the distance southwards. He could just about make out the outline of the twin gothic mortuary chapels with their central triple archway, ornate crocketted pinnacles and broach spire.

"There's quite a large flat area both in front of and behind the chapels," said Leo, "at least there is Newcastle."

"Enough space to land an airship?" asked Bull.

"Depends on the size of the airship," said Leo, "but it's quite a big space."

"We don't frequent the cemetery so much," said Bull, "so we don't know the topography too well."

"Understandable," said Leo, leading the way along the main avenue up towards the chapel building, which they soon reached. Leo stopped in front of the central arch and looked around for any clue as to where Doctor Toad might be.

"What time is it?" asked Leo. Bear pulled out his pocket watch and squinted at the face, angling it as best he could towards what was left of the moonlight.

"It's about two minutes to five as far as I can tell," he said. "So, let's just wait here and see what happens."

"That's wise," agreed Bull. "I fancy Doctor Toad is a most punctual sort and will arrive exactly at the appointed time."

"That's assuming he actually saw the smoke signals," replied Leo, "and we can't be sure that he did."

"Well," said Bear, "let's not succumb to any negativity; it's not even five yet, so let's just wait."

"Shall I sing something?" asked Bull. "To pass the time."

"No," said Bear very definitely, "the time will pass itself well enough, without any help from you. Let's just enjoy a few moments of quiet contemplation instead!"

"Very well," mumbled Bull sulkily.

As they waited in the icy air, the moon gradually disappeared completely behind the clouds, and it once again started to snow.

CHAPTER NINE

EXCEPTIONAL RELATIVITY

A S THE SECONDS PASSED, the snow fell heavier and heavier. They continued to look around, but there was no hint of an airship. Bear pulled out his pocket watch again but quickly gave up on trying to see what time it was as by now, there was almost no light at all. As Leo's heart began to sink at the thought that Doctor Toad had not seen the smoke signals, and was not going to come, he heard the faint sound of music coming from somewhere in the distance. The sound was scratchy and faltering, but Leo nevertheless recognised the tune – it was for sure a favourite of his father. All three of them looked around, trying to identify the source.

"It's coming from over there," said Bull, pointing with his right hoof. They walked towards the central arch, and as they did so, they began to be able to make out what appeared to be a rectangle of light suspended in mid-air about thirty or so feet in front of them. The rectangle was about two feet across and five feet in height and as they passed through the arch it came towards them before coming to rest with its bottom side just an inch above the snowy ground, a little more than three or four yards in front of them. They paused motionlessly. The light-line of the rectangle got wider towards its right side and within moments showed itself to be an opening door which as it gradually opened revealed a room which did not exist behind it in the space of the cemetery. A man of about three feet in height stood in the entranceway to the room. He had a green face, blue hands and wore a yellow tunic with black and red striped trousers. His hair was short, jet black and incredibly spiky as if gelled.

"Good evening, gentlemen," he said, "do come in out of the cold." He stepped back, allowing the three of them to enter. Leo went first, who, being only about five-feet tall himself, was able to pass through the doorway quite easily. Bull and Bear followed after him, who, both being much taller and wider, found the doorway a bit of a squeeze. Once they were inside, the green-faced man closed the door.

The room they had entered was quite large, possibly as much as ten feet in width and well over twenty in length, and was not at all what any of them would have expected the inside of an airship gondola to look like. In addition to the door by which they had just entered, there were a further five doors, two on either side and one at the end. There was nothing in the room at all other than a mahogany hallstand with an oval mirror and a tile back which stood between the two doors on the right. The floor was tiled in black and white squares, like a chessboard.

"I am Slingsby," said the green-faced man, but he didn't offer his hand.

"Bull, Bear and Master Leo," said Bear. "We have a meeting with Doctor Toad."

"Yes," said Slingsby, "the Doctor is expecting you. I will show you through to his library... but I warn you, do not attempt to speak to him until his aria has finished; otherwise, he may be upset, you know." They all looked at each and nodded. The music they had heard from outside continued to play and seemed to emanate from behind one of the doors to their left.

"You may leave your hats, coats, scarves et cetera, here," said Slingsby indicating the hallstand. Bull and Bear removed and deposited their respective hats, neither of them wore coats or scarves, and Leo took off, and then likewise hung up his flat cap, scarf and overcoat. Slingsby led on, knocked on the door and then opened it without waiting for any answer. He entered the room in silence and beckoned to the three of them to do likewise which they did.

The room they had entered was immense, and they were all quite astonished as they looked around while waiting, as directed, for Doctor Toad's aria to finish. The aria was being played on what appeared to be a very old wind up gramophone which had a large and quite ornate horn in distressed brass. The room itself was extremely tall, mostly of wooden panelling and, on the far side, had several arched windows which were complemented by pairs of thick velvet curtains. Above the windows, and all around the room, ran another mezzanine floor about four feet deep and supported by ornate cast-iron brackets. It was accessible from an iron spiral staircase in one corner of the room.

The walls of the main room were filled mostly with bookcases and pictures, below which was a continuous run of wooden drawers such as one might find in a museum archive or science laboratory. Leo started to look out of one of the windows and curiously, given that it was pitch black outside, he could quite clearly discern the trees and the headstones of the cemetery as though they were being illuminated from somewhere – which he knew they were not because he had just come from the outside. Additionally, everything visible through the window had a bluish, ultraviolet tinge to it.

After a few seconds, the aria, which was being sung in German, finished and a greyish-greenish looking toad stepped out from behind a large red fabric wingback chair which, while he had been sitting, had completely concealed him from view. Doctor Toad was about four feet tall and, like Bull and Bear stood upright on his back legs. He wore a red fez hat with a black tassel on his head – which was slightly skewwhiff, a black frockcoat over a white-winged collar shirt, a paisley print green waistcoat with matching cravat tie, grey pinstriped trousers and black and white brogue shoes. He also wore a gold pocket watch chain across his waistcoat. A pair of gold-rimmed pince-nez on a black cord hung about his neck, and a very elaborately patterned crimson and green silk handkerchief flopped from the breast pocket of the frock coat. He approached the three of them and took a small deferential bow.

"Doctor Toad, at your service," he said, holding out his four-fingered right hand to Leo.

"I'm Leo," said Leo.

"Delighted, Sir," said Doctor Toad cordially. They shook hands.

"And Mr Bull and Mr Bear," said Doctor Toad, also shaking hands with each of them, "how very nice to see you both again… it has been a few years since we last met, I believe?"

"Yes, I think so," said Bear, "maybe as many as three or four."

"Tempus fugit," said Doctor Toad. "Or, as Slingsby often says: time flies when one flies." Doctor Toad chuckled as did Slingsby. Bull, Bear and Leo didn't quite get what he meant.

"Miss Jency will not be joining us, then?" queried Doctor Toad.

"Unfortunately not," said Bear, "there was another meeting called due to the earlier disappearance of Mr Punch, so she thought it better not to risk drawing attention by leaving as well."

"Oh, I do see," said Doctor Toad, "what a pity; I do so like Miss Jency, she is such a vivacious and amiable young lady… and as for Mr Punch disappearing, what a dreadful business that is."

"It's believed he's been kidnapped," said Bear.

"How very frightful," said Doctor Toad, "and has a ransom demand been made?"

"Not that we've heard of yet, Doctor, no... I don't think so," said Bear

"We had to leave to meet you, so we didn't get the full story," added Bull.

"Well, no doubt time will tell, as it always does," said Doctor Toad. "Let us all be seated, then, and we can discuss the matter at hand," he added, indicating a large highly polished rectangular wooden dining table. There were four chairs either side and an extremely curious-looking sort of highchair made of a combination of dark oak and gunmetal with many levers, switches, pullies and springs on it at the head of the table. Doctor Toad approached the highchair and tapped the seat with his finger, which then lowered to a height at which he could easily sit on it. After he had sat, the seat moved itself up again such as to give him the same seated height as the other three who had also sat down, Bull and Bear on the left, and Leo on the right with his back to the windows.

"Would anyone care for some refreshment?" asked Doctor Toad. "I shall have a cup of Earl Grey myself with a twist of lemon, I fancy."

"I'll have the same, please," said Leo.

"Also for me," said Bear.

"Me too," said Bull.

"Very good," said Slingsby, and he turned and left.

"Now then, Miss Jency's smoke signal – relayed by that old sea dog Captain Bellamy, I believe – was quite brief, though I understand the matter to be of some urgency?" queried Doctor Toad.

"Yes, indeed," started Bear, and he began recounting to Doctor Toad the precise details of the entire day, starting from the time immediately before Leo had arrived when the fog had descended unexpectedly. Bull also assisted with the notes he had taken about which things were the same in both versions of reality and which were different. He mentioned the Boat & Horses Pub, the Guildhall, Saint Giles' Church and many of the other similarities such as the layout of the roads. From his knowledge of when things were built, Doctor Toad concurred with Bear's earlier assessment that it appeared that both Altcastle and Newcastle shared a common, or at least an identically parallel, past, as buildings built before the later nineteenth century were common to both realities.

He was also fascinated by the observations they had made in Emma's parlour about various works of literature, such as the Sherlock Holmes and Alice books, being common to both Altcastle and Newcastle, although he was not able to pin down the divergence in the two timelines any more precisely than between 1870 and 1900 without additional information, which he suggested they could get in the case of Altcastle from the library, but that would be lacking in the case of Newcastle as they did not have access to Newcastle's library and Leo could not supply details about the publication dates of the various Sherlock Holmes stories.

Finally, Leo explained his concerns about his parents wondering what might have become of him, if in fact time was not stationary back in his own reality. He also showed Doctor Toad his wristwatch and mobile phone and explained how a mobile phone worked which Doctor Toad was very interested in. During the briefing, Slingsby returned with a tray, and everyone was served with Earl Grey tea in rather exquisite Wedgwood china cups and saucers. It took well over an hour to go through the whole matter during which time Doctor Toad took down a great many notes.

"A most interesting and perplexing sequence of events," he said, once Bull, Bear and Leo had completed the tale.

"So, Doctor, what are your initial thoughts?" asked Bear. Doctor Toad raised a finger to the air.

"One must think about such matters," he said, "for a while at least… in order to first organise such a great many facts into relevancies and irrelevancies; and only then I fancy, try to make some reasonable assessment of what has gone on, and how this young gentleman has come to be here in Altcastle." He stroked his chin and sipped some tea. "Hmm…" he mused, looking up at one his bookshelves.

"I must consult one manuscript…" he soon said, getting up and taking a papyrus scroll from one of the shelves entitled *Posidonius Liber IV.* He placed his pince-nez on his nose and started going through the scroll. "Aha!" he said finally and returned to his seat.

"So… I think we may be almost entirely certain, Sir," he said looking at Leo, "that you crossed into this reality, we shall call it *the Alternate Reality,* when you crossed the Lyme Brook bridge and more than that: exactly halfway across, when you noticed that the tarmac, as you call it, changed to cobblestone – that much I think is certain."

"And what do you think the significance is of most of the place names beginning with *Alt* here in Altland?" asked Bear.

"It is indeed, as we discussed, a most curious thing…" said Doctor Toad "…and of course not something which any of us has ever queried before, as we are all just used to it, and have never known anything else, but now that we understand the place names are actually so entirely similar in both realities, other than that here the beginning of each word starts with *Alt,* it leads one to the view that it is, in fact, Leo's reality which is… how shall I put it? *The original reality*, and that this one has been changed somehow… *ALTered*, perhaps I should say."

"Yes," concurred Bear, "that is what I was thinking… it is as if someone has spilt this reality off from the original and then changed all the place names to Alt-something."

"But why?" asked Bull. "And who could have such incredible powers to do such a thing?"

"A most singular enquiry, for sure," mused Doctor Toad.

"Also," interjected Leo, "if Altcastle has been split off from Newcastle to go its own way and follow its own path, as we now all suppose, why has time stood still here in Altcastle since that happened?"

"How do you mean?" asked Bear. "I thought we had all now agreed that it is the year 2018 here, exactly the same year in every way as it is in your reality?"

"Yes," said Leo, "but even though it is also 2018 here, it is as if it were still 1880 or 1890 or something like that: everything is just as it would have been around the end of the Victorian era. It seems there has been no technological progress of any sort. Almost none of the things that exist in my reality exist here – they've never been invented here. Doesn't anyone ever invent anything here?"

"What sorts of thing?" asked Bull.

"Well, as far as I have seen so far, there are no fridges, no television, no computers, no telephones, no aeroplanes, no motorcars – literally nothing that has been invented in the last 120 to 130 years exists here, even though it's 2018 here the same as in my reality."

"Yes, yes," mumbled Doctor Toad, "I should like very much indeed to understand a good deal more about some of these things which you have mentioned. Why none of them has been invented in this reality, I cannot rightly account for entirely, although one obvious reason is that they have not been allowed to be invented by the powers that control each of the boroughs or indeed nations…"

"You mean the Countess has stopped them from being invented, for example?" asked Leo.

"Yes, I would suppose so in the case of Altcastle, and whoever the equivalent of the Countess is in all the other places around the world," surmised Doctor Toad.

"Curious, indeed," mused Bear.

"Anyway, let us discuss this further later on, and for now return our attention to Leo's present predicament," suggested Doctor Toad.

"Indeed," agreed Bull.

"So, the time at which you crossed into this reality, Leo, was 10:34, and that is why both your watch and phone show 10:34 even now. As to the question of if time has stood still in your own reality whilst you have been here in this reality, I think the answer must be a resounding *yes*."

Leo nodded and looked very relieved.

"Why do you think so, Doctor?" asked Bear.

"There is a section here in Posidonius' Fourth Volume – I have the only copy in existence incidentally," he said proudly, "all others were lost when the great library of Altexandria was burned down – in which the author relates an incident involving a similar mist in Celtic Galatia – that is now in northern Altkey."

"Really?" commented Bull.

"Indeed," Doctor Toad continued; "one damp day Posidonius crossed a river by boat which was covered in a thick mist or fog; which, as per Leo's experience, emanated from the surface of the water itself. When he crossed over it was midday on a Monday. He spent several days on the other side, in a different reality to his own, before working out how to get back again to his own reality… he did so on the morning of the fourth day. When he did return, he naturally expected that it would be Thursday, but in fact, it was still Monday and more than that: it was still midday – so no time had elapsed at all while he had been in the alternate reality."

"That's great, Doctor," said Leo. "So time has stopped in my reality?"

"Relatively speaking, *yes*… we shall not need to concern ourselves with the essence of relativity at this juncture, although the subject undoubtedly warrants a more considered discussion when leisure allows… but, as far as you may be concerned, *yes*, time has stopped in your reality, relative to time still progressing here," confirmed Doctor Toad.

"So everyone in Leo's reality is just frozen in time, and cannot move or do anything?" queried Bear confusedly.

"Not exactly," replied Doctor Toad, "to those in Leo's reality, everything is absolutely normal – time has not stopped *absolutely*, it has only stopped *relative to here*… it is a case of what one may call, hmm… *exceptional relativity*."

"So," mumbled Leo, trying to take on board what Doctor Toad was explaining to them, "as far as I'm concerned, here in Altcastle, time in Newcastle will not move forward?"

"Indeed, I am quite sure that when you get back, it will be 10:34 on Saturday 15th December 2018 and no one will have missed you at all."

"And how will I get back?" asked Leo. "Must I go through the mist again?"

"Hmm… in short…" said Doctor Toad thoughtfully, "I believe so. *The Lyme Brook Mist*, if I may call it that, is, in fact, the material out of which what we may call the inter-dimensional portal is made; the mist is the fabric of the portal, just as wood is the fabric of a doorframe."

"But how can we re-create the mist?" asked Bear. "Because when we walked back along the same route… only about thirty minutes later… the portal had gone, even though it was still quite foggy. So, how do we get the portal back?"

"A most interesting question… a most singular matter!" exclaimed Doctor Toad, once again raising one finger before resuming his study of the ancient papyrus scroll. The three of them remained silent, not wishing to disturb his thought process. Slingsby again entered the room at this point.

"More tea, gentlemen?" he asked expectantly.

"Indeed!" answered Doctor Toad without looking up.

"And possibly your pipe, Doctor?" asked Slingsby.

"Indeed… indeed, again," said Doctor Toad. Slingsby nodded and departed.

"Hmm…" mumbled Doctor Toad. "The answer is most certainly here!" He looked intently into Leo's eyes and pouted his lips. "Here for sure, I say!"

Leo nodded but said nothing.

"Is there anything we can do to help?" asked Bull.

"Nothing but your quietness will be needed," replied Doctor Toad. Bull was quiet, as were they all. Minutes passed, as Doctor

Toad continued to move up and down the scroll – which appeared to be many yards in length – backwards and forwards, the whole while panting and sighing.

"Aha!!" he exclaimed finally. "I need more tea!"

Just then Slingsby returned with more tea, on a silver tray, and additionally a briar pipe, a box of matches and a few ounces of tobacco on a small silver dish. Slingsby poured everyone more tea, while Doctor Toad filled his pipe and lit it.

"Now then," he mused, while puffing on his pipe, "I fancy the answer may be plain enough."

"Is it?" questioned Bear.

"I fancy it may be," replied Doctor Toad.

"And what is it then?" asked Bull.

"I am not yet entirely sure," said Doctor Toad, "… at this moment, at least … but I have the distinct impression that the solution is only a matter of moments away… if only those moments can be so elicited to reveal it!" Bull, Bear and Leo looked at each other blankly.

"Slingsby!" cried Doctor Toad emphatically.

"Doctor?" replied Slingsby keenly.

"The Tannhäuser again!" said Doctor Toad. Slingsby immediately went over to the gramophone and started the recording again. Everyone remained in silence while Doctor Toad imbibed the melodic strains of his aria, *O du mein holder Abendstern,* seeming to be almost in rapture. Thankfully the piece was brief, and after about three and a half minutes it had finished. Doctor Toad leapt from his seat on the last note and retrieved a book from his shelf entitled *Féth Fíada et Magicae Caligo* – from the look of the cover and binding, the book appeared to be very old indeed.

"How slow I have been!" he exclaimed, once again putting his pince-nez to his eyes and delving into the book. "Do you know gentlemen, what a Magic Mist is?" he asked, lifting his head up and looking at each of them in turn over the top of his pince-nez.

They all looked at each other and then at him and shook their heads.

"… they came without ships, without boats or rafts, across the sea they travelled through the air, in clouds of fog, in a magic mist, commanded by the might of their Druidry…" Doctor Toad closed the book. "So, there we have it!" he said. He turned to Leo. "You have been transported through a Magic Mist which, I dare venture, was created by a druid or druids for some specific and express purpose."

"Fascinating," mumbled Bear.

"But for what purpose?" asked Bull. "And by what druid? Does Altcastle even have druids?"

"I don't believe we have ever met a druid," added Bear. Doctor Toad once again raised his finger and allowed his pince-nez to drop from his nose.

"There is certainly one druid… I know the fellow… but I cannot imagine he would have done this, as it seems a most clumsy business to inadvertently trap Leo in another reality and there cannot have been any intention to do it, as it serves no purpose that I can see and in any case, if it had been intentional then the initiator of the mist would most certainly have been waiting for Leo to arrive, which he was not. I deduce therefore that the mist was created for some other purpose, and that Leo just happened, by pure chance, to cross the Lyme Brook during the time at which the portal was open."

"I see," muttered Bear.

"I fancy that the portal may have extended for quite a length of the midline of the brook and that when Leo accidentally crossed the middle of the brook on his bridge, the initiator of the mist was up to no good on one of the other bridges, or indeed even a temporary bridge that such an initiator had placed himself – it was for whatever was happening on that other bridge that the mist had been summoned."

"So can the mist be recreated to get me back home?" asked Leo.

"Elementary," replied Doctor Toad, "you must ask a druid to conjure a magic mist."

"But as Bear said, we don't know any druids," said Leo.

"But as I said, I do," smiled Doctor Toad. "On Saturday morning, the annual Mipas Poetry Competition will take place at the Sipby Theatre and Asiex the Woodcutter will certainly be in attendance – he always enters and often wins. Asiex, the woodcutter, is actually none other than Asiex the Druid. He is of an ancient Celtic bloodline and operates as a woodcutter merely as a cover."

"Really?" said Bull.

"No wonder the fellow can see us!" exclaimed Bear.

"You know this Asiex?" asked Leo.

"Yes, we've met him a few times," said Bear, "he lives somewhere in Altchurch Woods, but we don't know where exactly."

"And we had no idea he was druid," added Bull.

"Not the type of thing one would wish to have publicly known, I suspect," mused Doctor Toad.

"Quite so," agreed Bull.

"So, Sir," said Doctor Toad, turning to Leo, "I suggest that after the poetry competition, you make yourself known to Asiex the Druid and ask him to conjure a magic mist and send you back. I feel sure he will oblige."

"Great!" said Leo. "So I can ask him tomorrow morning."

"Not necessarily," said Bear. "It will probably be Friday again tomorrow…"

"It may be Friday for another few days yet," mused Bull.

"It will depend on how much money the shops have taken in, Leo, as I explained to you earlier," added Bear. Leo looked suddenly disappointed again.

"When is it decided what day it will be tomorrow?" asked Leo.

"The Mayor sends his clerks around all the shops every evening to ask what sales have been made and how much money has been taken. He then adds it all up, both from the town and all the outlying villages, and then he reports the figure to the Countess. She then decides if the day and date will advance or not," said Bull.

"She probably doesn't decide until quite late at night," said Bear, "but the people only find out at six o'clock in the morning when the Daily Tale is published or when the Town Crier starts his rounds announcing the day and date, and that all is well... that's around seven."

"It's completely mad," sniped Leo.

"Well, Sir," said Doctor Toad reassuringly, "at least you now know that no one in your reality is missing you, so you may as well relax and enjoy your experience in Altcastle. It is not every fellow of your age who gets to visit an alternate reality, you know."

"True," said Leo with a smile. "It is an interesting place."

"And you have additionally been fortunate enough to happen upon these two fine chaps and the dear Miss Jency," added Doctor Toad persuasively.

"Yes," agreed Leo, "that was very good luck, or I don't know what I would have done. I'd have been in a right mess."

"And probably arrested for beakery!" added Bull.

"Yes, probably," Leo laughed, "imagine if I'd met the Constable first!"

"Doesn't bear thinking of," said Bull.

"That is the spirit, Sir," advised Doctor Toad. "Once one has done everything one possibly can to rectify an unexpected experience, one should just try to make the most of things and at least learn whatever one can from it."

"You're right, Doctor," said Leo. "Another day or so won't hurt, and I'll no doubt see many more interesting things."

"Indeed you will," said Doctor Toad. "Now tell me a little more about this internet and worldwide web and how it is accessed from your device, if you would: I find it all most fascinating."

"Will you all have more tea while you chat?" asked Slingsby.

"Why not," said Doctor Toad, and Slingsby collected up the two empty teapots and went off to sort out some more. They continued talking about the internet, computer games and technology in general for quite some time, during which Doctor Toad made copious notes in his notebook about everything Leo told him. They had more tea and yet more again before the subject was exhausted, and Doctor Toad was satisfied that he had a good grasp of everything that Leo had explained.

"Well," said Doctor Toad, consulting a large grandfather clock next to the door, "I had better let you gentlemen go back to Miss Jency as it is almost eight o'clock and time for supper. I have most enjoyed our chat, Sir," he said, directing his comment to Leo, "the information you have given me is truly enthralling… mesmerising, in fact!"

"It's been my pleasure," said Leo. Leo liked to explain things to people and was always willing to discuss computer games, in particular: a matter which Doctor Toad had taken a great deal of interest in.

"I should very much like to discuss these matters further," said Doctor Toad, "if only the opportunity arises… as you can see, I am a Toad who likes talking to a chap who likes to talk!"

"For sure," agreed Leo. He, Bull and Bear stood up. Doctor Toad likewise got up and went over to one of the drawers below the bookcases. He opened it and took out what looked like an old metallic radio transmitter.

"Take this, Sir," he said, giving the device to Leo; "you will find it much more convenient to contact me using this than you will by using smoke signals… so old fashioned, you know, those smoke signals. As you can see, some of us do have, some very basic, minor inventions!"

"Thanks," said Leo, taking the radio transmitter from him and inspecting it closely. It had a cranking handle on its side, a dial and some buttons and switches. Bull and Bear regarded the device suspiciously; neither of them had ever seen anything that used electricity.

"The operating instructions are on the back," said Doctor Toad. "But after what you have just shown me on your device, I fancy you will find this quite easy by comparison… unlike on your device, there is no battery, and the power is produced using a dynamo rotated by that handle. Unfortunately, there is no… how did you put it… USB connection? So you will not be able to recharge your device from it."

"It's OK, Doctor," said Leo, "my battery is still at a half charge, and I've switched my phone off now; I won't need it again until I get home to Newcastle."

"Very well," said Doctor Toad. Slingsby opened the door to the hall, and they all proceeded towards the rear door of the airship, collecting their things from the hallstand on their way.

"Thank you very much for your help, Doctor," said Bear, shaking his hand.

"Yes, thank you," said Bull, also shaking his hand.

"Well, Sir," said Doctor Toad to Leo, clasping his hand, "it has been my great pleasure to meet you and hear all about the remarkable technology of your reality. Do not hesitate to contact me should you require any further help, and if for whatever reason your departure is unduly delayed, or indeed, should you visit Altcastle again in the future – which I very much hope you will do – then please do contact me so that we may continue our conversation."

"I will, Doctor," said Leo warmly, "thank you very much."

"And please do convey my warmest regards to Miss Jency," said Doctor Toad. "For now, I bid you a good evening and good luck!"

"Good evening, Doctor," said Bull and Bear as they squeezed back through the door and into the now two-inch deep snow of the cemetery.

"Good evening, Doctor," said Leo.

"Good evening, Sir," he said with a wave, as the three of them set off back towards the cemetery's main gate.

Doctor Toad closed the door, and the light disappeared, leaving the cemetery in total darkness other than for the faint glimmer of the reflected moonlight on the snow.

CHAPTER TEN

A WATCHFUL
GAZE

───

A S THE THREE OF them emerged from the drabness of
Friars' Street into Penkhull Street, they were greeted with
a scene akin to something from a Dickensian Christmas
card; there were carol singers with lanterns, sellers of hot pies and
pastries, shoppers carrying parcels, the brass band on the stage in
front of the Guildhall, and it was all suitably topped off with a fresh
layer of light, crisp snow that glowed beautifully in the light of the gas
lamps. It was well below freezing point, but everyone was wrapped
up warmly, the shops were all still open, and there was a friendly,
convivial atmosphere to the town as men, women, children, dogs
and horses scurried around happily. The sky had cleared, and the
quarter moon shone clear and bright over the rooftops.

"It looks nice," said Leo.

"Mipas is the best time of year for me," said Bull as they
proceeded northbound along the High Street towards Red Lion

Square. Just at the end of the Ironmarket, they saw the Town Crier coming along ringing his bell, but much less vigorously than previously.

"Don't forget the protest tomorrow morning, young Sir," he said to Leo as they passed him.

"I won't, Sir," said Leo.

"That's the protest against savers," said Bear. "It's tomorrow at nine."

"You must explain that to me some time," said Leo.

"We will," said Bull.

As they reached Red Lion Square, they saw that a large tree had been erected next to the weights and measures booth in the centre. It was beautifully decorated and lit with lanterns. There was a band of clowns blowing fire from their mouths in front of the tree, and a group of revellers were standing outside the Globe Commercial Hotel, next door to Emma's shop, with tankards of hot punch singing while they watched the antics of the clowns.

They were soon back inside Emma's shop where a customer was just leaving with several varnished boxes tied with string.

"Good evening, Mr Smith," said Emma to the departing customer.

"Evening, Miss Jency," he replied cheerfully.

"So, gentlemen," said Emma, turning to the three of them, "do go into the parlour and warm yourselves, then you can tell me all that Doctor Toad had to say."

"He sent his warmest regards to you," said Bull.

"How nice," smiled Emma. They all went into the parlour, and Leo took off his outdoor clothing and hung it up. Emma put some more coal onto the fire and an extra log. Nevermore was not on his perch, and there was no sign of him.

"Is Nevermore not here?" asked Leo.

"No, he has gone to deliver a card for me in Altmerend," said Emma. "He shall be back soon enough, I fancy. Is it still snowing?"

"No, it's stopped, but there's a nice blanket now – looks very pretty," said Bear.

"I do so like the look of Altcastle in the snow," she said. "It gives it a sort of magical, ethereal feel."

"I know what you mean," agreed Leo. "I think it looks very pretty too." Bull and Bear sat down in the armchairs next to the fire; Leo and Emma sat down at the table.

"So," asked Bull, "what happened regarding the kidnapping of Mr Punch and the squeaky voice once we left?"

"Well," sighed Emma, "it was quite a spectacle to behold: the meeting at first continued to proceed in the same pantomime fashion as before, with the Magistrate jumping up and down and the Constable running around aimlessly trying to arrest a voice. Eventually, however, someone at the front identified that the voice was coming from inside the Punch and Judy booth and shouted out: "the voice is in the booth". There then followed about five or six exchanges of "Oh, no it isn't!" and "Oh, yes it is!" until the Constable eventually managed to unlock the back door of the booth and open it; at which point he caught Judy *in flagrante delicto* half way between saying "Oh, no…" and "…it isn't!" and attempted to arrest her."

"Did he succeed?" asked Bear feverishly.

"Not at first," said Emma. "He tried to handcuff her, but because of her small size, the handcuffs did not fit properly, and she was easily able to free herself straight away. She then attempted to make off and had to be chased all around Penkhull Street and High Street by the Constable, the Mayor and all the prompters, until she was eventually apprehended outside the entrance to the Market Hall. During the entire duration of the chase, the Magistrate continued standing at the lectern shouting, "Beakery! Beakery! Arrest that puppet!" and banging his gavel. It was a most astonishing exhibition; I have to say. I do not believe anyone in Altcastle has ever seen the like of it."

"I can imagine," said Bear.

"What a pity we missed it all," said Bull.

"What happened next?" asked Bear.

"Well," said Emma, "because the handcuffs would not fit, the Mayor suggested that she be tied up with the orange and black bunting from the stage awning." Bull and Bear laughed out loud.

"What a sight it must have been," giggled Bull.

"Oh, indeed it was!" said Emma. "Once Judy had been restrained and tied up with the bunting, she was carried off to the police station under Constable Cuffem's arm for questioning. After that, it started to snow heavily, and the meeting was terminated."

"So what of Mr Punch?" asked Bear.

"No one yet knows," said Emma, "so I believe we must consider him still missing."

"Anyway," said Bull, "I fancy we shall hear no more about it tonight, it's almost half-past eight."

"Yes, it's getting late," confirmed Bear. "What is the plan, Emma, now that we know Leo is stuck here at least for tonight?"

"I fancy I will prepare some supper for us both," she said. "You are most welcome to stay here in my spare room, Leo; if you would like to?"

"Or you can stay in our underground hideout in the woods?" said Bear with a sly wink.

"If you don't mind a two-mile walk that is!" added Bull. Emma looked at Leo and smiled.

"I think I'll go with Emma's offer," said Leo.

"You've chosen wisely," said Bear. "Our guest room is currently in the care of some weasels anyway."

"They might have been somewhat put out at being evicted," added Bull. Just then, the shop's doorbell tinkled.

"Another customer?" questioned Emma. She went to look. Emma's shop didn't get many customers as demand for tins and boxes in Altcastle was not substantial; most of the townsfolk already had as many tins and boxes as they needed, and they were not the types of item that ever wore out.

"Oh good evening Mr Brownnose," said Emma from the shop.

"Evening, Miss Jency. How goes it?" he asked.

"It's only the Mayor's minion," said Bull, "come to see what sales have been made today."

"I have served two customers today," said Emma, "for a total of fourteen shillings and ninepence."

"Very good… not a bad day then by your standards… not enough for a change of date though, I fear," he said.

"I expect not," said Emma.

"Still, it's the protest tomorrow… that will hopefully get things moving on a bit better… we all hope so anyway," he remarked.

"I do hope so," said Emma.

"Anyway it's just started snowing again, and it's got cold, it has… people are going home, so it'll be all right to close up for the day now if you like, then you can get your supper… it's his Worship, Mayor Woodhay, who says so," said Mr Brownnose.

"Very good, then. Thank you. Good night to you," said Emma.

"Good night, Miss Jency," he said. Mr Brownnose departed into the snowy night, and Emma turned over her *Open* sign to read *Closed* and locked the shop door for the night.

"Just Mr Brownnose," said Emma returning to the parlour.

"Yes, we heard the damned sycophant," said Bear.

"Oh, really, Mr Bear," sighed Emma, "he is such a pleasant and polite fellow. I am quite sure there is no harm in him at all. He is only doing his job." Bear pulled his face and shrugged.

"Now that I have locked up the shop for the night, I can prepare some supper. Will you two gentlemen be staying for supper?" she asked, directing her question to Bull and Bear.

"What have you got?" asked Bull.

"Hmm… I have some sliced lamb," said Emma diffidently.

"Oh, what a despicable thing!" exclaimed Bull. "I just cannot comprehend how you humans can eat sweet, cuddly, lovely, fluffy, innocent, little lambs?"

"What a plethora of adjectives, old boy," mused Bear. "Anyway, I fancy we'll be off for some cabbage and berry soup."

"Beautiful soup?" queried Emma mischievously.

"Oh, please, don't get him going on that again!" complained Bear. "He'll be singing the infernal ditty all the way home now... and it's two miles, you know!" They both stood up.

"So, we'll be back in time for the protest," said Bull. "You won't want to miss that, Leo!"

"Yes, about half-past eight," said Bear. "We'll collect a copy of the Daily Tale on the way, then we can tell you what day it is."

"OK," said Leo. He stood up also; Bull and Bear moved towards the door of the parlour.

"Good night, then, Leo," said Bear.

"Thank you so much," said Leo. "I'm sure I would have been in a terrible mess if I hadn't met you two."

"It's been our great pleasure," said Bull and he put his hooves behind Leo's back and hugged him, after which Bear did likewise – though with paws, rather than hooves, obviously.

"Good night," said Leo with a smile. Bull and Bear walked on into the shop and then straight through the door as if it wasn't there.

"I must find out how they do that," mumbled Leo; he turned back into the parlour. Emma had gone to the kitchen and was busy preparing supper. Leo was about to sit down again when Nevermore tapped on the window.

"Shall I let him in?" asked Leo.

"Yes, please," replied Emma, with her hands full. Leo went to the back door and opened it. Nevermore jumped straight onto his hand.

"Hello, hello... hello again," he said in his inimitable croaky voice.

"Hello, Nevermore," said Leo.

"Cold it is," said Nevermore.

"I'll take you to the fire," said Leo and he walked back into the parlour, took a seat in one of the armchairs and placed Nevermore down on his knee. Nevermore extended his wings which were well over three feet in span.

"Better it is," he said, looking over his shoulder at Leo, as the fire crackled away in front of him.

"Will you want supper, my friend?" Emma called out.

"Just a little, if you please," he replied.

"It is sliced lamb with potatoes and carrots," called back Emma.

"Extra sauce for me!" he called back.

"Very good," said Emma.

"So, you deliver cards, do you?" asked Leo.

"I do indeed," he replied: "cards, letters, small parcels – whatever needs delivering, I am the bird for that! I know every address in Altcastle Borough!" Emma came back into the parlour with cutlery, napkins, side plates and glasses; she placed them all down on the table before taking a tall, octagonal wooden box from the sideboard and putting that down also on the table.

"Do you need any help?" asked Leo politely.

"Yes, please," she said, "there are a few more items to bring in." Nevermore fluttered onto the other armchair and Leo went into the kitchen with Emma.

Leo collected the mint sauce, which was in a delightful little china jug with a silver spoon, the plate of sliced lamb, two dinner plates and one soup plate. He took them to the table and returned.

"The water is on the step," said Emma. Leo opened the back door to retrieve it; it was in a glass bottle with a cork and was very cold. He took that to the table also.

"Hmm…" he thought "…no fridges here: how do they manage in summer?"

"Supper soon," chirped Nevermore, flying from the armchair onto the table and placing himself directly in front of the octagonal box, which Leo deduced had been put there for the express purpose of raising his plate high enough for his beak to get at.

Leo again returned to the kitchen, and Emma handed him a china serving bowl with boiled, minted new potatoes and carrots in it. She followed him through into the parlour but paused before reaching the table to collect an elegant glass, silver-plated claret jug with a beautifully designed decorative floral and foliate mount, scroll handle and a good-sized thumbpiece, from her sideboard. They both sat down, and Emma poured herself a modest glass of claret. She then proceeded to serve Nevermore using the soup plate and putting him a generous serving of the mint sauce as per his request.

"Please do help yourself, Leo," she said. Leo served himself while Nevermore tucked into his portion.

"It's very kind of you to let me stay," said Leo; "and to give me supper."

"Not at all," said Emma; "Nevermore and I will be very interested to hear what Doctor Toad had to say and then after, if there is time, we should both also be interested to hear about your Newcastle-under-Lyme and how it differs from Altcastle."

"Indeed we would," confirmed Nevermore.

They spent quite a while at supper chatting about the meeting with Doctor Toad mostly and what had been said. Leo also showed Emma and Nevermore the radio transmitter which Doctor Toad had given him, and explained to them how it, and radio communication in general, worked. After supper, they continued talking for over two hours. Emma, like Doctor Toad earlier, was fascinated to hear as much as possible about Leo's Newcastle, the internet, electricity, telephones and every manner of thing that did not exist in Altcastle.

At a little before midnight, Emma saw Leo off to bed as he was really very tired by then. She had left him an old fashioned nightgown on his pillow, but he never put it on; he just dropped his clothes over the back of the chair in his room and got straight into bed. Exhausted by such a strange and busy day, he went to sleep immediately, under the watchful gaze of Nevermore who had insisted on going up with him in case "he woke up lonely in the night and missed his parents and own bed" – what a thoughtful raven.

Chapter Eleven

The Wealth
of Boroughs

HE NIGHT PASSED PEACEFULLY in Altcastle, and all was
quiet. More snow fell overnight, and the temperature
remained below freezing. At about half-past seven,
Nevermore woke Leo up by gently pecking his nose, and Emma
brought him a cup of tea in bed. He was unaccustomed to such
treatment and thought it rather charming. His room was quaint,
but to his liking. There was a single bed with crisp white cotton
sheets, woollen blankets and a deep-red, patterned eiderdown on
top; the pillows were of feather and very comfortable. The floor
was of varnished wood with a nice Persian rug beneath the bed on
which also sat a mahogany nightstand. There was a wardrobe, chest
of drawers and a small fireplace with a cast iron grate which had
been lit when Leo went to bed but had gone out during the night.

Leo sat up to drink his tea and quickly realised that without
central heating, a bedroom can get very cold in winter; he quickly

decided to put on the nightgown that had been provided. Emma shortly returned with some morning sticks for the fire, which she soon kindled, and a china jug and bowl for him to wash with. She also provided him with a wooden toothbrush and a tin with tooth powder. Leo found the entire experience extremely novel; the only major drawback was that Emma's toilet was outside at the bottom of her yard, which given the outside temperature was not ideal. There was of course also no electricity, so he had to take a hurricane lantern with him to hang on a hook in the toilet.

Once Leo was washed and dressed, he descended the stairs and went into the parlour where Emma had laid the table out for breakfast. Nevermore was already at the table and pecking at the yolk of a boiled egg.

"Lovely day for a protest," he said, as Leo took his seat.

"Yes," agreed Leo, "I've only ever been to one protest before, so it will be interesting."

Emma soon appeared with two plates of bacon, scrambled egg and fried bread for their breakfast.

"Thanks," said Leo. He was not used to such a fastidiously set out formal breakfast and usually ate brioche rolls at his computer desk. This was more like a hotel, he thought. The three of them continued to chat about Newcastle, and Nevermore was somewhat concerned to learn that ravens didn't live in houses in Leo's reality. As they continued their breakfast, the by now familiar sound of the Town Crier's bell could be heard in the street.

"Oyez! Oyez! Oyez! All protestors to the Guildhall for nine o'clock!" he shouted.

"Will you be going to the protest, Emma?" asked Leo.

"Happily, I am exempted," said Emma. "Shopkeepers do not need to attend protests; the Countess excuses us on the basis that we would need to close our shops in order to attend, which would be bad for business."

"Another illogical rule," retorted Leo.

"How so?" asked Emma.

"Well, if everyone other than shopkeepers has to attend, then that means there would be no customers left to go into any of the shops, as they would all be at the protest. So there's no point in exempting shopkeepers as they will do no business anyway during a protest due to the lack of customers," said Leo.

"Hmm… that is a good point," mused Emma; "I had never thought about it like that… and I would suppose that neither has the Countess. Best not to mention your observation to anyone else I fancy, as I would much prefer to stay in my shop in front of the fire than stand in the snow with a placard for an hour."

"I'll keep quiet then," he agreed. Emma collected up the breakfast plates, and Leo served himself and Nevermore another cup of tea each. Just then there was a knock at the shop door, but before Emma could come from the kitchen to unlock it, Bull and Bear just walked through it.

"It's only us," called out Bull.

"Do come into the parlour," Emma called back.

"Good morning chaps," said Bull to Leo and Nevermore.

"Did you have a pleasant evening?" asked Bull.

"Very pleasant," said Nevermore, "I want to get a Nintendo Wii." Leo smiled at the thought of a Victorian raven playing Mario.

"A what?" asked Bear.

"I fancy it may take a little longer to explain than time will allow for," said Emma, bringing two extra cups and saucers. "Will you have tea?" she asked.

"Yes, please; it's cold out," said Bull.

"I'd say a few degrees below freezing," added Bear. "Hopefully it will warm up, once the sun gets a little higher in the sky."

"Is it still snowing?" asked Emma.

"No, it stopped while we were walking into town. There's a nice blue sky now," said Bear.

"Oh good, that will suit for the protest then," she said. Bull and Bear sat down at the table, and Leo poured them some tea. Bull took out that morning's copy of the Daily Tale.

"As expected," he said; "it's Friday the 14th again!"

"Probably all day," added Bear.

"I still think it's mad that the date can change halfway through the day!" said Leo. "That's even madder than making it the same day every day for several days!"

"It's the Altcastle way," said Bull.

"I think this is the fifth day of it being Friday now," said Emma, "sales must be really bad this year."

"Well, hopefully, the protest will shame a few into spending some money," said Bear.

"I do hope so," said Emma, "or Mipas will never come… and what of this morning's headlines?"

"I was just about to reveal the latest news!" said Bull excitedly. "The top story is all about Mr Punch, and about Judy too."

"What does it say?" asked Leo.

"It says that Judy has been fined two shillings for hiding in the booth and making a mockery of the Constable and the Magistrate, and a further fourpence for damage caused to the Countess' bunting by needing to be tied up with it," said Bull.

"And what of Mr Punch?" asked Emma.

"Judy has made a statement to the Constable that Mr Punch has not been kidnapped at all but has run away of his own accord because the audience didn't clap loudly enough yesterday, and he felt underappreciated."

"My goodness, what a turn of events," said Emma.

"But is it true?" asked Leo. "Or is it fake news like we have in my reality?"

"Fake news!" spluttered Bear, scandalised. "My dear fellow, this is the Altcastle Daily Tale we're reading from – it does not contain fake news, as you call it! Its articles are at the very pinnacle of journalistic endeavour and truthfulness."

Bull just smiled wryly.

"So, is it confirmed that Mr Punch has run away?" asked Leo.

"Well," said Bear, "to be absolutely fair, I suppose it's too soon to say for sure until he's been found."

"It's a hamstery business for sure, though," said Bull. "I can still see all those sneeped children in my mind's eye."

"Quite so," agreed Bear.

"Well, gentlemen," said Emma, "you had better be off to the Guildhall."

"Indeed," said Bull, "looking at the mantelpiece clock." Leo collected his coat, hat and scarf from the coat stand and made himself ready to venture out. Emma went into her shop, unlocked the door and turned her sign round to *Open*.

"See you all later, then," she said, and the three of them set off for the protest.

The snow was at least two inches deep but had already been powdered by footfall along most of the route. The streets were busy, and it seemed that the turnout for the protest would be very good indeed. As they reached the front of the Guildhall, they saw that the Mayor and some other dignitaries were already on the stage waiting; there was no sign of either the Magistrate or the Constable, though. They took their positions in the assembled crowd and Leo looked around for his crate to stand on and also for the two old ladies, Gladys and Vera, but there was no sign of any of them. As the clock struck nine, the Mayor banged his gavel and called for order; the crowd fell silent. There were no trumpeters or prompters present.

"Good morning," said the Mayor, to which the crowd replied as usual in a school assembly type manner. "Welcome to this latest *Protest Against Savers!*" he continued. "It is heart-warming indeed to see that so many concerned citizens have braved the snow and freezing temperature to make their disgust known!" he yelled. "Disgust, I say! Disgust at those terrible savers, who, rather than support the local economies of our dear town and villages, hoard their money in the abominable banks!" The crowd broke into spontaneous applause, and the Mayor paused for a moment or two to savour the adulation. "So, dear citizens let us betake ourselves to the banks and protest until half-past ten, at which time we shall reconvene here to distribute chocolate biscuit coupons to all those good people who have so zealously participated in this great and noble cause!" The crowd once again broke into applause and cheering – it seemed that Mayor Woodhay's speech was going down well.

"Down with the banks!" shouted someone, and everyone cheered again. It was quite a spectacle to behold.

"Free cocoa will be served to all protestors!" shouted the Mayor. "Kindly donated by the Worshipful Countess herself!" This latest information was greeted with the most enthusiasm of all, and some people even through their hats up into the air.

"Four cheers for the Countess," shouted another member of the crowd. "Hip, hip…" he yelled, and the crowd yelled back: "hooray!" This was actually repeated a total of six times rather than four, as the fellow evidently either couldn't count or had got too carried away with the excitement of it all.

"Truly bizarre," mumbled Leo.

"Placards will be distributed in situ!" shouted the Mayor. "So, off you go, and good luck to you all!" There were several more cheers as the crowd split up and started drifting off towards the banks.

"Which bank do we have to protest outside?" asked Leo.

"Oh, any you like," said Bear, "people can choose for themselves."

"We may as well just stay in Penkhull Street, the National Provincial Bank of Altland Ltd is just behind us," suggested Bull. They turned around and started walking the short distance to the bank.

"How many people have savings in the banks?" asked Leo.

"Oh," said Bear, "Altcastle is quite an affluent town; I fancy most people would have at least some savings with one of the banks."

"So, all these people are actually protesting against themselves," mused Leo.

"Hmm… yes, basically," said Bull, "that's true."

"So that's mad as well, then!" griped Leo. "It's crazy to protest against yourself!"

"Well, it's Altcastle, you know, old boy," smiled Bear.

"Anyway," added Bull, "the Countess ordered a protest, so a protest there must be!"

"But doesn't the Countess have savings?" asked Leo.

"Oh, yes, she'll have hundreds of pounds – she's very rich," attested Bear. Leo just shook his head in disbelief at the whole affair, but he hadn't yet seen the half of it.

The National Provincial Bank was a popular choice; at least a hundred protestors were there already when the three of them rolled up. Within moments of their arrival, at least a dozen of the Mayor's minions turned up with placards. They gave one to Leo which read:

DOWN WITH SAVING!
WITHDRAW TODAY
AND
BUY MIPAS GIFTS!

~ This Placard was Kindly Donated by ~
The Worshipful Countess of Altcastle-under-Lyme
The Right Honourable Lady Debra Sipby

"Remember, Leo," said Bull encouragingly, "the more people who withdraw and spend, the sooner it will be Saturday!"

On that advice, Leo held up his placard proudly, resting its pole in the snow.

They stood for several minutes, but no one either went into or came out of the bank. It was quite cold despite the sunlight and Leo shivered a few times. Happily, once all the placards had been distributed, the Mayor's minions turned their attention to the distribution of piping hot cocoa which had by then arrived in a large vat on the back of a horse-drawn cart; the cocoa was served in white enamel tin mugs with red rims. Leo was amongst the first to be given his cocoa and also received a chocolate biscuit for his trouble.

People were laughing and chatting away, and as usual in Altcastle, despite the inherent madness of the whole exercise, everyone seemed to be perfectly happy, and a general party atmosphere once again prevailed. Before too long, one trumpeter and one prompter turned up. The trumpeter blew his trumpet, and the prompter opened his folio to show "All Quiet!".

The chatter abated, and everyone watched the prompter. He next showed "Down with Savers!" and everyone simultaneously shouted: "Down with Savers!" while screwing their faces up and waving clenched fists in the air. The prompter then displayed "Withdraw and Spend!" and everyone shouted that. He then displayed "Chant!" and then kept flicking between "Withdraw and Spend!" and "Chant!" alternately, until he had everyone chanting "Withdraw and Spend! Withdraw and Spend! Withdraw and Spend! Withdraw and Spend!" continuously for several minutes. Leo even joined in himself, but only so Saturday would come.

As all this was going on, a chap came out of the bank; from the way he was dressed, Leo surmised he must be the bank manager. Strangely enough, no one seemed in the least bit angry with him, and he was even-handed a mug of cocoa by one of the Mayor's minions. Even more oddly, he started going around the crowd shaking hands with some of the protestors and speaking with them.

"Is he the bank manager?" asked Leo discreetly.

"Oh, yes," said Bear, "and the people he's talking to will be customers of this bank."

"Crazy!" muttered Leo.

After a few more minutes the brass band appeared, marching up Penkhull Street from the direction of Brook Lane. They were obviously playing some kind of seasonal carol although Leo didn't recognise it. As they drew closer, many of the protestors started waving to them, and they paused in front of the bank and performed several requests.

"It's all very festive here," commented Leo. "Everything's completely mad but in a sort of harmless, inoffensive kind of way."

"That's a good way of describing it," said Bull.

Once the bank manager had finished his cocoa, he handed back his mug and took a placard himself, which read:

DOWN WITH THE BANKS!
DON'T DEPOSIT – SPEND!

~ This Placard was Kindly Donated by ~
The Worshipful Countess of Altcastle-under-Lyme
The Right Honourable Lady Debra Sipby

Soon enough, a very opulently dressed older lady walked up and went into the bank; the bank manager handed his placard to someone else and followed her in.

"That's Mrs Mittens," said Bull. "She owns the Hats and Gloves shop."

"I think she'll be making a withdrawal," said Bear; "let's see."

"But how will we know?" asked Leo.

"Well, she's sure to tell everyone when she comes out," said Bear.

"Why would she do that?" asked Leo.

"Because she'll want four cheers, of course!" said Bull.

"Anyway," said Leo, "why do people in Altcastle get four cheers instead of three?"

"Why *instead of three*?" asked Bear. "It's always *four cheers.*"

"No, it's *three* cheers in Newcastle," said Leo.

"Well then, we might just as well ask you: *why do people in Newcastle only get three cheers instead of four,*" quipped Bull. Leo thought about it for a few seconds then said,

"Hmm… yes, it's a good point you've made."

Mrs Mittens soon came out of the bank again holding up two bright green pound notes quite demonstrably.

"Four cheers for Mrs Mittens!" cried out a man in the crowd. Mrs Mittens stood still and smiled to everyone assembled while she received her four cheers. "Are you going shopping now, Mrs Mittens?" asked the same man.

"Indeed I am," she said. "I shall be going to buy Mipas presents for my grandchildren!" Everyone applauded at this news, and many people whistled and cheered. Some people got so excited that they spilt their cocoa, leaving brown stains on the snow. Leo found the whole affair utterly bizarre, but Bull and Bear both appeared to be utterly delighted by it all.

"I do hope she spends both pounds," said Bear. "That will give a considerable boost to the figures!"

"Oh, she'll get an award from the Countess for that kind of expenditure," said Bull.

Upon the conclusion of Mrs Mittens' cheers, she waddled off up towards the Guildhall still beaming in self-congratulatory narcissism.

The prompters betook themselves to prompting again, and the crowd once more descended into frenzied chanting, this time with the slogan "Spend! Spend! Be a lovely friend!"

Within minutes a cart pulled up, loaded with hay bales, and a stout, ruddy-faced fellow stepped down from the seat.

"Ah, it's old Farmer Radish," said Bull.

"Will you be making a withdrawal, Farmer Radish?" asked a lady from the crowd.

"Aye, me dear, I fancy I will," he said, ambling into the bank to the applause and adulation of the protestors.

"Things are looking up," said Bear jubilantly. "I fancy he's quite a well-heeled fellow, old Farmer Radish."

"Yes, things are getting exciting, old boy!" said Bull effusively.

The crowd went back to chanting until Farmer Radish, at last, emerged jingling a bag of shillings over his head.

"Are you going shopping, Farmer?" shouted a boy.

"Aye… I'll just be delivering me hay bales, then I'll be doing a bit of shopping for Mipas," confirmed Farmer Radish.

"Four cheers for Farmer Radish!" shouted the fellow who had by now established himself as the Master of Cheers. The crowd eagerly obliged.

The same pattern of events continued for the duration of the protest with more people coming to make withdrawals, more chanting, more cheering and not unnaturally for Altcastle, more cocoa and chocolate biscuits being handed out to all and sundry. Within what seemed like no time at all, the hands of the Guildhall clock had moved round to ten twenty-five, and people started to head back to the Guildhall to receive their handouts of biscuit coupons.

Bull, Bear and Leo also headed back to the Guildhall, as Leo could see no reason why he should not receive his fair share of chocolate biscuits, the same as everyone else. The protestors coming up Penkhull Street were soon joined by those who had chosen other banks, and the fine citizens of Altcastle soon once again coalesced in front of the stage. Leo was delighted to see that Gladys and Vera had at last turned up, and were standing in their usual spot.

"Let's go over there," he said to Bull and Bear, pointing to a spot just behind the two old ladies. "It's a pity someone moved my crate," he muttered. The three of them went over to stand directly behind Gladys and Vera.

"Ooh, I hope the Countess didn't miss me at the protest, Vera," said Gladys, "only it was ever so cold for me old bones this morning, so it was."

"Ooh, I know, Gladys," said Vera, "it was bitter out, it was… I never made it meself, I didn't… was a bit early really, if truth be known."

"Ooh, it was, Vera," agreed Gladys. Leo smiled to himself.

"Now, this is proper Altcastle entertainment," he thought.

At exactly half-past ten, the Mayor banged his gavel and called for order. The crowd quickly settled down, and the Mayor's minions started running around handing out the coupons.

"Order! Order!" shouted Mayor Woodhay. "I have a very important announcement to make."

Everyone fell completely silent.

"Further to the piece in this morning's edition of the Daily Tale," he continued, "which reported that Judy had told the Constable that Mr Punch had run away of his own accord, I can now tell you all, by way of an update, that shortly after ten o'clock this morning, while decent, respectable people, like all of you, were out protesting, that awful, beakery-perpetrating, badber Punch was apprehended while trying to flee by our very own valiant and assiduous Constable Cuffem." The crowd gasped at the news and cries of "Beakery!" and "Damn the hamster!" could be heard in the cold morning air.

"Four cheers for the Constable!" shouted the Mayor; then he himself led the *hip-hips* with great enthusiasm.

"What's a *badber*?" asked Leo.

"It's the opposite of a *goodber*," retorted Bull.

"And just remind me again what a *goodber* is," said Leo. "I know I've heard the word before, but I don't remember where."

"It's very straightforward," said Bear: "a *goodber* is a person who does *good* things – like joining a protest ordered by the Countess… and a *badber* is a person who does *bad* things – like Mr Punch, who ran away in the middle of a performance."

"Right," said Leo squinting, and with an expression of otherworldliness.

"Order! Order!" shouted the Mayor. The crowd fell silent once more.

"The Magistrate has decided that the hamster Punch is guilty of various beakeries and in consequence, he will be put on trial this very morning, in just under an hour from now – at half-past eleven."

"Quite right!" shouted a man.

"He's a hamster!" shouted another.

"Ooh, I always said he was a badber, Vera," said Gladys.

"Ooh, you did Gladys... you really did," said Vera.

"You could tell he was a hamster by that big nose he's got," said Gladys.

"Ooh, you're right about that Gladys," agreed Vera, "there was a lot of beakeries up that nose, there was."

"And he looked Altalian, he did," added Gladys.

"Ooh, you can't trust them at all," said Vera, "they're always after ice-creams and spaghetti, they are!"

"Ooh, they are, Vera," said Gladys.

"Order! Order!" shouted the Mayor, banging his gavel again.

"The trial will take place at the Sipby Theatre in London Road. A small entrance fee will be payable – naturally – as the trial promises to be most entertaining!"

"How much is it?" shouted a woman.

"Just a ha'penny for adults, and a farthing for children and pensioners," shouted back the Mayor. "And refreshments will be served during the trial!"

"Ooh, they'll have refreshments, Gladys," said Vera.

"Ooh, it'll be well worth a farthing, it will," said Gladys.

"So, that's all for now," said Mayor Woodhay. "See you all at the Sipby Theatre at half-past eleven!"

A swell of chatter rose from the crowd as he finished speaking, and there was a palpable feeling of excitement in the air.

"We had better let Emma know about it," said Bull, "though I doubt she'll be able to come because of leaving the shop for so long."

"It will be a pity to miss it," said Bear, "it promises to be most entertaining."

"But what has Mr Punch done that's illegal?" asked Leo.

"Well," said Bear, "he sneeped the children…"

"But doesn't he have a right to quit if he doesn't like his job," said Leo. "He's not a slave, is he?"

"Well, not exactly," said Bull, "but he's probably under contract or something like that."

"It all sounds most unfair to me," said Leo.

"Anyway," said Bear, "he'll be represented, so let's see what his lawyer has to say about it."

"Hmm," said Leo, "it will be interesting, I suppose, but I don't think it will be very fair from what I've heard already."

"Well, let's see what happens," suggested Bull, "before you make your mind up. In the meantime, we had better go and tell Emma."

Leo and Bear nodded, and they all headed back to Emma's shop.

CHAPTER TWELVE

ANNABEL'S FREE

———

ULL, BEAR AND LEO soon arrived back at Emma's shop and relayed to her all that the Mayor had said.

"It sounds from what has been said so far, that Mr Punch might well need some moral support at his trial," said Emma, "but I shall have to find someone to watch the shop if I am to attend as it will no doubt go on for some time and I might miss customers if I close up."

"Can you think of anyone?" asked Bull.

"Hmm... let me see," said Emma, running through all her friends and acquaintances in her mind. "Possibly, my friend Annabel?"

"I do so like Annabel," squawked Nevermore. "She speaks to me nicely... not like most other humans!"

"Yes, Annabel will do very well then," said Emma. "That is, of course, if she is not too busy."

"Shall I fly to ask her," asked Nevermore.

"Please do, my friend," said Emma. Emma let Nevermore out from the kitchen door, and he flew off without delay.

"I do hope your friend can accommodate," said Bear; "it would be such a pity to miss an entertainment like this!"

"Well," said Emma, "I rather believe that we should attend to lend some moral support to poor old Mr Punch, such that at least a few people in the theatre are not shouting out that the poor puppet is guilty even before any evidence has been presented – which is what normally happens at ticket trials!"

"Hmm…" puffed Bear. "He's guilty anyway." Bull compressed his lips and nodded.

"What's a *ticket trial*?" asked Leo.

"When someone is guilty of a particularly outrageous or entertaining beakery," explained Bull, "instead of the normal short proceedings in front of the Guildhall, which anyone can attend for free, the Countess capitalises on public interest by holding the trial in a theatre and getting people to buy a ticket to attend."

"For a trial like this," added Bear, "she should do very well indeed."

"Absolutely, old boy," agreed Bull. "At a ha'penny a ticket she should collect up two or three pounds at least!"

"But shouldn't a trial be held in a court?" asked Leo.

"But there wouldn't be enough room for the audience!" said Bull.

"But is a trial really supposed to have an audience? I mean, it's not an entrainment is it?" complained Leo.

"Not an entertainment?" exclaimed Bear incredulously.

"That's the whole point of a trial," added Bull: "to entertain the good people of Altcastle… it's the Mipas season, you know, and people expect it."

"I don't suppose it will be very entertaining for poor Mr Punch," opined Emma.

"Well," said Bear dismissively, "it's not as if he'll get any serious punishment… and to be fair, he did run off in the middle of a performance causing widespread sneeping."

"I still think a trial should be in a court and not a theatre," insisted Leo.

"Anyway," said Bear, "Altcastle doesn't have a court – as Bull just said, justice is normally dispensed on the stage in front of the Guildhall because most beakeries are dealt with within a few minutes."

"And why is that?" asked Leo.

"Well," replied Bear, "because everyone is guilty, of course, so there's no need to drag out the proceedings."

"So why are Mr Punch's proceedings going to be dragged out?" asked Leo, still not convinced by the logic of the system.

"I suppose there must be a witness in this case," suggested Bull.

"But don't all cases have witnesses?" asked Leo.

"Of course not," said Bear. "If everyone is guilty, what need is there for any witnesses?"

"I don't get it," said Leo. "So, if everyone is guilty, then that means that Mr Punch is guilty?"

"Correct!" agreed Bull.

"So, if he's already guilty, then why is there any need for a witness?"

"The Countess must have decided that the witness is going to say something entertaining that will interest people, and make her more popular for organising a good show," said Bull.

"Given she's charging a ha'penny," added Bear, "there may even be several witnesses!"

Just then Nevermore came tapping on the window; Emma let him back in.

"Annabel is free; she will be here in a few minutes and will be able to stay as long as necessary," said Nevermore. "She is not interested in going to the trial as she would prefer to finish her poem for the poetry gala and talk to me, she said."

"She may well be taking the better part," said Emma, going over to the coat stand and collecting her coat and bonnet.

"You see, Bear," complained Bull, "even Emma's friend is going to enter the poetry competition, and you never encourage me in the slightest bit or give me any time to compose a suitable piece."

"Oh, please don't start off with all that again," said Bear, "and in any case how could you possibly recite your poem, when almost no one can either see you or hear you? The whole idea of it is preposterous!"

"I rather fancied I might be able to elicit the co-operation of a human to read out my work actually," said Bull.

"I rather doubt it, old boy, no one will be so keen to make a fool of him or herself," quipped Bear.

"How rather unkind, Mr Bear," admonished Emma. "I think if Mr Bull wishes to write a piece for the competition, then he should be afforded every possible opportunity and encouragement to do so."

"Hmm…" scoffed Bear. "Perhaps *you* would like to read out his poem in front of two thousand people?"

Emma's eyes glazed over.

"Well," she coughed, "I did not necessarily mean myself, naturally…" Bear, Leo and Nevermore all laughed. "I am not accustomed to public speaking, you understand," she added. Bull looked a little disappointed; it may well have been that he'd had Emma in mind as his reciter.

"Anyway, shall we go?" asked Bear, looking at the time on his pocket watch. "I don't think anyone will come into the shop while the trial is on, and there'll be a queue at the theatre for sure, so we'd best be lively."

"Then lively let us be, Mr Bear," agreed Emma. "I will see you later then, my friend. Do keep an eye on things until Annabel arrives," said Emma to Nevermore.

"Of course," said Nevermore. "Have a fine time!" He tilted his head to one side as he was apt to do.

"Do we have enough time to drop the book back in, which I borrowed from the library?" asked Leo. "Only I did promise Mr Zenodotus I would get my card stamped today, which of course I don't have, and as we don't need the book anymore, I could just take it back instead."

"Yes, of course," said Emma, "we can go that way, it will only take a few minutes extra – Mr Zenodotus will no doubt be very pleased that you have adhered to your promise."

So, the four of them left the shop and headed swiftly off down the High Street and into the Ironmarket towards the library. No more snow had fallen, but it was still below freezing, and the existing snow had become quite slippery due to compression. Nevertheless, they proceeded at haste as Bear was undoubtedly correct in his estimation of a large queue to get in; this was to be only the second ticket trial of the year, and was thus sure to be very popular with many Altcastlers.

CHAPTER THIRTEEN

THE TRIAL PART I:
THE BEAKERIES OUTLINED

"I T'S AN INCREDIBLE BUILDING," said Leo, "there's nothing like this in my Newcastle."

"It was only completed a few years ago," said Bull.

"It's equally impressive inside," added Bear, "as you'll soon see, but there's hardly ever anything on worth seeing... the Countess always edits plays before they're performed in case there's anything subversive in them."

"Ruins the plots, you know," added Bull.

"I see," said Leo.

The *Sipby Theatre*, obviously named in favour of the good Countess herself, was a fine building indeed – certainly the finest in all of Altcastle and definitely much better than anything that existed in Leo's Newcastle. Its grand façade was of red brick and sandstone, which had been quarried in the nearby Alteak District and imported into Altcastle – something in itself most unusual.

The architecture of the building was exceptional in every detail, and no expense had been spared in its construction. The nearby Holy Trinity Church, with its blue brick facia – an impressive building in its own right – and the school next door to that, were entirely dwarfed by the size of the theatre, which spread from what in Leo's Newcastle was Grosvenor Road all the way to Vessey Terrace, neither of which existed in Altcastle, giving its frontage a length of well over three-hundred feet. With a capacity of over 2,500 seats spread across five levels – the Stalls, Dress Circle, Grand Circle, Lower Balcony and Upper Balcony – the Sipby Theatre was a substantial auditorium indeed.

The front of the building was set back about fifteen yards from the main London Road, behind a line of ornate flower beds and small fountains; in the centre-ground – ten yards in front of the main doors – was a twelve-foot high statue of the Countess and her faithful hound, *Princely Paws*, in beautifully hand-cut white marble. The statue was surrounded by a small moat in which floated fresh orange rose petals and gardenias. Either side a torch burned in tribute.

They reached the front of the theatre and joined the huge crowd that was waiting to get in. Despite there being no less than seven front entrances and two at either side, it took quite a while to gain entrance due to the number of people wanting to see the spectacle. Emma paid a ha'penny for herself and a farthing for Leo – Bull and Bear, being invisible, obviously got in for free.

By yet another fortuitous coincidence, Gladys and Vera were just on the stairs up to the Dress Circle as the four of them entered the foyer.

"Let's go this way," said Leo, keen to follow them. The whole group complied, and they followed the two old ladies up to the Dress Circle where they found seats in row 'F'; Leo and Emma were able to find seats directly behind them in row 'G', and Bull and Bear remained standing in the aisle at the end of the row. Being invisible, they found that at such events, people would often sit on them, which they found very disagreeable. Next to Leo was a well-dressed old man who seemed very pleasant and smiled at him when he sat down.

The theatre was indeed huge and had a large stage that looked to be over forty feet wide, the main area of which was obscured by a black velvet curtain with detailed orange embroidery. The stage's apron extended at least five feet beyond the proscenium arch and in front of that was an orchestra pit with a full orchestra in it – at least sixty or even seventy musicians. The orchestra's conductor was an oldish looking man with a shiny bald head, surrounded on the sides and back by crazy white hair that stuck out in frizzes. He was wearing a black tailcoat, the tails of which were flying around behind him as he energetically conducted Rossini's Thieving Magpie Overture from his podium while the people came into the theatre.

Numerous gaslit, crystal chandeliers hung from the ceiling, providing a warm ambience throughout the grand building. The main extravagance of the auditorium was a large dome, which was ornately detailed and sat above the Stalls, Dress Circle and much of the Grand Circle. The seats were upholstered in orange velvet, which also topped their mahogany wooden armrests.

Quite a while passed as people continued to come in, and the orchestra played another Rossini overture when the first one had finished. Eventually, every seat in the house was taken apart from one of the private boxes to the left; it was the best box for sure and closest to the stage. Leo saw that Ebenezer Cromwell and some of his friends had taken a box on the right, although the corresponding box to the vacant one on the left was occupied by what appeared to be smartly dressed military officers in bright orange and black tunics. One of the men in Ebenezer Cromwell's retinue also looked somewhat military in terms of his hat – a black bicorn which he wore athwart, and which had a red, white and blue cockade attached to it. "Hmm..." thought Leo "...is it just me, or does that guy look like Napoleon." Of course, Leo didn't actually think that he was Napoleon, although he'd come to appreciate that in Altcastle almost anything could be possible.

Finally, two trumpeters appeared on either side of the apron, while the main stage area remained concealed behind the black velvet curtains – and seconds later, three prompters also entered on each side of the apron, holding their folios ready for action.

The Mayor appeared in due course, once the orchestra had finished playing, and everyone clapped without being prompted. The Mayor waved to everyone and gesticulated for everyone to simmer down after enjoying about a minute's worth of applause.

"My dear citizens," he started loudly and clearly – Leo had been initially concerned that they might not be able to hear very well, given the huge size of the theatre and the obvious lack of any microphones or loudspeakers, but in fact the acoustics were excellent, and he could hear the Mayor perfectly – "Welcome! Welcome to you all! And what a treat we have in store for you today!" As he was speaking, ice cream vendors appeared all over the place with fully laden usherette trays – this resulted in yet another round of applause.

"One ice cream or cake per person is included in your ticket price…" announced the Mayor. This latest announcement was met with such appreciation by the assembled townsfolk that the word *applause* could not do justice to the audience's reaction – hats were thrown in the air, some stood up and cheered, others banged their feet – it was a frenzy of unabashed delight. "…provided by the Worshipful Countess herself!" added the Mayor. As he spoke, the Countess appeared in the vacant private box to the left, much to the delight of the audience – well, at least most of the audience as Leo noticed that Ebenezer Cromwell and his party were not clapping or cheering very eagerly.

It was the first time that Leo had seen the Countess. She was surprisingly young-looking to occupy such a position of power, he thought, and looked only about thirty to thirty-five years old. She wore a long-sleeve, jet black, silk bustle dress with a button bodice and frilled lace collar, finished with accents in orange silk. About her neck was a shiny silver chain with an octagonal spiderweb pendant, similar to the crest which Leo had observed earlier, and which was set with diamonds large enough to be seen sparkling even at the not inconsiderable distance between row 'G' of the Dress Circle and the private box in which she now stood waving with the back of her hand. Over her jet black hair, she wore a tiara, also of silver and also set with diamonds which led, on either side, up to an apex that was set with a dazzling orange sapphire. The Countess was accompanied by a military officer in a black cocked hat, who stood a little behind her, and a black and white dog who wore a green silk waistcoat and had tassels hanging from his collar. From what Leo could see, the dog appeared to be a whippet – the same one who had been featured in the marble statue outside, no doubt.

"Four cheers for the Countess!" shouted one of the military officers in the righthand private box. "Hip, hip," he proposed, and everyone replied "Hooray!" with great enthusiasm.

As the four cheers proceeded, in which Emma and Leo only participated to the extent that they did not wish to look out of place, Leo noticed that Ebenezer Cromwell was also not very keen.

"The Countess seems popular with most people," muttered Leo to Emma.

"Oh, yes," said Emma, "she is... and especially when she provides free ice cream; although she will still no doubt make a profit on the whole affair, notwithstanding."

"Ooh, doesn't she look lovely, Gladys!" said Vera as the cheering concluded.

"Ooh, she does Vera," agreed Gladys.

"And she never looks a day older, does she, dear?" added Vera.

"Ooh, she doesn't," concurred Gladys, "it's as if she's never aged a day in all these years!"

Leo and Emma smiled to hear them.

Some people started to leave their seats to collect their ice creams and cakes, others remained seated; the whole ambience seemed relaxed and party-like once more. The Countess and her military escort took their seats.

"Who is the officer next to the Countess?" asked Leo.

"That is Major Schutem from the Altcastle Barracks," said Emma.

"So the barracks is still a barracks in Altcastle?" questioned Leo.

"Oh yes," said Emma, "there are about fifty soldiers stationed there officially, although rarely more than a few in residence at any given time – mostly the officers you see here live there so that they can enjoy the officers' mess for free!"

The trumpets sounded again.

"Order! Order!" shouted the Mayor, waving his hand about aimlessly – obviously missing his gavel on some subconscious level. Two prompters, one either side, displayed "SILENCE" and the audience simmered down, although people continued to go to and fro between their seats and the vendors, albeit quietly.

"We shall now commence the trial of Mr Punch," yelled the Mayor, "who is guilty of sundry beakeries. The Honourable Magistrate, Mr Justice Bender, will be presiding!"

"Shouldn't the Mayor wait until the trial is over before saying Mr Punch is guilty?" asked Leo quietly.

"I fancy he should," said Emma, "but unfortunately, I belong to a very small minority!"

The Mayor left the stage and soon reappeared in the Countess' private box where he took a seat behind her. The curtain soon rose to reveal the main stage, laid out almost exactly like a courtroom. Leo had never been in a courtroom, but he had seen courtrooms in films, and what he now beheld was an extremely realistic imitation. The judge's chair was at the far back, behind a raised up bench which had on it: a gavel and block, some law books, a large cut crystal wine glass and an impressive claret jug – Leo could see that it was a claret jug due to its similarity to the one he had seen Emma using at supper the previous evening.

In front of the Magistrate's bench were two small writing desks at both of which sat clerks, also in gowns and wigs; one was very tall and very thin, the other was quite short and rather stocky. To the left side was a wooden box, raised up with some steps leading to it and there was a similar one on the right side, but that had a door on it. Leo surmised that the one on the left, with no door, was the witness box and the one on the right, with the door, was the dock. At the front of the stage were a further two desks which had chesterfield type swivel chairs, and at which sat two other men who also wore gowns and wigs. The only thing which was obviously missing was the jury box.

"Where do the jury sit?" asked Leo.

"The audience is the jury," replied Emma.

"What everybody?" asked Leo.

"Yes," said Emma, "that is how it works here." Leo looked quite surprised by this.

"This court is now in session!" shouted the tall clerk, standing up. Everyone else on stage also stood up, but no one in the audience bothered except for those anyway wanting ice cream and cakes, the distribution of which continued unabated despite the trial starting. "The Honourable Magistrate, Mr Justice Bender presiding!" continued the clerk.

The Magistrate staggered onto the stage, swaying as usual from side to side as he came, and the orchestra once again sprang into action, this time playing the frenetic kettledrum theme from Borodin's Polovtsian Dances, which added yet another level to the extreme madness of the whole show.

As the Magistrate ascended the raised judge's area, he slipped over before making it to his chair and disappeared behind the bench. Gasps and laughter rose from the audience as both clerks rushed behind the bench and dragged the Magistrate up and onto his chair.

"He's drunk again," whispered Leo.

"He is – very!" said Emma.

"Order! Order! Silence in court!" yelled the Magistrate, banging his gavel in a frenzy. The prompters again displayed "SILENCE", and silence there soon was. The tall clerk laid some papers before the Magistrate and then returned to his place, as did the short clerk.

"Now then, Punch," said the Magistrate sternly, while looking down at his papers. "What have you got to say for yourself?" He looked up and over his spectacles at the dock – which was, of course completely empty. "What's this?" shouted the Magistrate in a crazed mania. "He's escaped again! It's beakery – beakery, I say!" The audience gasped unprompted.

"Ooh, Vera," said Gladys, "you can't believe he's that bad! Now, he's ruined the show by escaping again!"

"Ooh, Gladys, he's a badber all right!"

The short clerk stood up.

"Excuse me, my Lord," he said as discreetly as he could, although everyone could hear him.

"Yes, yes, what is it?" asked the Magistrate.

"The prisoner hasn't been brought up yet, my Lord?" he said.

"Oh, oh, quite, quite," mumbled the Magistrate, reaching for the claret jug and pouring himself a generous glass. "Order! Order!" he shouted after taking a slurp. "Bring up the prisoner!" The short clerk went into the wings and almost immediately returned followed by the Constable who was carrying a large birdcage with Mr Punch inside it. The audience gasped again at such a sight. The Constable placed the birdcage into the dock, but it wasn't tall enough for anyone on either the stage or in the audience to be able to see it, so he took it out again and placed it on the corner of the dock so Mr Punch could be seen.

"What's this?" shouted the Magistrate. "I've never seen anything like it! It's contempt, I say! Beakery, that's what it is! The prisoner must stand in the dock, not in a birdcage! He's not a canary is he?"

"He is a flight risk, m'Lord," answered the Constable. Leo laughed but then put his hand over his mouth to conceal it.

"Do you get it, Emma?" he whispered: "birdcage – flight risk?"

"Oh, Leo, what a sense of humour you have," she whispered back.

"I mean to say, m'Lord," the Constable went on, "every time I release him, he tries to make away, he does, and the handcuffs don't fit him 'cus he's got such little hands. That's why I've had to keep him locked up in this here birdcage, you see."

"Yes, yes," mumbled the Magistrate, again squinting over the top of his spectacles, "I do see... quite so." He poured himself some more claret. "Good thinking, Constable! Very wise!" he added more definitely, once he had been refreshed by another large slurp.

"Oh no, it isn't!" said Mr Punch, in his swazzled squawking voice.

"What's that?" demanded the Magistrate. "What did you say?"

"It's not *very wise*!" protested Mr Punch. "It's cruel to put me in here! I'm innocent!"

"Innocent?" cried the Magistrate. "Don't be preposterous! It's the maddest thing I've ever heard; of course, you're not innocent! Everyone knows you're guilty!"

The audience erupted into cheers and shouts of "Guilty! Guilty!"

The prompters all looked at each other in a daze – they hadn't even had time to display their pages with "GUILTY" on, and already everyone was calling out "Guilty". Emma called out "Not guilty!" but no one could hear her over the din.

"There you are!" said the Magistrate, once the audience had settled down a bit. "I told you so! You're guilty as charged, Punch."

"But I haven't even been charged with anything!" said Mr Punch.

"Ridiculous!" cried the Magistrate. "That's no excuse! You're guilty as charged whether you've been charged or not!"

"I can't be guilty as charged if I haven't been charged!" protested Mr Punch. "It's not logical!"

"Logical?" screamed the Magistrate in a fit of pique. "I'll be the judge of what's logical! These charges are… are… these charges… these charges… where are the charges?" he asked the Constable rifling through all the papers in front of him in total confusion.

"Here, my Lord," said the tall clerk, standing up and handing the Magistrate another paper.

"Exactly as I thought," blabbered the Magistrate. "It says right here that you are guilty of seven counts of beakery! It's right here in black and white, and there's no denying it!"

"But I still haven't been charged with anything!" Mr Punch continued to protest.

"Well, we can soon fix that!" screamed the Magistrate. "There's no doubt at all in anyone's mind that you're guilty as guilty can be!"

"It's not true!" complained Mr Punch. "It's all lies, big fat lies!"

"You'll be quiet in court if you know what's good for you, or I'll be minded to double the sentence!" warned the Magistrate.

"But I haven't had a sentence," said Mr Punch.

"Will you shut up!" ordered the Magistrate. "Your lawyer is supposed to speak, NOT you!"

One of the men in wigs at the front of the stage stood up.

"If it pleases the court, my Lord…" he started to say.

"And who are you?" demanded the Magistrate.

"Mr Xavier Skuze, my Lord… representing Mr Punch."

"Make a note of that clerk!" ordered the Magistrate and directing his instruction to the short clerk.

"Yes, my Lord," said the clerk.

"Very well," said the Magistrate, "see to it that Punch doesn't keep interrupting the proceedings, will you."

"Yes, my Lord," said Mr Skuze, putting his forefinger to his lips and directing the gesture towards Mr Punch. Mr Punch just sighed and pulled his face – which is no easy matter when one's face is made from painted wood. Mr Skuze sat down again.

"Now then…" said the Magistrate "…let's get on with the matter, shall we: where was I?"

"The charges, my Lord," said the tall clerk.

"Ah, yes… the charges… indeed," said the Magistrate. "Now then… as I was saying before I was so rudely interrupted: the hamster Punch is guilty of seven counts of beakery. And the beakeries he is guilty of are as follow:

Beakery Number 1: The sneeping of innocent children.

Beakery Number 2: Breach of contract with the La Falot Puppet Company Limited.

Beakery Number 3: Making away during a performance.

Beakery Number 4: Pretending to be kidnapped.

Beakery Number 5: Hitting his wife with a string of sausages.

Beakery Number 6: Avoiding arrest.

Beakery Number 7: Attempting to escape from custody."

"Objection, my Lord," said Mr Skuze, jumping up.

"Oh, really… already?" asked the Magistrate irascibly.

"Sorry, my Lord, I do apologise… but Beakery Number Five: *Hitting his wife with a string of sausages*, is not a real beakery and is just part of the Punch and Judy show."

"What? Are you mad?" retorted the Magistrate with boundless incredulity. "I've never heard anything like it! It's the most shocking excuse I've heard in over thirty years on the bench! There are at least twenty witnesses who will swear in court that Punch beat his poor wife almost senseless with sausages!"

"Yes, my Lord, I do understand that: but when he did it, it was during the show…"

"Aha!" shouted the Magistrate, interrupting him and pointing his finger directly at Mr Skuze. "So, there we are then! You're his lawyer, and even YOU admit that he did it! That's it: case proven!"

The six prompters all displayed "GASP", and the audience gasped – some shouted "Guilty!" or "Punch is guilty!" while others started to clap.

"Ooh, I always said he was guilty, Gladys!" said Vera.

"Ooh, you did Vera, and now it's proven, it is," said Gladys.

"Order! Order! Silence in court!" shouted the Magistrate. The prompters changed their folios to read "SILENCE".

"Let the record show," continued the Magistrate, "that Punch's lawyer admits that he did it." The tall clerk scribbled it down. "Now then... as to the other matters... as the miscreant has already been found guilty, there's not too much to say... but, as all these good people have come here in the cold and snow, we shall better hear some witnesses to make it worth their while."

The audience broke into spontaneous applause even before the prompters could display "CLAP", which they soon did in any case, and the orchestra once again played the kettledrum theme from Borodin's Polovtsian Dances, but even more loudly and feverishly than the previous time.

CHAPTER FOURTEEN

THE TRIAL PART II:

THE CASE FOR THE PROSECUTION

"WHO IS STANDING FOR the prosecution?" asked the Magistrate. The other bewigged man, who was sat at the front of the stage, on the opposite side to Mr Skuze, stood up.

"Good afternoon, my Lord," he started – by now, it had passed midday. "Donald Oliver Nathaniel Key, my Lord, for the prosecution," he continued in a rather pompous, monotone, upper-class voice.

"Ah, yes, Mr Key…" said the Magistrate, viewing him over his spectacles, "…indeed, most gratifying to see a barrister of your stature in court today."

"Thank, my Lord. Most kind," said Mr Key, giving the Magistrate the ostentation of a small bow.

"How many witnesses will you be calling, Mr Key?" asked the Magistrate.

"Four, my Lord," said Mr Key.

"Ooh, Gladys, they've got four witnesses, they have," said Vera.

"Ooh, I know! Isn't it wonderful! And only a farthing as well," said Gladys.

"You may call your first witness, Mr Key," said the Magistrate, pouring himself more claret.

"The prosecution calls Monsieur Pierre La Falot, of the La Falot Puppet Company Limited," called out Mr Key, who then remained standing while Monsieur La Falot came down from the private box where he had been sitting with the entourage of Ebenezer Cromwell, and onto the stage – it was the man whom Leo had noticed earlier and whom he thought looked like Napoleon.

"Ooh, he sounds a bit Altrench, he does, Vera," said Gladys.

"No wonder then that he's thick as thieves with that Altalian," said Vera.

"He's probably going to give evidence about smelly cheese, Vera," suggested Gladys, perfectly seriously.

"Ooh, he is… I think so," agreed Gladys.

"Please take your place in the witness box," said Mr Key as Monsieur La Falot appeared from the wings.

Mr Punch sneered as Monsieur La Falot passed his cage. The audience quieted themselves and sat in silent anticipation, although some still went to collect more ice creams and cakes. Monsieur La Falot took his place in the witness box and removed his bicorn hat, folding it flat and placing it under his left arm. The short clerk approached him and gave him a card to read from.

"Please recite that in a loud, clear voice," said the clerk.

"I solemnly affirm that the evidence that I shall give, shall be the truth, the whole truth and nothing but the truth," said Monsieur La Falot; he handed back the card.

"Now then, Monsieur La Falot," asked Mr Key, "are you a

resident of the ancient and loyal Borough of Altcastle-under-Lyme?"

"Indeed, I am, Sir," he replied, with a French accent.

"But you are not a native of the borough?" Mr Key continued.

"No, Sir. I immigrated here about ten years ago with my company and puppets."

"And what is your company, Monsieur?" asked Mr Key.

"It is the La Falot Puppet Company Limited, Sir."

"And where exactly is that based?" asked Mr Key.

"In Altignall End, Sir," said Monsieur La Falot.

"And how does your company operate?"

"It is a travelling puppet theatre, Sir. Each week… or maybe two weeks, I move from village to village to entertain the people," explained Monsieur La Falot.

"I see. And how long as the prisoner worked for the La Falot Puppet Company Limited?" asked Mr Key.

"I am not exactly sure, Sir, but I estimate it is over one hundred years at least," replied Monsieur La Falot.

"That is a singularly long time, Monsieur La Falot; how do you account for it?"

"The company was founded in southern Altrance, Sir, over one hundred years ago by my great-grandfather, also by the name of La Falot, and Punch was one of his original puppets," he replied.

"I see. And does your company have a contract with Punch?" asked Mr Key. Monsieur La Falot unbuttoned his coat, reached into his inside pocket and pulled out a tatty looking piece of paper with handwriting on it.

"Yes, Sir," he said, holding up the piece of paper. The audience gasped.

"And may I take it, Monsieur La Falot, that this contract does not allow for Punch making away during a performance?" asked Mr Key.

"You may, Sir," said Monsieur La Falot with gravity and certainty. The audience gasped again.

"It's all lies!" shouted Mr Punch. "That's his shopping list, not a contract!"

"Silence!" yelled the Magistrate banging his gavel several times. "The prisoner will keep quiet while we hear the evidence!" Mr Punch looked down, forlorn.

"So, here we have it, my Lord," said Mr Key turning towards the Magistrate. "It's clear as crystal: Punch is guilty of a shocking beakery!" The audience erupted into chatter.

"Ooh, Gladys, *a shocking beakery*," said Vera.

"Ooh, I know," said Gladys.

"Why doesn't Mr Punch's lawyer ask to see the paper?" commented Leo to Emma.

"Perhaps he will," said Emma.

"Order! Order!" shouted the Magistrate. "Silence in court!" Mr Skuze stood up.

"Objection, my Lord," he announced.

"What's that?" asked the Magistrate, squinting at him.

"The court should examine the paper to verify that it is a contract and not, in fact, a shopping list as has been suggested by the defendant," said Mr Skuze. The tall clerk stood up and whispered something over the bench to the Magistrate, who took another slurp of his claret.

"Very well," he said after a few seconds. "Please let me have the paper, Mr Key." Mr Key and Monsieur La Falot looked at each other shiftily; they also displayed a nervous demeanour. Mr Key hesitantly took the paper and handed it to the tall clerk, who briefly inspected it and handed it in turn up to the Magistrate. The Magistrate looked at for a few seconds.

"This does not appear to be in Altlish," he said finally. "What language is this?"

"It's Altrench, your Lordship," said Monsieur La Falot, "because the company was originally from Altrance."

"I see. What does it mean when it says: huit oeufs, beurre, pain, fromage, vin, lait?" asked the Magistrate, completely mispronouncing all of the words.

"They're important terms in an Altrench contract, my Lord," said Mr Key convincingly.

"No, they're not," squeaked Mr Punch. "They're a shopping list!"

"Order! Order!" shouted the Magistrate. "Silence in court! I won't have it, I won't!"

"My French isn't very good," said Leo to Emma; "but it sounds like eight eggs… and something about cheese, bread and wine."

"I fancy so," agreed Emma.

"Anyway we've heard enough about this," said the Magistrate sternly. "Next witness!"

"Objection!" said Mr Skuze.

"Now what?" demanded the Magistrate irascibly.

"I would like to cross-examine the witness, my Lord," said Mr Skuze.

"Certainly not… objection denied… sit down!" shouted the Magistrate.

"But I haven't asked the witness any questions, my Lord!" complained Mr Skuze.

"And what does that have to do with the price of fish in Altrimsby?" demanded the Magistrate. Mr Skuze looked somewhat confused by the question.

"Hmm… nothing at all, my Lord… not as far as I can see," he said confusedly.

"Precisely: nothing!" yelled the Magistrate. "So why bring it up, if it's completely irrelevant? Now sit down, or you'll be in contempt of court!"

Mr Skuze sat down; Monsieur La Falot left the witness box and headed back up to the private box where Ebenezer Cromwell sat glowing with delight.

"Next witness," shouted the Magistrate.

"The prosecution calls Mrs Judy Punch," announced Mr Key. The Magistrate poured himself more claret and started messing with his papers. Judy walked onto the stage and up into the witness box; unfortunately, due to her small stature, she could not be seen over the wooden sides. The short clerk nevertheless went over and gave her the card to read.

"I solemnly affirm that the evidence that I shall give, shall be the truth, the whole truth and nothing but the truth," said Judy.

"Where is the witness?" demanded the Magistrate.

"I'm here," called out Judy's squeaky voice from inside the witness box.

"Is this supposed to be some joke?" demanded the Magistrate and directing his comment to the tall clerk. "It's beakery, I say! The witness is making a mockery of justice!"

"I believe the witness may be short, my Lord," said the clerk.

"Well, I won't have it! The court can't take evidence from witnesses who can't be seen!" yelled the Magistrate. Just then a stagehand ran on from the wings carrying a wooden footstool. He placed it down inside the witness box and helped Judy up, on to it.

"May I proceed, my Lord," asked Mr Key. The Magistrate nodded while beckoning to the stagehand to refill his claret jug. "Now then," continued Mr Key, "are you the wife of Punch?"

"Yes, Sir, I am," confirmed Judy.

"And on Friday the 14th of December of this year, did Punch hit you violently with a string of sausages?"

"He did, Sir... he did it three times." The audience gasped loudly, and many shouted *Down with Punch, Shocking, Send him down*, or some other disparaging slogan.

"Ooh, just look at him in that cage, Gladys! He stands there as if butter wouldn't melt in his mouth, and all the time, he's a wife-beater!" said Vera.

"Ooh, I know Vera, just to think of it makes me giddy," said Gladys.

"Order! Order!" shouted the Magistrate. "Silence in court!" The audience became again silent.

"And what did Punch say when he beat you violently with the sausages?" asked Mr Key.

"He said: '*Take that! Take that! That's the way to do it!*' in his usual horrible swazzled voice… and he kept on hitting me again and again, all the while shouting: *That's the way to do it!*" testified Judy. Many members of the audience could again be heard gasping, and there was much head-shaking and shouting out.

"Order! Order!" shouted the Magistrate. "Silence in court!" But so scandalised was the audience at this latest evidence, that it took not only the banging of the gavel but also the jumping up and down of all six prompters with their "SILENCE" pages displayed, to quieten everyone down. After some seconds, the noise level abated.

"If it pleases the court, my Lord, the prosecution can call an additional twenty witnesses who will all tell the same sorry story?" said Mr Key.

"Thank you, Mr Key, but that will not be necessary: his own counsel has already admitted that Punch is guilty…"

"It's all lies!" shouted Mr Punch, interrupting the Magistrate again. "It was just part of the show! I say '*That's the way to do it!*' because it's part of the show, that's all!"

"Objection, my Lord," called out Mr Skuze again getting to his feet. The Magistrate banged his gavel frenetically.

"No more! No more!" he yelled. "He's guilty! Guilty! Guilty!" Just then the stagehand returned with a full jug of claret and the Magistrate refreshed his glass. The Magistrate glared at Mr Skuze menacingly, and he sat down again. "Next witness!" he yelled after quenching his thirst. Judy stepped down and disappeared back into the wings.

"The prosecution calls little Tommy Tucker," announced Mr Key. A smallish boy of about five years old came hesitantly onto the stage and was again helped onto the footstool by the stagehand.

The short clerk swore him in – although he fumbled some of the words and couldn't read most of them. Mr Justice Bender didn't seem in the least bit bothered, however.

"Now then, Tommy, there's no need for you to be at all nervous: everyone knows you're a goodber," said Mr Key. Tommy Tucker smiled at this. "How old are you, Tommy?"

"I'm five, Sir," said Tommy.

"I see," said Mr Key in a kind and reassuring tone. "Now, please tell us in your own words what transpired yesterday, at the Punch and Judy show."

"Well, Sir…" started Tommy Tucker "… I were in town with me mum and dad, I were… we was doing a bit of shopping for Mipas, we was… then I said to me dad… I said: *can we watch the Punch and Judy show,* I did… and me dad said *we can… it's only a ha'penny* he said… *so it's all right,* he said…" Tommy started to look around the auditorium, filled by so many people listening to him, and he started to look uncomfortable.

"Please don't worry about all these people," said Mr Key, "they're all friends, Tommy, and fellow citizens of yours; they're all on your side." Tommy smiled again. "Do go on, Tommy," said Mr Key.

"So… we sat down, Sir, and the show started, it did… Mr Punch and Mrs Judy was hitting each other with a big lump of wood and some sausages… they was falling about all over the place, they was, and me and me mum and dad was laughing at them, we was… it was very funny, it was… everyone was laughing, Sir."

"And what happened next, Tommy?" asked Mr Key.

"There were a crocodile and a policeman as well, Sir… and Mr Punch hit them with sausages as well… he hit everyone with sausages… even himself!" Tommy laughed as he recalled it.

"And then?" asked Mr Key.

"Mr Punch went off the stage, and then the crocodile were fighting with the policeman, and then they said *Mr Punch is coming, he is…* that's what they said, Sir: *Mr Punch is coming back*… but he never come… they said it a lot of times they did: *Oh dear*, they said, *here comes Mr Punch*… but Mr Punch never come, he didn't…"

"And after that?" asked Mr Key.

"We waited a long time… we was a bit bored of waiting, we was… then a man came out – that's the man with the big hat," said Tommy pointing up at Monsieur La Falot in the private box. "Well he come round, and he said the show was over 'cus Mr Punch had gone missing."

"I see," said Mr Key with all due sympathy and compassion, "that must have been very upsetting for you, Tommy?"

"Oh, it were, Sir… I were sneeped, I were," confirmed Tommy.

"And what did your parents have to say about the matter?" asked Mr Key.

"Me dad was angry, Sir… he said it was beakery, Sir… he said it was a fraud, Sir…"

"A *fraud,* you say?" asked Mr Key vehemently.

"That's what me dad said, Sir."

"And why was that?" asked Mr Key.

"Well, Sir, me dad had paid a ha'penny, he had… that was for the whole show… but we only got half a show," said Tommy mournfully.

"So, my Lord," said Mr Key, turning towards the Magistrate, "the prosecution respectfully submits that not only is Punch guilty of cruelly sneeping children; he is also guilty of a fraud, in that he obtained money by deception in so far as he had people pay for a whole show, but only delivered a half show – or even less than half in fact." The audience again broke into chatter, jeering and shouting slogans against Mr Punch.

"Order! Order!" shouted the Magistrate. "Silence in court! Make a note clerk: Punch is guilty of an eighth count of beakery – that of obtaining money by deception!"

"Yes, my Lord," said the short clerk, scribbling it down.

"I'm innocent!" shouted Mr Punch. "I never got any of the money. That hamster La Falot keeps all the money!"

"The prisoner will be silent!" yelled the Magistrate.

"May it please the court," said Mr Key, "I can call upon at least another seven children who have all been sneeped and all been defrauded!"

"Is it the same testimony that we have just heard, Mr Key," asked the Magistrate.

"More or less, my Lord," replied Mr Key. The Magistrate looked up at the Countess in her private box; she shook her head, and the Magistrate nodded.

"There'll be no need for that then; it will be too dull," said the Magistrate. "Clerk, let the record show that as many as eight children have testified that Punch both sneeped and defrauded them and that the charge is proven beyond doubt!"

As he finished speaking, the kettledrums kicked in again for another ten seconds of the Polovtsian Dances – it seemed that every time the Magistrate said something sufficiently dramatic, it needed to be followed by the banging of drums and the frenzied sound of Borodin's great dramatic theme.

"Objection!" shouted Mr Skuze; but he didn't bother to stand up.

"Overruled!" shouted back the Magistrate. "Next witness!"

"The prosecution calls Mrs Edith Fruitcake," called out Mr Key.

"Oh no," said the old man next to Leo, nudging him, "she's as mad as twelve hamsters!" Leo nodded. Mrs Fruitcake soon appeared from the wings, but she was walking backwards and fell over. Mr Key rushed over and helped her up, aided by the stagehand. They more or less dragged her into the witness box, turned her around the right way and sat her down on the footstool, which was just high enough to make her reasonably visible to the court.

Mrs Fruitcake was an old woman of at least seventy. She wore an unremarkable old fashioned ladies coat over an equally unremarkable old fashioned dress. A black bonnet adorned her grey hair.

"Are you all right, Mrs Fruitcake?" asked the Magistrate.

"Ooh, no, Sir... I mean your Lord..."

"That's all right, Mrs Fruitcake," said the Magistrate, "please speak freely."

"Well, your Lordship... I can't look at him... not at his horrible little beak, I can't... it gives me the terrors, so it does... that's what I was walking backwards for, 'cus I can't look at him, you see... not after what he's done."

"I see," said the Magistrate sympathetically, looking down at his papers. "Yes... yes... indeed... I can see you've had quite a shock from the Constable's notes." The Magistrate took a slurp of claret. "So, Constable, hide the prisoner inside the dock so that Mrs Fruitcake doesn't have to look at his *horrible little beak*, as she put it."

"Yes, m'Lord," said the Constable, taking the cage with Mr Punch in, and putting it inside the dock so it couldn't be seen.

"I'm innocent!" shouted Mr Punch. "Innocent, I am, and my beak isn't horrible! You can't treat me like this: it isn't fair!"

"What an outrage! I'll decide what's fair!" yelled the Magistrate. "Clerk, add another count of beakery!"

"Yes, my Lord?" answered the short clerk.

"Beakery number nine: giving decent folk the terrors by having a horrible beak!"

"Yes, my Lord," said the clerk; he made a note of it.

"Some say I'm pretty," came the squawking voice of Mr Punch from inside the wooden sides of the dock. "Some do say that... anyway, it's only a matter of opinion if my beak is pretty or horrible, and I can't be guilty of a matter of opinion."

Mr Skuze looked as if he was about to get up and object again, but the Magistrate looked at him sternly and raised his forefinger; Mr Skuze stayed put and silent.

"So, Mrs Fruitcake," started Mr Key, "please describe in your own words what happened and how the prisoner tried to avoid arrest."

"Well duck," said Mrs Fruitcake, "I'd been in Castle early on to fetch some oatcakes for me dinner…"

"Let me just stop you there for a moment," said Mr Key. "When you say *Castle* you are referring to Altcastle?"

"Yes, duck, I am… sorry about that, I meant Altcastle," said Mrs Fruitcake.

"It's quite all right," said the Magistrate, "and by dinner, you mean lunch?"

"Yes, duck… I mean your Lordship… only I'm a simple woman."

"You can say that again," mumbled the old man next to Leo. Leo smiled.

"That's quite all right, Mrs Fruitcake, please feel free to address me as *duck* if it makes you more comfortable," said the Magistrate in a most accommodating manner. "Please remember that it's the miscreant Punch that we're interested in today, not the vocabulistic vagaries of your diction."

"Ooh, thank you, your Lordship," said Mrs Fruitcake, "you're a fine gentleman, you are." The Magistrate nodded and smiled condescendingly.

"Please go on, Mrs Fruitcake," said Mr Key.

"Well… where was I… oh yes… while I was in Castle fetching some oatcakes, I heard from people that Mr Punch had been kidnapped… they were talking about it, you know…"

"Who was talking about it?" asked Mr Key.

"Well, everyone was… it was big news, duck… a kidnapping! I mean, you don't hear about things like that in Altcastle. Not since her Ladyship took over anyway. Everything is peaceful and orderly, isn't it? Old people can go about their business since we've had the Countess in charge… the streets are safe… there's no beakery…" The Countess looked down with a smug smile.

"Do please go on, Mrs Fruitcake," said Mr Key.

"Well, I'd got me oatcakes… but it made me think about my Sidney, it did…"

"What made you think about your Sidney?" asked Mr Key.

"Here we go," mumbled the old man next to Leo.

"The kidnapping did... you know, Mr Punch being kidnapped," said Mrs Fruitcake.

"Who is your Sidney, may I ask?" asked Mr Key.

"He was me hubby, he was... until he was kidnapped, that is."

"I'm sorry... so, your husband was kidnapped?" queried Mr Key incredulously.

"I do miss him, you know," lamented Mrs Fruitcake.

"I'm sure you do, Mrs Fruitcake, but when did this happen and was the prisoner involved?" asked Mr Key; he looked quite confused by Mrs Fruitcake's testimony.

"Ooh no, I don't think so. Me hubby was kidnapped above thirty years ago."

"I see... so, if we could just focus on your testimony regarding the prisoner and what happened this morning, that would probably be better."

"Ooh... all right duck, as you wish... so where was I?" said Mrs Fruitcake confusedly.

"About Mr Punch," said Mr Key somewhat impatiently.

"Ooh... it was horrible, Sir, horrible," said Mrs Fruitcake.

"What was horrible?" asked Mr Key.

"Well, Sir, I saw him running across the road, I did. It was at the top end of Queen Street, near Sidmouth Road, that's where he was running; and I thought to meself, what's he doing running across the road when he's been kidnapped..."

"And this was at about what time this morning?" asked Mr Key.

"Well, I got to Castle early on, so I fancy it would have been about half-past nine by the time I got up near Sidmouth Road," she replied.

"Very well; what happened next?" asked Mr Key.

"Well... I didn't think too much of it, I suppose... I thought perhaps he hadn't been kidnapped after all, or perhaps he'd escaped from the kidnappers… or something like that… so I carried on walking up the hill towards the Brampton… but then I heard the Constable's whistle, and I thought something's going on, it is… and then that's when it happened, Sir!"

"But what was it that actually happened?" pressed Mr Key.

"Ooh… it was horrible, Sir, horrible, it was" said Mrs Fruitcake again.

"Yes, we understand that is was horrible, Mrs Fruitcake; but what was it that happened?" asked Mr Key.

"Just as I was passing under a tree, he jumped out of the tree and straight into me shopping basket and landed on his back, right on top of me oatcakes…" The audience gasped in horror, and Mrs Fruitcake broke down in tears.

"There, there, Mrs Fruitcake," said Mr Key in a comforting tone of voice. Mrs Fruitcake continued to sob, and Mr Key gave her his pocket-handkerchief.

"Oh, thank you, duck…" she said, wiping her eyes "… but he was there in me basket just looking up at me… it's true, duck… there he was with his horrible little beak starring up at me… I'd never seen the like of it, I hadn't…"

"It's not true!" shouted Mr Punch from within the dock. "I didn't jump; I fell! I just lost my footing and fell!"

"Order! Order!" shouted the Magistrate while banging his gavel. "The prisoner will remain silent and not tell more lies while we hear the evidence!" The Magistrate poured himself more claret while shaking his head in consternation. "Clerk!" he said, to the short one.

"Yes, my Lord?"

"Add a tenth count of beakery, please: jumping into a shopping basket uninvited and generally contrary to good manners!"

"It's all lies," mumbled Mr Punch.

"Right away, my Lord," said the short clerk, writing it down.

"And what happened next, Mrs Fruitcake?" asked Mr Key.

"I screamed, Sir, I did… I just froze in terror and screamed… *Oh, me oatcakes!* I screamed…"

"*Your oatcakes?*" queried Mr Key.

"They was fresh, Sir… for me dinner, you know," said Mrs Fruitcake wretchedly.

"But what about your oatcakes?" pressed Mr Key.

"Well, duck… I mean, I just don't agree with it… you can call me old fashioned if you like, but I just don't agree with that sort of thing…"

"But what sort of thing don't you agree with, Mrs Fruitcake?" asked Mr Key.

"Jumping onto a person's oatcakes with dirty shoes on… I mean, it's not hygienic is it… you don't know where they've been, do you… it's not right is it, where food's concerned… I mean, what would your wife say, Sir, if someone jumped onto her oatcakes?"

"I imagine she'd be very unhappy about it, Mrs Fruitcake," agreed Mr Key solemnly. He turned around to look at the Magistrate. The Magistrate banged his gavel three times.

"Shocked, I am!" bewailed the Magistrate. "I've never heard of such beakery in all my years on the bench! Clerk, add yet another count of beakery."

"Yes, my Lord. This will be beakery number eleven," he said. The Magistrate nodded.

"Recklessly endangering the edibility of oatcakes!" declared the Magistrate.

"Ooh, Vera, *recklessly endangering the edibility of oatcakes*, that's a beakery we've never heard of before," said Gladys.

"Ooh, it is, Gladys. You can't believe anyone would do such a thing," said Vera.

"Just fancy doing that to somebody's oatcakes, Vera," added Gladys.

"Ooh, I know," said Vera.

"Order! Order!" shouted the Magistrate. "Silence in court!" The audience simmered down once more. "Carry on Mr Key… we may as well hear the remainder of this sordid matter."

"Yes, my Lord," he replied and then turned back to Mrs Fruitcake. "Now then, after you had this terrible shock, and started screaming: what happened next?"

"Well, duck... I dropped me basket, I did... I just dropped it... then it... I mean *he*, he jumped out of the basket and ran back into the trees, he did..."

"And was this the point at which Punch transformed himself?" asked Mr Key.

"Objection!" shouted Mr Skuze, jumping to his feet. "Counsel is leading the witness, my Lord."

"Overruled," shouted the Magistrate, banging his gavel and waving to Mr Skuze to sit down again, which he did. "Please carry on, Mrs Fruitcake," he said encouragingly, "your testimony is most interesting."

"Yes, your Sirship... so, where was I? Oh yes... so he ran into the trees and then I heard a lot of noises and then he ran out again after he'd turned into a reptile." Gasps of shock and horror rose from the audience.

"You say that Punch transformed into a reptile, Mrs Fruitcake? Are you certain of this?" asked Mr Key.

"I am Sir... I'm hundreds of them cents things certain... as I live and breathe, Sir, that's what happened: he turned himself into a reptile." Yet more gasps could be heard.

"Ooh, the poor dear... she must have been terrified out of her wits," said Gladys.

"Ooh, she must have been," agreed Vera.

"And what did this reptile look like?" asked Mr Key.

"Ooh, it was horrible, Sir, horrible," said Mrs Fruitcake, dabbing her eyes with the handkerchief again.

"Make a careful note of this matter, Clerk," said the Magistrate and add yet another count of beakery: changing into a reptile!"

"Yes, my Lord," said the short clerk.

"So, what happened next, Mrs Fruitcake?" asked Mr Key.

"Well, Sir, after he came out of the trees – after he changed into a reptile, I mean… he just stared at me… it was terrifying, Sir, truly it was… I thought I were done for, I did… I remember saying to meself: *that's the end of you Edith Fruitcake, you're a goner for sure…* that's what I thought, duck."

"It must have been a truly terrible and shocking experience," said Mr Key.

"Ooh, Sir, I can't describe the fear I had… I was sure he were going to eat me; I were."

"Eat you?" asked Mr Key.

"Oh yes, Sir, that's what he wanted to do… I could see it in them evil eyes of his… he was looking at me as if I were a tasty treat, he were…"

"It's all lies!" shouted Mr Punch. "I never tried to eat anybody. I'm innocent!"

"Order! Order!" shouted the Magistrate. "Silence in court! Go on Mrs Fruitcake, don't be put off by that brigand Punch!"

"Well, Sir, he had evil eyes, like I said… and all them horrible, big, sharp, white teeth… there was hundreds of them, there was – white teeth, I mean – all lined up, they was, and just waiting to eat me… he wanted to eat me alive, he did!" Members of the audience gasped with such gasping gusto that several fainted from lack of oxygen, children dropped their ice creams to the floor, some folks shouted out, but most remained in such bitter and deep shock they were transfixed in a stupor. The Magistrate shook his head again.

"The longer this trial continues, the worse it gets," he said dolefully. "I've never heard of such beakery in all my life; the very thought of turning into a reptile in order to devour a poor old lady is more than the ears of an aged man such as myself can stand without something a little stronger than claret…" he banged his gavel timorously, as though in shock "…bring me some brandy, Clerk, or I fear I shall not survive more of this evidence."

"Yes, my Lord," replied the tall clerk, beckoning to the stagehand who had remained waiting in the wings – possibly for just such an errand of mercy.

"Ooh, Gladys, I shall be afraid to walk home," said Vera.

"Ooh, I know… you just can't credit it: people being eaten alive in the Brampton," said Gladys.

"No wonder her Worshipfulness has brought the military with her!" said Vera.

"Ooh, she's wise doing that all right… what with people being eaten and all, and I fancy she's much tastier than Mrs Fruitcake, you know," opined Gladys.

"Ooh yes, with all her money, she must be," agreed Vera. The stagehand returned at this point with an extremely generous glass of Brandy which the Magistrate downed in one.

"Right," announced the Magistrate. "Silence in court! Please continue Mr Key."

"Thank you, my Lord," said Mr Key. "Now, Mrs Fruitcake; after you were terrified by the prospect of the prisoner eating you, what happened next?"

"I ran, Sir… ran for me very life, I did… all the way back down Queen Street, I ran; and I never looked back," said Mrs Fruitcake.

"And then?" asked Mr Key.

"I were so lucky, duck… it were a blessed chance it were… I bumped into the Constable coming up the other way. He saved me from the monster, he did! If I hadn't met him, I'd have been eaten for sure, Sir!" The Constable looked proud of himself on hearing this, and he puffed his chest out.

"And what did the Constable do?" asked Mr Key.

"After I told him all about what had happened, he went into St. George's and asked Reverend Basher to look after me, and then he went off to catch Punch," said Mrs Fruitcake.

"And did Reverend Basher look after you?" asked Mr Key.

"He did, Sir… he were very good, bless him… he gave me some tea and biscuits, he did."

"And then?"

"After about an hour, the Constable came back and told me he'd caught Punch and he'd put him in a cage."

"I'm sure you were glad to hear that, Mrs Fruitcake," said Mr Key.

"Ooh, Sir… I can't tell you what a relief it was to me… 'cus I'd been worrying about the Constable as well, I had," said Mrs Fruitcake.

"About the Constable?" enquired Mr Key.

"Yes, Sir… in case he was eaten himself or bitten… I asked the Constable soon as he come back if he'd been bitten, but the Constable told me that by the time he found him, Punch had already changed back from a reptile into his normal body… if you can call such a horrible thing *normal*, that is!"

"Quite, quite," said Mr Key. "Well, my Lord," he added turning to the Magistrate, "given all we've now heard, the prosecution has no alternative but to ask for the addition of a thirteenth count of beakery, namely: attempting to eat an old lady!"

"I quite agree… add another count as described, Clerk," said the Magistrate.

"Yes, my Lord," said the clerk.

"It's lies!" shouted Mr Punch again. "I never wanted to eat anybody!"

"Silence in court!" shouted the Magistrate. "I've told you already, Punch: keep quiet!"

"And that concludes the case for the prosecution, my Lord. As everyone can see: Punch is guilty of no less than thirteen beakeries of the foulest and most vicious nature, as I will describe more fully in my closing argument at your convenience, my Lord."

"Very well," agreed the Magistrate. "You may make your closing argument right away, and then I will pass sentence."

The kettledrums sounded again to mark the end of the prosecution's evidence, and the orchestra once again treated everyone to a few seconds of Borodin.

"Objection!" shouted Mr Skuze, again jumping to his feet.

"Oh really, Mr Skuze!" scoffed the Magistrate. "Now what?"

"If it pleases the court, my Lord, can I please cross-examine just this one last witness? Please? I haven't even been allowed to question one witness yet!" begged Mr Skuze with his hands joined together before his chest, as if in prayer.

CHAPTER FIFTEEN

THE TRIAL PART III:
THE CASE FOR THE DEFENCE

T HE MAGISTRATE LOOKED UP at the Countess who waggled her head from side to side undecidedly before puffing out and nodding grudgingly.

"Very well," agreed the Magistrate. "But be quick about it, as I must get on to the sentencing!"

"Thank you, thank you, my Lord," said Mr Skuze elatedly. Mr Key returned to his seat, throwing a sneer in the direction of Mr Skuze as he went. Mr Skuze approached the witness box.

"Now then, Mrs Fruitcake, please can you describe this reptile you were referring to in more detail?" asked Mr Skuze.

"Well, Sir... it was horr..."

"We all accept that *it was horrible, Sir, horrible...* but what did the reptile actually look like in terms of its size, colour, shape, et cetera?" he asked, interrupting her.

"It was green, Sir… with a long beak full of white teeth… yellow eyes and it was the same size as Punch," said Mrs Fruitcake very definitely.

"I see," said Mr Skuze. "Is it possible that what you saw was, in fact, a crocodile?"

"Ooh, no Sir, it was a reptile, Sir," said Mrs Fruitcake.

"It may interest you to know that a crocodile IS a reptile, Mrs Fruitcake," said Mr Skuze.

"Objection!" shouted Mr Key, jumping up. "Everyone knows that there are no crocodiles in Altcastle. Or does Mr Skuze now want us all to believe that the Lyme Brook has miraculously turned into the river Nile?" The audience laughed; the Magistrate banged his gavel.

"Order! Order!" shouted the Magistrate. "Where is this leading, Mr Skuze?" he asked.

Mr Skuze walked back over to his desk and collected a folder. He then walked back to the witness box, opened the folder and took out a photograph of the Punch and Judy show's crocodile. "Was this the creature that you saw?" he asked, holding up the photograph to her.

"Ooh, yes," winced Mrs Fruitcake, "that's exactly it! That's what Punch turned into." The audience again gasped in shock.

Mr Skuze handed the photograph to the tall clerk, who in turn handed it to the Magistrate.

"The defence offers this item as exhibit one, my Lord," said Mr Skuze. "We further submit that what Mrs Fruitcake actually saw coming out of the trees was, in fact, the Punch and Judy show's crocodile, who had gone to look for his co-actor, Mr Punch, in an attempt to force him back to the puppet theatre and back on stage. The two of them got into a scuffle over the matter, resulting in the crocodile appearing out of the treeline after the noise that Mrs Fruitcake says she heard. Mrs Fruitcake then mistakenly concluded that Mr Punch had turned himself into the crocodile, or a reptile, as she puts it, because she saw only the crocodile and not Mr Punch, who was still at this point within the treeline."

"Hmm… I see," said the Magistrate, closely inspecting the photograph.

"He's a good lawyer," whispered Leo to Emma.

"He is," agreed Emma, "but I fancy it will not make any difference to the outcome."

"Why is that?" asked Leo.

"You shall soon see," said Emma knowingly.

"Objection!" shouted Mr Key again; he had remained standing. "This evidence is not admissible!"

The Magistrate banged his gavel several times, and then shouted: "Objection sustained!"

"Objection!" shouted Mr Skuze. "Why is the evidence not admissible?"

"Because it does not agree with the verdict, of course!" yelled Mr Key. "If the evidence is admissible, then it proves that Mr Punch did not turn into a reptile!"

"Exactly!" confirmed the Magistrate. "So it's not admissible; it's obvious to anyone."

"But Mr Punch is innocent, my Lord. He actually, in fact, did not turn into a reptile!" insisted Mr Skuze.

"It's irrelevant!" yelled the Magistrate. "He's guilty until proven innocent!"

"Isn't that the wrong way round?" whispered Leo to Emma.

"No, not in Altcastle… everyone is presumed guilty," replied Emma quietly.

"But the photograph does prove him innocent," said Mr Skuze.

"Not if it's not admissible, it doesn't!" shouted the Magistrate.

"Perhaps, my Lord," suggested Mr Key, "you meant to say earlier that *he's guilty EVEN if proven innocent?*"

"That's exactly right!" exclaimed the Magistrate. "*He's guilty even if proven innocent!* So he's just guilty, and that's all there is to it. Now sit down, Mr Skuze, or you will be in contempt of court." Mr Skuze sat down as ordered, but in quite a huff. Mr key also sat back down, but with a satisfied smirk on his face.

"Thank you very much for your testimony. You may step down," said the Magistrate to Mrs Fruitcake, who did as invited. She disappeared back into the wings. "Now then," he continued, "we'll turn our attention to the sentencing…"

"Objection!" shouted Mr Skuze, again jumping up.

"Oh, for heaven's sake, man!" said the Magistrate irritably. "Whatever now?"

"My client is entitled to present a case for the defence before sentencing," said Mr Skuze. The magistrate puffed out his lungs contemptuously and shook his head. He looked up at the Countess again who nodded but held up five fingers to him as if to *say Punch can have five minutes for his defence.*

"Very well," said the Magistrate. "Call your witness then… but make it quick, will you!"

"The defence calls Mr Punch," announced Mr Skuze. The Constable lifted the birdcage containing Mr Punch from inside the dock and carried it over to the witness box where he again rested it over one the corners so that everyone could see Mr Punch give his evidence. The tall clerk came over with the card and swore Mr Punch in.

"Now, Mr Punch: first of all, please tell the court if you are guilty of the alleged beakeries," said Mr Skuze.

"No, Sir, I'm not – I'm innocent!" he exclaimed. The audience jeered and hissed loudly at this.

"Outrageous! Disgraceful!" shouted the Magistrate. "That's yet another beakery. Write it down Clerk: claiming to be innocent when you've already been found guilty." The clerk wrote it down.

"There's no justice to be had here!" shouted Mr Punch. "It's not fair! It's because I'm a puppet! Equal rights for puppets! That's what I say!" Gasps and moans rose from the audience.

"That's a revolutionary slogan!" shouted Mr Key, leaping excitedly to his feet. "It's beakery! He's trying to start a puppets' rebellion, my Lord!" The Magistrate banged his gavel vigorously.

"There'll be no revolutions in this court!" he shouted. "All puppets will continue to know their place in society and be about themselves and carry on with the show! There'll no rebelling, making away during a performance or any other form of hamstery business! Add another count of beakery, Clerk: trying to start a revolution!"

"Right away, my Lord," said the clerk scribbling down the latest beakery. The audience again erupted into angry chatter.

"Ooh, Gladys, as if he hasn't done enough already!" said Vera.

"Ooh I know: there's no end to his beakeries… he's never satisfied, is he?" replied Gladys.

"Ooh he isn't, is he! Now he's even started a revolution – the streets aren't safe to walk," added Vera.

"Put the prisoner back on the dock," ordered the Magistrate. "We've heard quite enough from him!" The Constable did as ordered while the audience clapped and cheered.

"There's no justice!" shouted Mr Punch as he was being transferred back to the dock. "I'm an innocent puppet!"

"Silence in Court!" yelled the Magistrate, banging his gavel.

"Poor old Mr Punch," whispered Leo. "They've hardly let him say anything in his own defence."

"I am afraid that it is quite the norm at proceedings such as this," replied Emma.

CHAPTER SIXTEEN

THE TRIAL PART IV:

CRIMES AND PUNISHMENT

"**O**RDER! ORDER!" SHOUTED THE Magistrate. The prompters displayed "SILENCE", and everyone settled down again for the sentencing. "It is now my painful duty to pass lawful sentence on the miscreant Punch."

"What happened to the verdict?" whispered Leo. "Shouldn't there be a verdict before there's a sentence?"

"Everyone already shouted *guilty*, so that will do," replied Emma.

"Giovanni Antonio Pulcinella, more commonly known as Mr Punch, you have been found guilty of fifteen beakeries, namely:

1: The sneeping of innocent children.

2: Breach of contract with the La Falot Puppet Company Limited.

3: Making away during a performance.

4: Pretending to be kidnapped.

5: Hitting your wife with a string of sausages.

6: Avoiding arrest.

7: Attempting to escape from custody by having hands that are too small for handcuffs.

8: Fraud, consisting of obtaining money by deception.

9: Giving decent folk the terrors by having a horrible beak.

10: Jumping into a shopping basket uninvited and generally contrary to good manners.

11: Recklessly endangering the edibility of oatcakes.

12: Changing into a reptile.

13: Attempting to eat an old lady.

14: Claiming to be innocent when already found guilty.

15: Trying to start a revolution.

And you are hereby sentenced to a fine of one shilling per beakery, plus thruppence ha'penny in court costs, and a further tuppence for whinging all through the case, so that's fifteen shillings and fivepence ha'penny in total," declared the Magistrate.

The audience roared in agreement, with many jumping up and cheering; the kettledrums sounded again, and yet again the orchestra played the third theme of the Polovtsian Dances from Prince Igor, but this time for a little longer to celebrate the handing down of the sentence.

"It's all absolute madness," muttered Leo. Emma smiled and nodded.

"Have you anything to say, Punch, now that sentence has been passed?" asked the Magistrate as the orchestra concluded.

Mr Punch started to sob loudly. He put his hand in his trouser pocket and pulled out a handful of coins which he started to examine through his tears.

"I haven't got that much," he wept. "I'll be bankrupt, I will... I've worked hard all these years, and now I'll be bankrupt..." he continued sobbing.

"Well, how much have you got?" sighed the Magistrate.

"Just two and six, my Lord," said Mr Punch. The Magistrate again looked up to the Countess in her private box. She took a quick look at Mr Punch, sobbing in his birdcage, and then nodded to the Magistrate. "Very well then, Punch; as it is the season of goodwill, despite your engagement in hamstery business, the court is minded to reduce your fine from fifteen shillings and fivepence ha'penny, to two shillings and fivepence ha'penny – that will leave you with one ha'penny so that you won't be bankrupt at Mipas. Now, hand the fine over to the Constable!"

Mr Punch put his hand through the bars of the birdcage and dropped the coins into the Constable's hand. The Constable counted them out and gave Mr Punch back a ha'penny in change as agreed.

"It's all here, m'Lord," confirmed the Constable.

"Very well," said the Magistrate. "Now, listen carefully, Punch! You've had a lucky escape this time and received a good deal of clemency on account of the season, but I warn you: you'd better be about yourself in future and entertain the children nicely and not run off halfway through a performance or else! Do you understand me?" Mr Punch wiped his tears away with his sleeve and nodded. "Good. Back to the puppet theatre with you, then!" said the Magistrate sternly. "And see to it you don't get lost along the way!" Mr Punch nodded again, and the Constable opened the door of the birdcage and put it down on the stage so that Mr Punch could go free.

"This court is now in recess!" shouted the Magistrate, banging his gavel.

"All rise," called the short clerk, standing up. Everyone else on stage stood up too. The Magistrate left the scene first, punctually followed by the other players. All six prompters displayed "CLAP", and a warm, appreciative, luxurious applause arose from the entire auditorium.

Mayor Woodhay soon appeared on the stage's apron, and as he did so, the black velvet curtain dropped behind him. After over half a minute of continual applause, he gestured for the clapping to stop and the prompters changed their prompts to "SILENCE".

"Well, my dear fellow citizens," he started enthusiastically, "that was quite a trial!" Many amongst the audience again produced a short burst of clapping and cheering, but it soon abated. "So, Mr Punch has gone back to the Punch and Judy booth, and after a night in his crate, he'll be back tomorrow for more slapstick comedy and shenanigans…" more applause was heard "… but in the meantime, I am delighted to announce that the Countess has decided to open the fairground from tonight…"

With such rapture was this news received, that he was unable to even finish his sentence. Most of the audience broke into clapping, cheering and hat throwing; some people even stood on their theatre chairs and started jumping up and down in a frenzy, they were so excited.

"I guess the fairground is good then?" asked Leo rhetorically.

"Yes, I would say that it is quite definitely popular," replied Emma.

The clapping and cheering went on well over a minute and such was the excitement of those assembled, that it would be hard to imagine that at least a few injuries were not sustained by people falling off the chairs or other things. One fellow became so energetic in his joy that he even toppled over the balcony of the dress circle; luckily, he was caught by some people in the stalls. Eventually, the euphoria abated, and the Mayor was able to carry on.

"So, dear citizens," he continued, "I am pleased to say that the fairground will open at four o'clock this very afternoon, and the Countess herself will be there."

"Four cheers for the Countess!" shouted a man in the stalls. There followed the usual *hip, hip, hooraying* for which the Countess graciously stood up in order to wave to her many hundreds of loyal admirers. Once that had finished, there was yet more cheering, shouting and clapping, until after about another minute the

Mayor again waved for people to be quiet and the Countess, after blowing several kisses to the audience, departed from the box with her complement of willing sycophants and her hound, Princely Paws.

"Well, dear citizens," finished the Mayor, "that's all for now: see you at the fairground later!" He bowed slightly and then disappeared offstage. As he went off, many people stood up and started queueing for the exits.

"We may as well wait here, for now, Leo," said Emma. "It will take several minutes at least for this theatre to even half empty." Leo nodded. "So, what did you think of an Altcastle court case?" asked Emma.

"Hmm... well..." said Leo "...where shall I start?"

"Was it so bad?" Emma smiled.

"The answer to that question can only be *yes!*" replied Leo. "I think it was truly outrageous, actually!"

"Well, of course, that is true," agreed Emma. "Though at least in Altcastle, the *beakery* of the system – if you will excuse my description of it as such – is all in the trial itself: the punishments are actually not too severe."

"Hmm..." mused Leo "... but Mr Punch has still lost all his money when he wasn't guilty of anything."

"Yes, that is a most unfortunate matter," agreed Emma. "So in your reality, is justice dispensed justly?"

"I don't know a lot about it," he said; "but from what I do know, no, I don't think it is. I think it's not as obviously corrupt as it is here – I mean they pretend it's all fair, at least ... and don't turn it into a joke like in Altcastle, but I think most people in my reality don't get any more justice than they do here... maybe they even get less."

"Really?" asked Emma.

"Do you have prisons here?" asked Leo

"Oh, no," said Emma. "There are no prisons; one only reads about that type of thing in old books from the library."

"So what happens if someone commits real crimes... you know, not joke crimes like your *beakeries*?"

"Hmm... well, the Countess would have you believe that these beakeries are very serious matters," said Emma with a smile.

"But they're not really," replied Leo. "I mean, no one actually believes that Mr Punch turned into a reptile or that every man in the town is guilty because someone left a toilet seat up... it seems it's all just a joke or done to entertain people."

"It may be so," agreed Emma. "But perhaps if one makes a big fuss about nothing, then no one will actually do anything very serious."

"Maybe," said Leo. "So, you don't have any murders or things like that?" he asked.

"Oh, heavens, no," said Emma. "I am certain no one has ever been murdered in Altcastle... certainly not during my lifetime at least."

"What about burglaries and thefts?" asked Leo.

"I do not believe they often occur either," said Emma. "Of course there were the famous kettle burglaries of a few years ago, and then there were also the button thefts before that, but I would imagine that one might not consider those to be very serious matters either."

"Yes, Bull and Bear told me about those... they think the Countess organised it all," he said.

"Really?" mused Emma. "Fancy that."

"What do you think?" asked Leo.

"I believe that thinking may be a thing best undertaken cautiously," replied Emma with another of her wry smiles. Just then Bull and Bear appeared in the seats immediately behind them.

"What did you think of it?" asked Bear.

"It was most entertaining, wasn't it?" said Bull keenly.

"Well," said Leo, "I think it was outrageously unfair actually: Mr Punch has literally had all his money stolen!"

"Well," said Bear, "he did sneep all the children…"

"And he really was guilty of that," interjected Bear.

"Well… maybe just that," conceded Leo; "but as to the rest, it was all complete rubbish. I mean, whoever in all their life ever heard of a crime called *recklessly endangering the edibility of oatcakes*? It's just pure nonsense!"

"It's a serious matter," said Bull, "*endangering the edibility of oatcakes* – and doing it *recklessly* is even worse."

"OK," replied Leo, "but how would someone do it *unrecklessly* – if that's even a word?"

Emma laughed.

"I am certainly not aware of such a word in Altlish," she said.

"Well, if it's not a word, then it most assuredly should be," said Bull very punctiliously.

"Indeed! I think it's a very fine word," added Bear. "And in any case, what other word could one possibly use to replace *unrecklessly*?"

"One might say that the opposite of *recklessly* is *carefully* or *thoughtfully*," suggested Emma.

"But that would be a worse crime," said Bull immediately.

"Indeed," agreed Bear, "if someone were to *endanger the edibility of oatcakes* recklessly then one might suppose that such a person didn't really mean to *endanger their edibility*, BUT if someone were to *endanger their edibility* carefully or thoughtfully, then that would surely mean that such a person had deliberately set out, or even planned in advance, to *endanger their edibility*, which would, of course, be much worse." A bewildered expression crept across Leo's face.

"What do you think, Leo?" asked Bull.

"It's hard to believe that I'm involved in a conversation about *endangering the edibility of oatcakes* actually – I had never imagined in my whole life, I would be. In fact, I think most people who have ever lived and died on this planet, have never discussed *endangering the edibility of oatcakes* in their entire lives."

"You make a good point," said Bull, and he nodded with an astute expression.

"So," said Bear, changing the subject, "shall we all be off to the fairground at four?"

"I would certainly like to go to the fairground," said Emma. "But it will not be fair of me to ask Annabel to watch the shop again while I am out, as she may want to go herself."

"Maybe Annabel won't want to go to the fairground?" suggested Leo.

"Well, that is possible," agreed Emma; "but it will be very rude to make such an assumption without consulting her."

"Of course," agreed Bear. By this time the theatre had more than half emptied.

"Shall we make our way back to my shop?" asked Emma.

"Well," said Bull, "we need to pay a brief visit to our friend Mr Badger, out at Barker Wood. It's his birthday, you see, but we can be back at the fairground by four o'clock quite comfortably."

"Very well, then," said Emma. "So, Leo… perhaps you will come back to my shop for a sandwich; then you can meet Mr Bull and Mr Bear at the fairground at four o'clock, even if I am unable to go myself?"

"OK," said Leo, "that's fine. Where will we meet?"

"We can meet outside the Loons Demented marquee," suggested Bear. "You cannot miss it: it has a large sign and will be very noisy."

"OK," said Leo.

"Good," said Bull, "we will see you there later, then."

"There is no point waiting for the rest of this queue to go, old boy," said Bear, "or walking through people – we may as well just go through the wall."

"Quite so," agreed Bull, and the two of them walked to the back of the dress circle and straight through the wall.

"It's incredible how they do that," said Leo.

"It is indeed", said Emma, "though I fear you and I will have to join the queue for the stairs with everyone else," she added, standing up.

It took quite a while for them to get out of the theatre and as they exited, it was again snowing. As they walked back up London Road, passed Holy Trinity and Well Street, Leo noticed the Militia Barracks to the right; the whole area around the barracks looked completely different to how it looked in his Newcastle.

They were soon back in Penkhull Street and quickly reached the stage in front of the Guildhall on which the brass band were playing carols. As they passed the Punch and Judy booth, they noticed a sign advertising two performances for the following day – one at 2pm and one at 4pm.

"Mr Punch will be back tomorrow, then" commented Leo.

"I fancy he has only avoided being back today because the grand opening of the fairground is set for four o'clock," said Emma.

They continued to walk along the High Street and soon arrived back in Red Lion Square.

CHAPTER SEVENTEEN

THE REMARKABLE ADVENTURE OF THE MOUSE AND THE MOOSE

S THEY ENTERED EMMA'S shop, Leo saw Annabel for the first time; she was behind the counter. She was a little younger than Emma, perhaps about nineteen or twenty, but wore the same type of formal Victorian ladies clothing as Emma, although her dress was a little more colourful and elaborate than Emma's. She had dark hair, blue eyes and a very pale, milky complexion.

"Hello Annabel," said Emma, as she closed the door.

"Hello dear," said Annabel, coming from behind the counter. Annabel kissed Emma on the cheek. "And you must be Leo," she said, turning to him and offering her hand, which Leo shook. "Nevermore has told me all about you… what an adventure you must be having; how terribly exciting it all must be!"

"Well," said Leo, "I suppose it is that."

"Although, I expect you will be relieved to go home once you meet Asiex the druid?"

"Yes, I will. Hopefully, I will meet him tomorrow at the poetry competition," said Leo.

"I am certain you will," said Annabel, "he never misses it and often wins, although I rather hope he does not win tomorrow as I am entering myself for the first time."

They all walked through into the parlour, and Emma and Leo took off their coats, hats, scarves and gloves.

"Hello, Emma... Hello, Leo," croaked Nevermore as they came through.

"Hello, my friend," said Emma.

"Hello, Nevermore," said Leo.

"Have you finished your poem?" asked Emma to Annabel.

"Not quite... but nearly: I think that it may require some further additional changes... perhaps I could read what I have so far to you after lunch, and then you can tell me what you think of it?" suggested Annabel.

"Oh, yes, that would be lovely," said Emma. "Have you made it nonsensical as you were proposing?"

"I believe so," said Annabel with a slight air of self-satisfaction. "I do hope that you will not consider me immodest if I were to say that I believe it may be as amusing as one of Mr Lear's."

"So it's like an Edward Lear poem, is it?" asked Leo.

"Oh, how very wonderful," she replied, "that you also know of Edward Lear; he is quite my favourite. What do you know of his?"

"I know *The Jumblies, The Owl and the Pussycat, The Table and the Chair, The Pobble Who Has No Toes*... hmm... and quite a few others I think."

"Oh I do so admire *The Pobble Who Has No Toes*," said Annabel.

"Yes, it's really funny and great," agreed Leo.

"Well," said Emma, "you two do seem very well suited to each other."

"Indeed," agreed Annabel. Leo smiled.

"So," said Emma, "shall I prepare some lunch?"

"Yes, please," said Leo.

"Cheese and cucumber sandwiches, again?"

"That will be fine with me," said Annabel. "Shall I help you?"

"No need, thank you," said Emma. "Why not let Leo relate to you the details of poor Mr Punch's trial."

"No doubt there was a serious miscarriage of justice?" said Annabel. "I should be most surprised if not."

"Oh, there most certainly was," said Leo, "complete with music!"

"How disgraceful," she said, sitting down at the table. Leo sat down too and started to give Annabel and Nevermore a comprehensive overview of what had gone on at the Sipby Theatre. Emma brought in the tea and sandwiches after a while, and they all had lunch. Just as they were finishing, the doorbell tinkled, and someone came into the shop. Emma got up and went through.

"Oh hello, Mrs Mittens," said Emma. "How nice to see you."

"Likewise, dear," said Mrs Mittens.

"How can I help you today?" asked Emma.

"I am looking for two good-sized boxes for my grandsons to keep their toy soldiers in. They have a good collection, but their mother – my daughter Mary, you know – has become a little wearisome of their leaving them lying around you see."

"I do see, yes," said Emma.

"I thought two nice painted or varnished boxes with hinged lids would be just the thing," added Mrs Mittens.

"Are they painted soldiers, Mrs Mittens?" asked Emma.

"Oh yes, indeed: hand-painted by Mr Lynemup from the toy shop in Altudley High Street," confirmed Mrs Mittens.

"Oh, yes, I know it… it is indeed a most beautiful toy emporium. Unfortunately, I do not often have the opportunity to travel up to Altudley these days."

"Yes, it is a bit of a distance, dear – especially on foot; not too bad by carriage. Though I fancy no carriage would make it with this snow," said Mrs Mittens.

"So," mused Emma, "perhaps boxes with a velvet lining might be just the thing, so the that the paint on the soldiers does not chip off?"

"Oh, yes, if you have such that would be ideal," agreed Mrs Mittens.

Emma came round from behind the counter and reached down two almost identical boxes from her second to top shelf. They were both of waxed oak; one overlaid in oak leaf patterns and the other in acorn patterns. Emma placed them down on the counter and opened them up. They were both lined with dark maroon velvet which was of a generous pile.

"Best, I would suppose if they are not exactly identical so that your grandsons will be able to tell them apart," suggested Emma.

"Yes, indeed," agreed Mrs Mittens inspecting them closely.

"They also both have a lockable catch," said Emma.

"They're very nice, dear, actually," said Mrs Mittens after a few seconds. "Who makes them up for you?"

"Mr Sandemwell… his workshop is near Altchurch woods," said Emma.

"Oh, good. I do not approve of any imports, you know," said Mrs Mittens very seriously. "I think our dear Countess is absolutely right in her view, that whatever can be made within our own borough, should be and that we all do whatever we can to support the economy of Altcastle and our lovely villages."

"I quite agree," said Emma, "although I fancy we shall still need to import our claret for the foreseeable future."

"Well, of course, dear, we can't do without that little necessity, can we," chuckled Mrs Mittens. "So, I will take both boxes. How much are they?"

"Ten shillings each," said Emma.

"And very reasonably priced, too, for such high quality," said Mrs Mittens. "It does pay to buy locally manufactured items, doesn't it? Do give the fellow my compliments when you next see him."

"I will indeed," said Emma as Mrs Mittens handed over to her one of the pound notes which she had taken from the bank that morning. Emma rang the sale into her till and gave Mrs Mittens a receipt.

"Would you be kind enough to wrap them, and drop them round to my shop in the Ironmarket – only I don't fancy carrying them myself in this snow in case I slip, you know… I'm afraid I'm getting on a bit, you know," said Mrs Mittens.

"Of course, I will wrap them in some nice Mipassy paper, and drop them in for you by the end of tomorrow, Mrs Mittens," said Emma. "Thank you very much."

"Thank you, dear," said Mrs Mittens leaving the shop. Emma returned to the parlour where Annabel had already tidied away the lunch dishes and made more tea.

"A whole pound note!" said Emma elatedly. "Mr Brownnose will be pleased when he calls later."

"Oh, it is very good, Emma. No one came into the shop at all while you were at the trial," said Annabel. Emma nodded comprehendingly.

"So, Leo," said Emma, "shall we have some more tea, while we listen to Annabel's poem?"

"Yes, indeed," said Leo. He poured four cups of tea while Annabel collected her notebook from one of the chairs near the fireplace, and then they all settled at the table again to hear Annabel's poem.

"Well," she said, "I do hope that you like it, but in any case, please be brutal in your criticism… it will be better to make a fool of myself amongst friends than in front of hundreds of people tomorrow… that is if, in fact, it is finally Saturday tomorrow! So my title is *The Remarkable Adventure of The Mouse and The Moose*. And here is the poem:

The mouse and the moose have set off for the moon,
But please do not fret – they shall come back soon.

They have taken twelve cakes and ten biscuits with jam,
And sixty-six slices of honey roast ham.
They have also taken nine crusty baguettes,
And apples and oranges stored in two nets.
The mouse and the moose may be hungry you see,
And even in space, they will still want their tea.

The journey is long, and will take several days,
And they earnestly hope not to meet with delays:
Like bumping their ship into fishcakes or stones,
Or running aground on some dinosaur bones,
Or breaking their rudder, or losing their way,
Or getting quite lost, or going astray.
They have never before, been to space you see,
So they cannot predict what problems might be.

The sails of their ship are orange and black,
And strong enough to get there and back.
So when the solar winds blow brisk,
They can keep full sail without any risk.
And when they finally reach the moon,
A meeting is planned with the Martian Racoon;
The Martian Racoon with the stripy tail,
Who flies around space on the back of a whale.

He had sent them a letter of invitation,
Delivered to them by an old dalmatian;
An old dalmatian with black-spotted coat,
Who delivers all things in a pale green boat,
A boat which is made out of pumpkin seeds,
The sort of boat that everyone needs,
The sort of boat that is fast and light,
O what a boat! What a beautiful sight!

The End!"

Leo, Emma and Nevermore all clapped.

"It's great!" said Leo.

"Although I am not an astronomer," mused Nevermore, "I feel confident there are no fishcakes in space… as to dinosaur bones, I cannot rightly say…"

"And what did you think of it, dear Emma?" asked Annabel.

"I think it is very good, actually," said Emma. "I especially liked the last stanza, where you say that it is *the sort of boat that everyone needs*… when of course, it is really the sort of boat that no one needs."

"Hmm… I am only a poor raven…" muttered Nevermore "…is that nonsensical, then?"

"Well, of course, ravens do not need pumpkin seed boats," said Annabel. "So, you may be forgiven for not wanting one." They all laughed.

"So, Annabel," said Emma, looking at the mantelpiece clock, "I intended to ask you regarding the fairground…"

"I do not wish to go today," said Annabel, interrupting her, "as I would like to go over my poem again… I am not entirely sure about some of the metre. So, if you and Leo would like to go, I will be happy to stay here and watch the shop. Perhaps we two could go together on Sunday?"

"Yes, that will be lovely. The shop will be closed, and we can spend all evening there," agreed Emma. "So, Leo, we must leave presently, if we are to meet our friends at four." Leo stood up and collected his coat, scarf and hat.

"Will you be out for supper, Emma?" asked Nevermore.

"Yes, I expect so," said Emma. "There is some cooked ham in the pantry… and some potatoes and broccoli…" She also stood up and put her outdoor clothing back on.

"I will cook your supper, Nevermore; please do not concern yourself," said Annabel. "And I will see you both when you return… please do not trouble yourselves about being late."

"We shall be back by eight, I hope," said Emma. "Mr Brownnose will no doubt call before that, so you may tell him: *two wooden boxes for one pound.*"

"Very good," said Annabel, as they all walked through to the shop.

"See you later, Annabel... see you later, Nevermore," said Leo.

"Do have a lovely time, then," said Annabel.

"Mind how you go in the snow!" said Nevermore.

Leo and Emma left the shop and set off back down the High Street. It was still snowing, and the fallen snow in some places was now over half a foot deep, though on the pavements it was compressed as the streets were very busy. As they passed the Guildhall and walked on into Penkhull Street, it seemed there were as many people coming into town as was were heading towards the fairground.

"How long will the fairground be open for?" asked Leo.

"Oh, from today until the end of the Mipas season, on January 6th," said Emma. "That is why I am sure a lot of people will not rush to go today, as there is no need... unless one wishes to hear the Countess' and Mayor's opening remarks."

As they rounded the bend of Penkhull Street and started declining the hill, down towards Brook Lane, Leo noticed a large poster on the side of one of the buildings.

"Is the election just for the Mayor's job?" asked Leo.

"Yes, just the position of Mayor," said Emma. "It is the only elected position in Altcastle; all other posts are filled by appointment."

"And it's the Countess who makes the appointments?" asked Leo.

"Technically it is the Mayor's role to make most appointments, but since the Countess controls the Mayor, then, yes, one could say that it is the Countess doing the appointing."

"Why does it say on the poster *Only Vote For This Party*? What party is it referring to, as it doesn't name the party that people are being told to only vote for?" queried Leo. Emma smiled.

"*Only Vote For This* is the name of the party," she said. "It is so called so it will always read *Only Vote For This Party* on all the ballot papers."

"How weird," said Leo, "that sounds like it should be illegal!"

"Well," said Emma, "that is an interesting point of view. Better to not mention it outside of our little circle of friends, though!"

"Hmm... right," agreed Leo. "So, how often are elections for Mayor held?" asked Leo.

"Oh, at least once a year... sometimes twice if nothing else interesting is happening," said Emma.

"Why so often?" asked Leo. "It's a very short term of office."

"Well," said Emma, "like most public events in Altcastle, elections are run to entertain and distract people rather than because they are needed, and as to the term of office, it is largely an irrelevancy as unless the incumbent Mayor upsets the Countess, the role is actually perpetual, as there is no conceivable way for the Countess' candidate to lose the election."

"Why not?" asked Leo.

"Well," said Emma, "there are two main reasons in point of fact. First and foremost, I suppose, is that most people actually like the Countess and will, therefore, support Mayor Woodhay because he is known to be her candidate."

"But why is that?" asked Leo. "The Countess seems like a dictator; why do people put up with it?"

"Almost everybody in Altcastle is happy," said Emma. "There is no real crime – just a few beakeries now and again – there is no poverty, there is plenty of food, plenty of housing, plenty of entertainments, and hardly anyone is ever ill – and even if someone is ill, the hospital is free, so most people just take the view that things are fine as they are. I think people will only rebel against a system of government if they are really unhappy about something, and hardly anyone in Altcastle is unhappy."

"Hmm... I see," mused Leo. "I suppose that sort of makes sense from what I understand about history... and what's the second reason her candidate can't lose?"

"The second reason is the design of the ballot papers themselves: as you will know, a ballot paper lists the candidates vertically with a box after the name of each for the voter to put a cross in, next to the candidate that they wish to vote for. However, on an Altcastle ballot paper, most of the boxes, other than the one after Mayor

Woodhay's name, are completely infilled in dark black such that even if someone did put a cross in one of them, it could neither be seen nor be counted. Boxes next to candidates from what you would term *crazy* parties are also left open so that they might get a few votes just for the sake of an interesting article in the Daily Tale. It is I fancy a most convenient method of eliminating unwanted voting patterns."

"That really is a total outrage against democracy!" cried Leo.

"I fancy one will not find too much of that in Altcastle," said Emma

"I get that most people are happy like you said, but I don't get that no one at all complains – someone must not agree with it," said Leo. "Especially when the ballot papers are like that, meaning the election is basically rigged!"

"Some do," said Emma, "there is a man – though I would hesitate to call him a gentleman – called Ebenezer Cromwell who is often quite critical of Altcastle's traditions and systems."

"Bull and Bear have mentioned him; they don't seem to like him," said Leo.

"Most people do not like him," said Emma, "and as he is the leading proponent of so-called democracy, the widespread dislike of him has the effect of supporting the status quo and the Countess' admittedly odd system of running the mayoral elections."

As Emma finished speaking, they arrived at the entrance to the fairground which had been set up just off Brook Lane, midway between Stubbs Gate and the Lyme Brook bridge. There was a gate with two large burning braziers either side of it and many more torches placed alongside in rows of light that looked very pretty. Over the gate was a large sign.

Two soldiers from the militia Barracks stood one either side of the gate, one was smoking a pipe while the other was drinking brandy, neither was armed with anything and they were handing out vouchers for some of the attractions.

"You look a fine young man," said the one with the brandy to Leo. "Do you fancy your chances on the rifles?"

"I think so," said Leo. He had never fired a rifle before, and he found the prospect quite exciting.

"There you are then," said the soldier, giving Leo a voucher for five free shots. "Best of luck to you!"

"Thank you, most kind of you," said Leo, trying to emulate Emma's manner of speaking so that he would not look out of place.

"And for yourself, Miss? Anything you fancy?" said the soldier drinking the brandy somewhat suggestively and with rather wider eyes than one might normally expect in such a discourse.

"She won't be fancying you matey, that's for sure!" laughed the other soldier.

"Oh really, gentlemen, that is indeed rather rude!" said Emma quite savagely and with a reproachful stare.

"Begging your pardon, Miss... it's the brandy talking," said the soldier. They both doffed their caps and looked suitably chastised; one of them put two vouchers into Emma's hand, and the other put three. They smiled and nodded inanely without saying anything further. Emma and Leo proceeded on through the gate and into the fairground proper. Leo looked at Emma and chuckled; she smiled back, clutching her five vouchers.

Chapter Eighteen

The
Fairground

T HE FAIRGROUND COVERED QUITE an area and was beautifully lit up by oil lamps of many various colours which hung both from poles hammered into the ground and from wires strung between those poles. By five minutes to four, the time at which Leo and Emma had arrived, several hundred people had already turned up, and a crowd was starting to gather at the far end of the ground where a stage had been erected, about level with the bottom of Occupation Street.

The fresh snow crunched underfoot as they started to make their way from the main gate. To the left of the main entrance, just to the rear of the Boat and Horses Pub, was a very large circular hook-a-duck stall, and to the right a coconut shy – something Leo had never heard of. Next to the hook-a-duck, stood the imposing "Herr Googmeister's Altavarian Sausages" stall which was a grand affair with numerous open grills and from which the delightful smells of bratwurst, frankfurters and fried onions were already wafting. On the opposite side, next to the coconut shy, stood "Auntie Oz's Cakes and Fancies" which had row upon row of all manner of cakes laid out, in every imaginable shape and colour. Next to that was "Nanny Bird's Berry Treats" which appeared to be a stall devoted entirely to pies and tarts made from forest fruits like blackberries and raspberries. Back on the opposite side, next to Herr Googmeister's, was "Karen's Cocoa Counter" which also advertised "Hot Eggnog" and next to that was "Mickey's Hot Mulled Wines"; large queues had already formed in front of both of the latter, no doubt on account of the continuing snowfall and freezing temperature, although Leo did notice as they progressed, that a good number of braziers had been set up and lit, above several of which people were busy roasting chestnuts, and others simply standing warming their hands.

In the centre ground stood the Carousel which was powered by a steam engine. It was by far the largest and most extravagant carousel Leo had ever seen and the ones he had seen, and rode on, in his own reality paled in comparison to it. To the right of the carousel was a rather Asiatic looking tent marked "Tatiana's Tarot", which looked somewhat mysterious, and to the left of the carousel, with its back towards Stubbs Gate, was their initial destination, a very large multicoloured, striped marquee with a sign made up again of multicoloured lettering which read "The Loons Demented". Outside the marquee stood Bull and Bear.

"Good evening, gentlemen," said Emma.

"Evening, Emma," said Bull.

"All well?" asked Bear.

"All well," replied Leo.

"How was Mr Badger?" asked Emma.

"Splendid in fact: we found him in inestimably good spirits," said Bear. "He had quite a few visitors, in fact."

"We have even partaken of a little of his hospitality," added Bull.

"I hope not too much, given the early hour?" replied Emma.

"Of course not," muttered Bear.

"Quite, quite," added Bull, "just a drop to be sociable, you know."

"Shall we go on towards the main stage?" asked Emma.

"Yes, indeed," said Bull, "let's find out what the dear Countess has to say for the grand opening." The four of them continued on towards the stage, passing another large marquee signed as "The Marvellous Magnetic Monkey" on the left and a hugely tall and wide helter-skelter on the right.

"This is quite a fairground," said Leo as they walked passed the first huge helter-skelter only to then see a second one which was even bigger. As they came to the end of the marquee of The Marvellous Magnetic Monkey, Leo saw "Grandad Joe's Rifles" and checked his voucher: that was the one he had five free shots for. Grandad Joe's Rifles was quite a grand affair with a counter that could easily accommodate at least twenty shooters at once and a very deep range which had both stationary and moving targets – powered by a steam engine and pulley system.

"The Countess always says it's the best fairground in all of Altfordshire!" said Mr Bull.

As they approached the stage and joined the back of the crowd already assembled, they saw a huge white marquee running along the opposite side of the fairground to the one which they had just walked up, with its back to the canal.

"That's a big tent!" said Leo. "What is it?"

"I am unsure," said Emma, "I have never seen it before – it must be new."

"Yes," said Bull. "That one has definitely never been here before."

The marquee was indeed immense, having a frontage of well over three hundred feet and a depth of at least a hundred. Both the entrance on the extreme left, and the exit on the extreme right, had as many as ten steps leading up to them, signifying that the maze was either on a raised platform or had at least two levels; the height of the marquee was in any case equal to that of a normal two-storey house indicating something far more complex than a simple set of mirrors placed on the grass. There was also evidence of some kind of mechanical workings, in so far as two steam engines were situated at the end of the tent, next to the swing boats, with pulleys and steam pipes leading off into holes in the side of the marquee.

"It looks interesting, anyway," said Bear, as they continued their approach.

There was a very large sign in front of the marquee:

~ Mr R. E. Flector's Mirror Maze ~
Do You Dare To Find Out,
If You Can Get Out?

BROUGHT TO YOU BY:
MR REGINALD EDWARD FLECTOR
~ ALTACCLESFIELD, ALTEEK & ALTUXTON ~
& NEW FOR 2018: ALTCASTLE-UNDER-LYME

IN ASSOCIATION WITH PIERRE LA FALOT & ASSOCIATES

The same message, but written just horizontally, ran along the top of the vast marquee also.

"Says something about La Falot at the bottom of the sign," said Leo. "He's the guy who lied at Mr Punch's trial and said the shopping list was a contract when it was obviously a shopping list!"

"Hmm…" mused Emma, "… so it does, Leo."

Just then the usual trumpeters and prompters appeared on the stage, and the trumpets sounded for everyone to be quiet.

The crowd soon settled down, and Mayor Woodhay promptly appeared in his usual top hat. The stage was similar to the one in front of the Guildhall, with a central lectern and an awning to keep the snow from falling on the speaker; it was flanked either side by more food, drinks and other stalls.

"Good evening to you all, dear citizens of Altcastle!" exclaimed the Mayor with great warmth and gusto. The prompters displayed "Good Evening Mayor Woodhay" which the crowd gladly recited in the normal school assembly type fashion.

"I will now ask our Worshipful Countess, the Right Honourable Lady Debra Sipby, to officially open this year's Mipas Fairground!" As he finished speaking, the crowd broke into spontaneous applause and cheering as the Countess appeared, and ascended the steps of the stage. She was closely followed, as she had been at the theatre earlier, by her black and white whippet, Princely Paws. As she walked onto the stage and carried on towards the Mayor, she waved to the crowd appreciatively. Once she reached the position of the lectern, the Mayor stood to the side, giving her the preeminent spot. She was dressed in a full-length white fur coat and a white fur ushanka-hat; while her whippet was similarly clad in a white fur dog coat and wore little orange socks on his paws, no doubt to protect him from the cold. After some moments of continuing clapping and cheering, she nodded to the prompters who changed their folios to read "SILENCE" and the crowd quietened down pretty much immediately.

"My dear citizens," she started, "it is once more the time of year for the Mipas celebrations to begin and for the fairground to open!" The crowd cheered at this but quickly resumed composure. "I am pleased to announce that we have had another successful year and our economy has once again, for the twenty-second consecutive year, grown by over two percent." The crowd cheered again at this news even more enthusiastically than before, not least because it was a good indication that the next day might finally be Saturday. "Because of our continuing prosperity, we have been able to add a new attraction to this year's fairground, and I am delighted to announce that for the first time in Altcastle we have a mirror maze…" She stretched out her left arm in the direction of Mr Flector's Mirror Maze, and the crowd once again cheered and applauded. "…and, as an opening night gift, entrance to the mirror maze will be free of charge today!" This statement was met with what can only be described as rapture, and many people threw hats and gloves, and even their coats, up into the air; others started hugging each other and twirling around.

"They're so easily pleased," muttered Leo. Emma smiled.

The appreciation of the Countess' kindness went on for some time, but she appeared to delight in it, letting it abate of its own accord, without the use of the prompters.

"As you will also see, my dear people," the Countess continued, "we have added a second, even bigger helter-skelter so that queues will be shorter and braver townsfolk can swirl down from even higher up. All things considered, this is the best Mipas Fairground ever, and I hereby declare it open!" The whole crowd now went wild with excitement and the Countess waved again and left the stage, going into one of the tents that Leo had by then noticed were erected behind it.

"What are those tents?" he asked Bear.

"They are beer, wine and food tents," said Bear, "for anyone who prefers to be inside out of the snow."

"Hmm… it's a really good fair, this is," said Leo.

"It is indeed," agreed Emma, "and now I think, we should all go and take full advantage of it! So, Leo, what do you want to do first?"

"Maybe, I'll try the rifles?" he shrugged.

"Why not, indeed," said Emma, "as we are so close." They all walked off towards *Grandad Joe's Rifles* which was already busy, though there was one spare slot.

"Will you have go, Emma?" asked Leo.

"Oh no, I do not think so," said Emma. Leo went up to the counter and handed the attendant his five-shot voucher. The attendant inspected it and then promptly gave him quite a heavy gas-powered rifle.

"Do you know how to use that, young Sir?" asked the attendant.

"I don't," replied Leo a bit sheepishly. He had fired a BB gun once or twice, but that was a mere plastic toy. The look and feel of this rifle were quite different.

"Well, then," said the attendant, "I'll show you." The attendant spent quite a while, not only showing Leo how to load and fire the rifle but also teaching him how to hold and aim it. After a few minutes, all was well, and Leo took his first shot at a stationary tin duck which was painted bright yellow, knocking the little fellow straight over.

"Well, done!" said the attendant. "Try one of the moving targets!" Leo reloaded his rifle and soon obliged, first scanning the object, a glass bottle, as the man had told him, and only firing once he was confident. The rifle fired and the bottle shattered.

"You've a good eye for this," said the attendant.

"Yes, indeed," agreed Emma, "you are quite the natural marksman!" Leo continued with his other three shots, only missing once – his last shot at a very small moving tin circle – it was only a couple of inches in diameter.

"I was too ambitious with that one," he said.

"Not to worry," said the attendant, "four out of five still gets a prize!" Leo and Emma smiled. "Now, what do you fancy?" The attendant pointed to a cabinet with glass doors to the left of the counter. Leo and Emma walked over, as did the attendant, taking care not to get shot by the other players on his way over. Leo was immediately struck by the quality of the prizes on offer; they were unlike anything he had ever seen offered as prizes before. There were small china fairings with hand-painted captions, match strikers, trinket holders, lighters, pens and all sorts of other things.

"What do you think, Emma?" asked Leo.

"I do admire that small wooden pen," said Emma, pointing to a small fountain pen with a silver nib. Leo looked at the selection for a few moments and then asked the attendant for the pen.

"There you go," he said cheerfully, giving Leo the pen. "Hope to see you again for another few shots before Mipas."

"Thank you very much," said Leo, putting the pen in his topcoat side pocket.

"He was a pleasant fellow," said Bull as they walked on towards the marquee of the Marvellous Magnetic Monkey.

"He was," said Leo: "very friendly." In fact, the fairground was filled with thrilled and cheerful faces, both behind the counters and in front. Jolly fairground attendants shouted "Roll up! Roll up!" while rosy-cheeked parents watched on with a cups of mulled wine as their children ran from one stall to the next, seemingly unable to choose what game to try their hand at next.

As they walked on, Leo looked to his left where the sun had long since set, and the last remnants of twilight were now disappearing behind the trees of the cemetery. The western, evening skyline was dominated by the two tall towers of the helter-skelters and the plume of white-grey smoke emanating from the steam engine that powered the carousel. Flakes of snow still fell gently, and they reflected back the light of the fairground as they drifted lower, sparkling like diamonds before they hit the ground and disappeared. All in all, Leo thought, what a beautiful and happy place this is.

"Shall we go in to watch the Monkey?" asked Bear, as they got to his tent. "It says next show in five minutes."

"I fancy so," said Emma. "He is such an entertaining chap; but do watch out for anything you have that is made of metal, Leo, lest you lose it – his powers of magnetism are quite astonishing."

"OK," said Leo, checking his pockets and buttoning the one with the pen in. Emma gave the attendant a penny, that being one ha'penny each. Bull and Bear, being invisible, as usual went in for free. They soon found some seats even though the attraction was busy. Although the outside of the marquee was of waxed canvass for waterproofing as one would expect, the inside had an interior of indigo-dyed velvet with silver and gold stars stitched onto it. After a few minutes, a man in a pink satin tailcoat, yellow and blue striped top hat and red trousers appeared holding a brass megaphone.

"Roll Up! Roll Up!" he shouted through his megaphone. "The show is about to begin!"

"You have buttoned your pockets, Leo?" asked Bull, checking that he had. Bear did likewise, and they both also checked their pocket watch chains. Leo nodded as Emma clutched her handbag very tightly on her knees.

"You all know the dangers you face!" continued the presenter in a rather sinister and malevolent voice – no doubt cultivated to add some dramatic effect to the proceedings. "You have seen my master at work before! I strongly advise you to secure your metal properties now before it is too late… and they are lost forever!"

Leo was quite excited by this point, as he had never seen, nor even heard of, a marvellous magnetic monkey, and he was extremely intrigued as to what such a creature might do. Just then, they heard a drum roll and a set of black curtains opened to reveal the eponymous showman. He was very well dressed in the attire of a Victorian gentleman – although, like the initial presenter, his top hat was striped in wild colours – and he was sitting on a tall metal stool stroking his chin.

Within seconds, he started gesticulating wildly, and all manner of metal objects started flying through the air towards him, where he had a bag marked "The Magnetic Monkey's Loot Bag" and into which everything disappeared. Inadequately secured jewellery, watches and pocket-change of the crowd all flew over Leo's head at some pace, towards his bag. Some people screamed in either terror or excitement at what was occurring, and a constable soon appeared by the monkey's side blowing his whistle vigorously while trying to catch the objects which were being pulled through the air by the Marvellous Magnetic Monkey's strange magnetic powers. Leo and Emma laughed at the sight of it, as Leo tried to make out if it was Constable Cuffem or not – it didn't look like him. After a few minutes, the monkey stopped gesticulating, raised his hat, bowed slightly and then he wiggled his small hairy digits at the crowd as if to say, "they're good, aren't they?".

Everyone started to applaud and cheer.

"It's insane!" said Leo. "People have paid a ha'penny to be robbed of their property by a crazy magnetic monkey, and now they're cheering about it! Why would anyone do it?"

"They enjoy it," said Emma, still giggling. "You must see that it is hilarious?"

"Well, I suppose it's a question of taste," said Leo. "But I will grant you, it is certainly a very impressive ability… I mean, some of those coins are probably not even magnetic and yet he's still got hold of them. But is that constable going to arrest him, now?"

"No, no…" said Emma. "He is part of the show!"

"Oh, I see," nodded Leo.

"The next part is also good," said Emma, as the Marvellous Magnetic Monkey stood up on his stool and the presenter came back on stage.

"Now then, now then, my dear friends!" he said in a clear voice. "You have witnessed my master's remarkable powers of magnetic attraction! Now your eyes will delight and will feast upon his remarkable powers of magnetic repulsion!" The drums rolled again, and a plethora of metallic tea trays flew out from the wings of the stage each holding a quartet of white rats with miniature-sized musical instruments. Each quartet had different instruments, with some having violins, some cellos, some double basses, some brass instruments, some woodwind instruments, some percussion and one with a grand piano, which had just one rat, slightly larger than all of the others and who was dressed in a black tail suit.

The Marvellous Magnetic Monkey used both hands to levitate the tea trays as they passed over his head. As they moved around in the air seemingly unsupported by anything other than the Magnetic Monkey's magnetic fields, the white rats played tunes like Mozart's rondo *Alla Turca* and the finale of Rossini's William Tell Overture. It was already quite a spectacle when some of the rats started letting off miniature fireworks which formed a canopy of iridescence on the marquee's roof. The whole feature lasted some fifteen minutes, after which the Marvellous Magnetic Monkey gradually allowed the tea trays to descend onto his stage at which point he jumped from his stool and took up a position in front of his rats; they all bowed, and the audience roared with applause and cheering. The rats then departed to the wings, and the monkey himself walked up the wall of the tent so perfectly naturally that it was as though he were walking on a normal horizontal surface. He finally disappeared through a small door, which had been placed in the apex of the roof.

"Pretty good," said Leo with a smile. "I've never seen anything like that before."

"Indeed," agreed Bull, "he's a most remarkable, fellow."

"A true master of the natural sciences," added Bull. "No one has any idea how he achieves such feats, though many have looked into it."

"It would I am sure rather ruin the entire spectacle," said Emma, "if someone were to find out the secret of it all. Some things, I fancy, are best left as mysteries."

"Quite so," agreed Bear.

"So, where to next?" asked Bull. "Shall we take in the Loons?"

"Perhaps a small bite to eat first," suggested Emma. "I feel sure, Leo, you will want to sample what you can while you have such an abundance of choice on offer."

"I certainly would," he said. "I think those cakes looked nice."

"Ah, yes," said Emma, "they are very good. Let us begin there."

So off they went, back into the snowy night and the buzz of the fairground. They were soon enough at *Auntie Oz's Cakes and Fancies* and Leo began surveying the wares in some detail while they queued.

"Hello!" said a lady as they finally reached the counter – it was a popular stall.

"Hello!" replied Leo.

"I'm Auntie Oz," said the lady. "What do you fancy?"

"Well, there's a lot of choice…" said Leo somewhat hesitantly. In fact, he had never seen so many cakes, doughnuts and pastries in one place in his life.

"Allow me to help you," suggested Auntie Oz. "Do you like a chocolate base or a fruit base better… as to the flavour, you know? Perhaps a combination?"

Leo thought for a moment:

"Yes… a combination, I think."

"Good… so white chocolate, milk chocolate, or dark chocolate."

"Definitely milk," he said.

"Now, what about orange, lime, lemon, apple, pear, strawberry, banana…"

"Strawberry… maybe lemon…" he said.

"Perfect, then what about a milk chocolate and strawberry fancy with fresh, lemon-tinted whipped cream?" suggested Auntie Oz.

"That sounds good," he agreed.

"And a few chocolate and vanilla flakes in the whipped cream too, eh?"

"Why not," he agreed. Auntie Oz did a little preparation then presented Leo which a large milk chocolate and strawberry fancy with a dome of cream on it, suitably embellished with flakes of vanilla flavoured milk chocolate.

"Thank you," he said, taking it.

"That's just three farthings," she said. Emma handed her a penny and took one farthing in change.

"It looks delicious," said Emma.

"Well, thanks for this," said Leo. "Are you not having anything?"

"I should watch my waistline, you know. I fancy dear old Nanny Bird's fruit pies are a good deal less fattening." Nanny Bird's stall was just next to Auntie Oz's Cakes and Fancies, so they moved over to that next.

"Ah," said Bull, "berry pies… now that's more like it, eh Bear?"

"Quite so, old boy," agreed Bear, giving Emma a penny. "Blackberry for myself," he said to her.

"Blueberry, for me," said Bull. Nanny Bird's stall was extremely busy, probably in view of the fact that most of her pies were served hot from an oven, and due to the cold night, people wanted something to warm them up. Emma joined the queue and immediately noticed that George, of George's Tailors, was standing a few places in front of her.

"Good evening, George," called out Emma.

"Oh, good evening, Emma," said George, turning round. "How very nice to see you. How did those clothes fit your nephew?"

"Very well indeed, thank you," she replied, pointing out Leo and beckoning to him to come over, which he did.

"Good evening, young man… Leo, I believe?" he said.

"This is George the tailor," said Emma.

"Hello, Sir," said Leo, remembering to be polite.

"Next please!" called Nanny Bird, and George went up to make his order before they had chance to get any deeper into conversation.

"Be seeing you then," called George, as he went off with some hot apple pie. "I do recommend Nanny Bird's pies taken hot with a little cream!" he added cheerfully. Emma and Leo nodded and waved goodbye to him, then Leo went back to Bull and Bear to finish eating his Auntie Oz's fancy while Emma continued queuing.

"Good evening, Nanny Bird," said Emma, as she finally reached the front of the queue.

"Oh, good evening, dear," she said, "what can I get for you?

"I would like one piece of your hot blueberry pie and two slices of blackberry, also hot, please?" said Emma.

"Of course, dear," she said. Bull suggested to Leo that he might help Emma carry the pies because it might look rather odd if she handed them their pies directly, as the pies would initially appear to be suspended in mid-air before slowing disappearing as they held them. It was a common problem they experienced with almost anything they picked up.

Leo obliged and collected Bull's pie while Emma took Bear's. They then proceeded to the rear of the stalls, next to the canal before handing them over. As Leo was able to see Bull and Bear, he could only imagine what such a phenomenon might look like to an unwise observer; although he considered, having just witnessed the exploits of the Marvellous Magnetic Monkey, and earlier the trial of a fully autonomous talking puppet, that such a thing would be a good deal more readily accepted as normal in Altcastle than it would be in his Newcastle.

As they ate their pies, Leo noticed a canal barge without lights, slowly approaching from the south. It was pulled by a black shire horse, under the guidance of a short man in a big overcoat and flat cap. As Bull, Bear and Emma merrily chatted about the quality of Nanny Bird's fine pies and where she might be getting her berries from, Leo continued observing the canal barge as it stopped behind Mr Flector's Mirror Maze. The short man tied up the barge very oddly indeed, with its bow on the eastern side of the canal bank and its stern tied up on the western bank, such that it formed a sort of bridge over the canal. Two men in dark clothing then got out of the barge and entered the maze from a rear entrance.

"So," said Emma, dabbing her lips with a cotton handkerchief, "do you fancy the helter-skelter now, Leo?"

"Oh yes," replied Leo, keenly. "I have never been on one!"

"Really?" said Emma surprisedly. "Well, then, let us remedy that now!" They all advanced to the first, smaller of the two helter-skelters where the queue was not as long as it was for the taller one. Leo asked Emma what the procedure for using a helter-skelter was, which she explained while they queued. The attendant at the top of stairs was accepting no hesitation from riders, and in fact, actually pushing off anyone who paused for more than a second, so the queue moved very quickly. Leo and Emma collected their hessian rugs and were soon spiralling down the almost frictionless steel slide before being ejected at the bottom into a pile of snow.

"That was great!" said Leo. "I'm really surprised it was so fast!"

"I think they have oiled the slide," said Emma, recovering her normal composure and dusting the snow from her topcoat. "Will you try the taller one?"

"I will!" exclaimed Leo. The taller helter-skelter was indeed taller, by at least some twenty feet and there was quite a queue with it being new that year. Fortunately, it was also being managed at the top by a no-nonsense attendant and the queue thus quickly went down as the attendant placed the hessian rugs and pushed people off to a flying start. Leo and Emma both screamed as they descended – as the extra height had been used not only for a slightly longer run of slide, but also to produce a steeper slope which of course resulted in a faster descent. They were again propelled by the terminal velocity into a pile of snow at the bottom which was being kept fit for purpose by another attendant with a rake.

"That was frightening, in fact! I feel dizzy," said Emma.

"It was great!" said Leo. Bull and Bear simply looked on with quizzical expressions.

"Where to next?" asked Emma. "The queue for the new mirror maze is enormous," she added, looking over at; the end of the helter-skelter slide pointed directly at the site of Mr Flector's maze.

"Well, it's new, and it's free," said Bull, "so of course, everyone will want to go in."

"I noticed some swinging boats," suggested Leo, "to the side of the mirror maze." They all headed off in that direction; the swing boats were located between Mr Flector's Mirror

Maze and Tatiana's Tarot, and again there was a small queue to overcome – as there was actually for pretty much everything. Emma explained to Leo the operation of swing boats and the importance of crossing the pulling-ropes over, as they queued. Soon enough, they were swinging away, and Leo pulled as hard as he could until Emma told him to stop, as he was doing far too good a job for her liking, and she was afraid he was actually going to pull the boat vertical. Leo suggested to her that there was probably some mechanism that would prevent that from happening, but it was not Emma's intention to put his theory to the test. After their five minutes was up, they got out, and Emma needed to adjust her bonnet.

"It's a pity we don't have those in Newcastle," said Leo. "They're very good!"

"I thought you would both fall out!" said Bear.

"Yes, indeed," agreed Emma grimacing slightly.

Just then they heard Mr Summoner's bell ringing.

"Oyez! Oyez! Oyez! Next Loons Demented in ten minutes! Join the queue for the next show!" he shouted loudly and cheerfully, the bell in one hand and a tankard of mulled wine in the other.

"Well, that is most convenient then," said Emma. "Shall we?"

"Indeed," agreed Bull. "It is a most singular presentation, Leo. I feel sure that you will have never seen anything to equal it!"

"Not even close, I fancy," added Emma. They crossed to the other side of the fairground, going between the carousel and the smaller of the helter-skelters; the queue was large but moving quickly.

"Why are they called the Loons Demented?" asked Leo as they queued.

"Hmm…" mused Bear "… very tricky to explain in words, actually."

"It is one of those things which one really needs to see with one's own eyes, I fancy," added Emma. "No amount of description could really do such a performance full justice, I feel."

"Quite right," said Bull. "You need to see it… and in a few moments, you will!"

They soon got to the entrance and put their ha'pennies in the hat; Bull and Bear of course gate crashed as usual. The inside of the tent was laid out almost exactly like that of the Marvellous Magnetic Monkey, with a large curtained stage at the far end and rows of seats for the spectators. There was just one notable difference: a continuous wall of large panes of glass which ran the entire breadth of the tent, thus clearly demarcating the spectators' seating area from the players' performance area. They found seats near the front, but Bull and Bear had to remain standing as the tent was filling to capacity.

The show soon started with a thunderous drum roll and as many as thirteen persons walking onto the stage with green wine bottles on top of their heads. Each bottle had a lit candle wedged in its top. The players were both male and female, but the female players wore top hats and tailcoats while the male players wore dresses; one wore a yellow and black striped outfit suit with wings attached to the back of it, and looked rather like a large bumblebee, as he was extremely fat. They formed into a line across the stage with the *bumblebee* in the middle, and then all shouted in unison: "It's time for some beakery!" The audience gasped, and the thirteen players soon started making weird noises and jumping up and down. The bottles on their heads started to wobble from side to side as they did so, and it was quite amazing that it took several seconds of this malarkey for all of the bottles to fall from their heads and smash onto the stage which they all soon did.

Next came out several additional players on stilts with teapots, who went around the stage very quickly, running in fact – despite being on stilts, and pouring tea over the original players' heads to cries of "more tea?" and "one lump or two?" The tea appeared to be quite hot as it was steaming when poured and the players started dashing around the stage and jumping such that at times their legs were perpendicular to their torsos. This went on for some time, and like crazed lizards they scurried back and forth screaming into teacups, jumping on each other, throwing themselves against the glass panes and generally engaging in other demented acts.

Leo found the entire spectacle utterly ridiculous – not being very keen on buffoonery anyway, but most of the audience seemed to enjoy it immensely, and there was much shouting out, clapping and cheering. Towards the end of the spectacle, the original players, including the bumblebee, started doing somersaults, cartwheels and jumping up and down in what can only be described as a frenzy, before attacking the players on the stilts and throwing them at the glass panes which thudded and wobbled with every impact. As a grand finale, they all set fire to their clothing, before running off the stage screaming. The audience again roared with appreciation, and the lights went up indicating the show was over.

"That was utterly bizarre," said Leo.

"I did so enjoy it," said Bull.

"It is a wonder that they do not injure themselves," sighed Emma. "I do hope they are all well after that."

"I'm sure they are fine," said Bear. "We've seen this show every year for decades; they're professional acrobats, you know."

"Quite so," agreed Bull. It took a few minutes for the tent to clear, and as they were towards the front, they had to wait a while to get outside again.

Directly in front of the exit to the Loons Demented's marquee was the carousel, which had conveniently just come to a halt as they had come out.

"Carousel next?" asked Bull with a big smile.

"Great!" said Leo.

Emma and Leo went up onto the carousel and soon found two suitable horses; Emma needed to be able to ride side-saddle, naturally. Due again to the number of people wanting to ride, Bull and Bear could not find places and Bull pulled his face somewhat, which made Emma laugh quite loudly, and loudly enough in fact that some other riders close by looked at her rather curiously, which also made Leo laugh.

Presently, they were spinning around at quite a speed, as their horses went up and down on the poles, and the pipe organ at the centre of the carousel played Johan Strauss' Tales from the Vienna Woods. Leo had never been on a steam-powered carousel before, nor had he ever heard the sound of an old-style fairground pipe organ. The tune, he thought, fitted perfectly with the snowy night, and the semi-discordancy inherent in the tune's transposition from violin to mechanical pipe organ only added to the ethereal magicality of the moment.

After about four minutes, the carousel stopped, and they alighted towards the north-western portion of the fairground from where the coconut shy beckoned them over.

"I do so enjoy the coconut shy," said Emma, "but I hardly ever win a coconut because my aim is so poor. In any case, I have three vouchers today!"

"I've never even played it," said Leo.

"Then now is your chance," said Bear.

There was not much of a queue, so Emma was soon at the front and handed over one of her vouchers in return for three balls. The coconut shy was of the traditional form and had four poles with coconuts placed in front of a large hessian sheet. Emma, as she had predicted, missed the coconuts with every throw and it was soon Leo's turn. Emma gave him the other two vouchers, so he obtained six balls in all. After the disaster of his first five attempts, Bull had the industrious notion of going and standing by the extreme left coconut which he then pointed to with a scheming grin. Leo threw his last ball at the coconut next to Bull, which missed, but just as the ball passed it, Bull knocked the coconut off the pole with his hoof, much to the chagrin of Emma.

"Oh really, Mr Bull!" she exclaimed. The attendant looked around and then at Leo, whom he fancied didn't look much like a Mr Bull.

"Well, done, sonny," he said to Leo, disregarding Emma's comment, though still displaying a demeanour of some confusion. The attendant collected the fallen coconut and gave it to Leo in a small string bag.

"Thank you, Sir," said Leo, with a smile. Bull returned to Bear, Leo and Emma, and they sauntered off into the fairground again while Emma gave Bull a good scolding for his cheating ways. Bull, Bear and Leo found Emma's moralising somewhat amusing, to say the least.

"What's the point of one being invisible if one cannot make a small advantage of the circumstance once in a while?" was Bull's final comment on the matter.

They walked back down the western side of the fairground passed Auntie Oz's and Nanny Bird's stalls again, and came upon the tent of Tatiana's Tarot.

"Do you fancy a card reading, Leo?" asked Bull. "Tatiana is very good. She may be able to give us some direction in terms of what may happen next and how you might get back home."

"I believe you already know her, Emma?" said Bear.

"I do indeed," confirmed Emma. "She is extremely keen on my services and goods."

"So, what do you think, Leo?" pressed Bull.

"Hmm... well... OK, why not," he said, and they all went over to the tent, where there were three people already waiting, and joined the queue. There was a small sign outside which read: "Tarot Readings – Five Minutes – Only a Ha'penny".

CHAPTER NINETEEN

THE FORCE
OF DESTINY

THEY QUEUED FOR SOME time before it was Leo's turn, but eventually, the lady who had been in front of them in the queue came out smiling, and the four of them entered Tatiana's tent.

"Good evening, Emma," said Tatiana, "and Messers Bull and Bear, also, how nice… and who do we have here?"

"She can see you?" whispered Leo to Bear.

"Of course," Bear whispered back, "she's a witchy one."

"This is Leo," said Emma.

"Please, all be seated," said Tatiana.

They all sat down, with Leo sitting directly opposite Tatiana at the other side of the table to her. The table was of the typical fairground gypsy style, covered in a black velvet cloth embellished with symbols representing the signs of the zodiac. On the table was an oil lamp, a silver tin with some coins in it, a crystal ball, and a very ornate, wooden, velvet-lined, hinged-lid box which was open to reveal a deck of tarot cards inside it. It was the type of box that Emma sold in her shop.

Tatiana herself was a woman in her mid-fifties, who wore a purple velvet dress and a black lace mantilla. She had a kindly, slightly chubby face; her most remarkable feature was her crystal-like blue eyes, which glinted like sapphires in the light of her oil lamp.

"I am afraid that we will not have the time to tell you Leo's whole story," Emma began, "and what he is doing here in Altcastle, as you have a quite a queue outside and it would not be fair to take up so much of your time. Of course, I will explain the matter in more detail when you next call into my shop, but for the moment, perhaps you might make a quick spread of cards for the purpose of telling us if there is anything which Leo should be particularly aware of on his journey?"

"Of course," said Tatiana, taking her cards out from the box. She shuffled the cards and placed them down in front of Leo; Emma dropped a ha'penny in the silver tin.

"Please cut the pack, Leo," said Tatiana. Leo cut the pack in about the middle, and Tatiana took back the cards and placed them down in front of her.

"Let's look first at what may lie on the immediate path ahead," she said, turning over the first card; it was the Magician. "The one you seek to help you on your journey… you will meet him sooner than you expected," she said.

"Hmm… interesting," mused Bull. Bear nodded.

Tatiana turned over the next card; it was the Empress.

"And one in authority will cross your path," said Tatiana. Emma, Bull and Bear all exhibited a surprised mien as they glanced at each other.

"And after that…" continued Tatiana, turning over the next card "…the Ten of Swords." Emma winced.

"And that one's bad, I guess," said Leo, first noticing Emma's reaction and then looking at Tatiana.

"Well," said Tatiana, "you will most assuredly face some problem... but allow me to continue, and let's see." She turned over the next card: Judgement. "In this context, Leo... I see that you will make a judgement about something... maybe change your mind over something... you shall see." She turned over the next card, which was the Jester. "But one who jests will help you..." said Tatiana with a smile.

"But how will Leo's journey end?" asked Bear. "Will he get home eventually?"

Tatiana cut the pack again and then turned over another card: the Sun. Emma smiled.

"So that's good?" asked Leo.

"All will end well," said Tatiana.

"But will that be tomorrow?" asked Bear. Tatiana turned over the next card: the Wheel of Fortune.

"Hmm... only time will tell..." she said "...the Wheel of Fortune is a card of chance in this context... but we also have the Sun, so in the end, all will be well."

"But that doesn't necessarily mean tomorrow?" asked Emma.

"No... not necessarily, but very possibly," said Tatiana, "when a wheel spins, who knows in what position any mark on its edge will face when it comes to rest."

"So what guidance would you give?" asked Bull. Tatiana collected up the tarot cards, placed them back into the wooden box and closed the lid. She then placed the crystal ball in front of her and asked Leo to put his hands on its wooden stand. Tatiana looked deeply into the ball for some moments. Everyone else remained silent.

"You must take from a floating bird, what the bird obtained from a sheep," she said. "I can tell you no more."

"What does that mean?" asked Leo perplexedly.

"It is what I see," said Tatiana, "but what it means, only you can discover."

"Well," said Emma. "That was quite a reading!"

"I see that Leo has come here from a long, long way away… and yet he has not travelled any distance at all… it is all very… very… misty, I would say… *misty* is the word I would use," said Tatiana.

They all looked at each other and stood up, perceiving that Tatiana had told them as much as she could.

"Well, thank you, Tatiana," said Emma.

"Do not worry – the Sun card indicates all will end well… despite some troubles along the path… have faith and all will be fine," said Tatiana.

"Yes, we will do," said Bear. Bull nodded.

"Thank you," said Leo.

They all said their goodbyes and the four of them left Tatiana free for her next client and returned into the snowy night.

"Well," said Bear, "that was rather remarkable!"

"Indeed," agreed Bull, "I fancy some mulled wine might be in order!"

"I think so," said Emma.

They all proceeded back towards the top end of the fairground where Mickey's Hot Mulled Wines was situated.

"As you do not drink mulled wine, Leo, why not get for yourself some cocoa?" suggested Emma, handing him a farthing.

"OK," he said, and he joined the queue for Karen's Cocoa Counter which was next to Mickey's.

"Hello, young man," said Karen. "Do you want cocoa?"

"Do you have hot chocolate?" asked Leo as he always found cocoa quite bitter.

"Of course," she said, "just a farthing for that."

Emma had carried on to Mickey's Hot Mulled Wines and soon obtained three enamel mugs full, one of which Leo came to collect once he had his hot chocolate. They then went over to Bull and Bear, who had gone to stand by the trees, on the far side of Stubbs Gate.

"Well, it was a most curious tarot reading," mused Bull, after taking a sip of his mulled wine.

"The magician referred to must be Asiex the druid," said Bear. "And if we are to meet him sooner than we expected, then that must mean tonight, as we expected we would meet him at the poetry competition tomorrow; so sooner than expected can in fact only be tonight."

"Very logical, old boy," agreed Bull.

"But how shall we be able to find him amongst so many hundreds of people?" asked Emma, looking from their position across to the fairground which if anything was even busier than it had been when it opened.

"That I cannot say," said Bear. "It would be like looking for a needle in a haystack."

"Maybe, if Tatiana is correct, we don't have to find him," suggested Leo, "maybe we will just bump into him?"

"Hmm... possibly so, dear fellow," said Bear.

"So what shall we do?" asked Bull.

"Perhaps we should just do whatever we were going to do, and see what happens?" suggested Emma.

"Yes," said Bear. "I think that's right... and what of the others mentioned: the Empress and the Jester?"

"Who could they be?" asked Bull.

"There are many people in authority in Altcastle," mused Bear.

"But only one is female," said Emma.

"The Countess?" suggested Leo.

"But Tatiana didn't specifically say *female*," said Bear.

"Hmm..." reflected Emma "...perhaps as per the Magician, we must just wait to find out."

"Could be... could be..." mused Bear. "So let's drink our drinks and then go back to the fair for some more amusement and see who we meet."

"Quite so," agreed Bull.

As per the consensus, they finished their drinks and went back over to the fairground to deposit their enamel cups in the wash buckets next to Mickey's.

"So, where to?" asked Bull.

"Well, I have two vouchers still for the hook-a-duck," suggested Emma.

"Hook-a-duck it is then," agreed Bear.

"But please, Mr Bull, no cheating this time; it is quite unfair to the stall owner if you do not know!" insisted Emma. Bull shrugged.

"As you wish," he agreed. They proceeded up towards the hook-a-duck stall, which was the closest stall to the entrance. Emma gave in the vouchers and obtained three hooking poles for herself and three for Leo. Due to Emma's chastisement, Bull and Bear remained out of the way and continued to chat about Tatiana's cryptic reading a few yards away.

Emma went first and took quite a while to get her three ducks hooked. When the attendant inspected their undersides, sadly none carried a winning mark. Next, it was Leo's turn. He was much more adept and very quickly hooked his three. As the attendant turned over the first one, Leo immediately saw there was a black star painted onto its underside.

"Well done, young Sir," said the attendant. "You's won a prize, you has!" He then turned the second duck over, and it too was marked with a black star. "Cor blimey," he said, "you's a lucky fella for sure." The third one, unfortunately, did not have a star, but nevertheless, according to the prizes' sign, two stars gave a good quality prize. "Now then, what do you want?" asked the attendant. Leo inspected the prizes which were on shelves in the centre of the hook-a-duck's circular wooden structure. There was a very good selection of things on offer, just as there had been at Grandad Joe's Rifles: pens, knives, fairings, wallets, sewing materials, balls of wool, small framed pictures – really a very fine assortment to choose from. As he scanned up and down the shelves, for some reason, his eyes kept returning to two large balls of black wool with knitting needles stuck in them. Although he couldn't knit, and in any case had no interest whatever in such a craft, for some reason the balls of wool attracted his attention.

"Can I have the wool, please?" he asked, after about a minute of looking.

"That is indeed an odd choice," whispered Emma. "I felt sure you might choose one of those useful pocketknives."

"You's a fine, lad, isn't you…" said the attendant, "choosin' somethin' to take home for your old granny… thoughtful, that's what it is!" Leo just smiled as the man handed him the balls of wool and the two knitting needles in a paper bag.

"Thank you, Sir," said Leo with a smile. "Goodbye."

"Bye, lad," said the attendant. Emma and Leo returned to where Bull and Bear were stood chatting.

"Well," said Leo with a satisfied smile, "I believe I have just done what Tatiana advised me to do: I have taken from a floating bird – a duck; what she obtained from a sheep – wool. I think that's what Tatiana was referring to."

"How clever you are!" said Emma with an astonished expression. "How ever did you manage to work that out?"

"It just came to me as I was looking at the prizes; I just thought that it can't be a coincidence that they would have balls of wool as a prize on a stall which has birds floating on water."

"I believe you are completely correct, Leo; but what are you supposed to do with the two balls of wool? I assume you are not able to knit?" asked Bear

"No, I can't knit… can you, Emma?" he asked.

"I fear not. I once tried as a girl, but I was terrible at it," replied Emma.

"Hmm… so we two balls of wool, but what of it?" mused Bull.

"Time, I imagine, will tell us," said Bear.

CHAPTER TWENTY

THE
MAGICIAN

"GOOD EVENING, ALL!" CAME a loud, chirpy voice from behind. "A fine gypsy lady says that someone might be looking for me!" They all turned around.

"By gad, Sir," exclaimed Bear. "What a business! We had anticipated meeting you after the poetry competition tomorrow, and now here you are!"

"Incredible!" mumbled Bull.

"A happy synchronicity!" said Asiex. "And you, Sir, must be Leo," he added, looking down at him with an inquisitive expression: "the well-known interdimensional traveller!"

"Not too well-known, I should hope," said Bear.

"I, of course, mean well-known by those people blessed with the mental acuity to know such things," said Asiex dryly.

Asiex was a very tall man in his early twenties with unconventionally long hair, at least by Altcastle standards, and a curiously unattended to, scraggly beard and moustache which, though oddly unstyled in themselves, seemed to suit his face deliberately, as they gave him an appearance of erudition which, due to his young years, he might otherwise have lacked. He wore a brown, ankle-length, hooded cape. "And how are you, Bull and Bear?" asked Asiex. "It has been some time indeed since our paths last crossed."

"Very well, Asiex, thank you," said Bear.

"I shall refrain from shaking your hands... I mean, paws. hooves... et cetera... otherwise, any incidental observer, upon regarding my shaking nought but the snowy night air, might consider me madder than they already do," he said.

"Quite right," said Bull. "It's a good point you've made!"

"Allow us to introduce our dear friend, Miss Emma Jency," said Bear.

"How do you do," said Asiex, shaking hands with Emma.

"It is nice to meet you," said Emma. "We have high hopes that you shall be able to help us, based upon the recommendation of Doctor Toad."

"I hope so," replied Asiex. "So, Leo," continued Asiex, offering his hand, which Leo shook, "what are you doing here in Altcastle, if I may be so bold as to enquire?"

"Well..." started Leo "... actually, I don't really know... I just sort of came here when I crossed the bridge over the Lyme Brook... in the mist, you know, yesterday morning..."

"Ah, yes, the magic mist of yesterday morning..." Asiex said, extending his forefinger and bringing it to his chin "... the creation of which was undoubtedly a most scurrilous and indecent act of beakery. So, allow me to be clear upon the matter: you were just walking along in your own reality, there was a mist over the brook, you walked over the bridge, and when you passed over the bridge, and thereby through the ganglion of the mist, you found yourself here in Altcastle – is that about it?"

"Yes, that's basically the story," confirmed Leo, a little shocked at how quickly Asiex had understood the whole matter.

"And then, by pure good fortune, you just chanced to meet these fine fellows, Bull and Bear, who in turn introduced you to Emma?"

"Exactly," said Leo.

"Hmm…I do see," mused Asiex.

"So, you know about the mist?" asked Bear.

"Indeed," confirmed Asiex. "It was no doubt created deliberately by some person or persons engaged in the black arts."

"The Indomitable Doctor Toad was of the same view," said Bear.

"But who would have done such a thing?" asked Emma. "And why?"

"That I do not know," replied Asiex. "Though to my estimation, we may have a secret Doctor Faustus dwelling amongst us, who may be tinkering with things that rightly ought not to be tinkered with, or worse still, another druid, or druids, but of the dark path. Methinks also that this recent mist was not, in fact, the first deliberately created mist we have seen this year."

"Really?" mused Bull.

"But what is to be done about such a matter?" asked Bear.

"I am presently unsure, though I think it shall be as well to discuss the matter in some detail with Doctor Toad in due course," said Asiex. "Especially now that we have, due to Leo's appearance here, absolute proof that someone is up to no good."

"But can you help me to go home?" asked Leo.

"I believe so," said Asiex. "In theory, creating a magic mist is not a substantially difficult thing to do – it was a common enough activity of druids many, many centuries ago and the principles will not have changed I believe. Although I have never summoned such a mist myself, I have seen it done – although not for the purposes of travelling between two different dimensions admittedly. I have numerous notes on the subject which I can refer to. I will need full details of where and most importantly, when, you came from – I will then prepare a suitable potion to send you back."

"Potion?" queried Bull.

"Indeed," said Asiex, "a suitable potion when poured into the Lyme Brook will recreate the mist, such that Leo may walk back over the same bridge by which he travelled here and return to his own reality – the only delicate part of the process is to combine the ingredients in the precise ratios to affect the desired outcome in terms of *when* Leo ends up when he re-crosses the bridge… an incorrect mixture will result in an incorrect time of reappearance in the other reality. That I believe is the only truly complicated bit."

"I see," said Bear.

"Well," said Leo, "I have my mobile phone and my watch at Emma's shop, and they both stopped at the exact time I came here and…"

"A mobile phone is a gadget that tells the date and time and which one can use in Leo's reality to speak to people over long distances," interjected Bear.

"I see. How very curious. I should like to see it," said Asiex. "Though I only need the exact information, which I assume you know?"

"Yes," confirmed Leo. "It was 10:34am on Saturday 15th December 2019 when I left my reality… it was that time on my watch and my phone."

"It is perfect that we have such precise information, as that is all which we shall require… together with the precise location of course, but that is a simple matter as it is literally just the same bridge which you crossed to come here."

"It's just the next bridge down the brook," said Leo, pointing towards the south.

"All is well then," said Asiex, taking out his pocket watch and checking the time. "I must be going alas, although I cannot help but feel I may have missed some minor detail as our intercourse has been so brief."

"Must you go far?" asked Bear.

"No, only into town to meet someone," said Asiex. "To the Red Lion in fact."

"Ah, we two can walk with you, then," said Bear, "as we are well aware of all of the facts relating to this matter."

"And we were in the valley at the time of Leo's appearance here," added Bull.

"Very good," said Asiex. "It will be as well to go over the whole story again." He turned to Emma and Leo: "it was nice to meet you, Leo… and you, Emma… I shall see you tomorrow morning after the poetry gala, together with the required vial of mist potion."

"Likewise," said Emma.

"Thanks," said Leo, "see you tomorrow."

"We shall be back in about twenty minutes," said Bear.

"Very good," said Emma. "We shall await you at this end of the fairground then. We may have another go at the coconut shy, while the possibility of cheating is absent," she added, looking pointedly at Bull, who just shrugged while sporting a roguish smile.

Asiex, Bull and Bear set off for the Red Lion in Penkhull Street, and Emma and Leo went back over to the coconut shy for another go.

After winning nothing at the coconut shy, both Leo and Emma were feeling a little peckish again and decided to visit Herr Googmeister's Altavarian Sausages stall while they waited for Bull and Bear to return.

"Good evening, young fellow, what can I get for you?" asked Herr Googmeister cheerfully. He was a tall and yet rotund fellow with spectacles and a closely shaven beard and bald head.

"Can I have a plain hot dog, please – no fried onions?" asked Leo. Herr Googmeister appeared distinctly confused and looked quizzically at Emma, who was standing next to Leo.

"Hmm… we don't sell any dogs," spluttered Herr Googmeister, "and certainly not hot ones!"

"He is from Altgerheads," said Emma explicatively. "He means a sausage in a bread roll… they call such dainties *hot dogs* where he is from, you see." Emma recalled the terminology from their conversation the previous evening about Subway, McDonald's and other eateries in Leo's reality.

"I see," said Herr Googmeister, still looking somewhat dismayed. "But why is a sausage in a roll called a *hot dog* in Altgerheads?" he asked.

"Oh, it's an American expression," said Leo nonchalantly.

"American?" asked Frau Googmeister bemusedly, who had overheard the conversation and come up to the counter.

"He means Altmerican," said Emma.

"I see," said Frau Googmeister hesitantly.

"Has Altgerheads been taken over by Altmericans then?" asked Herr Googmeister.

"Not exactly taken over," replied Emma. "*Influenced*, I fancy might be a better description."

"I'm surprised the Countess has let it happen," said Herr Googmeister. "Whatever next?"

"Well, dear, we haven't been there in more than five years, so I suppose it doesn't matter too much," opined Frau Googmeister.

"No, probably not, dear," agreed Herr Googmeister as he sliced a bread roll and put a frankfurter in it.

"I will have the same, please," said Emma, placing a penny on the counter. Herr Googmeister obliged.

"Thank you very much," said Emma.

"Thank you," said Leo also.

"Thank you, and good luck, young fellow," said Frau Googmeister, "with those Altmericans, you know!" Leo and Emma nodded politely while trying to refrain from laughing.

Herr Googmeister and Frau Googmeister continued to look at them as they walked away, still chatting as they watched – probably about what a business it was that Altgerheads had been taken over by Altmericans.

"Oh, Leo..." laughed Emma "...I do fancy that you might have quite affected that poor couple with your *hot dogs*; they will probably be talking about it all night long. And in any case, why ever is a sausage in a bread roll called a *hot dog* in your reality?"

"Hmm... actually, I don't know," he said; "but at least Herr Googmeister understands it's a name for a sausage in a bread roll and doesn't believe that I want to eat dogs."

"Then we must be thankful for small mercies," replied Emma, "for when he next talks to a person who really does come from Altgerheads, he may well consider that he met two mad people this evening!"

"Probably... but I didn't realise..." said Leo lightheadedly "... maybe I'll ask him for a pizza or a kebab next time I see him!"

"Oh, Leo," said Emma. "What a rascally creature you are!"

CHAPTER TWENTY-ONE

THE
EMPRESS

L EO AND EMMA SOON finished their hot dogs but continued to stand near to the Brook Lane entrance of the fairground, while they waited for Bull and Bear to return. While they were waiting, one of the soldiers who was manning the front gate came over to them – it was the same one who had previously been drinking brandy when they first arrived.

"Evening again, Miss," he said, doffing his cap.

"Oh, good evening," said Emma suspiciously, a little startled by his sudden approach.

"I hope you've been having a lovely time?" he asked.

"Yes, thank you," replied Emma, "the whole evening has been very agreeable so far."

"Good, good… and have you managed to attend all the attractions?" asked the soldier, politely.

"All, I think," said Emma, "apart from the new mirror maze as the queue was very lengthy… I expect on account of it being new and also free tonight. I fancy I will try it on another occasion, rather than stand queuing for a long time."

"Oh, you'll be coming again then?" asked the soldier.

"Yes, indeed," replied Emma, "I shall be returning with my friend another evening."

"Well," said the soldier, "let me give you two free entry vouchers for the maze then… they're no good tonight as it's free anyway, but you can use them another night, with your friend." He put his hand into the satchel that hung around his neck and started going through his pile of vouchers. "There you are," he said finally, "one each for you and your friend… oh, and there's a voucher to skip the queue also, but I've only got one of them left, I'm sorry… but take it anyway as I may have another on the night you come back."

"Well," said Emma, taking the three vouchers from him, "you really have been most kind, I must say."

"It's been my pleasure, Miss," he said, doffing his cap again. "I'm Corporal Chatem, by the way, Miss… in case you want to ask for me anytime."

"Miss Jency," replied Emma with a small nod of her head, "and my nephew, Leo," she added, looking at him. Corporal Chatem looked down at Leo and smiled. "Well," she said, "I am sure we have taken up quite enough of your time. Thank you once again." She smiled again, as did he, though a good deal more enthusiastically than Emma had. Emma walked off, grabbing Leo's hand to lead him off too, and as quickly as possible at that.

"I think he quite likes you," said Leo, once they were out of earshot.

"I am quite sure that he does not," said Emma contemptuously. "And in any case, he has no right to go about liking people without being invited to do so!"

Leo giggled.

"What are you laughing about?" asked Emma brusquely.

"I just think it's a bit funny," said Leo, still sniggering away inanely.

"Emma!" called Bear from behind them.

"Oh, Mr Bear, I am so pleased that you are back!" she replied, turning around.

"Have we been so long?" asked Bear.

"No," said Emma, "I am just finding this end of the fairground rather tiresome now." Bear looked down at Leo with a wry smile, sensing that there may have been a little more to it than that. "Shall we walk down to the new mirror maze," suggested Emma.

"Of course," agreed Bear.

"Did either of you win at the coconut shy?" asked Bull, as they all walked on.

"I am afraid not," said Emma.

"I nearly knocked one off," added Leo, "it just needed a little extra push!" Bull just smiled.

"So, is Asiex fully conversant with all necessary details?" asked Emma, changing the subject.

"Yes, yes, we do believe so," said Bear.

"He is very confident that he will be able to get Leo back to his own reality at exactly the designated time," said Bull. "He seems to have had some previous experience in such matters."

"Although, he was not entirely forthcoming about the circumstances," added Bear.

"I fancy he is a character of some discretion," said Emma; "so that is to be expected."

"Yes, quite so," agreed Bull.

"There will probably be a large queue still at the mirror maze," said Bear.

"I fancy so," said Emma, "although it is worth a look."

"Emma has a voucher to skip the queue," said Leo; "but only one."

"Really?" commented Bear.

"Yes, only one I fear," confirmed Emma.

As they passed the first of the two helter-skelters, they could see that the queue stretched all the way from the far end of the marquee where the entrance was, all the way back down towards the exit which was at the opposite end. There was an attendant at the back of the queue organising those wishing to join and advising of the expected queuing time.

"What do you anticipate the queuing time to be?" asked Emma once they reached the back of the queue.

"Well, I'm explaining to folks that it depends how quickly the people in there find their way out, you see, Miss," said the attendant. "Mr Flector only allows twenty people at once in the maze... due to the weight on the floors, you see... so if those in there take a while to find the exit, it can be quite a bit of wait, you see."

"I see," said Emma, "but what do you suppose the average queuing time has been?"

"It's about forty minutes, I'd guess, Miss... but like I say, it's a bit variable, it is."

"Hmm... rather too long to stand still in the cold," mused Emma. By this time the snow had stopped falling, and the sky was clear and starry, but the temperature had dropped to well below freezing. "I have a voucher here," she said, taking it out, "which says *Immediate Entry Dignitary Pass – No Need To Queue*, is that of any use?"

"Oh, yes, Miss," said the attendant looking at it, "they're issued by his Worship the Mayor for the great and the good, them is... just go right up to the entrance and hand it over, they'll let you straight in."

"Very good, thank you," said Emma. She walked on towards the entrance, and the other three followed her. "It will be a pity for you to miss the maze, Leo. As you will be leaving tomorrow, you had better take the *Immediate Entry* voucher and go in with Bull and Bear. I will go to one of the reception tents and have a glass of claret to warm myself up a little."

"But are you sure?" asked Leo. "It is your voucher."

"It is a pity we have only one, but I do have the two free entry vouchers for when I come again with Annabel. The queue will also, I hope, be much smaller on Sunday, as the attraction will have been seen by many people already and will not be free any longer. So, I think you should take this voucher tonight," she said, handing it to Leo. "I advise you not to let Bull cheat by walking through the mirrors and finding his way out first, by unfair means!"

"Very well," said Leo with a smile.

"Shall I take your bags?" asked Emma. Leo still had his string bag with the coconut in it and the paper bag from the hook-a-duck.

"OK," said Leo. He handed her the string bag and was just about to hand her the paper bag also when a thought flashed into his mind about Theseus and the labyrinth. "I may need these," he said, taking out the two balls of wool and the knitting needles, and stuffing them into his pockets. Emma smiled knowingly and took the empty bag from him.

"Good luck then!" she said. "And at least you will have the minotaur as your confederate in this maze," she added with a smile.

"Minotaur? How scandalous!" protested Bull.

"See you later, then," said Bear. Emma left, and Leo walked over to the entrance stairs and handed his voucher to the attendant who was standing at the bottom.

"All right, young Sir, up you go and wait just inside the first door. The man there will explain everything when it's time," said the attendant directing Leo to the door at the top of the stairs. Leo did as directed and entered what had the layout of a waiting room with about twenty chairs in it. He was the only one there other than another attendant who was reading the Daily Tale and didn't take much notice of him, other than just looking up and acknowledging his arrival with a nod and smile.

Bull and Bear followed him through but didn't speak as it would have looked odd to the attendant when Leo replied to them. Less than a minute passed, and some other people could be heard talking as they ascended the stairs to the waiting room. The door opened and Leo looked up aghast as he saw first Major Schutem, then the Countess with her dog, and then finally Mayor Woodhay walk through it. The attendant immediately jumped to his feet.

"Good evening, your Worshipfulness," he said very enthusiastically, "and to you, your Worship, and to you, Major."

"Good evening," they all replied cheerfully.

"I shall be able to let you through just as soon as the last people in there find their way out," said the attendant. "It will only be a few minutes now, I believe."

"And is this young man, also waiting?" asked the Countess, pointing to Leo.

"I can put him through the next time," said the attendant.

"Not at all," said the Countess. "If the maze accommodates twenty people at a time then he might very well come in with us."

"As you like, your Worshipfulness," said the attendant. Princely Paws came over to Leo and started to sniff him. Leo put out his hand to stroke him, and he responded by raising his head backwards slightly. Leo stroked him over his eyes and between his ears, which he seemed to appreciate.

"He seems to like you," said Major Schutem.

"Indeed," said the Countess, looking over at Leo. "I do not believe I have seen you before, young man, do you live in town?"

"No, in Altgerheads, your Worshipfulness. I'm here to see the fairground with my aunt," he replied, being careful to be both polite and fully on story.

"Oh, I see," she said, in a tone that seemed to indicate, at least to Leo, that she was not entirely convinced. "I rarely go there. It is a nice village but very far from town, so I go only once a year at most, and only in the summer months," she added. "And is your aunt not with you tonight?"

"She has gone to warm herself with some claret," replied Leo.

"Ah, very wise," said Major Schutem. "I fancy we shall all do the same once we've seen this contraption." Leo immediately wondered why the Major had referred to the maze as a contraption; he also noticed that the Countess intermittently glanced to either side of him, each time she looked in his direction.

"I'm sure it will work very well," said the Mayor. "Mr Flector has assured the planning committee that it has been fully tested."

"And by now, over three or four hundred people have been through it without any problem at all," added the Countess.

"Hmm... all the same, moving floors, ceilings and walls by pulleys is a strange business if you ask me," insisted the Major. Leo realised as he spoke that the layout of the maze must be dynamic rather than fixed, and that was why the steam engines were required – to power the moving of the constituent parts.

Just then, a bell rang; it was hanging over the door, which led to the mirror maze proper.

"Well," announced the attendant, "everyone inside has now found the exit and the maze is empty."

"So, we can proceed?" asked Major Schutem.

"Yes, Sir," said the attendant, opening the door to the maze; "and good luck to you all!"

The Countess clicked her fingers, and Princely Paws immediately ran back to her side. Major Schutem entered first, followed by the Mayor, then the Countess and Princely Paws, and finally Leo, with Bull and Bear closely behind him.

All the walls of the maze were of either mirrored or plain glass; the ceilings were only of mirrored glass. The floors were made of wooden boards which had been painted with various patterns, stripes and colours; these looked quite impressive in the mirrors and served to add further ocular confusion. Each corridor of the maze was lit by a paraffin lamp suspended from the high ceiling, which provided only a dim light such that the lead adventurer had to hold out his hands in front of him to avoid walking directly into a plate of glass.

"Quite impressive," said Major Schutem. Princely Paws saw himself in a mirror and started to bark as if another dog were there.

"Lead on, Major," said the Countess.

"Yes, my Lady," he said and walked directly into a glass pane. "No, that's not it!" he muttered.

After a few minutes, they seemed to have made some progress and Leo had the sense that they had managed to travel a few yards at least towards the exit. Then they heard a noise from underneath the wooden boards which sounded like machinery, gears possibly, shifting.

"What the devil is that?" asked the Major.

"It sounds like the cogs are shifting," said the Mayor.

"But I thought you said that the maze layout changes only when it's empty so people can come again and again and always find that the way out is different… so it never gets boring?" asked Major Schutem.

"Yes, that's correct," confirmed Mayor Woodhay.

"So why do we hear the sound of machinery while we're in here?" retorted Major Schutem.

"Well… I don't know exactly," said the Mayor.

"Let us proceed, Major," said the Countess. "We can ask these questions once we have completed the maze."

"Yes, my Lady," said the Major.

They continued to wander around for several minutes, but Leo got a distinct impression that they hadn't actually got anywhere. Still, although all of them had by now developed a sense of awe at the intricacy of the maze, none of them was as yet at all suspicious that something untoward was going on, or about to happen. That was until, all of a sudden, a mirrored glass plate dropped from the ceiling, directly vertically and split the Countess, Princely Paws and Leo up from the Mayor and Major Schutem, on the different sides of it. The mirror barely missed Princely Paws' nose, and Leo, who a millisecond earlier had been looking at the back of the Mayor, was now looking at himself in a mirror.

"What just happened?" demanded the startled Countess.

"A mirror just dropped in front of us," said Leo objectively.

"Hello?" shouted the Countess, banging on the mirror. "Mayor Woodhay? Major Schutem? Are you there? Can you hear me?"

But answer came there none.

CHAPTER TWENTY-TWO

THE TEN
OF SWORDS

B ULL AND BEAR LOOKED at Leo, who shrugged, and then
at each other.

"You walk through, old boy," said Bear. "I'll stay here
with Leo, in case."

"In case of what?" asked Bull.

"I don't know," said Bear. "But it seems to me that this isn't
quite right!"

"Hmm... quite so," said Bull. He walked towards the mirror
as though to walk through it in the normal manner in which
either of them usually walked through solid objects, but instead
of walking through the mirror, he just banged into it and was
recoiled backwards.

"Strange," said Bear, "let me try." Bear tried, and the same
happened.

"Very odd," said Bull.

"Indeed," said Bear. "Very!"

The sound of gears, pistons and turning cogs could then be heard beneath the wooden floor.

"Better to go back to the entrance?" queried Bull.

"I fancy so," said Bear, moving in that direction.

The Countess took a coiled up leash from her pocket, latched it onto Princely Paws' collar and pulled him tight to her leg, so there was no space at all between the two of them. Then she took hold of Leo and pulled him too close to her.

"They're trying to split us up," she said.

"Who are they?" asked Leo.

"I don't know," said the Countess, "but this is not normal at all: my voice should be audible through these mirrors, as should the voices of the Mayor and the Major; but they didn't hear me, and we can't hear them!"

"She's right," said Bull.

"I am," said the Countess.

Bear turned around at this point with a flabbergasted expression on his face.

"You heard him?" he asked, glancing first at Bull, then at Leo, before fixing his gaze on the Countess.

"And I can see you too," she said. Bull and Bear were dumbfounded.

"But h…" started Bull, only to be silenced by the fall of two mirrors, which fell simultaneously to form a triangular trap together with the mirror he was standing against, around him.

"Go quickly and get help!" the Countess ordered Bear. "Go back to the entrance now, while you can, and run!" Bear looked at Leo for a moment as if very reluctant to leave him.

"Go," said Leo. Bear turned and ran; he could run very quickly actually and did so. Within seconds he had disappeared, but they could hear mirrors dropping in the corridor, and see at least one had fallen just behind him, blocking them from following after him.

"Is he trapped as well?" asked Leo.

"He could be," said the Countess. "We should assume the worst." Leo banged on the glass of the mirrors that had just entrapped Bull.

"Bull! Bull!" he shouted. "Bull, can you hear me?" But there was no answer.

"I should never have let an outsider build this," lamented the Countess.

Just as she spoke, the mirror that had separated them from Mayor Woodhay and Major Schutem rose again, just as quickly as it had fallen. Neither the Mayor nor the Major was on the other side, but Leo thought he could see a clear way forward.

"Shall we go?" he asked.

"I'm not sure," said the Countess. "It could be a trap."

"But aren't we trapped already?" retorted Leo. "Anyway the route back to the entrance is now blocked, so it's either that way, or we stay here."

"Hmm… I'm not sure," said the Countess again. "Where have the Mayor and the Major gone… they were in that corridor?"

"Maybe they've gone on," suggested Leo. "Maybe it's just a mechanical malfunction in this part of the maze, and they've gone on and got out now?"

"It's possible," agreed the Countess. "But it seems too coincidental that we've been so effectively all split up… it does not seem random to me."

"No… maybe not," agreed Leo. "So, what shall we do?"

"We may as well try the way that's opened up then," said the Countess after a few seconds of thinking about it. Leo nodded and led on; the Countess with Princely Paws stayed very close behind. Fortunately, the turns in the maze which Leo took did not lead to dead ends, and after about ten junctions they seemed to be making some progress as they entered what looked like quite a long corridor. But just as they were feeling more hopeful, the gears and cogs turned again, and another mirror fell in front of them, once more blocking their path.

"Shall we go back to the last junction?" asked Leo.

"We must," agreed the Countess, pulling Princely Paws round to face the other way again. Leo led on towards the junction they had just passed through, about ten feet back. The junction was four-way, and previously they had gone straight ahead, Leo remembered, so straight ahead again would be back where they had come from.

"Left or right?" he asked.

"Your choice," said the Countess. "You've been lucky so far."

"I feel right is North towards the exit…" said Leo "…but, I don't know why."

"Sometimes one has to trust one's gut," said the Countess. They went right and carried on until the next junction, then left, then right, then straight ahead, then left again, then straight ahead again, then left. Then they heard the machinery again and more mirrors falling and lifting.

"The maze is changing," said Leo. "We'll be going round in circles."

"I fear so," agreed the Countess.

"Wait!" exclaimed Leo. "I have some wool here." He took one of the balls of wool out of his pocket.

"Good idea!" said the Countess. Leo and the Countess looked around for something to tie the end of the wool to, but every surface was completely smooth; there were no nails, hinges, gaps, handles – literally nothing to tie the wool to. Then Leo had another idea; he took one of the knitting needles out and checked the point on it.

"If I can drive this between two of the floorboards," he said, "we can tie the wool to that."

"Is it made of steel?" asked the Countess.

"I think so… it's a strong metal at least," he replied. He put the point to the best gap he could find, but the boards were well cut and fitted together very precisely, so it was not easy to drive it in. After some seconds he managed to get the needle into a small crack, but he was unable to get a good fix.

"Use the sole of one of your boots," suggested the Countess. Leo took off one of his leather boots and started hammering the needle with its sole. It was wasn't easy, but fortunately, they were hobnail boots, and there was a metallic horseshoe on the heel as is typical of Victorian men's boots, so each time he managed to strike the horseshoe against the knob of the needle it did go in further. After about a minute of trying, it was halfway in and secure enough to tie the wool to.

"What is the length of your yarn?" asked the Countess.

"It says 150 yards," said Leo.

"That should do then," she said. The job was soon done, and they set off again, with Leo taking the lead, but this time unravelling the ball of wool as he went. He used his instinct again to choose which way to go at each junction, and they proceeded for over a minute at quite some speed, making sure always to stay very close together so that a suddenly falling mirror would not split them up.

"I think we're getting somewhere," said Leo, but just as he spoke they heard the sound of the machinery beneath the floor again, closely followed by the thudding of falling mirrors and the whooshing sound made as mirrors were slid up.

"Let's continue anyway," said the Countess. Leo nodded stoically and carried on as before. They went through another four or five junctions and then came to a corridor where a length of black wool ran straight across the floor. It emanated from underneath a mirror on the left-hand side and disappeared again under a mirror directly opposite, on the right-hand side.

"So this corridor we're in ran the other way before," said Leo.

"And therefore the space ahead we have not been in, as a mirror was there before," added the Countess.

"Agreed," said Leo, again leading the way. At the end of that corridor was a mirror blocking the possibility of going straight ahead, but the path to both left and right was open, neither way had black wool in it.

"Left?" asked Leo.

"Your choice as usual," replied the Countess. They went left and soon came to another four-way junction with black wool lying straight across it; they obviously carried on straight, but within a few yards, it was a complete dead end. They went back to the previous junction then back again to the one before that. They then went right at that junction instead of left, but the same thing happened again: a four-way junction with wool running left to right and another dead end in the straight-ahead direction.

"It's hopeless!" said the Countess. "The mirrors have trapped us in a loop… someone is doing this intentionally so that we can't get out!"

"But who would do such a thing?" asked Leo earnestly. "And why?"

CHAPTER TWENTY-THREE

JUDGEMENT

―――――――――

"WHAT DID YOU MEAN before, when you said you shouldn't have let an outsider build the maze?" asked Leo.

"I know everyone in Altcastle," said the Countess, "I know who's a badber or a goodber, who to trust with a project and who not to… but Mr Flector is not from Altcastle; I don't know him at all."

"So why did he build the maze and not someone from Altcastle?" asked Leo.

"I wanted something new and different," said the Countess: "something unusual to delight the people. No one from Altcastle came forward with anything we didn't have already… Mr Slider built a new, taller helter-skelter which is very good by all accounts, but a new helter-skelter is not very novel really. So Monsieur La Falot suggested someone he knew in Altacclesfield who was a specialist in creating mirror mazes."

"Hmm… I don't think Monsieur La Falot is a very reliable person," said Leo.

"I see that now," said the Countess. "This Mr Flector of his has constructed a monstrosity right under my very nose, and now I'm trapped, and goodness knows what his plans are. Princely Paws hasn't even had his supper yet," she added, stroking his head.

"But why did you trust Monsieur La Falot in the first place when he's such a liar and a cheat?" asked Leo. "I mean, his evidence at the trial of Mr Punch today was complete rubbish, especially when he gave in a shopping list and said it was a contract!"

"I didn't know what a damn hamster he was!" said the Countess, defensively.

"But why put Mr Punch on trial in the first place – he hadn't really done anything to deserve being put on trial for, had he?" challenged Leo.

"Well, he's a badber anyway: running off in the middle of a show and sneeping the poor children who'd already paid their ha'pennies!" insisted the Countess.

"Even so," retorted Leo, "it was rather extreme to have him put in a cage and then fining him all his money."

"Well, La Falot insisted upon it," said the Countess. "He'd had a lot of problems with Mr Punch and wanted him to learn his lesson."

"Yes, but why go along with him?" asked Leo.

"I had little choice," said the Countess somewhat emotionally. "The Borough of Altcastle has debts to some large banks in Altanchester; La Falot, because he travels with his puppet theatre outside the Borough, was involved in arranging loans and helping to get finance for projects like this mirror maze and the repairs to the girls' school. Altland was never supposed to work like this, but some things have started to go wrong in the last few years… it's very complicated and a long story…"

"So, you put poor Mr Punch on trial just because you owe money via La Falot to keep him sweet?" scoffed Leo.

"I'm a goodber," maintained the Countess. "There was no real harm done to Mr Punch; it was just an afternoon, that's all. In any case, he's not human, is he? He's just a puppet!"

"But that's not the point; he still has feelings, and he seems to be alive – I'm not sure how or why – a lot of strange things happen here that I can't understand."

"Ahaa, so, you're not from here, then!" responded the Countess. "I thought as much when you told me you were from Altgerheads, yet you were with those invisible creatures, Bull and Bear, and you could see them."

"But how could you see them?" asked Leo. "Is it something to do with this maze? Is that why they can't walk through the mirrors?"

"I've always been able to see them, in fact. I have no idea why they can't walk through the mirrors; I didn't know they could walk through solid objects anyway. I've never spoken to them before, but I've often noticed them chatting away at the back of events – I even saw them in the theatre earlier."

"Why have you never bothered to speak to them, then?" asked Leo.

"Why should I have?" asked the Countess. "They do not interact with many citizens, and they seem to mind their own business and do no harm, so I have just let them be and wander around as they do."

"But how come can you see them?" asked Leo again. "They're invisible to almost everyone."

"Well, how come you can?" replied the Countess.

"They said it's because I'm wise, and only wise people can see them," answered Leo.

"I see," responded the Countess aggrievedly. "So, you think I'm stupid, do you?"

"No," said Leo, somewhat abashed. "I didn't mean it that way; I just didn't… well, I didn't…" Having had chance to consider the matter, he was struggling to think of some polite way of explaining that he never imagined the Countess to be a member of *the wise*, but he was pretty stumped for ideas. Not that he was too bothered, for having now spent half an hour with her, trying to get out of the maze, he considered her a great deal more normally human than he had done previously, and he certainly didn't find her in any way threatening.

"Well?" she pressed.

"I just thought you weren't wise, that is not stupid – but not exactly wise… it's just because of the way you behave and run the town with so many odd rules and customs," he said finally.

"So you don't find my governance of this borough very wise then?" she inquired.

"Well… it's none of my business really, as I'll be leaving soon, but if you must know: I do not actually," he said very definitely.

"You're a very cheeky young fellow, indeed, are you not?"

"My father often says so," said Leo. "And so do some of my teachers."

"I do not find that at all surprising," she said.

"Well, I have to stand up for my rights, you know," was his answer.

"No wonder you like Mr Punch," said the Countess, "you seem to be another revolutionary!"

"I might be," said Leo. "It seems to me there is a lot to revolt against!"

"You mean, here, in Altcastle?" asked the Countess.

"Well, I suppose so… and in general… in the world in general, that is – both in this reality and in my own," he said.

"So, where is your reality? Where are you from?" she asked.

"I am from here exactly, but in my reality, this is Newcastle-under-Lyme," said Leo. The Countess did not appear to be in the least bit surprised by his answer.

"Newcastle… hmm… I see… and what is your name?" she asked.

"Leo Marcus," replied Leo.

"And I suppose, Leo, that you came here yesterday in that fog?" she replied. Leo squinted his eyes.

"Yes, but how do you know about that?" asked Leo.

"The Lyme Brook runs through the fields to the rear of my house," she said, "I watched it forming and then disappearing from my library window. I know well enough what it is… it's now the fourth such mist this year."

"Where do you live?" asked Leo.

"Altlayton Hall," she said. Leo looked surprised.

"That's my school," he said, "in my reality, it's called Clayton Hall Academy."

"How terribly strange…" she mused "…what a thought."

"But what do you know about the mist?" he asked.

"I suspect it is created by vile and nefarious dark magic," she replied, "with an intention to aid in the perpetration of some terrible beakery, although I haven't yet fathomed how or why, nor who created it."

"Do you think it may be related to our present situation?" asked Leo.

"Hmm… I had not considered it, but yes, it is certainly a possibility," she replied with an astute nod.

"And how do you intend to get back to your reality?" asked the Countess.

"I saw a druid," said Leo, not wanting to disclose the identity of Asiex.

"Asiex the druid?" she asked. Leo was again taken aback; she seemed to know a lot more about things than he had imagined.

"Yes, but I hope I am not getting him into trouble," replied Leo. The Countess laughed.

"How is a simple woman like me going to make trouble for a powerful druid?" she retorted. "I know well enough what Asiex does in any case, I have consulted him myself regarding these mists – yesterday's was not the first as I said, and you are not the first person to have come here from Newcastle-under-Lyme either… but I will say no more of that as I am bound to secrecy."

"I understand," said Leo. "But you do know of my reality then?"

"Oh, yes," she said thoughtfully. "That is why this reality is so much better – we who are in control have learned by the mistakes of your reality; we shall not repeat them here in so far as it is in our power to prevent such!"

"What mistakes?" asked Leo.

"All your misguided technologies, your insane wars, your poor health and diseases, your terrible greed, your abuse of nature… I could go on almost indefinitely," she said.

"But here, even though the year is 2018 it's as if it's still 1900, or even earlier and…"

"Yes, earlier," she said, interrupting him.

"How much earlier?" he asked.

"The timelines of this reality and yours were made to diverge on 31st October 1889," she stated very definitely.

"But why?" asked Leo.

"There were many reasons," said the Countess. "Far too many to go through here."

"Well, give me an example then," said Leo. As they were stuck in the maze anyway, he considered the time might be best used by finding out a little more about how Altcastle had come to exist.

"Very well. Have you heard of Nicola Tesla?" asked the Countess.

"Yes," said Leo, "my father is a fan of his!"

"A fan?" she asked.

"An admirer," explained Leo.

"Oh, I see," she said.

"So, what about Nicola Tesla?" asked Leo.

"During the 1880s electricity started to be used in the larger cities, but it used direct current and was both unreliable and difficult to supply over longer distances. Nevertheless, those who were wise enough could see that the world was on the brink of huge changes. Even as early as 1883, alternating current electric lighting was in use in the Austro-Hungarian Empire. Have you heard of that?"

"Yes, I know a lot about history," answered Leo. "I know all about the Austro-Hungarian Empire and the Central Powers and the Double Entente."

"That's good," said the Countess. "Also in Altondon... London to you, the first electrical power station opened in 1882."

"Really? I didn't know it was so early," said Leo.

"Yes, it was 1882, but it became a failure because of the cost to run it, and in 1886 the streetlamps that had been run from the electricity produced by that power station were converted back to gas. Some thought that perhaps that might be an end to it, but then came Tesla on the scene. He was a real genius; he developed the alternating current system so quickly and to such an extent that it became clear to the wise that even within a decade, it would change the whole world forever, and it did. The *Paris Exposition Universelle* of 1889 was the last World Exposition to be lit by gas, the next one in Chicago in 1893, just four years later, was lit by alternating current electricity and so it was that the modern world that you know came into being. But Altland had been created by then, and the timelines had split – in this reality, the Chicago Columbian Exposition never even happened – the last one in our history books was the one in Paris in 1889."

"But why do that?" asked Leo. "Why stop all innovation and progress?"

"Is it progress?" asked the Countess contemptuously. "More pollution, more greed, poisons in the air and the water and the food, more violence, more wars... what sort of progress is that? In your reality, there are crimes all the time. There are wars and diseases, and people struggle to pay their bills and feed their families, but in Altcastle there is no crime, no poverty, no hunger, no wars, there are no diseases – no one even catches a cold here, because there is no one to catch a cold from, as no one in Altcastle has a cold. Which reality do you think is better?"

"Hmm... I don't know, now that you put it like that," mused Leo. "But surely having electricity wouldn't lead to crime, and it would eliminate the need for all those men I have seen, who have to go around lighting the gas lamps every night."

"Well, electricity, as per your request, was just one example – I could give you dozens more, like aeroplanes, weapons, poison gas, bombs, and as regards to the gas lamps, do you know that throughout the whole borough, including all the outlying districts and villages, there are fifty-eight lamplighters employed."

"That's what I mean," said Leo, interrupting her, "they wouldn't be needed if you had electricity."

"But have you not considered that those men might want to be needed?" asked the Countess. "They all have families to provide for; what would they do if they were no longer needed to light the gas lamps?"

"Hmm… I hadn't thought about that… couldn't they do some other job?" asked Leo.

"Possibly, but then that job would become automated, and then the job after that, and after that, and so on, until everything became automated as it will be in your reality one day, no doubt – maybe it is that way now, I don't know as I am out of touch with how things have developed."

"It's sort of getting like that, yes," said Leo.

"Well, it seems to me that such developments simply mean more profits for the companies and fewer jobs and livelihoods for the people – no thank you, not in Altcastle: we will keep our gas lamps."

"OK, on that point, then," agreed Leo, "I'm not sure I completely agree, but I take your point, but what about all the crazy laws here?"

"Are the laws really so *crazy*, as you put it?" she retorted. "How can you judge what *crazy* is? The worse thing that might happen to someone here is they may be fined a few shillings for some beakery – and only then if they are hamstery, otherwise life is perfect."

Just then their conversation was interrupted as they heard a very loud thud and the breaking of glass about 20 yards away.

"Something new is happening!" said Leo. "Maybe Bear or even the Mayor and Major Schutem have got out and are now opening an escape route for us. That was certainly the sound of somebody smashing one of the mirrors." As he finished speaking, there was another thud and again the sound of breaking glass.

"I think you're right!" said the Countess. "They are smashing the mirrors to get to us!"

CHAPTER TWENTY-FOUR

THE
JESTER

E MMA FINISHED HER CLARET and walked back into the
cold night. She walked on past the entrance to the mirror
maze, where there was still a large and now seemingly
restless queue, and up to the far end of the marquee where the
exit was. After waiting for about fifteen minutes for Leo, Bull and
Bear to come out, she decided to ask the attendant at the entrance
how long he thought it might take. As she passed the front of the
queue, she could hear people moaning about how long they had
been queuing.

"Do you remember my nephew?" she asked the attendant at
the bottom of the stairs which led up to the entrance. "He had an
Immediate Entry voucher."

"Oh, yes Miss: I do," said the attendant.

"Well, it must be over half an hour ago that he went in, and he
still has not come out," said Emma.

"Hmm… so it's him who's holding the queue up then," said the attendant. "Some folks have been waiting above half an hour now; that's why they're getting restless, see."

"Is it normal to take so long in there?" she asked.

"Oh no, the queue moves along about every five minutes usually… sometimes a little longer, but certainly not half an hour," said the attendant.

"Perhaps there is something wrong?" suggested Emma.

"Hmm… but what could be wrong? He must just be finding it difficult to get out," said the attendant. "But by all means, go up and ask the attendant on the entrance door if you're worried."

"Thank you," she said, "I will do that." Emma walked up the stairs and soon found the other attendant, who had fallen asleep in his chair. "Excuse me!" called out Emma, quite loudly.

"Hmm… hmm… what's that…" he muttered, coming to.

"Excuse me," said Emma again. "I am looking for my nephew who has been in the maze now for over half an hour."

"Half an hour, you say?" he replied surprisedly. He stood up, pulled out his pocket watch and checked the time. "Hmm… more than half an hour, in fact," he said. "Very strange – the maze isn't set to a difficult level because of the queues and it being the first night and all… they should have all come out by now… long since, in fact."

"How long is it supposed to take?" asked Emma.

"Five minutes is about right; some folks have taken a little more… but yes, generally about five minutes… and now your nephew and the Countess have been in there for easily nearly thirty-five minutes," he remarked.

"The Countess?" asked Emma.

"Yes, didn't you know?" asked the attendant. "Your lad went in with the Countess, the Mayor and that army geezer, what's his name? You know, in charge of the barracks…"

"Major Schutem?" suggested Emma.

"Yes, that's the fella," said the attendant. "So there was four of them altogether."

"Well," said Emma, worriedly, "I think that you had better go in and find them then: because something strange must have happened for them to be still in there after all of this time!" The attendant scratched his head and puffed his lips, then he nodded:

"Yes, I fancy you might be right, Miss," he said, trying the door handle. He opened the door, leaving it open, and walked into the maze. Emma remained in the waiting room but could see in. The first corridor appeared to go on for only about five yards and then there was a mirror at the end which Emma could clearly see both the attendant's and her own reflection in. The attendant had soon reached the mirror at the end, and looked around bemusedly before walking back towards her, while constantly checking the mirrors to both his left and right by pushing against them.

"Most peculiar," he said, returning to Emma's position, "there's no way through... I'm sure that end mirror wasn't there before... I went through the maze myself, I did, around half-past three... before we opened, you know, just to check it wasn't set up too difficult... and I was out the other end in well under five minutes."

"What do you mean by *set up too difficult*?" asked Emma.

"Well, Miss, the maze is changeable, you see... I mean it's not fixed if you get me..."

"You mean that the mirrors can be moved to change the layout of the maze?" queried Emma.

"Yes, Miss. Mr Flector said it would be a more interesting attraction that way, because if it were all fixed then once somebody had been through it once or twice, then they would know the way out, and it wouldn't be interesting anymore; but if the route around the maze changed every day then people would still come back because the way out would always be different," explained the attendant.

"I see," said Emma. "So, the ease with which one can find one's way through is what you refer to as *the difficulty*?"

"That's right, Miss; because it's such a large area, the way out can be a simple U-bend with almost no dead-ends, or it can be set up with hundreds of junctions and dead-ends."

"And it is supposed to be easy today?" asked Emma.

"Yes, Miss, otherwise it would take too long to get out, and people would have to queue for a long time which wouldn't be good."

"So, what has happened?"

"I don't know, Miss," replied the attendant, "I will have to go downstairs into the workings and find Mr Flector... something must have gone wrong with the workings because the maze isn't supposed to change while people are in it – it's dangerous, you see."

"Dangerous?" demanded Emma. "How?"

"Well, the mirrors lift up into the ceiling area and drop down... they're all on pulleys, you see, and they're controlled by winding gears underneath the maze, so if people are in the maze then you can't really start dropping mirrors down, or they could hit someone."

Emma looked startled by this latest information:

"But if you say that the end mirror was not there earlier, then the maze is changing while people are in it!"

"Yes, it seems so," agreed the attendant.

"Then you had better go and find this Mr Flector right away!" insisted Emma very forcefully. "I am going to find the Constable."

"Right," said the attendant, and he hurried off down the stairs. Emma followed him down and asked the other attendant at the bottom if he had seen Constable Cuffem that evening. The attendant said that he had seen him, and thought he had gone for a pint in one of the tents behind the stage. Emma rushed over to the tents and started to search them all. Meanwhile, the attendant who had gone to find Mr Flector did, in fact, locate him, exactly where he expected, in the control housing underneath the mirror maze. He was there together with Monsieur La Falot and another man, whom the attendant had never seen before, and who was wearing a long, black hooded robe; the hood was up concealing most of his face.

"There's been a problem," he said to Mr Flector, and he explained what had happened. Mr Flector told him not to be concerned and that everyone was safe and well, and that there had simply been a few technical problems with the winding gear which Monsieur La Falot and the other man were helping him to address.

Although not completely satisfied with the explanation, the attendant nevertheless accepted it and went back up to report to Emma. Just as he got back up into the waiting room, Emma arrived back with the Constable who demanded a full explanation as to what was going on. Once the attendant had explained everything and relayed Mr Flector's advice that all was well, the Constable seemed less flustered, but Emma was not at all satisfied.

"But what if one the mirrors has already injured someone?" she insisted. "Constable, how long do you propose to allow Mr Flector to go on fixing things before you take decisive action?"

"Hmm..." mumbled Constable Cuffem "...what sort of decisive action do you have in mind if you don't mind me asking?"

"You must do your duty!" declared Emma. "You must go into the maze and rescue the Countess and my nephew!"

"Hmm... well, I don't know about that exactly," he said, mumbling again.

"I should not have to remind you, Constable, that if any harm befalls the Countess, you will now be held entirely responsible!"

"Hmm... yes... I suppose you're right... do we have a fire axe?" asked Constable Cuffem, directing the question towards the attendant.

"We do, yes," he said, "shall I fetch it?"

"You better had," confirmed Constable Cuffem.

"Righto!" he said, and he headed back down the stairs to fetch the axe.

"I do hope you're right about this, Miss Jency," said Constable Cuffem. "I shall not be popular for unnecessarily damaging the latest attraction."

"Better safe than sorry, I fancy," said Emma, dismissive of his concern.

"Right," he said, and he was just about to say something more when the sound of an incredibly loud thud emanated from the maze through the still open door, which was quickly followed by the sound of smashing glass. "Here, here, what's going on? I told him to bring the fire axe, not do it himself!" Just then, the attendant returned, panting, and holding a large red-handled fire axe. "What's going on?" asked Constable Cuffem.

"You wanted a fire axe?" retorted the attendant.

"But didn't you just hear that thud and the sound of breaking glass?" asked Constable Cuffem.

"I did, but…" He was interrupted by the sound of another large thud and again the sound of glass breaking.

"Somebody else is breaking the maze," said Constable Cuffem.

"But who could that be?" asked Emma. Constable Cuffem shrugged.

"Maybe it's this Flector fellow," he suggested.

"No, he's downstairs," said the attendant. Just then they all heard another thud and yet more breaking glass, this time accompanied by the shaking of the wooden floorboards on which the maze sat: the whole structure shook in fact.

"That's never right," said Constable Cuffem.

"Off you go, Constable," said Emma, seizing the fire axe from the attendant and thrusting it into Constable Cuffem's hands. "I shall be right behind you!"

"Right," he said, with bulging eyes and a large gulp. He entered the maze and swung at the mirror at the end; the glass cracked, but the mirror didn't shatter.

"Again and harder!" shouted Emma.

"Right, Miss," he said, lifting the axe again. He took another swing but still didn't manage to shatter the mirror, although the crack did appear very marginally bigger.

"Again!" she ordered. Constable Cuffem puffed; he was not a fit man. Again he tried as best he could, but yet again there was no noticeable further damage. Emma went back and collected the attendant who was much younger than Constable Cuffem. "You do it!" she demanded. The attendant took the axe from Constable Cuffem and took a running swing at the panel which then shattered almost completely, but left a sheet of bare steel where the mirror had been.

"Are these mirrors placed over sheets of steel?" asked Emma. The attendant inspected the steel plate, which now presented where the mirror had been.

"It would appear so," he confirmed.

"Then hit the steel," she said. The attendant looked at her dubiously but nevertheless had a few goes. There did appear to be some slight denting of the material, but that was all.

"These mirror panes seem to me to be very suspiciously overengineered," declared Emma.

"You mean, they're too strong for what they're meant for?" asked Constable Cuffem.

"Precisely," confirmed Emma. "I fancy this Flector fellow has some answering to do!"

"Shall I go and arrest him?" asked Constable Cuffem.

"I fancy that might well be a good idea!" agreed Emma.

"Right then," said Constable Cuffem. "Show me where he is!" he ordered the attendant, who nodded, held out his hand towards the waiting room and led on. Constable Cuffem followed him. As they left, Emma picked up the axe and took a few swings at the steel herself, but she could make no impression upon it at all. At least five minutes passed, during which time Emma tried a few more swings of the axe and called out "*Leo, can you hear me?"* quite a few times; none of which actions produced any result. Eventually, Constable Cuffem returned:

"No sign of the beggar," he said panting. "He was there only a few minutes ago, now he's not. We've looked all over for him, but I fancy he's scarpered, I do... the attendant is still looking..."

"Have you looked outside?" asked Emma.

"Yes, Miss, but a thick mist has come up from the brook, you can't see more than a few yards," said Constable Cuffem.

"Mist?" said Emma incredulously. "At this time of night and in freezing temperatures? How is that possible?"

"It's strange all right, I'll grant you, but you go and look for yourself, it's like trying to look through pea soup," stated Constable Cuffem. Emma rushed off through the waiting room, down the stairs and outside. Sure enough, an incredibly dense mist had formed, and it was not even possible to see the helter-skelter which she knew was directly in front of her.

"Hmm... this is not normal," she mumbled to herself. "But who can help?" She started to run through every possibility in her head: "Bull and Bear – trapped in the maze themselves; Asiex – nowhere close, he is in town; the Countess, Major Schutem and Mayor Woodhay – trapped in the maze; Constable Cuffem – useless; Doctor Toad – probably miles away... who else?" she thought. "There must be somebody who could break down that steel!" Then she had an idea: "the Marvellous Magnetic Monkey! Yes, yes," she thought to herself, "steel is magnetic!"

She ran as quickly as she could across the fairground, which was no easy matter considering the thick mist, and soon arrived at the tent of the Magnetic Monkey. Fortunately, there was no show in progress, so she went into the rear entrance of his tent and soon found him, drinking tea with three of his white rats. He seemed surprised to see her, as did the rats, but after they had all introduced themselves to each other, and the rats had offered her a cup of tea – which she declined, they all listened very intently to the whole story.

"Hmm... well, then, it would appear that there is no time to lose!" said the Magnetic Monkey. "Leopold, please accompany me," he added, and one of the white rats leapt immediately onto the Magnetic Monkey's multicoloured-striped top hat.

"Ready for action!" declared Leopold.

"Let us be off then; the game is afoot," declared the Magnetic Monkey.

"Indeed," added Leopold, "there is beakery abroad in Altcastle this night!" So Emma, the Magnetic Monkey, and Leopold on his hat, all chased back across the fairground and into the tent of the mirror maze. Constable Cuffem was still trying to get through the mirrors, and by the time Emma returned, had smashed the glass of another one of the mirrors in the corridor, but he had made no impact at all on the steel sheet underneath.

"I have brought assistance!" declared Emma.

"Ah, Mr Magnetic Monkey," said Constable Cuffem. "Good thinking, Miss Jency!"

"Stand back!" said the Magnetic Monkey as he raised his hairy fingers toward the steel plate at the end of the corridor. Seemingly without too much trouble, the steel plate raised up into the ceiling, revealing another corridor of mirrors behind it.

"I shall investigate!" declared Leopold, and he jumped down from the Monkey's hat and scampered swiftly off down the corridor, making a left turn at the end. The rest of them waited with bated breath; within seconds, Leopold returned and reported that the way was blocked by another mirror, but otherwise, there was no danger. Accordingly, they all proceeded along the corridor to the next mirror, which the Magnetic Monkey also easily lifted with his strange powers. As soon as the mirror lifted, swirls of mist started to appear at the end of the next corridor and blew towards them.

"The maze must be open to the outside somewhere," said Emma.

"Indeed," agreed the Magnetic Monkey. "Possibly one of the accomplices of this Flector fellow has smashed his way in from the other side, and that was why you heard the sound of breaking glass."

"It'll be very difficult to find them now with this mist," said Constable Cuffem. Leopold again scurried off and ran into the mist, quickly disappearing from sight.

"It will," said the Monkey. "I am afraid my magnetic powers cannot help with that."

"There's a trail of yarn!" called out Leopold. "We can follow that!"

The Magnetic Monkey, Emma and Constable Cuffem all hurried into the mist to join Leopold, and sure enough in the corridor around the corner from the one they were in, a line of black wool ran straight across the floor from left to right.

"So this corridor must have run perpendicularly to how it does now," said Emma. "If you can lift each panel as before we can just follow the wool until we reach the end."

"But only one end will lead to your nephew," said the Magnetic Monkey; "the other end will lead to whatever the wool was first tied to."

"But even if we choose the wrong path, we will still find them by then simply retracing our steps back to here and then going the opposite way," said Emma

"Very good, Miss," agreed Constable Cuffem. "Over to you, Mr Monkey!"

"So left or right to start off?" asked the Monkey.

"Let's try left," said Emma. The Magnetic Monkey easily lifted the mirror, just as he had the others, and they followed the trail of the wool along corridors and around corners – the Monkey lifting the mirrors whenever one blocked the trail. As each corridor was opened, they found some were full of the mist, while others had no mist at all. Finally, the Magnetic Monkey lifted a mirror which revealed the Countess, Princely Paws and Leo – still holding his ball of wool.

"Thank heavens!" exclaimed Constable Cuffem. "Are you all safe and well?" Princely Paws barked in reply, and the Countess and Leo looked extremely relieved.

"Yes, we three are fine," said the Countess. "But we have been split up – deliberately I believe by that hamster Flector. We do not know where the others are."

"It was near the beginning of the maze that we got split up," added Leo; "but when the mirror was lifted up again, the others weren't there anymore."

"So, in fact, the mirrors have been falling and lifting while you have been in the maze?" asked the Magnetic Monkey.

"Indeed, Mr Monkey," said the Countess. "It was quite dangerous. I have to tell you; one of us could quite easily have been chopped in half!"

"So, what shall we do to find the others then?" asked Constable Cuffem.

"I do not suppose it is possible for you to lift all the mirrors at the same time, Mr Monkey?" asked the Countess. The Magnetic Monkey shook his head.

"They are too heavy," he said, "only one at a time."

"And it's impossible to break them as they're all steel-backed," added Constable Cuffem. "I tried very hard with a big fire axe, but I made no impression."

"Wait," said Emma, "if Mr Flector was controlling the mirrors to trap you, then there must be a way to lift all the mirrors from the maze's control room."

"Good thinking!" said the Magnetic Monkey. "Let's go! Do you know where it is?"

"Follow me!" said Constable Cuffem. "I've been there already when I was looking for Flector."

"Did you find him?" asked the Countess.

"No your Worshipfulness, he'd already run off, I fancy."

"Hmm… what about that other rascal, La Falot?" she asked.

"Also missing," said Constable Cuffem.

"Anyway, we can worry about finding them once we have rescued the others, let's go. Lead on Constable," said the Countess. Constable Cuffem went off, preceded by Leopold who knew the way out better than him, closely followed by the Countess, Princely Paws, Leo and finally Emma.

"Bull and Bear?" whispered Emma as they walked.

"Trapped also," said Leo.

"Hmm…" sighed Emma.

They were soon back in the waiting room and descending the stairs to the outside. The mist had cleared somewhat since Emma had fetched the Magnetic Monkey, and the helter-skelter's lights had become visible again. There was no longer a queue for the maze as the attendant had told everyone there had been a mechanical failure; a sign had also been put up saying *Closed for Repairs*.

They all went around to the side of the tent, where they found the attendant who had been searching for Flector and La Falot.

"Any luck?" asked Constable Cuffem.

"I'm afraid not," he said. "I've been all around this tent and the whole fairground… there's no sign of them anywhere."

"Hmm… ah well, we need to lift all the mirrors up… should have thought about it before but it never crossed me mind. Do you know how the controls work?" asked Constable Cuffem.

"No idea, I'm afraid: Mr Flector was very insistent that only he or Monsieur La Falot was allowed to touch the controls," said the attendant.

"Not to worry," said the Magnetic Monkey, "you wait here, I am confident I shall be able to work it out." They left the attendant and proceeded through the door at the side of the marquee and then went on into the control housing. After little more than three or four minutes of inspecting and sample trying various levers, the Magnetic Monkey seemed to have worked it all out.

"They have jammed the mechanism," he said. "Absolute fools – they could not even operate their own invention!"

"Then it was one of Flector's men who was breaking the mirrors," mused Emma.

"But why if he wanted to trap us, did he then start breaking into the maze?" asked the Countess. They all looked at each other and shrugged.

"Aha!" exclaimed the Monkey. "The steam valve is not turned up enough... insufficient pressure to lift the weight of the mirrors was their problem – they could drop them well enough under their own weight with gravity, but not lift them every easily; hence they needed to try to break them."

"No doubt they found that as difficult as we did," said Emma.

"No doubt," agreed the Monkey, twisting the steam valve without touching it. "That should do it," he said, tapping the pressure gauge. He then used his mysterious magnetic powers to pull, one after another, an entire bank of large levers situated along the backside of the tent. Sure enough, a huge whooshing of steam could be heard as gears turned and pistons pumped, and they could hear the sound of the mirrors lifting through the floorboards above their heads.

"I'll run back up, in case they're alarmed," said Constable Cuffem, and off he went.

"I'll do the same for Bull and Bear," said Emma.

"Very good," said the Countess.

"They will all be lifted in the next seconds," sighed the Monkey. The Countess seemed quite relieved that the Magnetic Monkey had been able to sort it all out.

"What's that you have Princely Paws?" asked the Countess, looking down at him; he had some folded paper in his mouth, which he had picked up from the floor. The Countess bent down and took it from him.

"What is it?" asked Leo.

"Hmm... it appears to be a ransom note," said the Countess nervously, and she read it out:

Dear Mayor Woodhay

My associates and I have kidnapped the Countess of Altcastle and taken her to an alternate reality to which you have no access. You won't be able to find her, so don't even bother looking!

In two days from now, you are to leave a chest containing ten thousand gold sovereigns, on the eastern side of the Lyme Brook bridge in Altlayton Lane near Altpringfields at exactly sunset.

Make sure to leave once you have placed the chest! And no tricks – no Constable Cuffem, no Major Schutem and no militia!

Be warned: if the gold is not delivered, the Countess will meet a very grisly end, and so will that dumb hound of hers! Altcastle will also be wrecked by the introduction of greed, crime, weapons and social unrest! The Altcastle you know will be destroyed!

Once we count the gold, we will send the Countess back across the bridge and close the portal.

You had better comply – OR ELSE!

Yours expectantly
R. E. Flector, Esquire

"How terrible!" exclaimed Leo. "So, that was the plan all along. It's very lucky that Emma, Constable Cuffem and the Magnetic Monkey managed to save us in time, before they got hold of you!".

The Countess gulped and looked most pale.

"It might only have been a matter of minutes!" she said sombrely.

"That's why they were trying to get to you: to kidnap you!" said the Monkey. "It's clear now! They used the pulley system to trap you in the maze after splitting you up from anyone who could help, and then they intended to take you out through the back. Luckily they were incompetent and did not understand that they needed more pressure for the pistons to lift such heavy panels."

"Just to think... poor Princely Paws... meeting a grisly end!" said the Countess sorrowfully while she stroked his head.

"As this Flector intended to hide you in an alternate reality, then he can obviously control the mist," said Leo.

"So it would seem; he must have some secret way of doing so," agreed the Countess.

"Can't you control the mist?" asked Leo.

"Not at all; I don't agree with it or want anything to do with it..." Just then the Mayor, Major Schutem and the Constable ran back in.

"What a relief," cried Mayor Woodhay.

"Indeed," agreed the Major. "I thought we'd all be stuck in there forever. After we got spilt up, we just went around trying to get out but actually got nowhere at all."

"The Constable has told me about Flector," said the Mayor, "I can't understand where he could have got to!"

"I will sound the barracks' bell," said Major Schutem, "and call out the entire militia – armed!"

"You will be wasting your time, I'm afraid," said the Countess. "Read this!" She handed the ransom note to Mayor Woodhay, and he held it up so that he, the Major and Constable Cuffem could all read it at the same time. They all read it quietly and with expressions of horror and shock.

"I can't believe it!" said Major Schutem. "The beakery of it!"

"It's incredible!" said the Mayor, handing the note back to the Countess.

"But how is it even possible?" asked Constable Cuffem. "This alternate reality business?"

"I must swear all of you to absolute secrecy!" said the Countess, very sternly. "We must not let a word of this matter reach the ears of any ordinary citizen – it will utterly destroy their happiness and peace of mind if they understand such foul creatures as Flector, and I suspect La Falot, can simply appear and disappear at will."

"Yes, indeed," agreed Major Schutem. Mayor Woodhay, Constable Cuffem and Leo all nodded.

"But there must be some way to prevent these devils from creating portals," said the Magnetic Monkey.

"Rest assured, I shall be looking into the matter in great detail," said the Countess. "Now, as things stand, Flector, and probably La Falot, have fled from Altcastle now that their wicked plan has failed, so we have some time to try to establish the full details of what has gone on and who else may be involved in this scheme."

"I suggest, Constable and Major, that you get witness statements from all the attendants of the mirror maze and anyone else who was involved in constructing it: find out if anyone else has been here or has been talking to Mr Flector... but as I said, under no circumstances mention anything about alternate realities and portals," said the Countess.

"Yes, very good," said Major Schutem. "We'll get right on it; I'll enlist the two soldiers on the gate to help."

"I'll start off with the attendant who helped me to look for the miscreants earlier; he'll know the whereabouts of all the other attendants I suppose," said Constable Cuffem.

"We shall have a meeting in the chamber of the Municipal Hall tomorrow after the poetry competition and Magpie March," said the Countess.

"Or shall we cancel them, now all this has happened; are you sure you feel up to such things while these hamsters are still at large?" asked Mayor Woodhay.

"I must be strong," said the Countess, "the people will immediately understand something is very wrong if we cancel such important annual events. We must continue as if everything is normal. We can deal with this matter in the afternoon."

"Very well," said Major Schutem. "Let's get on then Constable." Major Schutem and Constable Cuffem then departed to carry out their instructions.

"Shall I order the carriage?" asked the Mayor.

"I fancy so," said the Countess, "I shall wait here with Leo."

As the Mayor left, Emma, Bull and Bear entered from the adjoining side – the side which backed onto the canal.

"I'm glad to see you two!" exclaimed Leo, with a big smile. Emma looked quite shocked. "It's OK," added Leo to Emma, noticing her reaction: "the Countess can see them."

"Really?" asked Emma. "I did not know that."

"I've not ever made it known," said the Countess. "Are you all right, gentlemen?" she then asked, directing herself to Bull and Bear who were now busy shaking hands with Leo to celebrate their return to normality.

"Yes, yes," said Bull imperturbably, "we're both quite fine now."

"It's very odd that we couldn't walk through the mirrors," mused Bear. "I suspect a spell of some sort…"

"But how would the caster of such a spell know of you in the first place?" asked the Countess.

"We were just discussing that outside," said Emma. "It would seem that whoever is responsible for all this had some assistance from a sorcerer or another druid."

"Well, it was Flector who was behind it all," said the Countess.

"How can you be so sure?" asked Bull.

"Princely Paws found this on the floor," she replied, handing Bull the ransom note. Bull, Bear and Emma all read it together while Bull held it.

"What an outrage!" exclaimed Bear, having finished reading.

"And he knows about the mist…" added Bull.

"And worse still, can control it!" added Emma.

"Which means he is no longer in Altcastle presumably," mused Bear. "So no one can catch him."

"But which alternate reality has he gone to?" asked Leo. "Has he gone to my Newcastle?"

"I very much hope not," said Emma.

"I do not understand the workings of it," said the Countess. "I must discuss the matter very fully with Asiex." Emma looked surprised again, but didn't comment this time; it seemed there was much about the Countess, and her associations with others, that the people of Altcastle did not know. Just then, Mayor Woodhay returned.

"Your carriage is here, your Worshipfulness," he declared.

"Very well, I shall take my leave of you all. As I have already said to Major Schutem, Constable Cuffem and Mayor Woodhay, it is imperative that none of this becomes known to anyone else, as such news would be most distressing to the general population."

"Quite understood," said Bear; the Countess just nodded, as obviously Mayor Woodhay could not see Bear or Bull and therefore addressing them in his presence might have looked rather odd.

"I trust you will all be able to attend the Poetry Competition tomorrow?" asked the Countess.

"It will still go ahead then?" asked Emma.

"It must," said the Countess: "otherwise it will look extremely odd to everyone. It has been a much loved annual event now for over twenty years; all public events this Mipas Season must continue exactly as planned."

"But will you be safe?" asked Emma.

"Do not worry," said the Countess, "Major Schutem and his militia will protect me."

"Very good; until tomorrow then," said Emma.

"Thank you for your help," said the Countess, shaking Emma's hand. "And thank you, Mr Monkey!" she called to him. "Please attend the meeting after the March tomorrow, and also please come for lunch at Altlayton Hall again on Sunday at one."

"I will. Good night," he replied, as he continued tinkering with the various bits and pieces of the maze's winding gear.

"And good night to you also, Leo," said the Countess, shaking his hand. "It was a pleasure chatting to you; I do hope we may be able to continue our conversation sometime."

"I hope so too," said Leo with a smile and a nod. The Countess smiled back, then she and the Mayor departed.

"Well," said Bear, "what an eventful evening it has been!"

"Indeed," agreed Emma.

"So, what next?" asked Bull.

"I fancy Leo and I should return to my shop," said Emma. "What of you two gentlemen?"

"I think we will walk up into town with you and see if we can find Asiex again. Then we can give him a full briefing on what has occurred," said Bear.

"Yes, because he will not know that the Countess can see us," said Bull.

"Or perhaps he will," mused Emma. "Because the Countess obviously knows that Asiex is a druid from what she just said about discussing matters with him."

"Yes, it seems there's much that we don't know," said Bear.

"Indeed," agreed Bull, "I was rather shocked that the Countess could see us, I never expected that at all."

"Nor me, old boy," agreed Bear. "Just to think: all these long years and we never knew!"

"It is quite shocking," said Emma.

"I think the Countess knows a lot more than you have all given her credit for," said Leo. "I had quite an interesting chat with her while we were trapped."

"Really?" asked Bull.

"Why don't you tell us all about it while we walk up into town," said Bear.

"I will," said Leo.

They wished good night to the Magnetic Monkey and headed off into the night.

CHAPTER TWENTY-FIVE

THE POETRY COMPETITION PART I:
A MOTLEY CREW

I T HAD SNOWED AGAIN overnight, and the temperature remained well below freezing, yet it was a bright and very beautiful morning; the sun had risen at a quarter past eight, and by the time Leo and Emma had finished their breakfasts, shone down from a clear blue sky over the snow-covered rooftops of Altcastle. As Leo looked out into the backyard from Emma's parlour window, he considered that it was indeed a most suitable day for the Mayor's Mipas Magpie March, whatever that was – for other than the poster advertising the event, which he had seen on his first day in Altcastle in the library, he had no real idea what the event entailed.

"Will you care for any more tea?" asked Emma.

"No, thanks," said Leo. "I think Bull and Bear are due any second." Emma continued to tidy away the breakfast dishes and Leo started to put on his outdoor clothing.

"I do hope Annabel wins this morning," said Nevermore. "She made a great many improvements to her metre last night while you were at the Fairground."

"I hope so too," said Leo. "I'm sure she has a good chance."

Just then there was a knock on the door.

"No need to bother yourself, Leo: they will walk through it," shouted Emma from the kitchen. Sure enough, within seconds, Bull and Bear walked into the parlour.

"Well, it's official," said Bear, holding up that morning's copy of the Daily Tale, "it is finally Saturday the 15th of December!"

"It was Friday for such a long time this week," mused Bull, "that I fancy I shall miss Friday now!"

"Do not worry," said Emma, coming into the parlour and collecting her coat from the stand, "no doubt the Countess will find the need for four or five more Fridays in a row sometime in the not too distant future."

"Yes, I suppose so," agreed Bull.

"On another matter," interjected Bear, "we did manage to meet up with Asiex again last night after we left you – he was still in town, fortunately."

"We told him about everything that had happened in the mirror maze, about Flector and La Falot, and about the mist in the maze and the ransom note," added Bull.

"What did he say about it all?" asked Emma.

"He could really throw no more light on it beyond what we had already all concluded ourselves," said Bear. "Although, in speaking to him further, it became clear that he is on quite friendly terms with the Countess in fact, and knows her rather well. As had already come up previously, the two of them were aware that several magic mists had been summoned in the recent past and they had already held discussions about the matter…"

"But not come to any definite conclusions, unfortunately," interrupted Bull.

"Asiex did ask that you bring your gadget and wristwatch to the theatre this morning, Leo… he will need them, he said, to carry out some sort of analysis of something… although he was quite vague on the details," said Bear.

"OK," said Leo, "I will just go up to my room and fetch them." Leo headed off up the stairs.

"What could Asiex need them for?" asked Emma.

"No idea," said Bull.

"He started to explain something about *grounding* and *relativity*…" started Bear.

"And some other long words," added Bull.

"We had no idea what he was talking about quite frankly, but he said he would explain the whole matter to us this morning, once he had seen the items," concluded Bear. Just then, Leo came back.

"OK," he said. "I have both in my coat pocket."

"Very good. Are we all ready for the literary treat of the year, then?" asked Bear.

"How big a thing is this poetry competition?" asked Leo.

"Oh, it's a stupendous affair, old boy," said Bear, "and the first prize is five pounds!"

"And when almost everything costs only a ha'penny, five pounds is quite a remarkable amount of money!" added Bull. "That was one of the reasons that I wanted to enter this year!" he added pointedly while scowling at Bear.

"Oh, please don't start off again!" spluttered Bear. "I've had to listen to the same complaint all the way here, you know," he added, turning to Emma.

"Well," said Emma, "perhaps Mr Bull, you might start to compose your poem a little earlier next year, and you, Mr Bear, might be so kind as to afford him the opportunity of doing so." They each looked at the other and pulled their faces. "So, shall we go?"

"Indeed," said Bear, glancing at the carriage clock on the mantelpiece, "we may expect quite a queue to get in, I fancy – it was packed last year, and I don't suppose this year will be any different."

"I'm surprised so many people like poetry," said Leo as they walked out via the shop and into the street. "I think if such an event were to be held in my reality, not very many people would turn out."

"Not everyone will be attending to hear poetry," said Emma.

"Why else would they attend?" asked Leo.

"To laugh at the entries!" said Bull. "I might include myself, actually!"

"Laugh?" queried Leo.

"It is always the case each year that some of the entries are not terribly good," said Emma.

"It's not very kind to laugh at people's poems though," commented Leo.

"Well, it's the Altcastle way," said Bear.

The snow was crisp underfoot, and the air cold; a light breeze blew. The streets were quite busy, and most people were headed in the direction of the Sipby Theatre.

"Will we meet Annabel at the theatre?" asked Leo.

"Yes, but after it is all over," said Emma, "those entering sit in the first row of the stalls and need to be there early."

"I fancy she may be there already," said Bear, looking up at the Guildhall clock: it was twenty-five to nine by this time. They continued on along Penkhull Street and into London Road where, as Bear had predicted, large queues had formed by all of the entrances.

"No doubt, you will wish to amuse yourself by sitting behind those two old ladies again?" asked Emma with a wry smile.

"Naturally," said Leo, "shall we try the same door as last time?"

"Of course," said Emma.

After just ten minutes of queuing, they found themselves inside, and Bull and Bear were dispatched to see if they could ascertain the location of Gladys and Vera so that Leo could indulge his sense of humour. Due to their unique abilities, they had no problem moving through the crowd and had soon found the dear pair on the stairs leading up to the dress circle. Within moments of relaying the information to Leo and Emma, they were following close behind and managed to sit pretty much as at Mr Punch's trial, with Emma and Leo on the row behind and just to the right of Gladys and Vera. Bull and Bear stood in the aisle as the theatre was full again, and there were no spare seats.

Ice creams, chocolate cakes and other tasty treats were on sale at the bottom of every aisle like last time. Looking around, Leo was surprised to see so many people of his own age and younger in the theatre; at least one in every five people were children. The orchestra was playing away in the pit, like last time too; the tunes for today were, appropriately, the *Poet and Peasant Overture* by Franz von Suppé followed by some orchestrations from Act III of Giacomo Puccini's *La Bohème*.

"I wonder why the Countess is not in her box yet?" remarked Leo, looking over to where she was sat last time; only the Major and Princely Paws were present.

"She always acts as one of the judges," said Emma. "So she will sit on the stage with the other judges."

"How many judges are there?" asked Leo.

"Usually five," said Emma: "Mr Zenodotus, the Chief Librarian; Mr Chipping, the Headmaster of Altcastle Boys School; Miss Fysch, the Headmistress of Altcastle Girls School; the Mayor; and of course, the Countess, herself."

"Hmm… actually sounds like a proper panel of judges," said Leo. "Some of them are even qualified to judge a poetry competition… not at all what I would have expected!"

Emma just smiled. After a few more seconds the usual crew of trumpeters and prompters walked onto the sides of the stage's apron, and the orchestra fell silent. The trumpets sounded and onto the apron also walked Mayor Woodhay, but instead of his usual attire of a frock coat, today he was wearing evening dress with a black tailcoat over a white shirt and waistcoat with a white bow tie. As usual, he was wearing his tall top hat.

Oddly, looking around, Leo, then noticed that an unusually large number of men and boys were also wearing black tailcoats that morning, and most of the audience's female members were wearing black dresses with white bodices – it was an unusually black and white display of clothing.

"Good morning, ladies and gentlemen, boys and girls!" shouted out the Mayor. Without being prompted, the audience promptly replied according to expectation.

"Now then," he continued both cheerfully and enthusiastically, "we have a real literary treat for you all today, and a record number of entries!" The prompters displayed "CLAP", and everyone obliged as usual. The Mayor stood for a few seconds, and then the curtain rose to reveal a large desk to the left-hand side of the stage and a podium with a lectern in the centre; the desk had five chairs and the panel of judges, composed exactly as predicted by Emma, were already in situ, with one chair left vacant – presumably for the Mayor. Mayor Woodhay eventually waved his hands, the prompters closed their folios, and the clapping ceased. He took out a folded paper from the inside pocket of his tailcoat and opened it up.

"This year's entries are:
Spidersocks by Billy Sweeper;
The Mayor of Kippington Passed a New Law by Frederick Von Miter;
The Old Man's Clock by Mr Tapochki;
The Man With The Nine-Foot Nose by Will Sniffer;
Simple Simon Gets a Pie by Patrick Biplanket;
The Turnipecs by Tommy the Tinker;
The Song of the Fox and Monkey Pie by Peter Pykovsky;
The Remarkable Adventure of the Mouse and the Moose by Annabel Lee;
The Toothbrush and The Pastry Fork by Jill Hill;
Only a Puppet by Asiex the Woodcutter."

The prompters displayed "CLAP" and "CHEER", and everyone did so. After a few seconds, the Mayor called for silence.

"As usual, each contestant will come to the podium in turn and announce the title of his or her poem, then give their recitation. Contestants may also say a few words about their poem by way of an introduction should they wish to do so. Good luck to all!"

Mayor Woodhay then went and took his seat at the judges' table with the others. Billy Sweeper soon walked up onto the stage and took his place on the podium; he had his poem in one hand and a snow shovel in the other. Billy smiled a lot as he prepared himself, and then went on to recite a bizarre set of verses about someone called *Spidersocks* who could walk up walls, but only if clad in the appropriate socks. When he had finished, he made a small bow, and most people clapped; albeit not very enthusiastically.

"Why don't the prompters display anything?" asked Leo.

"The Mayor will only direct them if the Countess tells him to because she thinks something is particularly good or particularly bad," replied Emma, "otherwise he will let the audience decide for itself." Leo nodded and looked over to Gladys and Vera, but they didn't seem at all moved by the poem and had nothing to say. Soon enough, the next contestant was at the podium, and the audience settled down again to hear his recitation.

"Good morning to you all," said Frederick Von Miter. "My poem is called *The Mayor of Kippington Passed a New Law.*" Frederick then went on, a little nervously at first, to deliver a strange ballad concerning the sucking of dogs' noses and how the eponymous Mayor of Kippington – no doubt a fictional town invented in his own crazed mind, had tried to outlaw such a practice.

The poem contained such literary treasures as "the sucking of noses throughout the whole area, is as common as snow in south Altavaria" and "the sucking of noses is horrid indeed, and those who do it cannot succeed"; the latter sentiment being one that the audience could probably identify with. As Frederick Von Miter finished, he also took a small bow and then looked around the audience apprehensively. A few people clapped, but not many, and a dim burble of muted commenting could be heard. Some people were sniggering, others laughing out loud.

"Ooh, Vera," said Gladys, "I've never heard the like, I haven't… I don't think her Ladyship will want people sucking noses, I don't!"

"Ooh, no Gladys," she replied, "it's a beakery for sure. I don't think he's right in the head, you know… and he's got a foreign-sounding name as well."

"That's what I thought," said Gladys, "it makes you wonder what that other fellow puts in his sausages, it does… you know, that Googenmuncher fellow… he's something to do with Altavaria as well, you know."

"You can't trust them, at all," opined Vera, "I fancy it must be the weather that affects them."

Leo and Emma, said nothing, preferring to be entertained by Gladys' and Vera's commentary.

Such was the continuing chatter that the prompters had to display "SILENCE" so that Mr Tapochki, who had now taken over the place at the podium, could start his recitation. He looked quite tense as he waited for the audience to settle, and he shook as he held his poem with both hands in front of him. Within seconds, silence was achieved, and Mr Tapochki began to recite his entry, *The Old Man's Clock*, which wasn't really very good but was mercifully short. Again there was only subdued clapping at the end, but much less chatter than last time, and at least no laughing.

"Ooh, that was a short one," said Vera.

"Thank goodness," retorted Gladys. "I didn't know what he was going on about, I didn't. I think he should stick to selling slippers in the Market Hall!"

"Ooh yes, he does do a nice slipper… very warm I find them," agreed Vera.

Emma and Leo looked at each other and shook their heads. Mr Tapochki looked somewhat dejected as he left the stage, passing

Will Sniffer who was coming up in the opposite direction. Will Sniffer was very well dressed and had an air of great confidence about him; he beamed with happiness as he unfolded the paper that his poem was written on. His poem concerned a man who had a nine-foot-long nose which, unsurprisingly, made it difficult to smell whatever food he had in front of him, although he had little difficulty in smelling other people's meals – particularly if they were sat about nine feet away from him, no doubt.

"I think the rhymes were a bit better in that," said Leo, as Will Sniffer departed. There were a few more claps for his effort than there had been for the previous entry, yet nothing very substantial.

"I fancy Annabel has a very good chance of winning from what we have heard so far," replied Emma smugly. Leo nodded in agreement.

Patrick Biplanket soon took his place as next in line and coughed several times to clear his throat. He had very large eyes, thick glasses and bore himself with what Leo thought was a somewhat crazed demeanour, as he looked about the audience licking his lips and smiling to himself.

"I've always felt sorry for Simple Simon," he suddenly shouted angrily, bringing everyone to an abrupt silence. "It's not fair! That's what I say! Here's my poem, it's called: Simple Simon Gets a Pie.

Simple Simon met a pieman,
Going to the fair;
Says Simple Simon to the pieman,
"Let me taste your ware."

Says the pieman to Simple Simon,
"Show me first your penny."
Says Simple Simon to the pieman,
"Indeed, I have not any."

Says the pieman to Simple Simon,
"Then you cannot taste my ware:
I can't let rascals like yourself,
Have pies for nought but air!"

Says Simple Simon to the pieman,
"I have a flintlock here."
The Pieman's face turned white as ash,
As he looked down in fear.

Says Simple Simon to the pieman,
"Now give me ALL your ware!
Don't try to run or get away,
You haven't got a prayer!"

So the pieman did as told,
And Simon took the pies;
He gave the chap a roguish wink,
There was laughter in his eyes.

Says Simple Simon to himself,
"This is the life for me!
Whatever I want at pistol point
Hard work I'll never see!"

So Simon gorged himself on pies,
And other pieman-wares.
Says Simple Simon to himself,
"It's theft, but no one cares!"

"I'll take what I like from wimps like that,
They'll never tell me nay;
They'll either give me what I want,
Or just cry and run away."

So Simon spent his life in crime,
And stole from whom he pleased.
But by the end, he'd grown too fat,
From gobbling all he'd seized!"

Patrick Biplanket, smiled madly again as he finished and looked around, seemingly in anticipation of appreciation. Almost no-one clapped, however, and a man two rows in front of where Emma and Leo were sitting broke down in tears and started to weep uncontrollably. Other members of the audience shouted "BOO!" or "GET OFF!".

"That is Mr Aspick," said Emma with a smile. "It would appear the poem has upset him: he makes and sells pork pies, you see."

"I see," said Leo.

"Ooh, Vera, he's a rotten sort, upsetting poor old Mr Aspick like that!" said Gladys.

"Ooh, he is… and Mr Aspick makes such lovely pies, Gladys; I had one yesterday in fact… it even had a little holly leaf on it in pastry."

"Disqualified! Disqualified!" shouted Mayor Woodhay, jumping up excitedly after briefly speaking to the other judges. "That is an outrageous poem! You are hereby completely disqualified and banned from re-entering the competition for three years!" He gestured with the back of his right hand for Patrick Biplanket to get off the stage, which he did but not without pulling his face, first at the judges and then at the audience as he went. "Next entry, please!" declared the Mayor, resuming his seat.

It was Tommy the Tinker's turn next, who quickly came up onto to the podium, holding an exercise book which he opened at about the middle. Tommy the Tinker seemed like a sincere and calm sort of fellow and had quite a soft and attractive voice which suited well with the theme and metre of his poem, *The Turnipecs*.

As he concluded, the audience gave his entry quite universal and warm applause – even a few cheers. Gladys and Vera seemed to like it too as they clapped without commenting. Emma looked a little perturbed, possibly considering it somewhat *Edward Learish* and thereby competing with Annabel's entry.

The next entry had been announced as being by a Peter Pykovsky, but in fact about ten people walked onto the stage, some of them with musical instruments. The panel of judges looked rather confused as the leader of the troop set about positioning them all.

"What's this?" asked Leo.

"I do not know," said Emma. "It is most unusual. The man in charge is Mr Pullem, the landlord of Ye Olde Fox and Monkey Inn… out on the Keele road. It would appear that they are going to set the poem to music."

"Now then," said Mr Pullem finally. "By way of introduction, I would like to explain that Mr Pykovsky has written his poem, *The Song of the Fox and Monkey Pie*, in the form of a song, much like Lewis Carroll's *Lobster Quadrille*… so without further ado here it is:

A Fox and Monkey Pie is a very fine thing indeed;
Our own dear Mayor himself eats one, whenever he needs a
    good feed.
If ever he calls for one of our pies,
And we have none left, the poor man cries.
Our singing waiters of loud, strong voice,
Will always praise a rightful choice.
When choosing on what they wish to dine,
Those who have let their wisdom shine,
And chosen a Fox and Monkey Pie,
Will hear their waiter heartily cry:

Chorus
"He's ordered a Fox and Monkey Pie!
And from the kitchen, it soon will fly!
Tasty, delicious and ready to eat;
Oh, what a pie! What a wonderful treat!
The finest pie that money can buy;
The finest delight to be seen by an eye!
Oh, the Fox and Monkey Pie!
Yes, the Fox and Monkey Pie!
The finest delight to be seen by an eye!"

And even the Worshipful Countess herself,
Has taken pies home from our kitchen shelf.
Such fresh potatoes, diced so fine,
And bound in a jelly of gravy and wine.
Such beautiful, tender pieces of meat,
Cased in a pastry of finest wheat -
Wheat deluxe of finest grind;
No one can leave such a pie behind!

& Chorus

The Countess herself long since ruled that:
"No plate must contain any gristle or fat!
For serving such is beakery pure,
And so all chefs must always ensure,
That no such thing can be found in a pie!"
The ACES, of course, will keep a close eye,
And report to the relevant authority,
Any such chef who so offends;
And there he will stand without any friends,
While Justice Bender hands him a fine,
His beakery to underline!

& Chorus

Both beasts of land and birds of air,
Can't turn their nosiks from pies so fair.
And sure, no man can well prepare,
For those terrible words, so few can bear:
"Sorry," we say. "There are no pies left!"
And the broken traveller leaves bereft:
Sad and hungry, with bitter tears -
On realisation of his fears.

& Chorus

There's no finer thing to put in your eye,
Than the sight of a Fox and Monkey Pie!
So saddle up, make fit your steed,
And from Altcastle ride at speed,
Along the road that leads out west,
Where pies are known to be the best.
Waste no minute! Proceed with haste!
Always imagining the lovely taste,
Dash on! With clopping horse hoof din,
To Ye Olde Fox and Monkey Inn!
Where Mr Gristleless waits to bake,
And serve you a pie of finest steak!"

Mr Pullem had acted as the soloist for the verses, with several of his waiters playing a tune that fitted in with the lyrics, while others joined in to sing the choruses. It was in truth quite a show and was met with very warm applause and much cheering from the audience.

"Hmm… shameful," mumbled Emma. "That was nothing short of a blatant advertisement for Fox and Monkey pies."

"Do you think the judges will like that one more than Annabel's?" asked Leo.

"I should most certainly think that it will be judged technically poor on account of the verses being of unequal lengths; I most certainly hope so, in any case," she replied disgruntledly.

"Shall we take the stagecoach out when the snow clears and treat ourselves, Vera?" said Gladys.

"Ooh, yes, why don't we, dear," replied Vera. "We haven't had one of those delicious pies for quite some time."

"There you are!" scoffed Emma. "Just as I said: blatant advertising. I should not be at all surprised if half the people in this theatre are not now discussing when they shall next go out to the Fox and Monkey Inn!"

The applause and cheering slowly abated and Mr Pullem and his troop eventually stopped smiling and waving to everyone, and left the stage.

It was finally Annabel's turn, and she made her way up to the podium. Unlike everyone else, she did not have a copy of her poem with her, preferring to recite it from memory.

"My poem is a tribute to Mr Edward Lear, whom I greatly esteem," she started. "It is called: *The Remarkable Adventure of The Mouse and The Moose.*"

Annabel then went on to give a very well delivered recitation which was almost identical, although a little more polished in terms of the metre, to the version which she had previously given in Emma's parlour.

The audience clapped quite loudly, but not as much as they had done for *The Song of the Fox and Monkey Pie*. There were also one or two cheers, but nothing more very significant. Annabel bowed slightly and smiled during the applause, then left the stage as the clapping abated, crossing on the stairs with the penultimate poet, Jill Hill, as she did so. Jill took up her position at the podium and unfolded the paper carrying her poem.

Jill's poem was truly bizarre, although clever in having a mirrored rhyme scheme, and told the implausible story of how a toothbrush and a pastry fork had fallen in love and decided to elope. In the second stanza, while on their honeymoon, they also came across a rather rude sugar spoon. After the conclusion of the piece, the applause was quite muted, and Jill looked somewhat disappointed. Many people were laughing again, and there was a lot of chattering.

"Ooh, Vera," said Gladys, "you wouldn't credit it, would you?"

"Ooh, no, you wouldn't at all," she said. "Fancy leaving them out like that… and then letting a thing like that happen! It's no wonder she couldn't cope!"

"I wonder where they are now?" mused Gladys.

"Ooh, it doesn't bear thinking about, does it?" replied Vera. Emma and Leo chuckled as they listened.

"Now," said Emma, "I fancy this next and last entry will be the biggest risk to Annabel's winning."

"It's Asiex?" asked Leo.

"Indeed, and most years he wins in fact."

CHAPTER TWENTY-SIX

THE POETRY COMPETITION PART II:

EQUAL RIGHTS FOR PUPPETS

A SIEX PASSED JILL AS she was returning to her seat and went on to take up his place on the podium.

"My poem for this year's contest is called:

ONLY A PUPPET

Only a puppet he was made,
From a block he came to life;
And if that wasn't bad enough,
He got Judy for a wife.

Every day she beats his head,
With sausages or wood.
There's not one day of peace for him,
Nor one that's any good.

In heat and cold, he must perform,
In summer and in winter.
Each day his face is slapped so hard,
His nose begins to splinter.

The crowd applaud, the children laugh,
The ha'pennies all add up.
But when the coins are all poured out,
Go little to his cup.

And when the shows have run their course,
Because it's getting late,
Off go the crowds, back to their homes,
But Punch goes in a crate.

No home for him. No fire. No hearth.
No place to call his own:
Just a broken, bashed-up crate.
No wonder he should moan.

One hundred years he's lived like this,
One hundred years or more.
Then one cold day he just got tired,
And headed for the door.

So, yes, it's true! He tried to flee,
To escape the puppet show;
But he was caught before too long,
As he had no place to go.

The Constable arrested him,
And put him in a cage.
They said he'd done some beakery,
Because he'd left the stage.

At trial, they said he'd done worse still -
He turned to a reptile:
Though actually it wasn't Punch,
It was the crocodile.

He "Equal Rights for Puppets" called,
But few there chanced to care.
They hardly even let him speak;
It wasn't very fair!

That "Punch is Guilty!" so said all.
They fined him all he had;
And sent him back to work again,
Although it made him sad.

And so today, as he was told,
He'll be back on the stage,
No matter if he wants or not:
A puppet's rights outrage!

So spare a thought for Mr Punch,
Before you leave to dine:
And maybe give him a little tip,
To buy a glass of wine."

As Asiex finished, no-one clapped at all, no-one that is except for
Leo and Emma, and just one more solitary, little pair of hands
a few rows behind them. They turned their heads to look who
it was, and there on the end of a row sat Mr Punch. The rest of

the theatre remained in stunned silence, waiting to see what the reaction of the Countess might be. Asiex turned to look at her and raised his eyebrows while smiling. The Countess shook her head and squinted at him, tight-lipped.

A few seconds passed, and then the Countess stood up... and clapped. The Mayor also started clapping at that point as did the other judges, and soon enough the applause spread around the whole audience. Much cheering could also be heard. The Countess conferred with the other judges for about a minute while the clapping and cheering continued, then stood up and made her way to the podium. Asiex stepped down to return to his seat, and she took his place. The prompters displayed "SILENCE", and everyone quickly settled down.

"My dear citizens," said the Countess, in a very loud and clear voice. "I have a terrible report to make to you concerning a beakery of the most astonishing nature!" The audience gasped. "Last night at the fairground," she continued, "it was discovered that the new mirror maze is defective!" The audience gasped again. "Yes! Defective I can tell you; and this the fault of the foreigner, Mr Flector, and our own former citizen, Monsieur La Falot, who has now fled from the Borough of Altcastle with his accomplice."

The audience remained in silence as the Countess glanced up at the private box where Ebenezer Cromwell was again sat with his usual entourage, minus, of course, La Falot. "We do not yet know who else may be involved in this beakery of supplying a faulty maze, but rest assured, we shall soon find out!" The audience at this point broke into chattering, and the prompters jumped up and down on the apron holding their "SILENCE" pages open.

"Nor do we currently know the whereabouts of Flector and La Falot but Mayor Woodhay shall this afternoon be writing to the Mayors of all the eight adjoining boroughs with a request to apprehend the two of them if seen. Also, I must announce that it has now come to light that Monsieur La Falot perjured himself yesterday at the trial when he lied about Mr Punch's contract: it was in fact, as Mr Skuze suggested, a shopping list all along."

Gasps rose from the audience, and people shouted, "Down with La Falot!" and "Damn the hamster!" Leo and Emma looked at each other and nodded.

"In light of Mr Punch's wrongful conviction based on the false testimony of that devilish hamster La Falot, together with La Falot's beakery in conspiring with Flector to defraud the Borough of Altcastle by charging money for a faulty maze, I have decided to confiscate all property belonging to both Flector and La Falot!" The crowd applauded loudly, and many people cheered as well. The Countess allowed the audience to vent their emotions and then continued: "The mirror maze will be handed over to Mr Magnetic Monkey and his white rats to own and run, and the La Falot Puppet Theatre will be handed over to Mr Punch, who will be the new owner. Mayor Haywood will attend to the necessary paperwork!" The audience once again erupted into wild cheering, with many people standing up and jumping up and down.

"Well," said Emma, "that is indeed a turn of events!"

"I told you last night: the Countess isn't all that bad. I think she means well, you know, despite her odd ways," said Leo.

"Perhaps you are correct," mused Emma. "Or perhaps the time you spent together has had a beneficial effect upon her?" she added with a wry smile. "But I do wonder with all of this going on, who has actually won the poetry competition; as it seems Asiex's poem has been very well received, even to the extent that not only has Mr Punch now been given equal rights, he is also the proud new owner of a complete puppet theatre."

"Ooh, Vera," said Gladys, "you can't believe how things can change in just a day, can you?"

"Ooh, you can't, Gladys... who would have thought the horrible little thing would be innocent after all?" said Vera.

"Well, he's still got a big nose though," added Gladys.

"Ooh, he has," agreed Vera.

The Countess made no attempt to calm the crowd, and the clapping and cheering persisted for some minutes before finally dying down of its own accord.

"Lastly then," said the Countess, "before I call upon Mr Zenodotus to announce the results of the Poetry Competition, I must warn you all to remain vigilant for both Mr Flector and Monsieur La Falot. If anyone should see them or hear of them, then they should report it immediately to the Constable or to a soldier or indeed to any representative of ACES; please do not delay in making a report as these vile creatures have stolen a considerable amount of money from our Borough and therefore from all of us! I will now ask Mr Zenodotus to take over." There was more clapping, cheering and chattering while the Countess returned to her seat and Mr Zenodotus took to the podium. After more prompting, everyone fell silent.

"As Chief Librarian of the Borough of Altcastle, it always gives me great pleasure to announce the results of this excellent annual contest, and of course as usual, a book containing all of this year's poems to be published and added to both the town, and all village libraries for the continuing enjoyment and literary edification of all." There was some small clapping at this point during which time Mr Zenodotus referred to his notebook, no doubt to check the results.

"So," he continued, "in reverse order as usual: this year's third prize goes to Mr Peter Pykovsky for *The Song of the Fox and Monkey Pie*." The audience clapped loudly, and there was much cheering, as Mr Pykovsky and Mr Pullem came up together to accept the certificate and a one-pound note, which a stagehand came from the wings to bring. Mr Zenodotus shook hands with them both and congratulated them on their entry. After they had stepped down, he continued with second place, which went to Tommy the Tinker for his poem *The Turnipecs*. Tommy also received a certificate and the princely sum of two pounds, waving to the audience who clapped and cheered as he returned to his seat.

"Hmm... I am surprised that Annabel has won nothing," said Emma; "as the first prize, I feel sure, will now go to Asiex, and I fancy Annabel's poem was better than Tommy's."

"Well," Mr Zenodotus carried on, "that brings us to the first prize, and for the first time, the judges have decided to award a joint first prize as we could really not decide at all between *The Remarkable Adventure of the Mouse and the Moose* and *Only a Puppet*. So, can I please ask Annabel Lee and Asiex the Woodcutter to make their way to the stage!" The audience again roared into applause and cheering, and many people waved their scarves as Annabel and Asiex collected their certificate and five pounds each.

"You may keep the certificate, Annabel, as there is only one... I have many already from previous years," said Asiex.

"O thank you," said Annabel appreciatively, "it is really most considerate of you."

Mr Zenodotus shook hands with them both and congratulated them on their entries.

"Well," said Emma, "this is a most satisfactory result I fancy, and how generous to give them each five pounds instead of having them share the first prize of five pounds between them."

"Yes, indeed," agreed Leo, "I think the result is very fair actually." The clapping and cheering continued for some time as Annabel and Asiex returned to their seats, and the Countess took the place of Mr Zenodotus at the podium. Soon enough, the prompters all displayed "SILENCE", and the audience simmered down.

"I do hope you have all enjoyed this year's competition. As Mr Zenodotus has pointed out, all of the Borough's libraries will have the book containing this year's entries by mid-January... minus, of course, Mr Biplanket's entry which was a disgraceful exhortation to theft and violence and greatly upset poor Mr Aspick and, I am sure, many other piemen present."

This condemnation of the poem *Simple Simon Gets a Pie* elicited some spontaneous clapping which the Countess soon gesticulated to calm. "It only remains for me then to exhort you all to join in the annual Mayor's Mipas Magpie March which will commence at eleven o'clock sharp in front of the Guildhall as usual. See you there soon! Thank you all!"

"Four cheers for her Worshipfulness," shouted a man in the front row of the dress circle, and he proceeded to lead the audience in the usual *hip, hip, hooraying*, which the Countess gratefully acknowledged before leaving the stage, with the other judges, at its conclusion.

"Well," said Emma, "that was all very good in the end!"

"It was," agreed Leo. "I'm sure Mr Punch will be very pleased now that he owns the puppet theatre himself."

"Indeed. So, shall we go to find Asiex and see if he has your mist potion?" she suggested.

"Yes, let's do that," said Leo.

CHAPTER TWENTY-SEVEN

THE POETRY COMPETITION PART III:

SOMETHING SPECIAL

L EO AND EMMA WAITED for a few minutes while the theatre cleared a little and the queues for the exits reduced, then they headed down to the main foyer. On the way, they met up with Bull and Bear who had been standing at the back as usual.

"We'll go to find Asiex," said Bull; Bear had already gone on ahead and was moving through the crowd – quite literally.

"Very good," said Emma. "Leo and I will just go to congratulate Annabel and then wait for you two and Asiex by the statue at the front."

"Perfect," said Bull, and off he went.

After only a few minutes of searching, Bull and Bear located Asiex close to the northern side entrance of the theatre where he was speaking privately with the Countess. The two of them seemed quite deeply absorbed in whatever they were discussing and didn't notice Bull's and Bear's arrival.

Major Schutem was loitering around close by and, very unusually, was armed with both a sabre and a revolver. The Countess's four-horse carriage was waiting for her in the side alley, and no less than six soldiers of the militia could be seen standing next to it; they were also armed, with rifles – also a most unusual circumstance for Altcastle, as weapons were usually only ever seen when the soldiers were on parade for some special occasion. The head of Princely Paws could be seen poking out of the carriage window; he was no doubt waiting for his mistress.

"Better not disturb him, while he's speaking to the Countess," said Bear.

"Quite so, old boy," agreed Bull.

Meanwhile, back in the foyer, Annabel had appeared from the stalls, and came up to Emma and Leo, holding her winner's certificate, which was now framed in a very ornate wooden gilded frame.

"Congratulations, dear," said Emma, hugging her friend and kissing her on the cheek.

"Yes, well done, indeed," said Leo, shaking Annabel's hand.

"I cannot describe how pleased I am," said Annabel, beaming.

"It is really very remarkable, dear, especially considering it is the first time you had entered," said Emma.

"And just to think, Emma, I will even have my poem published in the annual yearbook of the competition as the first poem – Mr Zenodotus has just told that he will place my poem before that of Asiex, as he has been first so many times before. He also gave me this lovely frame for my certificate."

"How nice," said Emma, "he is such a lovely gentleman."

"Are you ready, Annabel?" came a voice from behind. It was Annabel's dear old mother.

"I am," she said. "I must be going, as I promised to have coffee with my mother and aunt before the Magpie March – my aunt lives just around the corner in Well Street. Shall I see you later at your shop?"

"Yes, we shall be there shortly after the opening of the March," said Emma, "around quarter past eleven… I do not think it worth staying any more than a quarter of an hour."

"Lovely," said Annabel, "see you later, then… see you later, Leo!"

"See you later," replied Leo.

Bull and Bear continued to wait while the Countess and Asiex finished their conversation. At the end of their chat, the Countess handed Asiex a small white envelope and then left the theatre and took up a seat in her carriage, escorted by the Major.

"Good morning, Asiex," said Bear, approaching him.

"And congratulations on your latest victory in the poetry competition," added Bull.

"I think it's at least your tenth win, eh?" enquired Bear.

"Good morning," said Asiex cheerfully. "I seem to have lost count now, I win so often, although it seems in future I shall have some worthy competition from Miss Annabel Lee."

"Indeed," agreed Bear.

"So, how has it gone regarding the magic mist potion?" asked Bull.

"Well enough, I believe," said Asiex. "I have prepared the potion in accordance with notes I had taken previously; it only remains for a small test to be carried out."

"A test?" retorted Bear.

"Indeed," said Asiex, "as I have never conjured up a magic mist before, it will be far too risky to send Leo into one without being absolutely certain that he will end up in the correct place and time; therefore I will need a volunteer to test the mist potion prior to using it for Leo."

"Yes, yes," agreed Bear, "quite right… good thinking!"

"I shall be happy to volunteer," said Bull.

"Or I," said Bear.

"Perhaps both of you then," said Asiex thoughtfully, "then if something is wrong, at least you will be together."

"And if something is wrong, what could happen?" asked Bear.

"Well," said Asiex, "the components of a magic mist potion can be many and various – some affect both space and time, some only space and some only time. In this case, I have used only those ingredients which affect time, and the time that the other side of the mist will give access to is the exact time which Leo specified. As to the space component, the alternate reality which the mist will open into will be determined by one last component which I will need to add. So, all should be well and go according to plan, but to answer your question, if something goes wrong, you could end up at the wrong time."

"I see," said Bull. "And what is the last component that you need to add?"

"Something that came from the reality we wish to gain access to," said Asiex. "A small hair from Leo's head should be ideal."

"Hmm," nodded Bull.

"Makes sense," said Bear.

"So, shall we go to Leo and Emma, they are waiting at the front, near the statue," suggested Bull.

"Yes, let's go," said Asiex.

The three of them soon found Emma and Leo, waiting as arranged. Asiex explained to both of them what he had already told Bull and Bear, and then took a small hair from Leo and added it to the mist potion which he had with him in a small glass vial. The potion hissed and smoked once the hair had been added, and then Asiex replaced the cork stopper and shook the mixture.

"There we are, then," he said. "We are ready to make the test!"

"Shall we do it on the same bridge that Leo used when he first arrived in Altcastle?" asked Bear.

"Indeed," confirmed Asiex. "Now, Leo, do you have your wristwatch and gadget?"

"Yes," said Leo, taking them both out. Asiex inspected first the watch, making sure that it was fully wound, and then Leo's mobile phone.

"How does it work?" asked Asiex. Leo took back the phone and showed them all how the side button switched it on. He explained all the symbols at the top of the screen, including which ones showed network and 4G connection. Asiex asked quite a few questions, always ensuring that Bull and Bear fully understood how to operate the phone and what the symbols meant. Once he was completely satisfied, he gave the wristwatch to Bear and the phone to Bull.

"Now then," he said, "when you pass through the mist, halfway across the bridge, the first thing you will need to confirm is that the ground beneath your paws and hooves has changed from cobblestone to the smoother type of surface that Leo has previously explained. Secondly, you will need to look at the second hand of the wristwatch, which should start moving again once it is back in its own reality, and also at the screen of the mobile phone, which should show both a network and an internet connection as Leo has just explained. All of this should happen in a matter of just a few seconds; in any case, whether these things happen or not, return to the Altcastle reality after no more than twenty seconds – I have calculated, based on the quantities of the ingredients I have used, that the portal between the two realities will remain open for only about forty seconds – if you do not return in that time, I will have to open another portal. Do you both understand?"

"Completely," said Bull.

"Absolutely," confirmed Bear.

"But what if something goes wrong?" asked Leo.

"Well," said Asiex, "that is why I am going to remain firmly in this reality – if there is a problem at least then I still have access to all my ingredients and notes and can try to rectify the issue… but I am quite sure I have not made any error – I just want to be one hundred percent sure before we send you through."

"OK," said Leo.

"I'm quite sure it will be fine," said Bear reassuringly.

"It's a pity we'll only get to see your reality for twenty

seconds when you've had such an adventure in ours," added Bull comically.

"I suppose so," said Leo, with a smile.

"So," said Asiex, "we shall go and conduct our experiment, and as I also want to make notes about how far the mist spreads either side of that bridge and for how long, so that I can try to glean more information to help me in the matter of those miscreants Flector and La Falot, shall we agree to meet at the bridge at midday?"

"Yes, that will give us enough time to see the commencement of the March, and go back to the shop so that Leo can change back into his Newcastle clothes," said Emma.

"Excellent," said Asiex, "that's sorted then. One last matter... further to the briefing I had last night from you two gentlemen, and the chat that I had this morning with the Countess, there are to be two meetings over this weekend regarding the appearance of these recent magic mists and the fiendish plans of Flector and La Falot. One meeting will be this afternoon in the Municipal Hall, after the Magpie March, which will be attended by the Countess, Mayor Woodhay, Constable Cuffem, Major Schutem and Mr Magnetic Monkey to discuss practical matters, and then another tomorrow lunchtime at the Countess' Hall in Altlayton, which will be attended by Mr Monkey and myself, to discuss the more esoteric, magical, aspects of the matter. The Countess did ask me to also invite you, Bull and Bear, and you also Emma, to the meeting tomorrow; because, as Leo will have left by then, you three will be best placed to provide any details of Leo's reality, as we suspect that may be where Flector and La Falot are now hiding."

"Really?" asked Emma, somewhat startled.

"I have thought long and hard about it all night," said Asiex, "and if you think about it, it makes quite good sense."

"How so, Asiex?" asked Bear.

"Well, consider this: these mists – which we think now number six in total, including the one in which Leo arrived here, and the one by which Flector and La Falot escaped last night –

were certainly created deliberately and for the express purpose of moving persons, and probably items, between realities. Now if, as we suspect, they were created by accomplices of Flector, then the one which brought Leo here obviously was created by them at some other point on the brook that was close enough to the bridge which Leo crossed to get here. Now, of course, if that is the case, then they, whoever they are, were crossing to and from Leo's reality – hence why he got caught up in their mist."

"Hmm… yes, yes," said Bear. "That all makes sense… at the same time that Leo came here, they were moving someone or something from, or to, Leo's Newcastle at some other point along the course of the Lyme Brook."

"Exactly," said Asiex.

"But that means that Flector and La Falot are now in Leo's Newcastle," said Emma. "That cannot be good!"

"It isn't," said Asiex, "but please bear in mind, that neither of them knows anything about Leo… not who he is, where he is from or what he looks like – they will never have noticed him, and they clearly could not see into the maze last night, so I believe there to be no risk they could recognise him."

"Hmm… makes sense," agreed Leo.

"So, the Countess believes that we here in Altcastle, could benefit greatly from some insight into the type of things that exist in Leo's reality and since you three must know a great deal about that by now, the Countess wants you to assist by joining our committee… so what shall I tell her?"

"Hmm…" mused Bear "…what an extraordinary turn of events."

"Indeed," said Emma.

"We've lived here for decades, just minding our own business, and didn't even know the Countess could see us, and now we're being invited to join a committee…"

"Perhaps we should be honoured," opined Bear.

"What do you think, Leo?" asked Bull.

"Perhaps you should read this, first, Leo," said Asiex. Asiex reached into his pocket and gave Leo the white envelope which the Countess had given to him earlier. "Open it up," he said. Leo opened the envelope; it contained a short handwritten note, another document, and two black and white photographs, one marked *R E Flector,* and one marked *P La Falot.*

"What does the note say?" asked Emma. Leo held it out so that they could all read it.

My Dear Leo

It was a great pleasure to speak with you last night, and also an interesting experience to hear your objections to some of my policies of governance! Notwithstanding our disagreements on some matters of such policy, I do hope that you understand that I always attempt to act in the best interests of the whole Borough of Altcastle-under-Lyme and its citizens.

With that in mind, and considering what Asiex will have told you concerning Flector and La Falot before giving you this note, I would like you to seriously consider accepting the enclosed appointment at a salary of four Altland shillings per week. Your first mission will be to locate the hamsters Flector and La Falot and report back whatever you can find out.

Yours truly
D Sipby

Rt. Hon. Lady Debra Sipby
Countess of Altcastle-under-Lyme

"My goodness," said Emma, "and what is *the enclosed appointment?*"

Leo opened the other enclosed paper:

AULSS
Altcastle-under-Lyme Secret Service

OFFICIAL APPOINTMENT WARRANT
Mr Leo Marcus
is hereby appointed a
Special Agent
of

AULSS

[Altcastle-under-Lyme Secret Service]

SIGNED THIS 15TH DAY OF DECEMBER, IN THE YEAR 2018.

N Woodhay	*D Sipby*
Rt. Hon. N. Woodhay	Rt. Hon. D. Sipby
Lord Mayor	Countess
of	of
Altcastle-under-Lyme	Altcastle-under-Lyme

"By gad, Sir," said Bear, "what an honour!"

"Quite so, old boy, and four shillings a week is very good indeed!" added Bull. "Imagine how many chocolate fancies a chap could buy with four shillings!"

"How typical," complained Bear, "with all that's going on, all you can think of is chocolate fancies!"

"Well, Leo, what do you think?" asked Asiex.

"But how am I to report back?" replied Leo.

"Assuming that the potion works – and I am very confident that it will – I will be giving you another bottle of the same potion which you can use in your Newcastle to come back here across the same bridge, or indeed any other crossing over Lyme Brook that you choose," said Asiex. "The potion simply creates a mist that forms a portal, so it works equally in either reality, simply creating a gateway between the two."

"I see," said Leo excitedly. "Actually I'm really glad to hear that because although, of course, I want to go home to see my mum and dad, I also like it here now… I was quite sad that I was going to leave today. The thought that I would never see Bull, Bear and Emma again was quite upsetting."

"Well," said Asiex, "fortunately, you will be able to visit your friends whenever you like."

"Very well then," said Leo, "I accept! And I assume these two photos are there so that I can identify them?"

"Correct," said Asiex. "I will let the Countess know later this afternoon that you are now Altcastle's first and only Secret Service Special Agent. And what about the rest of you?"

"Hmm…" said Bear "…well, as Leo is now a Special Agent, I think it will be best if we join the intelligence committee to help out as best we can."

"I agree," concurred Bull.

"As do I," said Emma.

"Excellent," said Asiex. "With all of us working together, we are sure to be able to defeat the evil machinations of Flector and La Falot, and whoever else might be involved in plotting against our peaceful way of life." He took out and checked his pocket watch. "We had better be off then, gentlemen, and let Emma and Leo get up to town before the Magpie March starts."

"Quite so," agreed Bear, and the three of them set off for Lyme Valley.

"We shall better be getting along, then, also," said Emma.

"Yes, let's go; I am very interested to see this Magpie March, it sounds completely mad!" said Leo.

"Oh, it is indeed," said Emma, and with that, the two of them headed up London Road, back towards the town centre.

CHAPTER TWENTY-EIGHT

THE MAYOR'S MIPAS
MAGPIE MARCH

A S THEY ARRIVED IN front of the Guildhall, they saw that
a sign writer had already been busy changing the plaque
for the puppet theatre in favour of its new owner, Mr
Punch. Instead of reading "La Falot Puppet Company Limited" it
now read "Mr G A Pulcinella Puppet Theatre Limited", Giovanni
Antonio Pulcinella being Mr Punch's real name, of course. He was
there watching, smiling and waving to everyone who passed by, as
the sign writer finished the job off for him.

"Well, he seems happy enough," said Leo.

"Indeed he does," agreed Emma. "Shall we wait over by the
Castle Hotel; the Magpie March will commence within minutes."
The two of them walked over to the Hotel, while more and more
people continued to turn up, largely dressed in black and white
clothing; most of the males wore black tailcoats over white shirts,
waistcoats and white bow ties – most also wore black top hats.

Females predominantly wore black dresses and bonnets with some sort of white bodice or scarf.

"Is it because they're supposed to look like magpies?" asked Leo, observing each newcomer as he or she joined the gathering in the square in front of the Guildhall.

"Precisely so," confirmed Emma.

Before too long, Mayor Woodhay turned up in front of the stage and started shaking hands with everyone. He was still dressed as he had been at the theatre earlier, but was now additionally wearing his gold chain of office. The Countess, accompanied as usual by Princely Paws, and her entourage of militia walked onto the stage from a set of backstairs which led directly the front doors of the Guildhall itself – obviously, she was taking no chances with Flector still on the loose.

She waved as she came up, and everyone in the crowd started cheering; she and Major Schutem took seats while the rest of the soldiers took positions at either side of the stage. Princely Paws lay down at the Countess' feet, and she covered him over with a blanket. Various other local dignitaries also joined the Countess on the stage, including Mrs Sarah Pod of ACES; her husband, Arthur – Leo assumed; Mr Zenodotus; Mr Chipping; Miss Fysch; Justice Bender – drunk and falling about as usual; and various other people who Leo didn't recognise. Mr Summoner, today dressed in a black topcoat rather than his usual red attire, was busy ringing his bell and shouting:

"Oyez! Oyez! Oyez! The Mayor's Mipas Magpie March is about to commence!"

Constable Cuffem was also very much in evidence as he went around, organising children and some dogs who had also turned up to take part in the frivolity.

The brass band soon appeared at the brow of Penkhull Street playing Johann Strauss' Emperor Waltz; they were joined on this occasion by members of the Sipby Theatre's orchestra and some members of the militia with drums, who were all wearing black tunics rather than the orange ones they normally wore. The whole group must have numbered more than a hundred players and made an incredibly loud sound. The crowd cleared a path for them as they approached, and there was much clapping and cheering. As they came to the area in front of the stage, the Mayor left the crowd and took up his position at the lectern. Trumpeters and prompters on stilts soon appeared as per normal on such occasions, and the Mayor waved to the trumpeters to sound their call to order. The prompters displayed "SILENCE" and the crowd and brass band soon complied.

"My dear fellow citizens!" exclaimed the Mayor in a loud but cheerful voice. "Welcome! Welcome, to the 99th Annual Mayor's Mipas Magpie March – a great and much loved Altcastle tradition!" The crowd roared with applause and cheering, spontaneously and completely unprompted. "As usual," he continued, "as Lord Mayor it will be my privilege to lead the March again this year, and we shall take the same route as is customary, finishing here again in about forty-five minutes… depending on numbers joining at the back as we go, of course. So, without further ado, let the band strike up and off we'll all go!" The crowd once again applauded and cheered as the Mayor came down from the stage and the Countess took over his position at the lectern. Mayor Woodhay put his hands behind his back, underneath the tails of his tailcoat, with his palms facing upwards.

An insanely loud drum roll then rose from the snare drums of the twenty or so militia soldiers, and the band started to play the overture from Gioachino Rossini's *The Thieving Magpie*. As the band started, Mayor Woodhay started to jump and hop down the High Street and into Penkhull Street in the direction of Brook Lane. As he proceeded, he bent forward and used his upturned palms to flap the tails of his tailcoat. Given his attire, hopping walk, and posture, he did, in fact, look rather like some kind of demented, giant magpie.

As he got off, people clapped and cheered, before falling into line behind him and doing exactly the same things as him in terms of flapping their tailcoats, dresses, shawls or whatever else they were wearing – everyone bending forward, everyone jumping, hopping and kicking their legs out to either side as they merrily advanced.

Just as the March got started, it began to snow again; the flakes were big and fluffy and fell oh so slowly, dancing playfully, like the marchers, in a soft, light breeze. Leo looked on in stupefied incredulity as more and more people joined the line and the Mayor eventually disappeared over the brow of Penkhull Street.

"Well," said Emma, "what do you think of it?"

Leo shook his head; his eyes were widened.

"Insane," he said. Emma laughed.

"I have not participated myself for some years now," said Emma with her typical wry smile. Leo looked at in her astonishment – he found it hard to believe that she had ever participated at all in such a spectacle. They continued watching as more and more people joined, and the Countess kept on waving from the stage, but once the line had topped over a thousand, they felt they had seen enough and headed off via the Ironmarket towards Red Lion Square and Emma's shop.

When they arrived, they found Annabel was already there, in the parlour, being congratulated by Nevermore for her achievement in the poetry competition.

"I suppose that you will be getting ready to depart now, Leo," said Annabel somewhat mournfully.

"I'm afraid so," said Leo, "but as I have been appointed a Special Agent of the Borough, I shall be returning before too long." He took out his warrant and showed it to Annabel and Nevermore.

"You had better change your clothes, Leo," said Emma, "I will relate what Asiex said earlier."

"Sure," he said, heading off up the stairs.

While Leo changed back into his normal Newcastle-under-Lyme clothing, Emma told Annabel and Nevermore everything that Asiex had said to them and how she, Bull and Bear had been invited to join a committee to help in defeating the malevolent plans of Flector and La Falot. Within a few minutes, Leo reappeared wearing the clothes he had arrived in.

"As I'll be coming back," he said, "I thought perhaps I could leave my Altcastle clothes in the wardrobe, Emma?"

"Of course," she said, "though I fancy I had better wash and iron the shirt, at least."

"Yes… I suppose that might be good… thanks," said Leo – he was not a great believer in handing in his laundry too frequently, "and before we go, I just wanted to give you a little gift for being so kind to me."

"Oh," said Emma humbly, and a little taken aback, "really?"

"Yes," he said, taking the wooden fountain pen, which he had won at Grandad Joe's Rifles, from his coat pocket, "you'll remember saying that you quite admired this… so I'd like you to have it."

"Oh, how lovely, Leo," said Emma endearingly and accepting it from him. "I shall keep it on my writing desk, it will remind me of the fun we had at the fairground. Thank you."

"My pleasure," said Leo. Emma placed the fountain pen down on her writing desk, next to her ink bottle. Annabel and Nevermore smiled. "I have also left the radio transmitter which Doctor Toad gave me in the bottom drawer of the wardrobe," Leo added; "so when you need to contact him, you can do so more easily."

"Oh, that will be very useful, yes," said Emma. "I fancy I shall remember how to use it when the time comes… and I suppose we had now better be going to meet Asiex… so, Annabel… may I ask you to watch the shop again while I am gone?"

"Of course, dear," said Annabel. "Do you want me to drop off those two wrapped boxes at Mrs Mittens shop in the Ironmarket also?"

"Oh yes," said Emma, "that would be most helpful. Thank you."

"Well, Leo," said Annabel, offering her hand, "it has been my great pleasure to meet you, and I am so pleased to know that you will be coming back."

"As am I," said Nevermore.

"I'm happy to be coming back soon, too," said Leo, shaking Nevermore's right talon, which he had offered by way of saying his goodbye.

"We shall go by way of Lower Street and Goose Street, Leo, so to avoid the Magpie March and your being seen in those clothes," said Emma.

"Very wise," commented Nevermore. Leo nodded in agreement, and they exited via the shop back into Red Lion Square and then headed west down Church Street.

They proceeded briskly despite the continuing snow, which was now falling much faster and thicker than before. They soon passed into Lower Street, which, as Emma had envisaged, was completely deserted.

"I do hope Asiex's experiment has been successful," said Emma.

"I think it will have gone OK," replied Leo, "he seems a very competent kind of chap."

"Yes, he does," agreed Emma. "No doubt it will be a great relief to you to be back in your own reality soon."

"It will," said Leo, "although it's odd really… I feel as if I've always been here in Altcastle even though this is actually only my third day here."

"Hmm… yes, it is interesting how the mind works… how quickly one gets used to a new situation… and to new people."

"It is," mused Leo as they continued to walk on into Goose Street.

"Do you fancy that you might be able to find Flector and La Falot back in your Newcastle?" asked Emma.

"I've been thinking about that," said Leo. "It won't be easy, I don't suppose. The first thing I thought was that they're probably not called Flector and La Falot in my reality – they will almost certainly go by other names, that's the first issue. Secondly, even if I did know what they were called, I don't work for the police or know anyone that does – it will be difficult to search for them without access to some sort of police database."

"And a database is a thing that exists on one of those computers you told me about?" asked Emma. "Like a directory in some non-physical way?"

"Exactly," confirmed Leo. "I suppose I could use Facebook or something like that to look for them but again, not knowing what they're called, will make that almost impossible."

"What about surveilling the Lyme Brook, around the spots where you know that they have been previously active?" suggested Emma.

"Yes, that could work," said Leo, "but the problem is I have to go to school in the week, and my parents will not be very happy if I go to Lyme Valley all night, every night in camouflage gear, carrying a pair of binoculars…"

"No, I suppose not," laughed Emma. "They may find it rather odd, I fancy."

"Hmm… but I can certainly walk up and down the brook a few times and look for clues, because the other thing that crossed my mind is that neither of them will be expecting anyone to be looking for them in my reality. They will not know that we have the ability to create a magic mist, will they?"

"Hmm, no, I would suppose not," said Emma. "They know nothing about you at all… they will have no idea that you were inadvertently conveyed by their mist into this reality, nor, as you say, that Asiex is capable of sending you back."

"Everyone just thinks he's a woodcutter, don't they?" queried Leo.

"Yes," said Emma, "I had never heard of any druid living in Altcastle before this last few days, and I am quite certain La Falot will not have done so either. As for Flector, he is not even from

Altcastle, and was only in the Borough for a few weeks while he built the mirror maze so he can know nothing."

"Shall we go through the fairground?" asked Leo, as they had by know walked halfway down Brook Lane.

"Better to go across the level-crossing, I fancy," said Emma, "and then take the path between the brook and the canal."

"OK," agreed Leo.

"So, I would consider it impossible that they would expect anyone in your Newcastle to interfere with them," concluded Emma.

"That will be my advantage then, in looking for signs of their activity along the length of the brook, as they have no reason to cover their tracks at all, and may well have left clues as to their recent presence."

"What sort of clues would you look for?" asked Emma.

"Well," said Leo, "my dad and I are big fans of Sherlock Holmes, and we know all the stories and how he works things out. So, for example, last night, before I got trapped in the mirror maze, I had a milk chocolate and strawberry fancy from Auntie Oz's stall, and you, Bull and Bear, had fruit pies from Nanny Bird's stall."

"Yes," said Emma, "and what of it?"

"Well," continued Leo, "due to our not wanting anyone to see the pies being handed over to Bull and Bear and then slowly disappearing, we went to the rear of the stalls, where it was dark to eat. I didn't really think too much of it last night, but now I'm here again, and I can see that canal barge again – the one that's tied up diagonally across the canal rather than at one side or the other – you see the one I mean?" he asked, pointing to their left.

"Yes," said Emma, "that one there… yes, you are correct, it is tied to this bank of the canal at the stern and to the far bank of the canal at the bow, how odd. I wonder why someone would do that?"

"To use the barge as a bridge over the canal," said Leo.

"My goodness, Leo," said Emma, with one of her astonished looks, "how clever you are: why yes, it is rather obvious now that you have pointed it out."

"Well, that's what I was saying: I saw this barge arrive last night while you, Bull and Bear were chatting about where Nanny Bird might get her excellent berries from. I recall now that two men got out of it and went into the mirror maze."

"Hmm... I see," said Emma.

"You will also notice that the barge is directly behind the mirror maze and that the stretch of canal behind the maze is the stretch that is closest to the brook and thus, I think, where they placed the portal."

"But there is no bridge over the brook here," said Emma.

"But in my reality there is," said Leo. "Yes! Yes" he exclaimed excitedly. "It's all becoming clear to me now!"

"Is it?" asked Emma.

"Yes," he said. "I've got it, and I think I know where to look for them!"

"How?"

"In my reality, there is small footbridge over the brook at, or near to, this exact point," said Leo, "and beyond that there is a fairly new housing estate that always has a lot of rental properties..."

"Aha, so you fancy that Flector and La Falot are renting one of those properties in your reality, so that they can use that footbridge to come and go between the two realities?" asked Emma.

"Yes, exactly," he confirmed. "It would be the perfect place for them to live in my reality."

"How very, very fascinating," said Emma. "You have it all worked out!"

"Yes," he said with a big smile; "I actually and really think that I do."

"Well," said Emma, "I hope so... but you must be very careful not to be seen by either of them; what they wrote in that ransom note was very unpleasant. I do not consider that they would think twice about actually doing harm to someone."

"Yes, you're right," he nodded, "I will have to be very careful."

"I fancy that during this last few yards there has been a bit of mist in the air," said Emma.

"Yes… maybe… a little, at least," replied Leo, "but not as much as usual when there is one of *those* mists."

"There is Asiex," said Emma, "with Bull and Bear – what a relief!"

"Yes, they must have been to my reality by now and returned, so all looks well."

CHAPTER TWENTY-NINE

UNTIL WE
MEET AGAIN

T HEY PROCEEDED WITH HASTE to where Asiex, Bull and
Bear were standing near the bridge, but as they got closer,
Leo could see that they did not look entirely at ease.

"Is something wrong?" he asked as he reached them.

"Well," started Asiex, "the good news is that the potion
worked: Bull and Bear have been to your Newcastle and have
come back safely to Altcastle. When they crossed the midpoint
of the bridge, the second hand on your watch immediately
started rotating as we expected it to, and your phone had both
a network and an internet connection within seconds – also as
expected."

"But look at the time, dear fellow," said Bull, holding the
mobile up towards Leo: 11:39.

The date still read Saturday 15th December, but the time no
longer read 10:34 as they were all expecting.

"But how can that be?" asked Leo. "That means that an hour has passed."

"Yes, an hour and five minutes to be exact," confirmed Bear.

"I don't understand," said Leo.

"Nor we," said Asiex. "Bull and Bear have recounted again everything that Doctor Toad said about time relatively standing still, and about the experience of Posidonius..."

"But if Doctor Toad was wrong, and time in Leo's reality has not stood still, then over two full days should have passed," said Emma, interrupting him.

"And not just an hour," added Leo.

"Yes, yes," muttered Asiex, "it is extremely perplexing."

"We suggested that maybe time has slowed down in Leo's reality, rather than stopped," said Bear, "but we can't fathom out any reason for that to be the case."

"Indeed," said Asiex, "one would think that either time would stop – relatively speaking – as the Doctor said, or it would continue as normal... but, as I said initially, the good news is that the potion works perfectly well and once you get through the mist, you will be in your own reality again... albeit a little later than we supposed."

"I fancy your parents will not have missed you for the sake of an hour?" asked Emma.

"I would think not. May I see the phone?" said Leo to Bull. Bull gave it to him, together with his wristwatch, which he put in his pocket. "Oh no, there are five missed calls... but, all from Sam – no doubt to ask where I am."

"So, it's not too bad, then?" asked Asiex.

"No... it could be a lot worse," conceded Leo. "Imagine if I'd been missing for two days!"

"Well, it's very strange," said Bear. "Doctor Toad was quite certain that time in your reality would stand still while you were here."

"Yes, I can't account for it at all," said Asiex. "I have no explanation to offer."

"Well," said Emma, "as you said, Leo, it could be a lot worse. When you come back here, perhaps now that we know Asiex and have a source of magic potions, we can make a series of tests at regular intervals to see what time it is in your reality."

"That is an excellent idea," agreed Asiex. "It will be useful both to work out how this hour has been added and indeed, to prevent Leo staying too long here and being missed in his own reality."

"Yes…" mused Leo, pensively, "that will be good."

"What else are you thinking, Leo?" asked Emma, noticing that he was distracted and pondering on something.

"Hmm… just about Flector and La Falot going through the mist to my reality last night…"

"What of it?" asked Bear. Asiex squinted thoughtfully and stroked his beard as if something on the matter was forming in his mind too.

"Well, if they went to my reality last night, surely they cannot have entered into frozen time? Can they? They would not be able to do anything," said Leo.

"Yes, that's a good point," said Asiex. "But, on the other hand, if the time in your reality stopped standing still only because they had entered your reality, then that does not account for the small change of one hour, as they left this reality last night."

"That's many hours ago," interjected Bull. "Well, over half a day."

"Yes, it is," confirmed Asiex. "And also, that must mean that both of them… and indeed any and all of their accomplices who went with them, and whose identity we do not yet know, belong to your reality because as we can see, Altcastle time has not been frozen because they have left it, as we are moving about in both space and time, even as we speak, and the time is getting later with each passing minute as one would normally expect."

"But if that is true, and Flector and the others are from Leo's reality, then how was Leo able to come here in the first place? Surely when they left Leo's reality, at least two weeks ago in Flector's case, then time would have been frozen there, and Leo would not have been able to cross the bridge in the first place?" asked Bear. Asiex shook his head and sighed.

"This will require a great deal of thought," he said; "it is not a matter we can resolve now."

"Indeed," agreed Emma. "But at least we can say for certain that Flector's leaving of Leo's reality does not freeze time there, because as Mr Bear has just pointed out, Leo would not have been able to come here otherwise."

"Yes, that must be true... it is extremely confusing how this works," said Asiex. "However," he continued, "the two main priorities for now, must be, one: for Leo to return to his own reality so that he's not missed by his parents; and two: to try to prevent Flector and La Falot from doing harm in Altcastle by either kidnapping the Countess, or indeed anyone else – as they planned, or doing something else that is going to destroy our peace and way of life."

"Yes," said Leo, "I agree: I must return now before any more time elapses and I am missed by anyone other than Sam. I will try to locate Flector and La Falot today or tomorrow while it is the weekend, and I don't need to go to school."

"Very good," said Asiex. He put his hand in his pocket, pulled out a glass vial and handed it to Leo. "Just two or three small drops will create a portal that will last about ten seconds, and that is long enough for you to pass through and also short enough such that no one else goes through hopefully. Only use it when you can be certain that no one else is close enough to your selected crossing point to cross through by accident."

"Understood," nodded Leo. "So, never in sight of anyone or when anyone is either in front of me or behind me."

"Exactly," confirmed Asiex.

"And I just drop the few drops directly into the brook?" asked Leo.

"Yes, you must release the drops upstream from where you want to cross… the flow of the water will then carry them downstream a little way – just under the bridge that you are crossing over… then the mist will extend only a few yards at most. That will be sufficient for you to pass through without creating a mist so large it will envelop too long a length of the brook. I assume that is what they did…"

"You mean they put too much in?" asked Emma.

"Yes, I believe so," said Asiex, "because that also fits with what Mr Magnetic Monkey said about their incorrect operation of the machinery in the mirror maze – they have gotten hold of what tools they are using from someone else I believe and are basically incompetent themselves. It cannot be from any deliberate intent that they created a mist that was so expansive that it could even be seen from Leo's house, as he described, which is over a quarter of a mile away from the Lyme Brook."

"It was fortunate that only Leo was caught in the mist, really, given its size," mused Bear.

"Indeed," agreed Asiex. "Anyway, you had better be going, Leo." Asiex shook Leo's hand and smiled. "See you soon, I hope."

"I hope so," said Leo. He then hugged Bull, Bear and lastly Emma, who also kissed him on the cheek.

"Take care, Leo," said Emma.

"See you soon, old boy," said Bear.

"Good luck," said Bull.

"Thanks for everything," he said to the three of them. "Until we met again, then!" They all smiled and nodded; Bull waved his hoof, with a tear in his eye.

Leo walked towards the bridge, leaving Bull, Bear, Emma and Asiex behind him. He got his vial of mist potion ready, walked forward onto the bridge and then paused at the midpoint to release three small drops of potion into the brook.

As soon as the first drop hit the surface of the water, thick swirls of white mist vortexed up and enveloped the bridge – so quick was the action of the mist potion that he never even saw the second and third drop reach the water; he glanced back, but could no longer see his four friends. Within only seconds, the bridge was shrouded in as a thick a mist as he had witnessed three days before, when he first came to Altcastle. He gingerly proceeded forward, glanced back again and called out "Goodbye for now!"

"Good…" was all he heard in reply – just half a word – and as he placed his left foot down, he felt the surface below – it was smooth, like tarmac, not cobblestone, and he felt no snow crunch beneath. He placed his next foot down – the same surface. He moved forward quite hastily then, until he could make out the metallic sign that read "Lyme Valley Parkway", which stood in his reality on the western side of the brook. There was no one else about, fortunately.

He turned around towards the bridge again and very soon the mist began to clear, just as Asiex had predicted. As the mist vanished in the wind and light drizzle, he could see the modern road and the hospital buildings in the distance beyond that. On the spot where Bull, Bear, Emma and Asiex had been standing in the Altcastle reality, now only an empty path remained.

"I'm back," he puffed. Then he stopped to check his mobile phone and wristwatch. The time on the watch was 10:34 – just as it had been in Altcastle – but of course, it was an analogue watch so the time would need to be changed manually – the second hand was moving though, as expected.

It took a few seconds before the network and 4G symbols appeared at the top of the screen of his mobile phone, and the date and time only refreshed once a network connection had been established. The date read Saturday 15th December and the time: 11.39. Still exactly the same time that it had been when Bull and Bear crossed over. "Hmm…" he thought "… so time has been frozen again in that period at least – weird!" Just then, his phone rang; it was Sam again.

"You alright?" said Leo answering it.

"Where've you been?" moaned Sam. "I've been looking all over Castle and the Valley for you – your phone was going straight to voicemail."

"Yeah," said Leo, "I've had a bit of an issue with reception… and I got held back with an unexpected problem."

"Well, where are you now?" demanded Sam.

"In the Valley; where are you?" replied Leo.

"I'm in Maccie's… in Castle," said Sam.

"OK. Who you with?" asked Leo.

"On my own," answered Sam. "Ollie's maybe coming later."

"OK, I'll be there in a bit," said Leo; "I've just got to go somewhere first."

"You kidding? You're late already…" retorted Sam.

"I won't be long," said Leo, not wishing to annoy his friend further, yet also keen to start his mission to save Altcastle.

"Right… how long will you be then?" asked Sam.

"Only about twenty minutes," said Leo.

"OK… in a bit…" said Sam "…and you'd better tell me what the problem was that's made you so late."

"Will do," said Leo.

He hung up and headed off briskly along the path which follows the line of the Lyme Brook, in the direction of the new housing estate and footbridge that he'd been telling Emma about. As he walked along hurriedly, his mind was spinning with thoughts and ideas.

"Hmm…" he mused "…first, I'll take a quick look for any sign of Flector and La Falot and get some plan in my head for later… I definitely need a proper plan before I do anything… I can't just go and knock on every door… or maybe I can if I have some plausible story, like washing cars to collect for a charity… perhaps that could work? Or maybe not… I don't have a badge or an ID card or anything? Hmm… I need to think first… and act only when sure… and should I tell Sam what really happened, or he'll think I've just made the whole thing up, or worse – gone mad? Then again, maybe he could help me with my first mission… hmm… what's best, I wonder?"

{ APPENDIX }

(FOR LOVERS OF NONSENSE POETRY)

YEARBOOK OF THE
22ND ANNUAL POETRY COMPETITION

With a Foreword by
Rt. Hon. Lady Debra Sipby
Countess of Altcastle-under-Lyme

Edited by
Mr Zenodotus
Chief Librarian

2018 Edition

Table of Contents

FOREWORD BY
THE RIGHT HONOURABLE LADY DEBRA SIPBY,
COUNTESS OF ALTCASTLE-UNDER-LYME.

Dear Citizens

It gives me great pleasure to once again write the foreword for the Annual Mipas Poetry Competition Yearbook. This year marked the 22nd anniversary of the competition, and it was held, as is now usual, at the Sipby Theatre on the morning of Saturday 15th December 2018.

This year saw both a record number of entries, 10 in fact, and a record attendance of over 2,500 poetry lovers. Unfortunately, one entry had to be disallowed by his Worship, Mayor Woodhay, for exhorting listeners to theft and violence, such things having no place in Altcastle-under-Lyme, and for that reason, that poem is omitted from the yearbook leaving a total of nine poems for this year – the same as last year in fact.

The remaining nine poems were of a very high standard indeed and so much so in fact that for the first time, a joint first prize was awarded as the learned judges could not decide between the poem of Annabel Lee and that of

Asiex the Woodcutter. A very well deserved second place went to Tommy the Tinker and third place went to Peter Pykovsky for his delicious – no pun intended – poem, *The Song of the Fox and Monkey Pie.*

I do hope that you all enjoy reading these poems for many years to come.

Yours truly
D Sipby

Rt. Hon. Lady Debra Sipby
Countess of Altcastle-under-Lyme

THE REMARKABLE ADVENTURE OF THE MOUSE AND THE MOOSE

The mouse and the moose have set off for the moon,
But please do not fret – they shall come back soon.
They have taken twelve cakes and ten biscuits with jam,
And sixty-six slices of honey roast ham.
They have taken as well, nine crusty baguettes,
And apples and oranges stored in two nets.
The mouse and the moose may be hungry, you see,
And even in space, they will still want their tea.

The journey is long, and will take several days,
And they earnestly hope not to meet with delays:
Like bumping their ship into fishcakes or stones,
Or running aground on some dinosaur bones,
Or breaking their rudder, or losing their way,
Or getting quite lost, or going astray.

They have never before been to space, you see,
So cannot predict what the problems might be.

The sails of their ship are orange and black,
And strong enough to get there and back.
So when the solar winds blow brisk,
They can keep full sail without any risk.
And when they finally reach the moon,
A meeting is planned with the Martian Racoon -
The Martian Racoon with the stripy tail,
Who flies around space on the back of a whale.

He had sent them a letter of invitation,
Delivered to them by an old dalmatian;
An old dalmatian with black-spotted coat,
Who delivers all things from a pale green boat,
A boat which is made out of pumpkin seeds,
The sort of boat that everyone needs,
The sort of boat that is fast and light,
O what a boat! What a beautiful sight!"

Annabel Lee 2018

Only a Puppet

Only a puppet he was made,
From a block he came to life;
And if that wasn't bad enough,
He got Judy for a wife.

Every day she beats his head,
With sausages or wood.
There's not one day of peace for him,
Nor one that's any good.

In heat and cold, he must perform,
In summer and in winter.
Each day his face is slapped so hard,
His nose begins to splinter.

The crowd applaud, the children laugh,
The ha'pennies all add up.
But when the coins are all poured out,
Go little to his cup.

And when the shows have run their course,
Because it's getting late,
Off go the crowds, back to their homes,
But Punch goes in a crate.

No home for him. No fire. No hearth.
No place to call his own:
Just a broken, bashed-up crate.
No wonder he should moan.

One hundred years he's lived like this,
One hundred years or more.
Then one cold day he just got tired,
And headed for the door.

So, yes, it's true! He tried to flee,
To escape the puppet show;
But he was caught before too long,
As he had no place to go.

The Constable arrested him,
And put him in a cage.
They said he'd done some beakery,
Because he'd left the stage.

At trial, they said he'd done worse still -
He turned to a reptile:
Though actually it wasn't Punch,
It was the crocodile.

He "Equal Rights for Puppets" called,
But few there chanced to care.
They hardly even let him speak;
It wasn't very fair!

That "Punch is Guilty!" so said all.
They fined him all he had;
And sent him back to work again,
Although it made him sad.

And so today, as he was told,
He'll be back on the stage,
No matter if he wants or not:
A puppet's rights outrage!

So spare a thought for Mr Punch,
Before you leave to dine:
And maybe give him a little tip,
To buy a glass of wine."

Asiex the Woodcutter 2018

THE TURNIPECS

"They are coming!" called an old man,
"They are coming from the sea!"
"The Turnipecs are coming here,
For everyone to see!"
Now, Turnipecs, one needs to know,
Are curious things indeed:
They have blue skin that is very rough,
And turns yellow when they feed.

And it is a well-regarded truth,
By all, both young and old:
That no Turnipec will ever do,
One single thing it is told.
They are very disobedient,
Even unto their own;
And rarely observe good manners,
Even when they are shown.

Many will say: "Oh Turnipecs,
Just turn them all away!"
But when they have travelled so very far,
It is not a kind thing to say.
Better to give them a warm "hello",
And offer them bread and cheese.
And hopefully, they might improve,
Once they feel more at ease."

Tommy the Tinker 2018

The Song of the Fox and Monkey Pie

A Fox and Monkey Pie is a very fine thing indeed;
Our own dear Mayor himself eats one, whenever he needs
    a good feed.
If ever he calls for one of our pies,
And we have none left, the poor man cries.
Our singing waiters of loud, strong voice,
Will always praise a rightful choice.
When choosing on what they wish to dine,
Those who have let their wisdom shine,
And chosen a Fox and Monkey Pie,
Will hear their waiter heartily cry:

> *Chorus*
> *"He's ordered a Fox and Monkey Pie!*
> *And from the kitchen, it soon will fly!*
> *Tasty, delicious and ready to eat;*
> *Oh, what a pie! What a wonderful treat!*

The finest pie that money can buy;
The finest delight to be seen by an eye!
Oh, the Fox and Monkey Pie!
Yes, the Fox and Monkey Pie!
The finest delight to be seen by an eye!"

And even the Worshipful Countess herself,
Has taken pies home from our kitchen shelf.
Such fresh potatoes, diced so fine,
And bound in a jelly of gravy and wine.
Such beautiful, tender pieces of meat,
Cased in a pastry of finest wheat -
Wheat deluxe of finest grind;
No one can leave such a pie behind!

Chorus
"He's ordered a Fox and Monkey Pie!
And from the kitchen, it soon will fly!
Tasty, delicious and ready to eat;
Oh, what a pie! What a wonderful treat!
The finest pie that money can buy;
The finest delight to be seen by an eye!
Oh, the Fox and Monkey Pie!
Yes, the Fox and Monkey Pie!
The finest delight to be seen by an eye!"

The Countess herself long since ruled that:
"No plate must contain any gristle or fat!
For serving such is beakery pure,
And so all chefs must always ensure,
That no such thing can be found in a pie!"
The ACES, of course, will keep a close eye,
And report to the relevant authority,
Any such chef who so offends;

353

And there he will stand without any friends,
While Justice Bender hands him a fine,
His beakery to underline!

Chorus
"He's ordered a Fox and Monkey Pie!
And from the kitchen, it soon will fly!
Tasty, delicious and ready to eat;
Oh, what a pie! What a wonderful treat!
The finest pie that money can buy;
The finest delight to be seen by an eye!
Oh, the Fox and Monkey Pie!
Yes, the Fox and Monkey Pie!
The finest delight to be seen by an eye!"

Both beasts of land and birds of air,
Can't turn their nosiks from pies so fair.
And sure, no man can well prepare,
For those terrible words, so few can bear:
"Sorry," we say. "There are no pies left!"
And the broken traveller leaves bereft:
Sad and hungry, with bitter tears -
On realisation of his fears.

Chorus
"He's ordered a Fox and Monkey Pie!
And from the kitchen, it soon will fly!
Tasty, delicious and ready to eat;
Oh, what a pie! What a wonderful treat!
The finest pie that money can buy;
The finest delight to be seen by an eye!
Oh, the Fox and Monkey Pie!
Yes, the Fox and Monkey Pie!
The finest delight to be seen by an eye!"

There's no finer thing to put in your eye,
Than the sight of a Fox and Monkey Pie!
So saddle up, make fit your steed,
And from Altcastle ride at speed,
Along the road that leads out west,
Where pies are known to be the best.
Waste no minute! Proceed with haste!
Always imagining the lovely taste,
Dash on! With clopping horse hoof din,
To Ye Olde Fox and Monkey Inn!
Where Mr Gristleless waits to bake,
And serve you a pie of finest steak!"

Peter Pykovsky 2018

SPIDERSOCKS

The people call him Spidersocks because he can walk up walls;
But only with his shoes not on, because otherwise, he falls.
But just in socks he's quite a chap, and walks up really well,
Why it is? They just don't know; no one can really tell.

They've done a lot of tests on him, on both his feet also;
But when they analyse it all, the answer doesn't follow.
Without his socks, he falls, and with his shoes, he falls.
So maybe it's the socks themselves, or maybe it's the walls?

They've tested both with other's feet, but no one else can climb,
They've done a lot of work on this and spent a lot of time.
And so for now, it's Spidersocks, as one and all agree,
The only chap who walks up walls for everyone to see."

Billy Sweeper 2018

THE MAYOR OF KIPPINGTON PASSED A NEW LAW

The Mayor of Kippington passed a new law,
"Let the sucking of noses be witnessed no more!"
In paragraph two of that excellent Act,
The Mayor, his good self, did state this fact:

"The sucking of noses throughout the whole area,
Is as common as snow in south Altavaria!"
Too many noses are now being sucked,
So the Mayor of Kippington must obstruct,

All further spread of this terrible matter
And silence any idle chatter,
That such a thing can be allowed,
Or praised at all in any crowd.

To suck a nose is extremely bad,
And makes all sighthounds very sad.
It is not good! It is not moose!
It's as useful as frozen orange juice,

At the North Pole, in a terrible blizzard,
To a hatless, coatless, shivering lizard,
Who wants some tea, that's nice and hot,
But is given ice in a dirty pot.

The sucking of noses is horrid indeed,
And those who do it cannot succeed!
It cannot continue, and must stop NOW,
All current nose suckers must take a vow:

"I do solemnly promise with all of my brain,
I will never suck a nose again,
And from that foul practice, I will abstain,
And if I don't, I won't complain,

When the Sheriff of Kippington and the Mayor
Take me down to the old town square,
And give me a ticket that says, "ONE WAY",
And the date of travel says "TODAY",

And off I will go to Kippington Station,
To take the train to my new destination:
Sneepington Junction, and there to collect,
At the Sneepster Suppliers, with due respect,

A sneepster's beak to be worn at all times,
In punishment for my many crimes,
Of sucking noses without respect,
Of which I am the chief suspect."

- *Frederick Von Miter 2018*

THE OLD MAN'S CLOCK

The old man's clock went tick-tock, tick-tock,
Tick-tock, tick-tock, all around the clock,
Ticking, tocking, never stopping,
Keeping time, never dropping,
Any minute, any second,
So the old man surely reckoned,
He could set all things by it,
And it would faithfully acquit,
Its function free of any fault,
And time the stars in heaven's vault
To rise and set, each in their place,
Timed by the hands, on that old face."

Mr Putyur Tapochki 2018

THE MAN WITH THE
NINE-FOOT NOSE

The man with the nine-foot nose could smell terribly well
   indeed,
But he always smelled other people's dinners, whenever he
   tried to feed.
He never smelled his own food once: not once in his whole
   long life.
He would always just say, "How does it smell?", to his poor
   long-suffering wife.
One day the man with the nine-foot nose, went out for a walk
   in the street,
And as he walked on, and looked all around, he started to
   smell a real treat!
He sniffed, and sniffed, and sniffed some more; he could smell
   the aroma of pork,
Nicely roasting with honey and sage, but unfortunately, it was
   in Alt York!

He'd smelled a roast three thousand miles away, over the
   Altlantic ocean.
"I wish I had a smaller nose", he thought, "now that's an
   attractive notion!"

Will Sniffer 2018

THE TOOTHBRUSH AND
THE PASTRY FORK

The toothbrush and the pastry fork decided to elope,
For when they'd told of their relationship, poor Jill could just not
    cope.
They'd developed quite a love you see, when they were left to dry,
One fine and sunny afternoon, after Jill had eaten pie.
For first she'd used the pastry fork, to put it in her mouth,
But the berries in that pie so fine had come up from the south;
And as anyone will tell you, about berries from the south,
The seeds can stick between your teeth as you chew them in your
    mouth.
So once she'd washed the pastry fork, after eating all her pie,
Next, she used the toothbrush, and then she put that too, to dry;
But when the two revealed their love, poor Jill just could not cope,
And this was the main reason which then caused them to elope.

The toothbrush and the pastry fork enjoyed their honeymoon,
Apart from a single incident with a rather aggressive spoon.
The fellow was out of order, and intolerably rude,
And for some unfathomable reason wouldn't stay at all near
food.
First, he left a souffle by jumping off the dish,
And then a pudding also, against the diner's wish.
The waiter most perplexedly inquired what be his wish;
The spoon replied abrasively that he did not like the dish.
He said he'd taken lessons in all matters linked to food,
And would not be used for afters, even if considered rude.
He said that his loving designers had made him a sugar spoon,
And he wouldn't be used for anything else, even on
honeymoon."

Jill Hill 2018

 **Matador**